The Heart

of Moab

"There is therefore now no condemnation to them which are in
Christ Jesus, who walk not after the flesh, but after the Spirit."
Romans 8:1 KJV

By Kara S. McKenzie

Printed by Createspace, An Amazon.com Company
Copyright © 2017 by Kara S. McKenzie.

ISBN-13: 978-1548470883
ISBN-10: 1548470880

Dedication

To Mary Ellen and Taylor

Cousin Kara ♡

The Heart of Moab

By Kara S. McKenzie

Chapter 1

Achsah ran ahead of the others in the golden wheat field while she laughed and tossed tiny bits of grain behind her. Three young men chased her as they ducked and dodged soft kernels she threw at them. Their eyes sparked with interest as they caught up with her.

She stopped suddenly, and a look a chagrin crossed her face. The shadow of a lone cloud fell over the sun in the blue sky and slowly moved over the plains to where she stood. Her eyes darkened.

The young men came to stand around her.

"Achsah, what is it? Is something wrong?" Jonathan reached out and took a piece of wheat from her hair. He threw it on the dry ground.

She rolled her eyes as she moved away from him and pushed his hand away. She ignored his question while she fingered the rose-colored amulet that hung from a golden jeweled chain around her neck. Then, she gave him and the others a bored look. "I don't think I want to play this game anymore. It's too hot."

The sun of the Moab plains beat down on them as they stood looking at each other.

A feeling of impatience ran through Achsah.

She blew back a strand of hair that had fallen into her face. Ha! The same games and men bored and wearied her. Their predictability never ceased to amaze her. She wondered why she continued to bother with them.

She looked out over the land to Mount Nebo which rose in the distance above the sunken valley of the plains. Vast prairie-like fields spread out across the land which were broken in the distance by prominent, rocky cliffs. It would take many lengths of a donkey to reach the great hills and mountains beyond. Grass and rocks littered the plains.

"May I get you water?" Jonathan's eyes never left her face, and he leaned close. "Sheerah has a vessel full at the edge of the field. I can go now, if you'd like?" He looked down the dusty path and out to the wheat fields where a light breeze swayed the tops of the mature grain.

Achsah brushed off her tunic. She turned and glanced at a thinner, wiry man on the other side of her.

She lifted her hand to block the morning sunlight that streamed into her eyes. Her speech was smooth. "Judah, could you go and speak to my sister. Tell her I want my sandals. I didn't bring any, and I've already stepped on one jagged pebble."

She looked down at her bare feet and scuffed the dusty path with them. Her toe toyed with a piece of wheat lying there. The finery of her ankle bracelets glittered as her foot moved in small, circular motions.

A taller, darker-haired man squeezed between Judah and Jonathan. "I'll do it." His eyes sparkled. "I was going that way to get a different threshing tool. There's no need for Judah to go."

"Hmm." Achsah put her finger to her chin as she eyed the eager group. "Maybe. Jonathan and Judah, you are both needed in my father's field. He'll not look well upon any of you, if you neglect your duties because of me. And since Hezro has plans to go that way, he can get them for me."

She turned and looked down her nose at Hezro. "My sandals are just inside the door. And tell Vashti I wish to speak with her. She'll leave her chores for my purposes."

"I'll get them, Achsah, and bring them back, and I'll send for Vashti. Then, you might spend time later with me." He turned and made his way down the path toward her home.

A wry smile formed on Achsah's face. Later? Hmm. Let him go and do her bidding, but his service to her would not amount to much on her part. She'd no time for his silly games. She'd had enough of all of them. She only wanted her sandals.

The other young men hadn't left. They were still looking at her.

"Well." Achsah's eyes narrowed. "Shouldn't you be with the other workers?" She crossed her arms.

Jonathan and Judah both nodded.

Judah gave her an apologetic look. "Yes sorry, Achsah Your father will be waiting for us."

Both young men nodded to her again and quickly stepped off the path. They went to the field as she turned back toward the town.

*****

From a distance, Toi stood behind the bench where he'd been working. He chipped away at a large stone and smoothed the edges, then he stopped to hold it in his hands. He couldn't help but notice the young woman across the path on the edge of the field. The colored linens from Egypt that she wore shimmered and danced in the sunlight while she moved past on her way to the marketplace. She pushed aside a strand of thick, brown hair that had fallen over her shoulder. Her back was straight, and she appeared almost regal as she turned away from the young men who had followed her so diligently.

He shook his head. The crafty Moabitess had every man in the vicinity following her like a flock of lambs. She seemed to derive pleasure in tormenting them.

She looked over at Toi.

When she noticed him, she tilted her head. She gave him a guarded look, yet it was not without some interest. She wrapped a length of hair around her finger and pulled on the end of it as she made her way across the path to a tent further away from where he cut stone.

Toi eyed the young man, Elpaal, who sold cloth out of the tent from where she had stopped to look.

The cloth seller smiled at her and immediately lifted fabric, in swatches, from his wooden stand, as the young woman fingered the material.

She leaned close to Elpaal and whispered in his ear. She giggled, and then she turned to the tent where Toi was. She gave Toi a quick backward glance.

Toi smiled as she turned to her task at hand. As lovely as she was to look at, it was obvious to him that she spelled trouble for those around her. Her opportunistic schemes were not lost on him as they were with the other men who chased at her heels. Poor fools. Unless, of course, they were aware of the wily games she played, Any man within a donkey's length of her would do well to leave her be.

The man at the cloth tent laid the purple swatch in her hand. Throughout the transaction, he never took his eyes from her. He smiled widely. Then he put up his hand and refused payment when she pulled a coin out of her jeweled handbag. A golden signet ring on her hand caught the sunlight as she quickly slipped the coin back into her money pouch.

Her eyes sparkled as she reached up to touch the side of his bearded chin. She smiled back at him.

The man nodded appreciatively, and he didn't take his eyes from her when she walked past his tent.

Before she left, she turned back to Toi one more time. Her attempts to capture him with her eyelashes, which fluttered seductively against her cheeks, didn't go unnoticed by him.

He gave her a knowing smile. He couldn't help but muse over the fact that she'd used the young cloth seller with the intention of sparking his own interest in her.

Her eyes narrowed as she turned to stare. She obviously didn't appreciate the fact that he wasn't buying her flirtatiousness and pretentious airs.

Toi chuckled. He sat down and went back to his work. He kept his eye on her while he chiseled off a piece of the edge of the stone. He wondered why she wasn't at her house helping with chores.

4

His friend Shobach quietly worked next to him. "She reminds me of those camel traders who came through here last week. Remember the one who tried to rob us in his double dealings?"

Toi watched her leave down the path. She brushed off her skirt as she went, and she smiled at the men who passed her on the road. Each of them tipped their heads and smiled back.

Toi's brow rose, and he laughed. "Ha! I'd say so, but maybe worse than that."

"A craftier lot than men who would steal for a profit?"

"Yes! My uncle has concubines that remind me of her. A man would do well to stay away from this woman."

"It's true."

"Do you know her name?"

Shobach turned to Toi. "Her name's Achsah. But I wouldn't get any ideas. She's very pretty, but she would most certainly bring you much grief."

Toi didn't answer his friend's advice. Instead, he laughed again. "Hmm. Adorned one? The name is quite fitting with all the jewelry and the fine cloth she wears."

He took the rectangular piece of rock in his hands and repositioned it so that the rounded end was on the side he worked on. He lifted his hammer stone and chipped away at the end of it. "You are aware, my friend, that I do appreciate a challenge, yet you won't find me devouring her pretentious words, or smiles, the way those other senseless fools around her do. I wouldn't allow my heart to be deceived by a woman such as her."

"I would hope not. Though I've no doubt that she'll have met her match, if the two of you ever crossed paths. Yet, I don't believe either of you would win a prize in the end for it." Shobach gave him a knowing look.

"I'm sure we wouldn't." Toi nudged his friend's arm jovially. "But it might be entertaining to try."

"Maybe for you, but I wouldn't pursue her." He suddenly had a look of concern. "You understand that Adonai warns against foreign women. You might consider this."

Toi set the tool he was working with on his lap. "You sound like my mother." He laughed. "Don't worry. I'm not in danger of falling for a woman's schemes."

"You shouldn't consider yourself resistant the troubles that might result from turning from the statutes. You should pray and listen to Adonai."

"Lately, I find myself too busy for such things." Toi looked down the dusty path between houses to where the young woman had disappeared. "She would draw my interest, for a time, but I'm sure I wouldn't be bringing her home in the end." He smiled and went back to his work. "The family's in no grave danger of it."

Shobach gave Toi a cross look. "It's well that you have no plans of it, for I'm sure it would bring you and your family grief, if you did. The thought of that foreign women, or any other, for that matter, in your household, brings a picture of great discontent to my mind." He shook his head wearily.

"Somehow, I couldn't imagine her breaking bread with Benaiah, or father, not to mention mother and my other siblings." Toi laughed.

Shobach carried another large stone from the cart next to the tent. He set it down on a low table and picked up his hammer stone as he began to shape it. "You've only just come to the field of Moab, in the last year, and you already have your eyes set on one of the strange, foreign women here? Did you not learn your lessons in Bethlehem?"

"With women?" Toi could not help breaking out into laughter again. "They're a mystery to me, and I'm sure they always will be. But despite, I cannot walk away from them. I'm intrigued with a pretty face and a sweet smile. I may just take a stroll when I'm finished with this stone. The afternoon sun will be upon us soon, and we've worked at this long enough. Where is her family's home?"

"You truly want to know? Do not say you haven't been warned."

"Where might I find her? You may as well tell me. I'll find out from someone else."

Shobach hesitated, then he spoke quietly. "There's an altar to Chemosh, on a hill, behind Achsah's family dwelling. They live in the last house. It's outside the gate."

"It may be the direction I take, I believe such a meeting would prove interesting."

Shobach sighed. "I'm sure for you it would, yet as I said, you were warned. The woman is trouble."

"Yes, I've heard your case. Now, it's time to get my things and go back home. Helping you today has put me behind there. And yet, your courtyard's closer to the marketplace."

"You're always welcome here. I'll see you another day."

"Peace, friend."

"Peace."

*****

Achsah looked down the small path that led through a courtyard to where her sister, Dinah, came toward her. Dinah held a pair of sandals in her hands.

A hot wind swept past Achsah. She drew in a breath of tepid air. It smelled like a mixture of meadow grass and smoke from burning oven fires. She wrinkled her nose as she observed Dinah.

Why Hezro sent this sister to her, rather than Vashti, she couldn't understand? Vashti was easier to deal with. Vashti stayed in the shadows and made no scenes.

While Vashti was sweet and accommodating, and was tender of heart, Dinah was completely the opposite. Dinah had the heart of a lion and was almost never content. Her ridiculous attempts to compete with Achsah were almost laughable. Achsah wondered why Dinah even bothered with it. Though Dinah was a very pretty, young woman, she took few pains with her appearance and had no control over her tongue.

Dinah stopped short of Achsah at the end of the path. Her clothes and fiery auburn braids of hair were in disarray. "There you are."

Achsah gave her a disconcerted look. "I told Hezro to send Vashti. Where is she? And why didn't *she* bring my sandals?"

"Mother needed her." Dinah's face scrunched up. She held out the sandals. "Vashti was helping her with the meal."

"But, why couldn't you have helped mother? I wanted Vashti to come." Achsah took the sandals from Dinah and sat on a nearby rock. She put them on and began to tie them.

"Because you don't always get everything you want, Achsah. You're not queen of the Moabites."

Achsah finished tying her leather laces and got up. Even though she was older than Dinah, by a year, Achsah was a couple inches shorter than her sister. She'd always been petite in size.

Achsah pointed her chin upward to look at Dinah. "Vashti delights in helping me. You, on the other hand, speak ill of me whenever you get the chance."

Dinah ignored her sister's accusations. Instead, she offered her own. "Where were you? Mother needed you to help in the courtyard."

Achsah didn't answer. She looked back at the small, stone houses that stood at angles to each other weaving patterns through the town.

A caravan of camels with traders passed through. The clomp of their feet on the path stirred up dust. A man with a toothless grin looked down at her from his perch as his cart ambled past.

She brushed off the edge of her skirt.

Some younger men, who were on another cart, caught her eye. They smiled as one of them clucked to a donkey who quickened his steps.

She looked at the men as they rode past and then turned back to the town. She suddenly remembered something.

8

She tugged on Dinah's arm and gave her sister a curious stare. "Never mind the house, or the chores, or mother." She tipped her head to the side. "Have you been to town lately?"

"I have." Dinah shrugged her off. "Why?"

Achsah turned nonchalantly. She pulled a long-stemmed, purple flower from the side of the road and brought it to her nose. She breathed in its sweet scent and looked over the top of it. "I wondered if you've heard news about any recent Israelite families who might have come from the west. Did any of your friends say anything?"

Dinah's eyes narrowed. She glanced at Achsah. "There are a couple of them, but they're not new. The last family has been here for at least a year."

Achsah looked curious. "I've not seen them."

"They only recently began to sell in the marketplace. They spent the better part, of their first year, in the fields and re-building and moving into one of the ancient houses here. There are three brothers and two sisters."

"What are their names?"

Dinah thought a moment. She looked puzzled. Then a knowing look came into her eyes. "Wait." Her eyes widened.

"What?" Achsah pursed her lips.

Dinah's eyes gleamed. "I know where your interest lies. I know why you're asking all the questions." She put her hand to her mouth, and she started to laugh. "It's that Israelite, who recently brought his work to town, near the cloth seller's tent. That's who you're asking about, isn't it?"

Achsah turned and watched a small dust devil suddenly lift into the air and spin across their path. The rushing wind raced by, and Achsah pushed a strand of dark brown hair away from her face that had swept into her eyes. The whirling dust spun into the field and then vanished into the air.

She turned back. Her voice was cool. "What you do mean? Who are you talking about?"

"The worker of stone, Toi. That's who. He hasn't been to town, until this week, but it's him who's drawn your interest, isn't it? You're pretending not to have seen him. He's been working with his friend and kinsman."

Achsah frowned. "I asked you about any new Israelite families, not about a stone worker. I don't know anything about him."

Dinah regarded her a moment. Then she laughed. "I see the look in your eyes, and I believe you're lying. You told me this morning you were going to the marketplace for cloth. Toi works near Elpaal's tent, and you saw how handsome he was. You wanted to add him to your list of admirers. He's the artesian. Ha! I knew it!"

Dinah's mouth lifted at the corner. "As if you don't have enough men vying for the scraps you throw at them."

"That's ridiculous." Achsah turned, and her eyes narrowed. "When I saw him, he was covered in dust. There was nothing appealing about him," she snorted. "I only wanted to know if he had sisters."

"You did see him! I told you!" Dinah burst out laughing. "And I know you better than that. Sisters? You want nothing to do with them. I saw him. The dust couldn't hide anything. He was handsome. I should've known he wouldn't have escaped your notice."

Achsah blinked. "You're impossible! I hardly saw he was there."

"You knew right away who I meant! You said it yourself!"

"I passed the courtyard where they worked, but it doesn't mean I was interested." Achsah looked away.

"No?" Dinah eyed her sister curiously. "Yet, you asked about his family."

"I told you. I wanted to know if he had sisters."

Dinah frowned. "When have you ever been interested in any man's family, Achsah? What other reasons…" Then she stopped short, and she laughed again. "Ah! I know it. You're upset because he isn't playing your games. He hasn't followed you around as those other fools do. I'd be surprised if he even looked your way. You *do* want to know about him."

"That's silly. I haven't even given him a thought. He's worth no more than a shekel in a basket to me. I've better things to think about."

Dinah laughed again. "Ha! A shekel in a basket? I don't believe it, and I know you don't want anything to do with his sisters. That would be the last thing you'd want. Israelite women are of no interest to you."

Achsah pursed her lips. She looked around. "Where's Hezro? He was supposed to bring Vashti back with him."

Dinah put her hands on her hips. She looked down the path. "Not every person in Moab has time to wait on you. I'm surprised mother let me come, although I shouldn't have. She'll find any reason to keep you out of the house with the trouble you cause."

Achsah began walking toward their home. "I know that she wants me out of the way, but I don't wish to be there either. And it doesn't matter if Hezro isn't around. I got the cloth I wanted, and I brought back another household god that mother asked for. I'll put it in the entrance. It's a silly looking thing." She held up a small carved image of a fish.

"Achsah! Why do you say the things you do?" Dinah drew in a breath. "Do you want to incite its anger?"

Achsah laughed. "You're no better than this absurd little thing, my dear sister. No wonder life is such a trial for you."

"With you as a sister, it is!" Dinah started to tromp back in the direction of the house, but then she stopped when she noticed Hezro coming toward them.

Dinah straightened her tunic, but he walked past her and went straight to Achsah.

He appeared chagrinned. "My apologies, Achsah. I meant to bring Vashti, but your mother..." He stopped short at her feet.

Dinah gave him a reproachful look and stomped off toward the house. Her mahogany braids swung back and forth behind her as she kicked up dust on the path.

Both Achsah and Hezro said nothing at first.

Then Achsah glanced at the house and wiped her brow. "It's no matter. I was going inside anyway. I'll see Vashti then. You can go now."

Hezro smiled. "But, what about us? Can I see you again later?" He suddenly turned as three other women across the street walked by. He seemed to be studying them with interest. Then he looked back at her.

"I'm busy. I've things to do." She frowned. She'd no intentions of meeting him again, and she wasn't about to give him any hope of it.

"Then I suppose I'll see you another time." He tipped his head slightly.

"Yes, yes, another time." She waved her hand at him as she watched him walk away.

She sighed. Now she'd need to go and help her mother. Maybe there would be a sewing task for her.

She despised the thought of physical work, where she might spoil her pretty tunic with dust, or where she might be overwrought with heat. She pushed a golden spangle further up her arm and smoothed out the folds of her shimmering tunic.

She needed time to think.

She might ask if she could go to the high places. Mother would surely encourage this. It might be one way to get out of the work at hand for the last few hours of the day.

But if she did, she'd need to get there before the sun lowered in the sky.

*****

Ruth looked out the window from her family's small, cave-like home, carved out of a rocky cliff. There were people at the Moabite altars, set high in the hills, giving sacrifices in the

12

distance. There was still time to worship Chemosh before the shadows grew long, but she'd lost interest as of late.

Orpah took her wrap from a stone bench and readied herself to leave. "Are you coming?

Ruth shook her head. "Not tonight. I believe I'll stay home this time."

"Are you sure? You haven't been there in a while."

Ruth smiled. She got up and went to Orpah. She took her sister-in-law's hands in her own and kissed both of her cheeks. "You go. I believe I've lost the inclination for it. Chemosh gives me no rest, and Mahlon's teaching me about the Torah."

Orpah opened the door to go out. She looked back one last time.

Ruth went to the table and sat next to an oil lamp that harbored a flickering light in the shadows of the room. A solemn look came into her eyes. "And besides, with the loss of Elimelech, everything's different here. Naomi needs someone to sit with her, and I'm tired. I spent the day gleaning in the fields."

There was a neigh of a lone donkey outside in the adjacent courtyard. Another animal made a scuffing noise with its feet.

Orpah nodded. "I suppose it was all so unexpected. It is true that Naomi is very downcast." She sighed. "Maybe it's best for you to stay here with her."

"Yes, we'll talk later. Mahlon and Chilion will be back from the fields soon. I'll help with the meal." Ruth pulled stems from the grapes which were in a bowl sitting on the table. She dropped them into an empty container next to it.

Orpah stepped outside. "Peace, Ruth! I'll not be long."

Ruth lifted her hand to wave. "Peace." She watched as Orpah made her way to the gate to let herself out.

She turned to the quiet of the household and its duties. Her thoughts went to her mother-in-law who would be coming back from the well soon.

Ruth sighed.

She hoped Naomi's pain would lessen in time as she grieved over her husband's death.

It would be good if, in the months ahead, Naomi would be able to go about her tasks without the deep sadness she suffered from daily.

Ruth would do what she could to help.

She finished pulling the last stem from the grapes on the table and set the bowl aside. She looked for the next task that needed to be done.

*****

Toi started up the rocky path past a terraced garden. He eyed the stone altars which were built for the Moabite's fish god. Hewn pillars to Chemosh were on the side of a hill, at the top, and under every spreading tree.

A bitter smell of sacrifice trailed past Toi's nose as he walked near the first offering.

Two young men and a woman burned incense on the top of a dark stone. They murmured chants to Chemosh in rote unison. The woman's face was cast downward toward the ground.

Toi moved past them.

Along with the chants and sounds of fires snapping wildly, there was a blended mass of song. The music was strange. It was an eerie foreign sound that wove its way down the paths and over the valley. Toi eyed the people with an impatient look as he made his way up the hill.

Farther along the path, in a grove of trees, after he'd almost made it to the top, he stopped short.

Shobach was right. The Moabitess, Achsah, stood in front of a shrine. The sun was still out, even though the day neared its end.

Toi leaned against a tree and pulled a tall piece of grass out of the ground as he watched her. He chewed on the end of it.

The young woman stared at trails of smoke that spiraled upward on the top of the altar while the dark plumes disappeared into the air above her.

14

Achsah intrigued him with her wide emerald eyes, thick lashes, and high cheekbones. Her features differed from the other women in the town.

Her skin was a beautiful tone and glistened in the sunlight that shone down on it. Two tiny braids held back the front sections of her thick, brown hair in which were tied in the back with a leather cord.

The tunic she wore was unusual. He eyed it with interest. The fabric shimmered in the sun and was cut and sewed quite different from the usual style in the land. Embroidered golden threads were woven into her silken, orange skirt in designs that flowed out from her tiny waist.

With her choice of colors and style, it seemed she'd made as many efforts to attract as much attention to herself as was possible. Her family must have been very rich as she lacked nothing in the way of precious stones and pieces of jewelry.

Though she sat at the altar, for quite some time, and stared at the top of it, she still hadn't spoken to the Moabite god, Chemosh. Instead, she leaned forward and blew on the incense when the flame began to wane.

She turned briefly toward the sun and then directed her attention back to the spiraling smoke on the altar. Her large hazel eyes were fastened on the golden flame as she sat there quietly as if entranced by the flicker of it. The small tip of yellow-orange fire twisted and snapped as it sent wisps of smoke into the air. She hadn't uttered a prayer, or a song, or chant, but sat unusually still instead.

When the flame finally died, she took a seat on the lower part of the stonework which surrounded the altar. She pushed her sandals from her feet and wiggled her toes while she stared at the jewels on them. A golden chain around her ankle slid down, onto the lowest part of her foot, and she reached down to turn it.

She appeared less interested in her duties to her god than to her baubles and trinkets which adorned her wrists, ankles, fingers, and toes. Her eyes danced as she admired the many glittering bracelets and rings.

Toi smiled as he watched her. He wondered what might have brought the young woman to the high places when it was clearly not her god who had caught her interest.

He spoke quietly. "What? No chant to Chemosh? No reverent words? Isn't it the custom of your people to sing or chant to your god?"

Achsah turned quickly. At first, she seemed surprised he was there. Then she put her hand on her hip as her eyes met his. "Excuse me?"

He laughed. "I apologize, but I've seen no sweet incantations coming from your mouth, nor heard any pious words. It appears you're more interested in the jewels on your pretty fingers and toes instead."

She quickly pulled her feet under her tunic and stared at him. "Why are you here?" Her eyes narrowed. "And why does it matter to you what I do? I didn't come to talk to you."

Toi laughed again. "I've taken great pains to learn about your people, since I've come, and about the Moabite women in particular as well." His eyes sparkled as he said it.

She directed a dead stare at him. She brushed off her skirt and sat up straighter. "Shouldn't you be at your temple, or altar, doing what your people do, instead of spying on me? I thought you Israelite men weren't supposed to talk to foreign women."

"My people wouldn't appreciate it." Toi looked at her with amusement in his eyes. He didn't move from where he stood. "But, sometimes I find it a dull affair to watch the priests burn the sacrifices, and I don't mind talking to you." He chuckled low. "Though, your devotion to Chemosh, or lack thereof, makes me wonder why you bothered to come."

Her mouth drew open. Then her eyes sparked contentiously. "I've taken time out of my day to walk up this hill and light the incense. It's more than you do for your God." There was an edge to her voice.

Toi gave her a wry grin. "At least I make no pretense of what I do. I wouldn't stand at an altar, unless I truly thought I might gain something from it."

16

Achsah's cheeks glowed heatedly. She quickly tied the laces on her sandals and went to him. "My own practices are my business, and there's no pretense in my actions. It matters little to me what you think. I don't know you and have no wish to."

She turned to leave, but he gently took hold of her arm. He pulled her around and smiled. "I believe you will wish to know me. I'm sure of it. But not be in the way you expect. I won't be chasing after you like those other fools in the marketplace."

Achsah stared at him and took her hand away. Her voice was quiet, yet she bit out her words. "I want nothing to do with you, or wish to hear what you have to say."

He laughed again. "Your temper won't do, if you wish to seek my favor, Achsah."

"Ha!" Her eyes glittered dangerously. "Why would you think I'd want anything of the sort?"

Then she turned, and a frown arched over her brow. "And how is it that you know my name?"

"Why wouldn't I?" He smiled. "It seems you're quite well acquainted with the townspeople in these parts. You seem to be the topic of many discussions."

He watched as a myriad of emotions crossed her face.

"I don't care what they say about me." She looked at the fields in the distance. She seemed to be contemplating his words.

Then she smiled as if a thought suddenly came to her. Her eyes held a gleam in them. "All this talk. I suppose there's little good that comes from any of it."

Her expression was suddenly coy, and she drew her mouth into a slight curve. She moved closer and put her hand on his arm. "My only wish is that we could be friends."

She looked across the path in the direction of the town. "I might stop at the marketplace tomorrow and see if you have any of those precious stones I might like."

"You wish to be friends?" Toi looked down at her hand which held many rings. "I'd be very pleased if you came to see me tomorrow." His smile widened. "Your pretty face would be a welcome sight at my workplace."

"Truly?" Achsah's eyelashes lowered as she tipped her head to him.

"There was humor in Toi's voice. "Yes." He took her hand in his. His eyes began to gleam as he looked at her. "But, there is something I must tell you first."

"What?" Achsah bent closer. The color of her green eyes darkened.

Toi leaned down and brushed her hair aside. He whispered in her ear. "You're welcome to visit me, Achsah, though I believe you should know that you won't be receiving any free stones while you're there." He let her go and watched her expression as he backed away.

Achsah cheeks brightened as her eyes met his. She quickly raised her hand to him.

"Careful." Toi smiled. He put up his hand and pushed hers away. "You need to watch what you do, if you want our friendship to continue. I liked it better when your words dripped with honey, and your tongue was smooth like silk."

Her eyes flashed as she attempted to pull her hand away. "You're ridiculous. Let go. I've things to do, and I can't stay here all day."

He pushed her gently away.

She glared at him as she caught her balance.

Then she turned and started down the path.

As she made her way to the village, she spoke over her shoulder. "Believe what you want, Toi." She spoke his name quietly. "But, I've no wish to know you. Understand that *you* were the one who came looking for me. I didn't follow you here."

*****

Toi leaned back against a tree. He didn't say anything, but he let out a low whistle as he watched her walk away.

18

She'd said his name. She must have asked about him. He chuckled to himself.

This woman Achsah had spirit. She wouldn't easily be swayed in his direction. He could be sure of it. She spoke with such confidence. There was nothing demure or unassuming about her.

He smiled again as she rounded the turn. She hadn't looked back.

He raked his hand through his hair. What Shobach had said was true. Achsah was trouble. Yet, she also held his interest.

He smiled again. He supposed that as long as he kept his heart from the woman, there would be no danger in pursuing her attentions.

He grinned at the thought of the man who would one day allow himself to be caught in Achsah's web. Though Toi might enjoy her smiles that she would cast his way someday, or take pleasure in her pretty looks, he was certain he would never yield himself ever to her in any way.

He watched as she disappeared out of his sight, and he spoke under his breath. "I must be mad to pursue the women I do. Yet it seems to be something I can't resist."

*****

Chapter 2

The next morning, Achsah stomped down the rocky path toward the marketplace. She'd finished her early chores and was on her way to buy cloth. Her ears were tuned to the sharp sounds of the bricks being shaped by stoneworkers and the calling out of the people in the market as the town came to life.

She bristled as she passed two traders with a slew of camels attached in rows behind them. One camel raised its head and let out a resounding wail over her head. The howl seemed to mirror her own dark thoughts.

She strode past the place where Toi worked his craft, and she set her eyes on the wheat field adjacent to him. That infernal stone cutter had left her sleepless the night before. She was determined to show him that she wanted nothing to do with him.

She planned to meet one of the field hands again, and Toi would know, very soon, that her interest lay elsewhere.

Ittai worked in the distance. Not that she particularly cared for this man, but she didn't see any other around to make her point.

"Ittai!" She waved to him from the edge of the field. She wrinkled her nose as he dropped the tool he used and wiped the sweat from his brow.

Ittai was tall. He had dark hair that reached to his shoulders. Though his beard was long, and somewhat wild, no one could deny that he was attractive. Achsah wasn't sure of her own thoughts of him. Sometimes the way he looked at her made her feel uncomfortable, but she supposed she'd need to overlook her feelings for now. She was determined to teach Toi that he was wrong about her and that she would not be looking his way anytime soon.

Ittai walked across the field to where she stood. "What is it, Achsah? I've no time for your games. I'm working for your father."

Achsah reached up and adjusted the edge of his tunic and smiled at him. "Are you certain of it?" She tugged on the tie that encircled his waist and walked away from him.

The tips of the wheat around them bent as the wind wisped over the tops and swayed them slightly.

She giggled as he pulled her back into his embrace.

He studied her warily. "What do you want?"

She reached up and touched the side of his face. "You didn't notice me watching you? I passed by and saw you working."

She glanced at Toi from a distance. He watched them. Good. He'd pay for his insolence the day before.

She turned back to Ittai. "Why do you look the way you do? I've waited to see you."

Ittai studied her warily, then his dark eyes suddenly gleamed, and he quickly leaned down to kiss her.

The sweat from the fields trickled down his face and soaked the front of his tunic. Heat from his body stole over her.

She moved back as his arms encircled her waist in a tighter hold. The smell of his damp shirt made her crinkle her nose. She suddenly wasn't so sure she wanted him this near to her. A drop of sweat fell onto her neck and ran down her chest. "Not so close."

Ittai's voice lowered. "What? You called me here. You took me from my work, Achsah." He frowned. "I won't have mixed messages anymore. Come now."

"Ittai."

"I told you I'm tired of your games. You'll not waste my time again."

Achsah pushed on his sweaty chest. She leaned further from him. "I wanted to talk, nothing more. My father...won't like this."

"Your father?" He gave her an annoyed look. "Don't bring him into this. He may own the field, but it doesn't mean he's going to come between us when you behave the way you do. There'll be no more talk. I'm through wasting my time."

She squirmed from his grasp, and tried to push him away again, but to no avail. "But you're dirty from the fields and from working." She eyed him distastefully. "I hadn't counted on it, and I told mother I'd be back soon."

She pried his fingers loose, and suddenly, when she realized he wasn't letting go, she smashed down on his foot with her sandal.

She managed to break free from his hold.

When she heard him groan and curse under his breath, she fled into the field of tall wheat. She was sure Toi had seen what had taken place between them, but she wasn't about to give him the satisfaction of calling out to him for his help.

Ittai's voice was low and deep. "Come now, Achsah. Come out." He stalked through the field after her.

She kept low and crawled away from him. Luckily, the wheat was at its full height, and she was able to stay hidden from him.

"Achsah please, I told you that I've no time for your games."

Achsah's heart beat wildly in her chest when she heard the soft padding of his footsteps nearby.

She drew in a breath as she parted pieces of wheat that were in front of her face. The grainy smell was pungent. She crouched further down as her knees pressed against the hard packed earth beneath her.

She frowned. She hoped her beautiful tunic wouldn't be ruined by the smelly dirt.

After a time, she heard nothing but the sound of the wheat swaying in the wind and the birds above her singing. She let out a breath and stood up. She brushed herself off and sighed.

It seemed Ittai wasn't one to reckon with. She supposed it would be best to stay away from him after this.

She began to walk back through the grass when a noise sounded behind her.

She turned around and froze in her spot.

Ittai had seen her, and his black-hearted smile widened on his face as his eyes fastened on her like a hawk.

She screamed and made an attempt to run, but she wasn't fast enough.

Ittai lunged at her from where he stood.

She shrieked again, and she held her arms out. Her heart beat wildly in her chest. "Ittai, no!"

He shoved her hands aside and took her by the shoulders.

It was one of the few times she'd actually felt fear, because he was stronger than she'd imagined.

"Stop, Achsah! I told you that I'm done with your games."

She tried to stomp on his foot again but missed. "My father will kill you!" Tears sprang to her eyes. "He'll be very angry with you!"

"I'm not worried about your father right now…" Ittai laughed.

She beat on his arms and tried to strike his face, but her attempts seemed futile. "Stop! Ittai! I tell you, you'll regret this!"

There was a rustle behind them, and a voice sounded. "Let her go." Achsah looked over her shoulder.

Toi had found his way to them.

She breathed a sigh of relief when he shoved Ittai aside. There was a veiled threat in his voice. "There's no need for this. Leave her, and go back to the fields."

Ittai eyes darkened when he saw Toi. "This isn't your business. It's between the two of us."

Achsah moved back, confused. She blinked as she rubbed the dust from her eyes. She pushed her disheveled hair behind her. Her breaths came in gulps. Tears stained with dirt fell onto her cheeks.

When she realized she was free, the panic in her died. Her fear was very quickly replaced with anger. She looked darkly at Ittai through narrowed eyes.

Though the man towered over her, he stood little chance against Toi who clearly had the advantage. Having worked the profession, he did, with heavy stones the day long, he was undoubtedly larger and more solidly built because of it.

Achsah straightened as she watched them.

There was a hard edge to Toi's voice. "I said to leave her be. You'll face grave consequences for such an act. There's no need for it."

Ittai scowled. "My problem isn't with you, but with her." He pointed to Achsah.

Toi turned. He stared at her. "It seems you aren't the only one who has a problem with her." He frowned, and then he turned back to Ittai. "But there'll be none of this. Go back to the field, and forget about this business."

Ittai eyed Toi as if he contemplated what he should do next.

Achsah backed away and rubbed her wrists. She wiped more tears from her eyes.

Ittai wagged a finger in her direction. "She'd better not do anything like this again." His expression was grave. "And if she says anything to her father, she'll wish she hadn't."

Achsah bit back a retort. She wanted to tear the man apart. If she were only stronger, she would. Her eyes flashed dark green and narrowed as she looked at him.

"No." Toi shook his head at Achsah as if he willed her not to speak.

Ittai looked irritated. Then he turned and went back the way he'd come.

Toi watched Achsah as she wiped back another tear. "You need to get out of the field." He let out a breath as she rearranged the jewelry on her wrist. "Come now, you're wasting my work time and my money."

Achsah straightened her skirt. She pulled the wheat out of her hair and combed through the dark strands of brown with her fingers. She clasped her hands together to keep them from shaking.

Toi reached out and tried to take her by the arm, but she quickly drew back, and her eyes widened as she looked at him.

He stared at her in disbelief. He put out his hand. "Please, I've had ample opportunities to take advantage of you, if I would have wanted to. I just saved you from this."

Achsah eyed him warily. She stepped forward and took his hand in hers.

He didn't say anything, but instead he turned and half dragged her along beside him as they made their way out of the tall grass.

She kept tripping as she struggled to keep up. "Slow down. I don't walk that fast." She gave him a disconcerted look.

He didn't vary his pace. "I should have left you with him. You didn't deserve my help for what you did. Did you think of what might have happened, if I hadn't have come? Why would you act like you did?"

Achsah pursed her lips together. Her face heated as she looked at him.

He moved quickly through the fields.

Neither spoke as they walked toward the road going into the town. They stopped when they got there.

She turned from curious stares of people who drove past on carts. She wondered how much they'd seen.

Toi's expression sobered as he looked at her. "You acted poorly and with bad judgment. Why haven't your parents taught you better than this? The games you play, and that temper of yours, will surely land you in a very bad place someday, if you continue this way. You must watch what you do and heed my words."

Achsah let out a breath. "*He* should have…"

"No, Achsah, *you* were wrong. I see how some of the men are tiring of your games, and you can't control their actions.

You can't defend yourself against them. If you hadn't called Ittai over, none of this would have happened. You were lucky I put a stop to it. Next time, you might not be so lucky."

She looked down, and she played with the gold spangles on her arms and wrists.

Before they crossed the road, Toi reached over and stopped her. "I met a Moabite woman today you should consider. This wouldn't have happened to her. She's respected. There's no reason for you to act the way you do."

Achsah put her hands on her hips. "What woman?" She turned to him.

Toi's lip curled upward. "A better one than you. Her name is Ruth."

Her brow rose a notch. "I know her."

"She has pure heart. You could never understand a woman like her."

Achsah drew in a sharp breath. "What do you mean by that?" She tugged on his arm. "You don't know me. You know nothing about my heart."

He pushed her hand off of him. "I might not, but I do know you aren't as she is. She makes wise choices and watches her tongue. She would have kept herself far from Ittai. Her heart belongs to her husband. It's what I meant when I said what I did."

Achsah pursed her lips. "It doesn't matter to me what she does." She shrugged. "And you're right. I don't understand her ways as I've reaped few rewards when I've taken the same paths she has. What gains are made, when a heart given, is trampled upon? Only a simpleton will risk such a thing."

Toi reached out to stroke Achsah's cheek, but she turned away. She wiped a tear that had dropped from her eyes onto her cheek.

"She's not so pretty," she said.

"Pretty? Vanity's unbecoming, my dear. Those who rely on it will be brought down in time. The men will tire of your antics, as Ittai did, in spite of your pretty face. You'll get no

26

respect from them and will gain nothing by the things you do. How can you expect to be cherished, or honored, by any man, when you do these things? Think on what I've said. You didn't even have the courtesy of thanking me for my assistance."

Achsah gazed at the mountain north of the town. She sniffed and wiped her eyes. She wanted to tell him she was glad he'd given his help, but something held her back. She started to talk, but her throat was dry, and she couldn't get the words out.

Toi put his hand on hers. "Achsah, I don't want an apology, unless you can say it with integrity. And you most likely cannot. It's best if you say nothing."

Achsah bit her lip. Though she was grateful that he'd offered his assistance, when he did, she couldn't bring herself to say it. She pulled her hand away.

"I assumed as much." Toi shook his head.

Achsah's brows formed an upward arch, but before she could answer, she heard a voice behind them.

She turned and groaned. "Oh, great grains! My sister. Will this day ever end?"

"Sister?" Toi rubbed his chin and turned.

Dinah's bright auburn braids flew behind her shoulders in disarray as she tromped up the path toward them. Her eyes were like fiery coals. She stopped at Achsah's feet. "Where have you been?"

Toi looked surprised. "She has a sister." He shook his head, and then he chuckled to himself.

Achsah directed an ill-tempered frown his way.

Dinah took a place beside them. She tugged on Achsah's arm. "I thought you said you didn't like him? You told me he was worth no more than a shekel in a basket."

Toi stared at Achsah. A surprised look crossed his face, and he laughed. "A shekel in a basket?" He gave Achsah a sideways glance. "That's what you likened me to?"

Achsah's eyes narrowed. She put her hands on her hips. "And with good reason, but I don't care what you think."

"Well, for not liking him, you sure are spending a lot of time around him and talking about him at the house."

Toi laughed again.

Achsah's cheeks flamed as a rage boiled inside her. This time Dinah had gone too far. Achsah was sick of her younger sister and the men around her. Dinah had no right to say these things for others to hear, and Toi should not have laughed at her because of it. Only moments before, she'd been made to suffer at the hands of that sweat-soaked, field worker, Ittai. What more was there to endure?

"Well?" Dinah put her finger on Achsah's chest and poked her with it. "What have you to say for yourself?"

Achsah could not contain the anger that exploded inside her. Dinah had gone too far. She pushed her sister's arm away. Then she shoved hard, and Dinah fell backward, into the field, taking Achsah with her.

Achsah's careful braid came loose, and her light brown hair spilled over her shoulders.

Dinah grabbed some strands of Achsah's hair and pulled it hard.

Pain shot through Achsah's head and neck. She couldn't see Dinah. She let out an injured sound and then screamed, "Stop it you, horrible girl! Let go, or you'll regret it!" She tried to pry her sister's hands from her as tears sprang to her eyes. Achsah's head throbbed, and she felt as if her upper jaw had been bruised.

They both tumbled on the ground while trying to hit each other with their fists.

Achsah felt Toi's arms around her. He gripped Dinah's hand tightly which caused her to let go of Achsah's hair, then he pulled the two apart.

He held them from each other while they both threw wild swings in each other's direction. His voice was a command. "Stop it! Both of you. Do it, or I'll take you both and dump you into the river! Is this what you want?"

28

The sound of the rushing waters of the great river, in the distance, was suddenly distinctly clear. Both young women quieted, yet they regarded each other with dark, narrowed eyes.

Toi tossed Dinah in a heap on the ground. "Go home!" He gave her a shove with his foot. "Quickly!"

Dinah got up with a dazed look on her face. She didn't seem to want to go against Toi's wishes.

She brushed her tunic off and straightened it. "You just wait, Achsah! Mother's going to hear about this!"

Achsah began to reply, but Toi held his hand over her mouth. "I said to stop. Leave it be!" His voice was quiet, yet it was not without a hidden threat.

Dinah ran back down the road from where she'd come.

Angry tears sprouted from Achsah's eyes. She gently pried Toi's fingers from her lips. "Let go of me. I'm not going to say anything to her."

Toi took a deep breath. The look on his face was one of disbelief. He set her down. "What do you think you're doing?"

"Dinah started it. Now, I have to go back home to her." Her face scrunched into a frown.

"You'll be all right. Just stay away from the field hands, and treat your sister with more kindness than you do. She's younger than you. You must teach her the better way."

Achsah gave him a discouraging look. She combed her fingers through her hair again and re-braided it. "How can I, if I don't know a better way. It's not something I can teach her. Who's to teach me?" A tear slid down her cheek, and she choked back a sob. "I'll never be Ruth, and I can't be what everyone wants me to be. It's not possible. There's too much I'll never know."

He turned to her in surprise. He reached out and tenderly brushed her cheek with his hand as if to rid her of some dirt there. "Well, my little Achsah. Did you just speak from your heart? Is it true? Is it possible for such a thing to happen? Do I see brokenness?"

She got up and studied him as she straightened her tunic. She took a step back and lifted her chin. Her voice was quiet, but not without an edge to it. "You can make fun of me if you want, but I won't listen to it."

She turned and looked down the path toward her home. There was a reluctant expression that stole over her face. "I'll be forced to endure the storm which is brewing in our home. I'm sure I've not heard the end of it."

Toi got up next to her. He had a serious look on his face. "I wasn't making fun of you. I'm glad you were truthful with me. I only wish I'd hear more of it."

He smiled. "You've given me an eventful morning. Though, I *am* glad I'm not going home with you. Do you have other sisters I should be aware of?"

"None that should worry you, not like Dinah."

"How many?"

She frowned as she looked back down the path. "Two of them, and a brother. Why?"

Toi looked toward the village. "I like to know the people in the town, for business purposes."

"Vashti's my mother's child, as is Dinah. Vashti's quiet, and she's almost ten years old. She's a good girl. One of my father's concubines has a daughter and a son. Helah, my other sister, and Vashti are near the same age and play together. My father's son, by this same woman, is Samla. I'm the oldest and am in trouble the most. Dinah and I are mortal enemies as you've seen." She gave him a chagrinned look.

Toi couldn't help but smile. "I'm lucky to have come out of the last battle alive. I can see what you're saying is truth."

"Yes well, I've avoided my home and chores long enough. I must go now. My parents will be none too pleased with me." She shrugged nonchalantly as she pushed a jeweled armlet that had slipped down, higher up on her arm. She retied her orange-gold sash around her waist. "But I've given up hope for that to happen. I'm sure it would be difficult to find good in one such as myself."

Toi put his hand on her shoulder. "Achsah, everyone has redeeming qualities. Your family must know them."

She shrugged. "If they do, I've not heard of them."

Then her eyes turned a deeper shade of green. She looked up at him. "I suppose even a stranger wouldn't have a lot of good to say about me."

Toi rubbed some dirt from her cheek. He didn't speak at first. Then he smiled. "It isn't difficult to see that you're quite capable of getting what you want." He chuckled to himself. "You're a woman of strength and fortitude, Achsah, and a beauty, with an ability to think quickly on your feet. I admire you for that. You don't give up easily and seem to be able to see others as they are. Yes, I do see redeeming qualities."

He studied her. "Though, I believe you possess these things, I'm sure you're a woman who's known little love, one who's been forsaken in a desolate land. How could you know how to love, when you've received little of it?"

She didn't say anything, at first, as she contemplated what he told her. Then she spoke quietly. "I didn't ask you this because I wanted anything from you. I only wanted to know what you'd say."

He gave her an amused look. "I assumed as such, and I don't want anything from you either."

She suddenly backed away and crossed her arms in front of her. "You don't like me, do you?" She eyed him suspiciously.

Toi laughed as he looked at her. "On the contrary. I like you very much, possibly more than I should. But a desert flower is bound to have thorns." His mouth turned up at the corner. "And I do fear beautiful things that might injure me."

Achsah gave him a reproachful look. "I think you should fear me."

Then she moved closer and reached up to straighten the edge of his robe. Her eyes suddenly turned a smoky green and slanted up at him. "Though you might find that the prize is worth the injury and wish to know me better. You seem one who would overlook such things for the sake of love."

31

She tipped her head upward. Her eyelashes fluttered at him. She'd heard the lies that came from the lips of men. Would he play the games other men did and tell her what he thought she wanted to hear?

"Achsah, I don't think it would be as it is for Ruth, or my family, for the two of us. I look to my own interests and nothing else. I don't believe I can love anyone. I've little faith in those things."

A silence pervaded the air as Achsah contemplated Toi's words. Save for the hot breeze, which hovered over the stirring grasses, the sounds of the marketplace had faded into the distance.

When she spoke, her voice was a whisper. "I've never loved anyone like that either, nor do I believe I would know how to… as it's much like the wind, within my grasp, but quite impossible to take hold of. Sometimes, I'm afraid of the thought of it."

She took a breath and looked away. "You spoke honestly. I suppose I might be able to trust you, because of this, which is more than I can say for most men."

Then, Achsah pushed his hand off her arm. "I need to go now. I believe enough has been said." She backed away from him. "No good ever comes from such talk. My family will be waiting for me."

"Achsah." Toi's voice softened. "I didn't mean to…"

She shook her head. "No please. No more."

When he reached out again to her, she shook her head. "I told you I don't want this."

She turned abruptly and looked down the path.

As she walked away, she could feel his eyes on her. She didn't turn back. He'd spoken the truth when she asked for it. She could admire him for that.

Despite, she'd secretly wished, in her heart, that he might have compromised the truth so that she would consider him, as she did the others, not worth her time.

But because he had not done so, she'd have to consider him differently, and she wasn't sure she was prepared for such a thing.

A wariness filled her heart at the thought of it.

*****

Chapter 3

It was as Achsah had guessed. Dinah had taken their troubles home with her and had caused a great stir among each and every member of their household. The family was once again torn apart and in an uproar.

Achsah looked up and took a breath as she eyed her father's fields on the edge of the town. She breathed in the fresh, sweet scent of barley and exhaled. The flat, rocky hills of the plains of Moab jutted up against the purplish gray mountains just south of the river Arnon. All was stark and dry today, yet in the valley there was a sense of quiet and peace.

It was surely a relief to be free from the disparaging remarks and looks of disapproval tossed her way that morning.

Over the course of time, she'd found ways of distancing herself from the others and evading her family. Today was no different. Walking the road to town proved to be her respite.

She supposed her mother and father welcomed the thought of sending her on errands, rather than keeping her there to finish her chores. With her gone, their source of contention was put to rest, and they could carry on their tasks with minimal difficulties.

She turned back and smiled. Dinah was most likely asked to take on extra duties for the sake of keeping the family peace. Her sister wouldn't be happy with it.

Ha! It served her right for what she did.

A picture formed in Achsah's mind of Dinah, sitting at the weaving loom, as she pulled the yarn tight with a bitter look on her face. Mother would be scolding her for it.

Achsah scanned the town in the distance. She was anxious to find her way to the cloth maker's tent. Elpaal might spare her another pretty swatch that she could add to her collection. She had ideas as to how she could construct another handsome tunic for herself.

She sighed impatiently. First, she'd need to purchase the goods for which her mother had sent her to town for. Then, she'd use what was leftover for her own things. If there was none left for her, she'd devise a way to have what she wanted. She could count on that.

She couldn't wait to get to the tent. She adored the markets and the swarms of people there. She might even stop for a meal at her friend's house, on the way back, as she had no interest in returning to her household until later that evening. There was nothing there for her but more trouble.

The sky was a bright blue, and the sun had arisen above the mountains. The glowing gold day moon sent spokes of bright, iridescent light over the plains and throughout the valleys. Birds sang quiet melodies as they found perches in the few trees along the path. The subtle warmth of the morning sun brought a rosy glow to Achsah's cheeks.

She smiled at the thought of her welcome escape from all that lay behind her.

She twirled around once and kicked a pebble down the path as she walked. She giggled with delight at the thoughts of the new purchases she planned to make and the excitement of the town.

Maybe Dinah had done her a favor. The day might just turn out to be better than she'd expected.

*****

Achsah looked down the road. It appeared Ruth was on her way to the market also. The path was busy with people on their way into the town from the houses that were etched into the stone cliffs off the road outside the gates.

"Good morning." Ruth waved shyly. "Wait, and I'll walk with you." Ruth drew her shawl around her and quickened her pace. Her large, almond-shaped eyes lightened when she looked at Achsah.

Achsah studied Ruth's clothing and the way she moved and spoke. She wondered why so many people had spoken so highly of Ruth and alluded to her beauty. She didn't see what others did. To Achsah, there was nothing in the woman's appearance that would suggest such a thing.

Ruth's tunic was plain. She had on a tan-colored piece of fabric with no embroidered designs or beadwork. She wore no jewelry or embellishments. Nor did Ruth bother with kohl around her eyes or other cosmetics. A simple rope was secured around her thin waist. Her hair hung straight behind her shoulders. The only hint of color, she possessed, was the natural pinkness on her sun-browned cheeks.

Ruth drew nearer. She took Achsah's arm and smiled widely. "What do you plan to buy today? Might I help you? I could carry a basket for you?" There was a warm look in her eyes.

Achsah let out a breath as she gently shook her arm free from Ruth's hold. "My mother needs things, but I plan to get fabric for myself."

"Oh." Ruth smiled again. "I'm going that way."

Achsah didn't answer, but she walked alongside Ruth.

Ruth stepped up her pace. "Mahlon asked that I bring back some feed for the goats. Our stores are low. Things have not been good since my father-in-law died. Naomi's very distraught, so Orpah and I are doing our best to be a comfort to her."

Achsah turned. "You've been with this family for some time. I suppose it was difficult for all of you." She eyed Ruth with a curious stare. "What's it like being married to an Israelite?"

Ruth shook her head. "My husband, Mahlon's, a good man. He treats me very well. His family has been generous with their affection."

"Even when you're a foreign woman? Isn't that what the Israelites think of us, that we are not their kind?"

"Mahlon doesn't." Ruth's dark eyes widened. "He's good to me. His whole family has been. I love Naomi and the rest of the family with all my heart."

Achsah stared at Ruth as if she wasn't sure she believed her, yet she couldn't help sensing what Ruth said was true.

"My husband cares for me very much. He's taught me the ways of his people, and I've adopted many of them as my own."

Achsah looked skeptical. "But, you're not Israelite."

"No, but they accept me as if I were, except than I'm unable go to their synagogue with them." Ruth smiled.

Achsah's eyes swept over Ruth as she walked beside her. She still couldn't imagine what it was that others saw in the woman. The plain drab apparel Ruth wore did nothing for her wispy shape. Her lack of cosmetics left her without color. She surely didn't resemble the Moabite women Achsah knew. Maybe Ruth would be accepted by the Israelites as one of their own with her quiet, demure ways.

"I suppose, if it were me, things would be very different." Achsah straightened. "They might not appreciate the things I say, or do, or my mode of dress."

Ruth looked shocked. "Oh Achsah, my husband and his family would surely accept you as you are. My husband would say that you have beauty in our Lord's eyes. He says that Adonai sees into your soul and that the Lord created you to be the way you are."

Achsah gave Ruth an odd look. She backed up a step. "Surely you say these things to flatter me."

Ruth reached out and put her hand on Achsah's arm. "No, I've no reason to, and I meant what I said with all my heart. You're beautiful to Adonai, because he created you. He's the Creator of all." Her dark eyes grew large.

"You truly believe this?" Achsah drew back.

"I do."

Achsah hadn't noticed the warmth which radiated from Ruth before this. There was something unusual about the woman. Her kind words and thoughtful actions were so very sincere and inviting. This loving God she spoke of seemed to have fashioned her very heart.

What had Ruth said? The Creator Lord saw into her soul?

Achsah regarded Ruth with a puzzled expression. "This Maker is different from Chemosh if such beautiful things can be said about him."

"It's true, but he's also just. He's not a god made with human hands, but the one true Lord. I've given up many of the ways of my people for Adonai."

Achsah looked skeptical. "You might have, but I don't believe I would. I'm sure your Lord wouldn't think the same of me, as he does of you, when my own kin can see no good in me."

"Achsah, even when your mother and father forsake you, Mahlon would say that, Adonai, would take you as his own. He loves with an everlasting love, and he can, because he's the Lord of all."

"Well then, if he does such things, I'm not so sure he's wise. Does he not know what I am and the things I've done?" Achsah tossed her thick brown hair behind her. She kicked a small pebble off the road as she watched it skip across the dry, desert sands. "If he gave more thought to the matter, he might consider changing his ways."

A quiet giggle erupted from Ruth, and she covered her mouth with her hand. "You're unaware of Adonai's abilities. He'll surely look at the motivations of your heart, over your actions, and he'd see what I do, a young woman of honest words and beauty."

Achsah couldn't help smiling. "You can believe it, but I'm not so sure. I think it's best I keep my mind on the cloth at the market instead. I must remember the town streets ahead. I've purchases to make."

Ruth smiled back. "Well then, it seems we must part ways. I believe we're headed in different directions."

"Yes, it's true. I hope your day at the market is profitable."

"And the same with you." Ruth patted her on the arm.

Achsah took a path that led to the marketplace. Ruth left to find grains to keep their goats fed and well.

*****

Toi shook his head. How Achsah managed to escape her home, to shop in the village, was beyond his ability to understand. If the same thing had happened to any of his sisters, they wouldn't have been allowed to leave the house for weeks. When they did, they would've been chaperoned. Either the discipline was highly lacking at her place, or she'd managed to find her own way to freedom. In Achsah's case, Toi supposed the latter was true.

After all that had happened, he would have thought Achsah would have learned from her previous experiences, yet she was holding a piece of highly ornate, shimmering fabric, in her hands, and plying Elpaal with her playful smiles. He hoped Elpaal wouldn't fall for her tricks this time. The woman seemed to have a way of stealing the hearts of men in this town. She would put Elpaal out of business, if he weren't careful.

Elpaal held up another swatch of fabric. It was less vibrant. He seemed to be attempting to persuade Achsah to take the lesser of the two. Toi was sure Elpaal's suggestion wouldn't go over well with the young woman. Achsah seemed to want the very finest in merchandise.

Toi watched as her eyes narrowed, and a petulant look crossed her face. Her eyes were fixed on the unwanted swatch of fabric. It seemed as if she were even more determined to have her way when Elpaal rejected her offer.

She shook her head and stomped her sandal down on the hard ground, and then she flipped a mass of dark brown hair behind her. Her antics weren't working.

Toi couldn't help but smile. He was pleased that Elpaal had caught onto Achsah's tricks. Otherwise, the man would have no business over the course of time.

Toi continued to shape the stone, beneath his hands, with his copper chisel. He watched Achsah, out of the corner of his eye, and chuckled. Her footsteps were quiet as she made her way into the courtyard where he worked.

He kept chipping away at the rock, to smooth the edges, and didn't look up, even though he heard her stop at his feet. Nothing would possess him to hand over any of his hard earned money for her own senseless purposes.

"You know that I'm here. You should look at me."

Toi tapped the stone he was working on, one more time with his hammer, and he looked up. He gave her an indifferent look. "Why did you come, Achsah? I've work to do. I need to concentrate on my trade."

She sat on the bench beside him and rested her hand on his. "Your business seems to be prospering. I see you take pride in your work." Her speech was smooth like the oil in his lamps.

He didn't say anything, but he looked down at her small hand and outlined it with his fingers. Such a delicate little thing.

Her eyes were wide when she looked at him. "It appears you do quite well." Her voice became soft like a song.

"I do. It's a very profitable business. I enjoy it. I've even carved some of those detestable gods, for your king, and was paid well for them."

Achsah looked interested. "The Moabite king?" She gave him a sly look. "You've made idols for him?"

"I've no problem making money any way I can." Toi shrugged nonchalantly. "As long as I don't find myself worshipping the abominable things, I can still sleep at night."

She looked annoyed at first, then she quickly remedied her expression. "You have coins during a time when the crops are dry?"

"My money pouch isn't without a good amount of weight." He lifted a full leather sack which was on the bench next to him.

He leaned closer to her, and his eyes sparkled. "It's enough that I'm able to spend my excess on my pleasures."

Achsah reached out and grazed his chin with her fingers. "Is this so?" Her eyes turned a brighter green.

40

Toi marveled at the way Achsah was able to draw a person in with her unspoken charm. For a brief moment, he even contemplated opening his money pouch for her, yet his thoughts were short-lived. It wouldn't do to set his heart on her.

"I must get back to my work." He put her hand aside. "You might want to stand back. The stone pieces sometimes break and fly into the air."

Achsah inwardly groaned. She smoothed out her tunic and stood. "You see that this skirt is beginning to fade. Elpaal has new cloth from the orient."

"Is that so?"

"Yes, some very pretty fabric. It's indigo colored with small gold pieces woven into it. I tried to get him to come down on the price, but he wouldn't."

He got up from the bench and moved closer to her. He smiled. "You like it very much?"

She tipped her head upward and nodded. "I do. My heart desires it."

"How much did he ask for it?"

"Ten shekels. I have only one coin. My father wasn't so generous today. He isn't in the best of moods after the other day." She looked up at him again.

Toi waited to see what she would do. Then he leaned down and whispered in her ear. "How do you think you might pay for it, Achsah?"

She lifted her eyes to his and smiled. "I thought, since you've done well, and have money, that you might feel an obligation to help me. I'd look very pretty in that fabric."

"I believe you would. He encircled her waist with his hands and drew her close. "You smell like Myrrh." He breathed in slowly and smiled.

"So, you'll help me?"

"It would be a good color for you." He smoothed back her hair and gave her an amused look. "But I don't believe it would be good to part with my earnings for your vanity's sake.

You must know that you're quite pleasing to me as you are." He chuckled as he said it.

Achsah's face suddenly reddened, and her eyes turned a bitter, smoky green. "You tricked me." Her voice held a threat. She pushed him away. "You shouldn't do these things."

"I thought you appreciated my attention." Toi straightened his robe and fixed his collar.

"I don't care about you. I only wanted the cloth."

He laughed. "I knew that, but I'm surprised you thought you could use your tricks on me. I knew the secrets of your heart and what you wanted before you came into the courtyard."

"And you did not say?" Her eyes narrowed. She put her hands on her hips, and her skirt flared as she swung away from him. "I thought I could count on your honesty."

"When you were playing games with me? I saw no reason for it." He smiled. "You should know that not everyone will do your bidding when you want them to. You cannot always get the things you want, when you want them."

Achsah eyed him with an angry look. "You think I can't get these things without you? I should have known better than to come here. I don't understand why I even wasted my time. There are others, who are more than willing, to accommodate me. Don't think I won't get that fabric, because I will!"

Toi stood watching her as she made quick steps to the gate and went out. She slammed the wooden door behind her. He wondered how long it would be before she was wearing the new tunic she proposed to make.

This Moabite daughter could not help but draw his interest. She would find a way to get what she wanted.

*****

Achsah sat down on a table, at Elpaal's stand, and she swung her legs beneath it. "You watch, Elpaal. I'll have your shekels. It won't be long. Put that fabric aside, and open the curtains of your tent."

42

Elpaal shook his head wearily. "Do what you wish, Achsah, but don't slow my sales. It's all I ask."

"I'll not hinder them. You'll have more than you would have had without me."

She waved at a couple of the men who walked down the road. "Jonathan! Come! Over here!" She pushed her long braid behind her.

Toi was watching. How long would it be for her to make her money to prove that she wasn't going home empty-handed? She needed nothing from him.

"Achsah, how good to see you. What is it?" Jonathan tied his gray donkey to a post and walked across the dusty road.

She tipped her head to him as he drew near. "If you give me a shekel, I'll give you a kiss."

Jonathan gave her a sideways glance, and then he smiled. "A kiss?" He adjusted his cloth headpiece, and he pushed the ties of the leather cord to the back.

"I need a few shekels to buy some cloth." She pointed at the shining, indigo fabric. "One shekel for you." She put her hands on her hips and laughed.

Two other men walked across the road and stood behind Jonathan.

"Here." Jonathan pulled a shekel out of his money pouch which swung freely from his waist.

He handed it to her. He rubbed his chin as he eyed her with a look of anticipation.

She smiled as she leaned closer to him and pecked the side of his cheek. "There...your kiss."

Jonathan laughed. "Come now, that wasn't what I thought you meant." His eyes sparkled when he looked at her. "Yet, you did offer a kiss. I suppose fair is fair."

He motioned to the others. "Jeuz, Gareb! This way! Let Achsah give you a kiss. She needs shekels to buy the pretty fabric."

A small crowd gathered at the tent while Achsah kissed Jeuz, Gareb, and Jobab twice, and Jair once on the cheek."

"How many coins do you have, Achsah? Is it enough?"

"Let's see." She pulled her own coin from her money pouch and added it to the others. She looked over at Toi and lifted her chin. She smiled. "With my own, it makes nine. I need one more."

She looked around. No one else seemed willing to give her more coins.

Then the crowd parted. There was a brief silence as the men under the tent stepped aside.

Ittai walked past them. He was taller than the rest of the men. His face was like stone. "It's my turn. You owe me, Achsah." His eyes were dark.

Achsah's heart began to pound. She looked up at him. "You shouldn't be here, Ittai. We were only having fun." She smoothed out her faded tunic as heat seared her cheeks.

"But you mustn't deny me my kiss." The sleeve of his dark blue robe almost covered his hand as he held a shekel out to her. "Here."

She regarded him warily.

"Leave her be, Ittai." Jonathan spoke quietly. "She's not serious. She only needs money for cloth."

Ittai shoved Jonathan aside and grabbed Achsah by the arm. "I told you, I'm next."

Achsah's eyes widened as she felt Ittai's strong hand tighten around her waist. She tried to push him away. "Ittai, please, stop this."

When Jonathan and Jair made a move toward him, Ittai put Achsah behind him. His eyes glittered dangerously. "Leave us be. She owes me."

"I owe you nothing." Achsah tried to get around him but couldn't. He shoved her backward again.

"I dare any of you to come closer."

None of them moved. He was much larger then the rest of them, and he was clearly at an advantage.

Achsah turned when Toi suddenly came into the tent.

The other men in the group stepped aside.

"Let her go." Toi's voice was low.

Ittai turned around.

Toi moved closer. His eyes darkened. "I thought I told you not to bother her again. I meant what I said. Go home, and keep your money."

Ittai gave Achsah a dark look. "I told her to stop her games, and she's back at them again."

Achsah's eyes narrowed, but she said nothing as she held her money to her chest.

Toi spoke again. "I won't say it again, Ittai. You know what you were told. Come now, she's not worth it."

Ittai's eyes narrowed. His complexion was dark, and a scowl spread over his face, but he let go of Achsah and took a step back. "I'll not fight for the likes of her. I've better prospects, in my sight, than a worthless daughter of Moab. I'll keep my coin and won't waste my time on her."

Achsah's eyes were like hot tar pits as she looked at him. She held her tongue, even though she wanted to throttle him.

Ittai scowled at her. Then he turned, and he pushed his way out of the crowd.

Achsah looked back at Toi.

*****

Toi held a silver shekel out to Achsah. "Now, here's your last coin."

Then he turned to the others. "Go home. She's done with this nonsense."

The other men, under the tent, grumbled as they left to go back to their work.

Achsah put out her hand. She tipped her head upward to look at Toi. Her eyes sparkled. "I'll have the fabric now."

Toi reluctantly dropped the coin in her hand. "I must be mad to give my hard earned money over to you."

"It's not so bad, is it?" Achsah looked down at her hands, which were full of coins, and she smiled.

She quickly moved past Toi. She took her money and handed it to Elpaal. "Here, I have what I need. I can purchase the fabric now."

Elpaal took it in his hands and laughed. "It seems you were right, Achsah. Thanks."

A delighted look came over her face as she held the shimmering material in her hands. She fingered it lovingly. "It's beautiful. It will make the prettiest tunic. I can't wait to wear it."

"Aren't you forgetting something?"

Achsah frowned. She turned around.

Toi stood behind her. A wry smile spread over his face. "I believe you owe me something for the coin."

She sighed wearily. Then she conceded. "Oh, all right. If I must, but I'm leaving soon. There are things I planned to do. Come closer so I can kiss your cheek, too."

Toi looked annoyed when she tipped her face to his. He took her by the shoulders while he studied her with an interested look.

Then he laughed, and he pushed her back. "Ha! I believe I'll forgo my payment. It seems I want none of this after all." He moved away as if he were ridding himself of the dust on the street. "If there's a time you give me anything, Achsah, it will be because you want to, and it will have meaning."

Achsah's lips formed a pout as anger spewed out of her. "If you think that will ever happen, you'll be waiting for a long time."

She took the fabric in her arms and turned from him. She made her way to the village path and started down it. She could hear his laughter behind her.

She didn't care what he said or did. He meant nothing to her and never would.

The man incensed her. She'd never been treated in such a way. What made him think he ever had a chance of winning her affection?

She'd go to Reuben's father's home. She'd been invited to the engagement meal for her friend, Sheerah. Reuben, an

46

Israelite man, had plans to ask Sheerah for her hand in marriage. Sheerah was a Moabite as she was. Achsah had known Sheerah from the time they were young.

The drinks would be flowing freely, and there would be dancing. At Sheerah's, she'd have no more thoughts of Toi. She'd put her mind on happy things and not on what he'd said to her. As it were, she had better things to do.

Let him go back to his silly carvings, and idols, and finding humor in the things others did.

Nothing would induce her to do as he had suggested. She had no interest in him, or in anything concerning him.

*****

Chapter 4

Achsah entered the party after the announcement had been made. People freely ate and drank. The great hall smelled of cooked lamb and fresh hot bread. Cheese was set out on platters with olives, dripping in oil, and bunches of grapes.

Jonathan went quickly to the door. "Sheerah's wanted to see you, Achsah." He took her arm and walked beside her to his sister.

Sheerah smiled when she saw Achsah. "Reuben and I are to be married. Father's agreed to it! Isn't it lovely?"

Achsah clasped her friend's hands in her own and drew her near. "I'm glad for you, Sheerah. I hope you have a long life and much happiness." She smiled as she noticed the light shining from her friend's eyes.

Achsah gently squeezed Sheerah's hands and then looked around at the other couples in the room. So many of her friends, younger than her, were now married. Their parents had secured positions of wealth and security for them. Surprisingly, most seemed happy with the choices that had been made for them.

Something, vast and hollow, stirred inside her when she spoke again. "Reuben suits you well, Sheerah."

Sheerah put her hand on Achsah's arm. "I wish it were the same for you. Reuben's good to me."

"It does appear that he treats you as he should. I hope it continues." Achsah's smile was suddenly cynical. She was better off without ties to any man, or his family, at least until she was forced into it. It seemed to be the quickest way to ruin, and she wanted no part of it. She cringed at the thought of any arrangement made by her parents for her sake. It was certain her own interests wouldn't be considered, and that it would solely be a business deal.

Reuben came to stand next to Sheerah.

"Good evening, Reuben." Achsah slanted her eyes at him as she played with her braided hair. "I must congratulate you for the choice you've made. I do hope you're faithful to my friend and do not allow your thoughts to stray." She gave him an inviting smile.

Reuben took a drink and stared at Achsah reproachfully.

A heated look came to Sheerah's face as she glanced from Achsah to her betrothed. "Achsah, please."

Reuben's eyes darkened. "Sheerah's a good woman and worthy of a faithful man. I'd do nothing to hurt her."

"I've no doubt that she'll be good for you. You'll have no worries with her as a wife. I only wish the best for my friend." Achsah shrugged and gave him a bored look.

"Here, Achsah." Jonathan came over to her. "Sit for the meal. Have a drink and make merry with us. My sister will want you to." He put out his hand and gestured to the mats where the guests sat.

Cakes of bread, bunches of raisins, summer fruits, and roasted grain were set out in clay bowls and baskets.

Sheerah spoke quietly. "Eat and enjoy the music and dancing, Achsah. It's a day to celebrate." A smile formed on her face as she looked at Reuben who had drawn her close.

"Don't think much about what I do, or say, Sheerah. Nothing could induce me to injure my good friend in any way. Sometimes, I'm interested to learn about others and what they will do, if given the chance, and nothing more." The light returned to her eyes once again. "I'm glad that you'll be happy. Now go greet your other guests, and enjoy the night. I'll make myself known to the others."

Sheerah and Reuben both tipped their heads as she walked away from them. She took a seat on the floor under a low table. She grabbed a silver chalice, which one of the servants promptly filled, and she raised it to the others around her. "Lift your cups to the happy couple."

Others nodded and raised their cups to her. They cheered. Some of the men gathered round and took a seat beside her.

Achsah glanced to the far corner of the room. She suddenly noticed Toi. He was standing next to a friend and was looking at her with an amused expression on his face. Somehow he'd found his way to Sheerah's celebration.

Ha! Let him watch all he wanted. She'd have her fun and be on her way. He'd know soon enough that her interest in him held no promise or desire attached to it.

She leaned closer to Jonathan, who'd taken a place at her side. She whispered in his ear. "I have the fabric for my new tunic. I'll wear it for you soon."

She dipped a piece of her bread in some wine vinegar and took a bite. She savored the grainy taste which was smothered in the tart liquid.

Jonathan took another drink and smiled widely. "I'll look forward to it."

*****

Achsah laughed as she danced to the timbrels in the middle of the floor. She eyed the people around her. Other than Reuben, with his new bride to be, most of the men watched her.

The room smelled of myrrh and cinnamon. The music permeated the air with the sounds of tambourines, harps, and gentle lyres. Laughter and conversation echoed throughout the great hall.

She giggled at a group of women standing at a distance. The dead stares they gave her did not go unnoticed.

She playfully dipped low as she smiled at Tamar, one of Sheerah's Israelite friends. Achsah was sure Tamar despised her with a passion. The woman was no better than Dinah, so full of hatred and jealousy.

Achsah's eyes danced as she turned again to Tamar with a playful expression. Was it her fault that Tamar was a plain, awkward little mouse? Maybe if the ridiculous woman wouldn't stand on the sidelines, with such a bitter frown, the men would notice her too. As it was, they did not. The only one she'd seen

50

near Tamar was Hezro, but he flirted with many women. Though it was clear he'd shown interest in the poor girl, he certainly had no intentions of attaching himself to her for longer than an evening.

After Achsah finished dancing, she made her way to collect her basket of wares, which she'd left on a stand earlier, at the back of the room.

When she passed the table, Tamar and the other women were at, she thought she'd heard her name. She stopped to listen.

Their voices were animated. So rapt they were in their conversation, they failed to notice her standing just outside their circle.

Tamar made a face. "Achsah thinks a bit too highly of herself, with her excessive jewelry and clothing, and her flirtatious looks. It's true that the men do watch her, while she puts on her show for them, but little does she know, that none of them would consider her for long."

"Maybe to spend the evening with." Rizpah laughed.

A woman named Abigail turned to her friend. "It's true. No one would marry a woman like her. She'll eventually be on the streets."

Tamar put her hand to her mouth. "Even her own family wants nothing to do with her. They'd have trouble giving her away in marriage. Men might show interest in her, because of her behavior, but a woman like that could never be cherished or honored in the marriage way."

They all began to laugh.

Sheerah put her hand on Tamar's arm. "You mustn't speak poorly of my friend. She doesn't realize the consequences of her actions. Reuben says that she's young and has not been taught…"

The group suddenly became silent, and Sheerah looked behind her. Her cheeks turned pink when she saw Achsah standing there.

Achsah bristled, and her eyes darkened. "I don't care what anyone says, or what any of the men would do. My future isn't tied up in any of them. No one can hurt me with gossip or slanderous talk. I'm not to be pitied."

"Oh Achsah, it's exactly what you want." Tamar eyed her coldly. "You know how to play the games, and everyone sees it too, even the men. None of us care what you say or do."

Achsah shrugged. "If I were you, I'd not be boasting. Hezro's the only man I've seen look your way, and he has no designs to be any woman's husband, if this is who you're setting your sights on."

Tamar crossed her arms over her chest. "Oh, go away. You're wicked and have no heart. Go back to the family who doesn't want you."

Sheerah spoke softly. She looked as if she might be sick. "I'm sorry, Achsah. I truly didn't mean for this to happen."

Achsah shook her head back and forth. "You said nothing hurtful. You mustn't despair over Tamar's words. I know you have a kind heart."

"Then please allow me to make it up to you someway."

Achsah shook her head. "Another time. The other women here think quite differently of me, and I realize I'm not welcome because of it. I know when it's best to leave. I've had my fill of feasting and dancing."

"Achsah."

Achsah gave Sheerah a genuine smile and put her hand on her friend's arm. "Please, I want your feast time with Reuben to end in a happy way. This is your evening to celebrate. Don't worry, because I'll welcome the night air and the walk home. What these women say means nothing to me. We'll meet another time."

"Truly?"

"Yes, you must celebrate, and we'll see each other soon." Achsah reached out and squeezed Sheerah's hand.

Sheerah nodded and smiled half-heartedly.

Achsah turned and made her way to the back of the room. She pushed the door open and stepped outside. She drew in breaths of the cool evening air. Relief threaded through her at the thought of the quiet path ahead of her.

The celebration had suddenly seemed less enjoyable, after hearing what Tamar and her friends had to say. Some of the things, that were aired before the others, were surely harsher than she deserved.

What had she done? Danced with a bit more zeal than these women had and enjoyed the smiles of the men who watched? Or delighted in the feasting and wine? But, why would they have scorned her for this?

She let out a light laugh. How could she not take pleasure in what was freely available to her? It was a celebration, a time of songs and merrymaking? Why had what she'd done caused the stir it had?

She lifted a brow, and a slight smile formed on her face as she remembered the pleasure she'd derived when she'd seen the expression on Tamar's jealous, brooding face as she danced.

She supposed some of the remarks, from the others she'd endured, had been brought on by herself and her actions, yet the women were crueler than she thought possible for such a minor offense.

She let out a breath. Vicious gossip is what it was. How she behaved in front of others, or what her parents thought of her, shouldn't have mattered to them. She surely hadn't deserved the measure of condemnation she'd received for enjoying the dance and music.

Achsah peered into the night as she drew her scarf tighter around her shoulders. Her mouth formed a pout as she thought of the other women.

What did they know? How could they understand, what she thought, or know the things she endured in her own home? Tamar was a dour, sulking she-devil. Everyone of her friends, save for Sheerah, could eat a bitter root and die, for all she cared.

She looked at the fields beneath the glowing moon. There was no movement on the road. All was quiet and still. The darkness kept her hidden from other travelers of the night. She didn't mind walking back alone.

She supposed, when she finally did make it home, her family would be sleeping, and she'd not have to contend with any of their cold stares or haughty remarks anyway. She'd had enough turmoil for one evening.

Maybe time alone would be good for her? Within the confines of the town's quiet paths, surrounded by the cricket's song, and swaying fields beyond, she would have an opportunity to ponder the events of the day. Lately there seemed to be much to consider.

*****

She took quiet steps, on the road, in the darkness. She looked down to keep from tripping over rocks and other objects and shifted the basket under her arm. Her heart churned at the thought of Tamar and what had been said.

A measure of guilt ran through her when she remembered flirting with Sheerah's intended, for the briefest of moments. She'd only wanted Sheerah to know the fickleness of men, and how untrustworthy they could be, yet Reuban hadn't fallen for the trap she'd set. Maybe he wouldn't be so bad after all.

She stopped and looked over a small rise. She sat down on a large, flat rock that jutted out of the landscape. She placed her basket on the ground and looked up at the dusky sky above.

So much had happened, as of late, with Ittai days before, and with Toi, her family, and the dinner party. There was much to think about.

In the shadows of the roadside, she had time to think. It seemed as good a time as any to weigh what had been said by others and consider her own reactions to it.

She straightened the edge of her tunic and smoothed out the wrinkles in her skirt.

She gazed at the fields as her thoughts turned to the women at Sheerah's gathering and what they'd said. It seemed recently she could scarcely draw a breath without someone scolding her, or lecturing her, about her depraved life and how she'd pay for it in the end.

She should've been able to live the way she wanted without others involving themselves in her affairs. Surely it would be easier for them, to worry about themselves, rather than thinking so much about the things she did.

The women at the party had repeated the same things Toi had told her, that others would have no respect for her, and that she'd never be cherished or honored by anyone, if she continued in her behavior. They'd laughed at the fact that no man would ever offer his hand in marriage to her.

Her eyes narrowed as she stared into the night. Why did it matter so much to them? Her happiness wasn't dependent upon any man. These women didn't know anything about what she thought, or how she felt.

She listened to sheep bleating in the distance. Shepherds were at fires in the fields. Their laughter and voices carried to where she sat as they conversed freely without constraint.

She wondered if men gave as much thought to the paths their lives would take and what their future would hold.

She sighed. If they did, they surely didn't seem weighed down by those around them because of it. They did as they pleased with little repercussion of others taking offense at their actions.

Achsah crossed her arms in front of her as she eyed the shepherds with an annoyed look. If only she could be so free. They determined their own futures, and families, and the paths their lives would take, while she had little say regarding it. She was forced to depend upon men for her very existence.

In spite of what Tamar had said, she was sure it wouldn't be long before she'd be taken in marriage, by whomever was selected for her, whether she wanted it or not. Her father would see to it. She'd be expected to be willing and obedient in whatever decision was made for her.

She pulled at the golden ties on her braided hair and twisted it in her fingers. She began separating the strands and sifting her fingers through it.

Tamar and her friends should've allowed her her freedom while she still had it. Didn't they understand that her dance and song were like a last breath for her? In time, there would most likely be no more of it.

The women were obviously looking for gossip and enjoyed making her the object of their contention. It had surely become a game to them.

As for Tamar, it was clear that she'd been jealous. One only had to look into her hate-filled eyes to know her thoughts. Tamar had caused more trouble for Achsah than any other woman she'd known. Achsah wasn't even sure what she'd done to cause the woman to despise her so vehemently. Whatever it was, she was convinced there was no remedy for it.

What did this pitiful woman know anyway? Tamar meant nothing to Achsah. Out of all the women, at the dinner, Sheerah was the only one worth her time.

Achsah took slow, uneven breaths of air. She closed her eyes. This morning, she'd slipped past her father, in efforts to dodge his usual disapproving looks, but she found she was spared them for once. He hadn't even looked at her when she'd left.

Dinah had screamed at her, and the others in the house had said nothing. They'd gone about their chores as if she weren't there.

Ittai and Toi had both agreed that she was worth little to them, within the hearing of all present at the cloth maker's table. Though she'd not answered to the slight, she couldn't deny that she wasn't affected by it.

None of the men had stepped forward to defend her honor at the dinner. Not even Jonathan, Sheerah's brother, had spoken in her favor against the others. He'd been silent.

Achsah shrugged. Maybe the women were right. The men had watched her with relish when she'd danced. They'd toasted her and plied her with more drink. They'd laughed and joked with her as she'd drawn them in with her flirtatious smiles. She supposed neither respect nor honor were necessary for such things.

She pulled her knees to her chest and wrapped her arms around them. She rocked in place as she eyed the hollow expanse of the fields below her. A chill breeze caused her to shiver.

She'd never considered anyone ever cherishing her, after all she'd done. What could she expect, when her own father and mother saw nothing good in her? A tear threatened to spill from her eyes, and she quickly wiped it away.

"Achsah? I wondered where you'd gone to?" A low voice sounded behind her.

It was Toi.

She didn't answer him. She looked away. Why did he come and follow her here?

He sat on the rock beside her and looked out over the valley. "Are you well enough?"

Achsah spoke quietly, yet a sob stuck in her throat. "Why wouldn't I be?"

"You're not so unfeeling as you'd have others believe." He turned to her with a look of interest.

A light breeze rustled the tops of the grasses in the field. Achsah listened to the quiet chirping of crickets around them as she wiped away a tear that had fallen onto her cheek. She looked up at him, but said nothing.

Toi reached out and outlined her fingers with his hand. "Come now, allow yourself to feel. Why are you so afraid of it?"

"I don't fear it."

"You hurt like others do." His voice gentled. "I believe that you are afraid."

Something hollow stirred inside her. She didn't speak.

Toi smoothed back the hair from her face. He put his arms around her and drew her closer. "The things those women told you were unfeeling. They shouldn't have said them," he said. "You did nothing to deserve their criticisms. You were enjoying the dance and the festivities."

Though earlier, he'd been harsh in his assessment of her, at this moment he was far from it.

More tears came, and she brushed them away, yet it seemed once they'd begun, she was unable to keep them inside. They ran down her cheeks as she lifted her shawl to her eyes.

Toi didn't say more, but he held her as she began to weep. She pushed on his arm.

"Stop, Achsah. Let me comfort you."

She couldn't speak and didn't want him to see her tear-stained cheeks. She held her shawl over her face resigned, and she stayed where she was as more tears streamed from her eyes.

She was there for a time. It seemed the evening stood still as the moon rose, and a heavy darkness descended over the land. The late night sky had awakened, and the sounds of crickets filled the valley with their chirping.

Achsah realized how long she'd sat there when she looked up and noticed how many more stars had flooded the expanse above them. A cloud drifted past, and the air grew colder.

She sniffed as she wiped the last of the wetness from her cheeks.

She suddenly eyed Toi suspiciously.

Where had the time gone, and how could she have trusted him the way she had? She shivered.

She suddenly pushed him away and got up. She brushed the dust off the side of her tunic.

He watched as she took a step back with a wary look.

The moon came out from behind a cloud. She could see his face clearly. "Why did you come here? Why did you follow me to this place?"

He stood and reached for her again.

She put out her hand. "No." Her eyes darkened. "You didn't come for me. What are you doing here?" She crossed her arms over her chest.

At first, he gave her a sympathetic look, but then his expression changed as she drew further away from him.

There was amusement in his voice. "Ah, it's my little Achsah." His eyes sparkled as he spoke softly to her. "I see that you've awoken from your troubles."

Achsah wiped her face and tipped her chin upward to look at him. "I asked what you were doing here?"

He didn't speak right away. The night was still. He broke off a piece of long grass and lifted it into his mouth.

Achsah reached out and took the plant stem and tossed it on the ground. "I told you, that you don't care for me. Why are you here?"

He suddenly laughed. "Do you trust anyone, Achsah? Maybe I'm not so bad."

"Tell me why you followed me?" She placed her hands on her hips. He'd come and offered her comfort, but he didn't do it for her. It was surely for reasons of his own as the women at the party had said.

"I heard those other women. I'm looking out for your interests."

Achsah eyes narrowed. "You're not here for me. Whatever you came for, it's surely to benefit yourself."

"Last time, you needed my help. A woman shouldn't be taking the road at night alone." Toi looked out over the plains. "What if Ittai had followed you?"

"It's a short walk, and the streets are empty. I didn't need you."

Toi shrugged. Something deepened in his eyes. "I suppose I did come for another reason, at least until I saw the state you were in."

Her eyes narrowed. "What do you know of it? Surely your gentle words, and the comfort you gave, were not for my benefit?"

"Ah, my little Achsah, you cannot say I was without feeling. When I see a woman in tears, I cannot help but be moved." Toi's eyes lightened again.

"I don't believe you care for me, and you mustn't call me that anymore."

"What?" He laughed. He looked thoroughly entertained as he watched her.

"You know very well what. I'm not yours, or anyone's, and I don't plan to be."

Toi took her hand in his. "Come now, don't be silly. You should listen before you say more. What I have to tell you could benefit you also."

Achsah rubbed her eyes and turned sharply. She gave him a wary look.

Toi smiled again. He lifted his hand to her cheek. "Since the dinner at Sheerah's, I've been thinking. An idea came to me, which I believe would be good for me, and might be agreeable to you also. I have a proposition, but I'm not sure how best to explain it to you."

She pushed his hand away. "Proposition? What proposition?"

Toi spoke again, this time in a slightly subdued tone. "One I believe you'll want to hear."

Achsah eyes narrowed. "Tell me. I can't stay here all night. I need to get home."

Toi put his hand on her arm. "Wait a little longer. What I have to say won't take long." He hesitated at first. "Achsah, I told you I believed myself incapable of the kind of love others give away so readily. My sentiments haven't changed."

A chill breeze swept across the plains. Achsah shivered at the sound of a wolf howl in the distance. She looked up at him.

"I wanted to ask you something that would benefit us both. It's why I came. I left the dinner party when I saw you go."

"What are you saying?" She frowned. "You hardly looked at me at the feast, or even when I danced."

"I might have seen more than you thought I did."

She drew the folds of her tunic around her. "Never mind that. What's this idea of yours?" She turned to look at him.

"I'll speak plainly to you." He stared at the night sky. "I know what those women at the feast told you, that the men would not have you as a wife."

"I don't care what they said. My tears were not for that. My mother and father will surely try and rid themselves of me eventually. They'll find someone who'll have me." She laughed to herself bitterly.

She turned to the sound of crackling underbrush and looked to see what it was. There was a small animal rooting about in the field grass farther from them. She watched as it disappeared into the thicket.

He moved closer and took her hand in his. "The women may say these things, but you must know you're not without prospects."

She eyed him warily. She wasn't sure what he was alluding to. "When you say 'prospects', what do you mean?"

The chirping of the crickets suddenly waned as the sound of the wind enveloped the dark night.

Toi's voice deepened as he spoke. "That I could take you as my own."

"Your own? What are you saying?"

"I mean that I would marry you."

Achsah turned abruptly. Her mouth opened as she looked at him. What was he up to? She broke out in a small laugh. "You? Marry me?"

He smiled as he watched her reaction. "Just listen."

"But you had no plans for this, with any woman, at this time?" She turned and gave him a look of disbelief. "What you're saying is ridiculous. I'm a foreign woman, a Moabitess, and I'm detestable in your family's eyes."

She suddenly pushed him away from her. "What do you really want from me? You aren't speaking the truth. You're making fun of me."

"No." Toi stepped closer. "I've given it careful thought. I'd take you from your home and provide for you. I'd give you the things such as that cloth you so admire. You could live with my family. You'd have a home."

She stared at him aghast. "But, you would want something from it? What would you be getting for such a marriage?"

Toi's look was one of interest. "You have a well-to-do father who has contact with the Moabite people. My business would benefit greatly because of it. I could do very well, and you're very beautiful. I wouldn't mind such an arrangement."

He reached up and took a strand of her hair in his hand. He eyed it with a smile and let it slip through his fingers. "I doubt either of us would find it a marriage we could not bear." He slid his hand around her waist, and he pulled her closer. "What do you say to it? You'd secure a home, and a husband, and you'd marry well."

Achsah sighed when she realized he was serious. Her eyes turned large and dark.

Toi gave her a curious look. "I've been honest with you. I've come to you with a proposal that would be to your advantage."

Achsah stared at him. "I thought the Israelites marry within their own people. Isn't this what your God wants?"

"So I've been told." Toi shrugged. "But, of course your ancestors did come from Lot. You cannot say we are not kin of a sort. And I don't always follow the path others consider right and true."

Achsah looked resigned. "I suppose it's what I could expect from you." She lifted her chin slightly, and then she shrugged. "And it's true that no decent man will have me. Everyone says it."

"No decent man?" He laughed.

The chilly, desert air swirled around them. Achsah shivered as she looked up. "I suppose I could do no better."

"No better?" Toi laughed again. "You must not consider it so bad."

Achsah rolled her eyes. "You know you're worse than bad, and I know it too."

Toi pulled her closer and smiled. "Maybe it would be better this way as I'd require little of you."

"And I'd have freedom to do as I wish?"

"Within the marriage, of course."

Achsah gave him an interested look. "It might please me to live this way, without the condemnation that comes daily, from those around me, for my errant ways."

"I'm hardly in a place to judge. Surely you'd have none of that."

Achsah's green eyes lit suddenly as a thought came to her, and she voiced it aloud. "If we did marry, I could invite Tamar and her friends to the wedding. They would see that they were wrong about me. I wouldn't mind such a thing."

She smiled with satisfaction in her expression. "It might make it all worth it. I suppose there would be benefits."

"All for Tamar, so that she might eat her words." He shook his head in disbelief and laughed again. "Would it be that terrible for us to be married?"

Achsah got up. She was suddenly quiet. "I don't know. I don't know you."

"But, you would consider it?"

"My father would need to be approached, though he'd give me away as soon as he could." She shrugged. "It might work. We might suit each other well."

Toi nodded. "I believe it too. It's why I asked."

"Then, I suppose it should happen." Achsah sighed. "When do you want the marriage to take place?"

"There's no time for a lengthy engagement. We'll marry quickly. I'll send my father in the morning. He'll do as I ask. The longer this business takes, the more difficult it will be for my parents to accept. I'll have mother prepare a feast two days from now, and then I'll send for you."

Achsah's eyes widened. "A couple days?"

"Yes, I've never been one for conventions. I can't imagine waiting a year when we know our plans."

Achsah lifted the indigo cloth out of the basket. "But?"

Toi took the fabric from her and put it back from where she got it. "There will be plenty more of this. Wear the orange dress with the gold threads stitched into it, the one I first saw you in. I've not forgotten how you looked in it."

Achsah was satisfied with his answer and with the expression on his face.

She thought back to Sheerah's engagement meal. What would Tamar and the other women say at the wedding feast? She couldn't wait to find out.

He laughed as he looked at her. "Already scheming, are you? I can tell by the look on your face. You seem to have a penchant for parties."

She ignored his remarks. There was excitement in her voice. "I must go to tell my father to make the necessary arrangements for our engagement. My mother will need time to prepare for it. I'll wait for you."

She turned and started to leave, but he stopped her.

"You gave those men kisses today, but where's mine? I proposed marriage to you. Wouldn't this be the time you might oblige me?" Toi took her hand in his.

She sighed. Then she quickly pecked him on the cheek. "There, you have yours." She started to take her hand from his. "Now, I must go. I've things to do."

Toi didn't let go of her hand, but he pulled her closer to him. He lowered his head and kissed her tenderly.

Achsah felt the warmth of his touch, and she kissed him back as emotions welled up inside her that she'd never experienced before. She didn't doubt at that moment that her physical attraction to him was beyond what she'd felt for others.

Yet, she'd heard his earlier words. He considered their arrangement a business deal. She was sure he'd have recognized the extent of her father's land and his possessions by this time. It wouldn't do for her to allow herself feelings for him.

She drew back as she studied his face in the moonlight. She sighed. "I believe you'll hurt me someday." Her words were a whisper. "I'm sure of it."

64

He smoothed back her hair which had strayed into her eyes. "Not if you don't want it. But you'll need to trust me."

She backed away. She didn't know what to say. To trust was to risk. Was she willing to go that far? She didn't know. She wiped more tears that had fallen onto her cheeks, and she glanced down the road that led to her home.

He didn't let go of her hand. "Here, let me take you back. I can do that much for you."

She nodded. She didn't particularly want to walk home at night by herself, even though the path wasn't far. "Let's go."

She walked with him in silence, past the hills and fields, to the gate of her family's courtyard.

After she went inside the door of her house, she looked back at his lone figure as he disappeared into the darkness.

Tomorrow, she'd prepare her things and wait for him to come for her. Her wedding would be a new day. Everything would be different.

*****

Chapter 5

Toi said it again. It was as if he were trying to convince himself. "There's a Moabite woman I wish to marry. Speak to her, father. I want her as my wife." He drummed his fingers against his dark blue robe. He got up and paced across the floor as he scuffed the sweet-smelling hay that lay scattered about on the floor under his feet.

He looked out through the open door and into the courtyard. Long shadows spilled out from the walls of stone that surrounded the house. The air was dry and warm. It would be a hot day.

He sat back down at a low, circular table in the center of the room and snuffed out the flame on the end of a flat, rounded stone lamp. The day was light enough to see without it. There was no use wasting the excess oil.

He took a piece of bread from a wooden platter and dipped it in oil. He placed it into his mouth. He allowed the warm, soft morsel to find its way to the contents of his stomach. It didn't settle well this morning. There was a raw, empty feeling that welled up in him.

Whatever possessed him, the night before, to ask Achsah to marry him, he could not know. She was a Moabitess, and she was one who could only spell trouble for him. The woman would surely be his downfall in the end.

He looked into his bronze chalice. It was filled to the brim with sweet smelling drink. He took a sip and let it trickle slowly down his throat as he thought back to the previous evening.

Maybe he'd had too much wine the night before. Or it might have been he'd overheard those women, in that home, and he didn't like what they'd said to Achsah. He had seen the lost expression on her face and had listened to her quiet tears on the moonlit footpath. Whatever it was, he couldn't know for sure.

Yet, it was morning. He'd promised he would marry her.

Now he was trying to convince his father to bring Achsah into their home, and he wasn't even sure of the decision he'd made. Everything had happened so quickly.

Though the words he'd spoken to her had not been in vain, Achsah, as difficult as she was, had accepted his offer quite readily. The deed had been done. He'd asked her, and she'd agreed to it.

What had she said? That telling Tamar would make it all worth it?

He took another bite and smiled. What was he thinking?

He almost laughed aloud. What had he'd allowed himself to get into? All for a pretty face and the wealth that came with it. He hoped she wouldn't cause too much trouble in the family.

Achsah would be waiting for him. He'd go through with what he'd agreed to. One redeeming quality, he did have, was that he was a man of his word. His father would need to understand this.

Josheb pushed the striped cloth headpiece behind his shoulders. The brow on his forehead wrinkled. "She's a foreigner, Toi. Why not choose to marry a woman among our people? You'll be placing yourself, and our family, in an unholy situation."

"I've already spoken to her. I'll not change my mind. Achsah's the woman I want. Don't tell mother I'm marrying a Moabite until the matter is settled. I'll have the servants prepare a feast and will tell her when Achsah comes. It'll be easier for Achsah and mother this way."

His father let out a prolonged sigh. The others in the household had left for their chores. A silence pervaded the room. "It appears you'll not change your mind."

Toi shook his head. "No father, I won't. I want you to go to Achsah's father for me today and discuss the arrangements. I wish to marry this week."

"This week?" Josheb stared at him.

Toi gave his father a determined look. "I won't wait. I told Achsah it would be soon. She expects it."

Josheb groaned, but he got up. His sandals made soft sounds on the hardened, clay packed floor as he walked to the doorway. He stood beneath the arched, wooden frame and turned back once. "I'll do this for you, but I've strong reservations about it. I'll bring some of the animals to give as a gift.

Toi nodded. He watched his father leave as the heavy, thick door closed behind him.

It would only be a matter of time when Achsah would be his wife.

*****

The cart ambled along the rocky path as it passed by rolling meadows and craggy cliffs in the distance. A tempestuous, hot wind was blowing up dust in the air. A storm was brewing in the west, but luckily it would not reach them until the ceremonies were over.

Achsah's family had left for Toi's home earlier. She was on her way to be given in marriage. There was to be feasting and dancing all day.

Her father had readily agreed to the marriage in the early morning hours earlier in the week. He was overjoyed with the betrothal gift of sheep, goats, and a camel from Toi's father. He'd left in a jovial mood that morning. It was obvious the arrangement was to his liking as he'd be ridding himself of his wayward daughter, and the household would finally have a chance for peace.

No matter. Achsah smiled. News went out to her friends, and others in the town, that Toi and she would be wed. She couldn't wait to see the look on Tamar's face after the ceremony had taken place.

Achsah smoothed out the folds of her silken, orange tunic as she looked out over the rocky terrain.

She sat upright in the cart and pulled a festal outer robe around her to keep her skirt underneath clean and fresh. Her hair fell freely down her back underneath one circular braid on top of her head. It was embellished by a golden headband of jewels that formed a crown. Though her hair had been well set, a few errant pieces had been loosed from the ride. She tucked them behind her ear.

She didn't spare her arms, ankles, wrists, and neck the embellishments afforded them. Many glittering, gold spangles, and chains of gold, jingled on them when she walked. A small, golden nose ring completed her jeweled ornaments.

She'd put on her best sandals and after bathing, had washed herself in the sweet scents of perfumed oils.

Lastly, she'd covered herself with a filmy veil of gold that had fallen over her face in gentle waves.

Even though Toi's proposal had not been one of undying love and devotion, Achsah was determined none would know of their arrangement of convenience. She planned to make it an evening of much food, high spirits, wine, and song. The dancing couldn't come soon enough for her.

*****

Toi lifted Achsah down from the wooden cart. He took her hand as he led her on the path to the gated entrance of his home. They stood on the other side of the stone wall that surrounded it.

Before they went through the door, she lifted her veil and took off her outer robe.

One of the household servants came out. "I'll put your things in the room that will be yours. It's in the second courtyard." The woman took the robe and veil and went into the house while Toi waited outside with Achsah.

Toi grasped her hand in his and squeezed it gently.

She was covered in golden jewelry and had on the shimmering orange tunic he'd asked her to wear.

His eyes sparkled as he looked at her. He smiled as he leaned down and whispered in her ear. "The bride I've waited for all my life."

Achsah gave him a disconcerted look. She pushed him aside at the entrance that led into the courtyard. She heard music playing amidst lively conversation. "Where will the ceremony take place?"

"In the courtyard. I'll introduce you to my family."

She looked through the stone arch of the doorway. Then she turned back to him and reached to fix the collar of his tunic. "You can't go in there like that."

He smiled at her as he allowed her to straighten it. "I hope this isn't a sign of what's to come."

"Oh, there'll be much more. You can be sure of it. A husband of mine will certainly not look the mess that you do."

His look was one of interest, but he didn't say anything. He couldn't resist as he stole a kiss, and he took her through to the outer recesses of the house.

She eyed him warily.

Toi smiled again. He wondered what his family would think of her. He hoped her sister, Dinah, and she would be on their best behavior.

*****

"Mother, this is Achsah. Achsah, my mother's name is Hannah. You met my father, Josheb, earlier."

Hannah had obviously been informed that Toi had chosen a Moabitess to marry. Though her expression was watchful, she didn't seem surprised. She bowed formally. "You're welcome in my home, Achsah."

Achsah tipped her head as she took Hannah's outstretched hand.

The mother didn't seem so bad. Her voice was gentle, and she appeared introspective in nature. Her rich, brown eyes were soft and kind. They were genuine.

Achsah could detect a hint of skepticism in the woman's face, yet she couldn't blame Toi's mother for having had reservations about her son's choice. Toi hadn't done what his people had expected. He wasn't marrying within his family's line and had brought a foreign woman into their home instead. Achsah was sure her jewels and highly ornate clothes were deemed a bit much, and her makeup was most likely considered overdone, yet the Israelites also adorned themselves for marriage.

"That Toi has chosen you to be my daughter, must tell me you're a good woman." She smiled.

Achsah's brow rose, and she fidgeted with her hands. She didn't say anything. She steadied them to keep the sounds of her bracelets from clinking together.

She looked at Toi who was staring at her as if he were thoroughly entertained. She shot him a dark look, and then she turned back to his mother.

Hannah gestured to the other family members. "This is Benaiah and Jorah, my second and third sons respectively.

Kezia, our first daughter is your age, seventeen. And Sapphira is our youngest daughter. She's fifteen."

Benaiah, the brother who was closest in age to Toi, gave Achsah a dark look. His eyes were the color of charred wood. He breathed a sound of disgust. "Ittai told me about her and the things she did."

Jorah backed up a step. Though lengthy in height, and having the same wide shoulders as his brothers, he was slightly leaner in build. He seemed quieter and more introspective.

Benaiah turned to Toi. There was a low, threatening tone in his voice. "What were you thinking to bring a Moabitess here to mother? And that one?"

Achsah had seen the look of some of the Israelite men who despised her people. Her cheeks flamed red, and she stared daggers at Benaiah. The brother had nerve. "You listened to Ittai? That horrible man?" She lifted her finger and wagged it at him. "He's worthless in my eyes."

A hush filled the courtyard, and some of the people turned to watch. Tamar, Rizpah, and Abigail all looked curious.

"Achsah." Toi took hold of her arm. He leaned down and whispered in her ear. "Hold your tongue, and try to gain my brother's good favor. This will lead to no good. Let us wed, and dance, and eat instead. This must be a good day."

She gave Toi a disconcerted look, but realized it would not be good to cause friction with his family before the ceremony. She let out a slow breath and moved closer to Toi. She turned to the others. "Ittai wasn't kind to me."

Benaiah was going to say something else, but his mother put her fingers to her lips, and she shook her head at him.

Kezia stepped forward and took Achsah's hands in hers. Though she was plain, in mode of dress, and her face held no distinctive qualities, other than a smattering of freckles bridging her nose, something sweet radiated from within her. She reminded Achsah of Ruth. Her long brown hair was in two braids which fell neatly over her shoulders. She leaned close to Achsah, and her voice was quiet. "Benaiah takes time to warm to the people of the land. Be patient with him. I welcome you to our home. You'll be my sister."

Achsah nodded. She wouldn't look at Toi's older brother again.

Jorah tipped his head cordially at her. He wasn't overly friendly, but he was polite.

Achsah smiled when Sapphira handed her a beautiful, purple flower.

The young woman blushed pink. "I picked it for you. You're pretty."

"Thank you." Achsah nodded to Sapphira. She smiled. This one seemed fun and was as welcoming as Kezia was.

Then Achsah looked back at Toi. "You can tell them to let the ceremony begin now. I want to dance."

Toi took her hand and led her across the space to where the priest stood. "We're ready. We wish to become husband and wife."

*****

Achsah swayed to the harps, and lyres, and other instruments with the other women as Toi stood at a distance while he watched. She couldn't help but think how handsome he looked in his dark robe of blue and his clean, white tunic beneath. He was talking to his friend, Shobach, and he was, as usual, finding humor in something they were saying. Both were laughing and enjoying the festivities.

Achsah scanned the area, and her eyes strayed to Tamar who was at a table near an outer wall. Tamar was eating. She had a disgruntled look on her face as she talked to Toi's sister, Kezia. Achsah hoped the two of them weren't close friends. Tamar didn't deserve someone as kind as Kezia for her companion.

Achsah gave Tamar a knowing smile, and then she strolled over in her direction. "Are you pleased with the celebration?" Achsah gave Tamar a coquettish smile as she said it.

Kezia came forward. She took Achsah's hands in her own. Her voice was soft and quiet. "I'm glad my brother chose to marry. I was worrying that he'd no plans of it."

Tamar gave them both a sullen look. "I'm wondering what she did to trap him into it. I thought he was more careful than this."

Kezia's cheeks burned a bright pink. "Tamar, you shouldn't say such things. Achsah's my sister, from this day on."

Tamar's mouth opened. There was a grating sound to her voice when she spoke. "You're too kind, Kezia. I hope, for your sake all, of this will end well."

Kezia smiled. "Oh, it will. Toi would not have wed, if he'd had any reservations about it." She let go of Achsah's hands.

Toi came across the floor and put his arm around Achsah's waist. He drew her close and smiled as if he were delighted. "How is my loved and cherished one?" He brushed a strand of hair from her face.

Achsah's brow rose as she looked at him, but she turned to Tamar and smiled as she intertwined her fingers with his and rested her head on his shoulder. "It seems I've stolen his heart. He can't keep himself from me." Her look was triumphant as she turned back to Toi with an adoring look.

Toi lifted her hand to his lips and kissed it. There was laughter in his eyes as he glanced at her.

Tamar shifted her stance. "Well, things do have a way of tarnishing in time. I'm sure it's still too early to tell."

"Which you won't know yourself until you have a husband." Achsah gave Tamar a wicked grin.

Tamar made a face. She had no response.

Achsah tugged Toi's hand. "Come, we've other guests to see. Enjoy the dance and food, Tamar. It's a day to celebrate."

Tamar was left standing and staring at them as they walked away.

Achsah whispered to Toi. "I do not like her. I waited all day for this time to respond to her silly remarks."

"The reason you married me." Toi commented. There was amusement in his eyes.

Achsah smiled. "That, and for all the things you said I could have." She reached out and smoothed out a wrinkle in his robe as she looked up at him.

He shook his head. His eyes twinkled as he spoke. "I hope your father is as rich as you say he is. I may need some help."

Achsah looked across the room.

Ritzpah and Abigail stood, side by side, in the corner of the room. They watched her.

Abigail put up her hand and whispered to her friend. They both gave Achsah dark looks as she walked past.

Achsah ignored them and turned back to Toi. The women in this place were certainly sulky and ill-humored.

74

Achsah's family was sitting on a feasting mat at the far end of the courtyard.

Toi pointed at them. "Come, you haven't gone near your family all night. You should see them."

Achsah gave him a disapproving look. "Since it will be expected, I suppose I must spare them a moment of time and throw a bone to our guests. But, if it were my wish, I'd much rather go my own way."

"I figured as much, but it would be right to do it."

"And expected."

"Precisely." Toi laughed. "Tamar's watching."

Achsah sighed and took his arm.

They walked over to the mat and stood at the end.

Achsah's father looked up when he noticed she was standing next to him.

He turned to Toi. There was a jovial tone in his voice. "Your father has provided us with a rich meal. It will be a good family for our Achsah. We didn't quite believe it when he came to our door."

Achsah frowned. Our Achsah? Hmm. A heightened color came to her cheeks. "And why wouldn't you believe it?"

Her father gave her a knowing look. "No particular reason, but I'm sure it'll all work to everyone's advantage."

Dinah piped in. "Mostly for ours."

The family began to laugh.

Achsah bristled. "You might consider what you say on this one day or how you treat me. It is my wedding day."

"It's Toi's also." Dinah sounded cross. "I would be thinking of my husband."

Mara chided Achsah as she lifted her finger in the air and shook her head. "As a wife, you'll need to learn to submit and use manners. You'll get nowhere acting selfishly the way you do." She turned to Dinah. "And as for you, you'll never marry, if you speak the way you do. No one will have you."

Rachel, her father's concubine, stood up. "How do you expect either of the girls to learn under you, Mara?" She turned to

Achsah's mother. "You yourself never submit, and you don't use manners."

Achsah groaned. "This again."

"Achsah, stay out of it." Achsah's father gave her a look of disapproval. "It isn't your concern."

Rachel, one of her father's concubine's eyes were dark. "Yes, Achsah, you must listen to your father and do as you're told."

"I don't need to do anything any of you say anymore. If father hadn't taken three women under his roof, there wouldn't be this squabbling."

"Achsah!" Rachel put her hands on her hips. "Must you start trouble at every turn?"

Mara shook her head. "Yes, Achsah. You said it yourself. It's your wedding day. You might take that sullen look from your face. Dinah's right. You should be thinking of your husband and not yourself. You seem to be able to find fault and complaint at every turn."

Achsah opened her mouth to speak, but Toi broke into the conversation. "I've no qualms with your daughter. She's beautiful today."

He squeezed her hand and kissed her cheek. Then he pulled her closer to him. "There are other guests we must see to. Please enjoy the feast and your time here. Come, Achsah."

Dinah rolled her eyes.

Achsah tried to speak, but Toi pulled her away from the table. "Let it be. It isn't worth your time."

"But, this is our wedding celebration. Can't they keep from feuding for one day? It's wrong."

"Obviously they can't, but you can do nothing about it. They don't see it as you do." He leaned down and brushed his lips against her hair. "The people here must know that you're happy and loved. Let's show them this instead."

Achsah let out a breath. She nodded. "I can't go near them. I'm not good with them."

"Then dance as it lifts your spirits. I'll talk to Shobach, and you'll forget all this and celebrate our marriage. Sheerah's friends will see you." He smiled.

Another woman handed Achsah a tambourine, and she took it in her hand. She shook it as she held it above her.

Despite the difficulties of the night, Achsah couldn't help the feeling of being carried away by the lively music and the heavenly scents around her. Sounds of people laughing and conversing happily raised her spirits. With dancing, and good food, it might turn out to be a better day than she'd imagined. At least Toi's parents had not spared anything in the celebration.

She dipped and swayed to the rhythmic beat. She tapped the musical instrument against her hips and smiled with the other young women as they danced together, in a circle around the room, in patterned steps.

She lifted her arms in the air and made slow, even movements. She swung back and forth in time to the lively music. She occasionally glanced in Toi's direction and relished in the fact that he was watching her with interest as he talked with the other men there.

After dancing, for some time, she left the middle of the courtyard and laid her tambourine on a low, wooden table. She looked around and fanned herself. The air was muggy. She took a breath.

When sounds of the instruments died for a moment, Achsah went to the second courtyard. This area was most likely for housing the women. She didn't go near Tamar, nor her sister, Dinah. She was determined not to cause another scene.

The courtyard had been warm, but the cool air, in the back of the house was inviting. She sat on steps that ran up to the roof and breathed deeply. It was dark, and the night was closing in. She stood there looking at the stars.

*****

Jorah, Toi's younger brother, got up and went to the main gate. He eyed the others as they celebrated. Toi was in the corner of the room, with Shobach, and it seemed Achsah had left the crowded courtyard.

Achsah's family sat quietly in the corner of the room.

Although, they appeared well-dressed and mannerly in speech and custom toward others, and outwardly there was nothing to discredit them for, something didn't sit well with Jorah as he watched them.

Throughout the ceremony and the festivities, Achsah's father had been cordial, when he was approached by other guests, but privately he seemed anything but pleased. He'd watched Achsah with a measure of distaste all evening while she'd taken turns around the room in a myriad of dances and merrymaking.

Occasionally, he'd make casual conversation with another guest, as his wives looked on, yet he seemed detached from both Achsah and her sister, Dinah, and from his wives. The three youngest children sat nearest him, and chatted happily, while Achsah's father occasionally smiled and patted one of them on the heads.

Jorah eyed Achsah's sister, Dinah. She was very beautiful, as were her other sister's, and yet she was quite different. She wore many bracelets and rings, just as her sister did, yet her choice of clothing and jewels were less ornate and simpler. Her dark, wild auburn hair flowed freely down her back. Two small front braids were bound together by a lavender tie which matched the darker purple of her fine linen tunic. A headdress encircled her head and glittered with large, golden jewels.

The young woman's wide dark eyes were marked with kohl lines. Her arms crossed in front of her, and her shoulders were set back as she watched her father's wives and listened to their conversation.

She turned suddenly, and a puzzled look came over her when she noticed Jorah studying her. She reached up and began to play with a long piece of hair that had fallen forward over her

78

shoulder as her eyes trailed the length of him and rested on his face.

Her expression suddenly lightened, and her pouty, red lips began to curve upward. She tugged on a second piece of hair and curled it around her finger.

Jorah quickly looked away.

Though this young woman was lovely to look at, she seemed rather forward for his taste. She was not the shy, modest woman of his culture.

He stared out into the night sky and let out a slow breath. Encouraging a young woman, such as this, would not end well for any man. He could only guess what trouble she could bring to a family.

A sick feeling ran through him at the thought of Toi attaching himself to such a family. What troubles might he spread to their own family because of it?

*****

Dinah giggled to herself when Toi's brother turned away. She'd seen the look on his face when she'd attempted to flirt with him. Even though moments before, he had stared at her in an appraising manner, her attentions had clearly unsettled him.

She laughed again. Was he afraid of her? Did she truly believe that she might cast some kind of Moabite spell upon him, right there in the room while he watched her?

She eyed the light brown waves of his hair which fell just over his ears. It framed his handsome tanned profile. His physique resembled the other men in her family. None of them lacked favorable traits. His dark green robe was newly sewn and fit squarely over his shoulders. It was tied with leather belt around his waist.

Dinah drew in a breath. Too bad the brother seemed more cautious than Achsah's husband. Though he had eyed her with interest, it was certain he had no intentions of allowing for more than a favorable appraisal. There surely were many wasted opportunities with these Israelite men.

She sighed and turned to the dancing when he didn't look back around. She guessed it would be a long evening. At least the food and music were to her taste. There seemed little else to be desired.

*****

Achsah looked across the fields in the distance to an oncoming storm approaching. A dark purple color lit the horizon. Heat lightning spilled slivers across the sky, and a low sound rumbled in the distance.

The music started back up. Lively chatter and conversation came from inside.

A voice startled her.

"You think you can come to our family and be one of us, a daughter of Moab, who worships that abomination, Chemosh?"

Achsah turned to the sound of Toi's brother, Benaiah. His voice was cutting. He'd come around the side of the house and was blocking the narrow passage that led to the party.

Achsah didn't answer him. She lifted her chin as she eyed him warily.

Benaiah leaned against the side of the house. Even though his powerful build and height were intimidating, she was determined not to let him know that she felt trepidation at the thought of being alone with him.

She got up from the steps. "Let me through. Leave me be." Her eyes narrowed, and flames shot into her cheeks. "I'm your brother's wife."

Benaiah's lower lip curled upward. "Ha! You insult him and our family with your presence." He scowled as he took a step toward her. "I heard what happened in the field with Ittai. He told me what you did. You're a despised woman."

"Ittai's lying! I did nothing with him. Toi was there! He knows the truth. Why don't you ask him?" Angry tears flooded Achsah's eyes.

Benaiah growled low. "I'll tell him. He should know what lies come from your mouth and what you've done."

Achsah gave him an angry look. Whatever he thought of her, she didn't care. He wasn't worth her time. She only wished he'd move so that she could go back into the courtyard where the festivities were taking place.

*****

Dinah went to the gate. Toi's brother was still staring at the night sky over the low part of the wall. She stood behind him. "You're one of the brothers? Which one are you?"

He turned and leaned against the wall as he watched her. He didn't answer.

She moved closer to stand next to him. "Achsah said that Toi had three brothers. You must be the youngest."

"I'm...Jorah. I overheard Achsah mention your name. You're Dinah, aren't you?" The sound of lutes and a harp played quietly behind them. He looked to where the people congregated. "You're not taking part the festivities and the dance?"

"Watching my father and his wives play games? Hardly." She combed her fingers through strands of her hair that framed her face. She gave him a curious look. "You don't seem to be taking part in the merrymaking either."

"I prefer a quieter setting. Social gatherings are not something in which I relish."

"Well, for your brother's sake, you should be celebrating."

"Maybe." Then he nodded in the direction of the home. Toi was coming out. "But, I believe your sister's keeping him busy enough. He's looking for her."

Dinah straightened the sash around her waist, and her lips curved into a smile. "I'll go help him find her. He looks lost." She began to walk away as she eyed Toi with interest.

"Oh no." Jorah noticed the eager look in her face as she stared at his brother from across the courtyard. "You're the last person he needs tonight."

He took her arm and held her by the crook of her elbow. "You leave him be. He's your sister's husband."

"I know that, but it doesn't mean I can't be of service to him." She attempted to shrug him off.

"But, he doesn't need you to interfere." Jorah leaned closer. "You stay here and listen to the music."

"I don't want to talk to you."

Jorah scoffed at the look on her face. "You'll leave my brother be. He and Achsah are busy with their own affairs. It's their wedding day."

Dinah tugged her arm away but didn't move from where she stood. "I planned to help him find her. I don't know why it would be a problem."

"I told you. He doesn't need your help. There's no reason for it, other than to come between them." He looked across the room to her family's table. "Do you want me to talk to your father and tell him what you're doing? I'm sure he wouldn't appreciate your trying to intervene in your sister's affairs on her wedding day."

Dinah's eyes narrowed, and her cheeks flamed. She tugged her arm free and began to rub her elbow. "I don't think he cares what I do. But, you would not go to him."

"I would." Jorah spoke quietly. "Because you're not going to spoil this day for Toi, nor Achsah. I won't allow it."

Dinah looked at the table where her father sat and then back at Jorah. She suddenly laughed aloud. "Ha! Achsah's already done that. She's spoiled the whole rest of their life."

Jorah couldn't hide the displeasure her words brought him. He frowned. "Then, as I see it, there will be no reason for you to add to the trouble. Now, go back to your father. I would like some peace."

Dinah didn't move.

He gave her a gentle shove. "Go, or I'll tell your family everything you said."

She brushed herself off and straightened her tunic. Her eyes narrowed again. "I'll sit with my father, but I'll have nothing to do with you, or your ridiculous family."

"Good, then we'll both be at peace." Jorah watched her sit back down next to one of her younger sisters. She crossed her arms in front of her as she looked at him.

He turned and looked over the stone wall and into the darkness of the night. The stars above had multiplied and spread over the shadowed mountains and valleys of Moab. At least quiet reigned somewhere. He wondered where Toi was and what kind of wife his brother had married. If she was anything like Dinah, he greatly pitied him.

*****

"Benaiah?" Toi came through the gate behind his brother. Achsah straightened and pushed back tears.

Toi went to her. "Achsah?"

"Tell him." Benaiah's voice was low and feral. "He should know what happened in the field with Ittai."

Her eyes narrowed. "I tried to explain, but he doesn't believe me." She looked up at Toi. "He's ruining things."

Toi stood between her and Benaiah. He wiped tears from her face. "This matter will be put to rest. You won't have to answer to my brother tonight. He has no right to say these things to you. You've done nothing to him."

He put her aside, and he turned to Benaiah. "You've slandered my wife on our wedding day."

"But, she's not telling the truth. I heard what Ittai said. If you knew what she did, you wouldn't be with her."

Toi shook his head. "I was there. I intervened before Ittai could hurt her. She doesn't understand the ways of men. He could have dealt with her differently."

"But she deserves consequences for her actions."

"Not what he felt he was entitled to. No one deserves such treatment."

Benaiah frowned. "But, Ittai, he told me..."

"Then, he told you wrong. He fed you lies. I told you; I was there."

"Toi, she's a daughter of Moab. Why would you marry her?"

Achsah looked up at Toi again. In her eyes there were questions.

He took her hand in his and stole a careful look at Achsah. "She's the woman I chose. It should be enough for you."

Achsah didn't say anything, but she looked out into the darkening sky. It didn't matter why he married her. He'd promised her that she'd have fine clothes and precious wares and that he'd take her from Dinah and the rest of her family. There would be benefits as he had said.

Benaiah gave him a look of disbelief.

"You'll respect her, Benaiah, and you'll treat her as you should. When you marry, I'll do the same."

"But, it won't be difficult for you. I'd never marry a Moabitess!"

Toi shrugged. "You do as you see fit, but leave Achsah alone. She's done nothing to you."

"For your sake, I'll say no more to her tonight. But I'll never accept her as my sister. Nothing will ever induce me to it."

Achsah's dark eyes flashed. "And you will never be my brother! You're no better than Ittai!" She suddenly wanted to rush at him and hurt him the way he'd hurt her.

Lightening crackled across the sky in the distance, and there was the sound of thunder. A wind had arisen, and dust swirled around them.

Achsah wiped the sand out of her eyes and made a move toward Benaiah, but Toi grabbed her before she could get past him.

She looked up at Toi, and she pushed against his arms.

"Achsah, he doesn't mean it. He doesn't know what he's saying."

Benaiah shouted, "I know exactly what I'm saying. A daughter of Moab will never be my sister!"

She glared at Benaiah and struggled to get away. "Let me go!" She turned and tried to hit Toi with her fists. "He can't talk to me that way!"

Holding her by the waist, Toi lifted her off the ground. "Achsah, stop! Settle down. You'll gain nothing by this."

Benaiah watched as Toi struggled to hold her still.

Achsah turned and struck him under the eye.

"Ow! Achsah!" He was having difficulty keeping her in his arms.

"It seems your wife has a temper, Toi." The expression on Benaiah's face suddenly brightened for the first time. He laughed. "Adonai be with you. It's the first day of your marriage."

Toi motioned to Benaiah. "Take the cart to town, or somewhere. Come back after the feasting's over. Leave us in peace."

Benaiah laughed again. He turned to go. "At least you'll pay for what you've done. I hope the rest of us are left out of it." He went through the courtyard and looked back one more time, before he went through the gate. He tipped his head to the both of them as a smile spread over his face.

"Achsah, quit fighting me. I've done nothing wrong. He's gone."

"You didn't let me go." Realizing she wasn't able to get loose, she settled in his arms and gave him an angry look. She wiped back more tears. "I wanted to get back at him for the things he said. You wouldn't let me."

"Benaiah's larger than *I* am. What do you think you could have done to him? You must listen to me. I'm your husband."

He put Achsah back down and then reached for her.

Achsah's eyes widened. She waited for his hand to rein down upon her. She quickly threw her hands in front of her and crouched down.

He stared at her. "Achsah, what are you doing?"

"I thought…"

He put out his hand and helped her up. He pushed back a piece of her hair that had fallen loose. Then he bent over and picked up the gold piece which had slipped off her head. "Here, I'm not going to hurt you." He handed it to her.

Achsah placed the jeweled piece back on her head. Her look was one of puzzlement. "But, I thought you would beat me for what I did. Why didn't you? I spoke rudely to your brother. It's your right as a husband to discipline me for such things."

Toi seemed surprised by her words. He looked through the doorway to the lit room beyond. "My father feels such measures aren't necessary, and I'm inclined to agree. My brother wronged you. He shouldn't have treated you this way."

Achsah didn't say anything. There were questions in her eyes.

"But, you must learn to control your temper. It gets you into trouble."

She reached up and touched the bruise forming on his cheek.

He winced. "I hope this is the end of it tonight. I'd like to keep my injuries to a minimum. I'm glad it's dark in the courtyard, and others were not witness to this display."

Achsah scrunched up her brow. She shouldn't have hit him, and caused such trouble, but she didn't have it in her to apologize. She felt as if she would be conceding defeat if she did.

The storm had turned its course and veered southward. She took hold of the stone wall outside the house. "Your brother's right, you know. You shouldn't have married me. You chose wrongly."

Toi eyed her curiously. He didn't respond to her remark, but he took her hand instead and tugged on it. "Come, there's still celebrating to do. Let's enjoy the music and feasting."

She went back into the house with him. She'd do her best to stay out of trouble for the remainder of the evening.

*****

Later that evening, after Dinah returned home, she laid her head down on her sleeping mat. She pulled her woolen blanket over her and turned on her side. Her fingers clenched around the edge of the covering, and she stared at the wall. She felt the heat come into her cheeks when she thought of Toi's brother, Jorah.

He'd threatened to speak to her father and had told her that he wouldn't have her spoiling Achsah's day. Ha! Truly? What did he know? Achsah was no innocent.

He'd no understanding of her feelings toward her sister and why she treated Achsah the way she did. He knew nothing of their relationship and what they'd endured in their family.

And it wasn't fair that she was left to fend for herself in this place. Achsah had somehow managed to find her way out of their nonsensical household and leave the whole crazy lot of them behind, including her.

Toi appeared to have come from a decent enough home and family. Achsah would have money and things. She would have a space of her own and a new life. Her sister had managed to marry well. Nothing seemed fair.

Dinah's eyes darkened as she regarded the stone wall of the house in the dark. The light of one lamp was still glowing on the table in the other room.

She closed her eyes and willed herself to sleep as she attempted to block that maddening brother of Toi's from her mind. He'd no right delving into her business, or deciding what she could or couldn't do. No one did.

She hoped she'd never see him again.

*****

Sapphira danced around the end of Achsah's bed the next morning. Her large, dark eyes shone beneath a shawl she'd wrapped around her thick, dark hair. "Come Achsah! You must see the new baby goat!"

Achsah rubbed her eyes. "Is the sun even up?" She groaned. One ray of light from a window, high in the room, was evidence of the morning rays shining through.

Toi had left earlier to go to town.

Achsah had planned to sleep longer, but it seemed his youngest sister wasn't going to permit it.

"Come Achsah! Get up! You must see this!"

A servant woman came into the room. She carried an earthenware platter. There was a cup of water on it. There was also a slice of barley bread, honey and curds, and a cake of raisin.

For having come from Bethlehem, where drought and famine had been common for most, Toi's family was not without the means to support themselves. Many of their household workers, family members, and livestock had come with them from Bethlehem. It seemed they still had many things.

Achsah looked around the room where she slept. The house was large and well furnished. Being crafters, of stone and wood, by trade, certainly put this family at an advantage.

The cool morning air made her shiver. She took a woolen fleece throw from the end of the straw mattress. She wrapped it around her and sat up.

"Sapphira, you must let me sleep longer after this, at least until the sun's over the horizon." She made a face.

"But the sun is up! And the goat was born. You must see it. Kezia's out with it in the courtyard." Sapphira's eyes shone with delight. "Toi said it was the only one that lived. The little thing is still having trouble walking." She reached over and tugged Achsah's arm.

Achsah took a bite of the raisin cake and savored its warm, sweet taste. She couldn't help but smile. She drank some fresh spring water and sighed. "I'm coming. Give me time, and I'll be out."

A huge smile spread over Sapphira's face. She laughed. "I'll go out with him. Don't take too much time. I want you to see him!"

"Go. I'll be there!" Achsah waved her hand toward the door. She let out another groan.

Sapphira laughed. She turned and dashed out of the room.

The young sister surely had energy. She was full of life. It appeared that Sapphira hadn't even taken time to comb out her hair. It had been in wild disarray, over her shoulders, and she'd not one adornment of jewels in it. This would clearly need to be rectified. She was no better than Dinah.

Achsah finished eating the meal the servant had brought. It was good Toi's family had many workers in the home. She'd help with chores later as it appeared Toi's sisters and mother were busy, and it was the day after her wedding.

Achsah reached for one of her tunics and slipped it on. This evening she'd find a spring, or creek bed, to wash in. It seemed there was no ritual mikveh bath at their home as of yet. She wasn't sure, if they did have one, or if she'd be allowed in it. Her clothes had all been neatly folded and put on a wooden shelf which was built into a recess of the stone wall.

She took a comb, which had been carved from bone, from the shelf. She ran it through her hair, and then she braided the length of it into two sections. She placed a tiny golden chain with dangling jewels of different colors, across her forehead, and tied it in the back with thin leather cords.

She slipped on her golden spangles and a jeweled necklace. Then she tied her sandals and made her way out to the courtyard to where the newborn goat was.

*****

"Come quickly, Achsah! You must see it!" Sapphira's voice was full of excitement. "Look! He has white fur."

Achsah rubbed her eyes and yawned. This was what she was to rise quickly for? She wrinkled her brow as she took steps across the courtyard. The morning sun streamed down on her. She squinted to see.

She couldn't help but smile when she noticed the excitement on Sapphira's face as she watched the little goat toddling around the courtyard. He was under a green olive tree, near the gate, that led to a third courtyard, where the animals were kept.

Kezia stood on the other side of him. She looked up and gave Achsah a shy smile. She was a meek looking, thin young woman. Her warm, brown eyes were like her mother's.

"He's little, but sturdy." Her voice was soft and quiet.

Sapphira moved around the tiny goat. She turned circles and laughed. She went to Achsah and took her hand. "Come, pet him. He's soft."

Achsah stared at the young woman. At fifteen, Sapphira had a lot of energy. Her spirit and heart were genuine. "But my hands are washed, Sapphira. He's newly born."

"He came in the night. I cleaned him off, and he's dry now. You must pet him once. Not long though, so he can be with his mother."

Achsah approached the goat warily and got down next to it. She petted its warm, dry coat. It made a sound and looked straight at her. Its silly face made her laugh.

Sapphira came to her side. "See how cute he is!"

Kezia nodded. "He's only just started walking."

"Sapphira! Kezia!" Benaiah's irritated voice sounded behind them.

Achsah and Sapphira got up, and they both turned.

Benaiah spoke harshly to his sisters. "Go back inside, the both of you. Get away from the Moabitess!"

Kezia stepped forward. Her voice was quiet. "We were showing Achsah the goat, Benaiah." A blush stained her cheeks.

"You mustn't spend time in this woman's company. She's foreign. She's not a good influence. Before you know it, she'll be teaching you her ways."

He gave Achsah a hardened look. It was clear that he wanted nothing to do with her.

Achsah let out a breath. She hadn't asked to spend time with his sisters. She was tiring of this brother of Toi's and would not answer to his insults.

"Her name is Achsah." Sapphira put her hands on her hips and turned. "She's Toi's wife. This makes her our sister." She made a face at him. "I'll tell mother, if you keep bothering us. She wants us to be kind to Achsah. I told Achsah to come out."

Achsah looked away. She couldn't help but smile. This sister of his wasn't going to allow her older brother to have the upper hand with her.

Although he deserved even harsher words than what he'd gotten, Achsah bit her tongue.

Kezia paled and appeared as if she would faint with fear. She didn't say anything, but she gave Achsah an apologetic look.

Achsah didn't want to cause the young woman more pain. She turned to both Kezia and Sapphira, and she ignored Benaiah completely. "I'm going to town. It might be best I leave soon. I've things to do."

"Ha!" Benaiah's eyes narrowed. "Spending my brother's hard earned money is what you'll be doing. It's what I might expect of you."

Achsah rolled her eyes. This ridiculous man was bothersome. Whether she planned to buy jewelry, or cloth, was her business. Sheerah was also waiting for her at her home.

She turned and stared brazenly at him. "I'm visiting my friend. I told her I'd go to town with her. Whatever else I decide to do, at the marketplace, will be added pleasure. I'll be back in time to find out what your mother expects of me."

Then she smiled and looked back at Kezia and Sapphira. "I'm glad I could see your little goat. He's a playful thing. I must go now."

Sapphira ran up and took Achsah's hands in her own. "I hope your visit with your friend goes well."

Kezia nodded and smiled. A spot of color came back into to her cheeks.

Achsah turned to leave. The spangles on her wrists and feet jingled as she walked past Benaiah. She could feel his dark eyes staring daggers at her. He couldn't hide the war that she knew was drumming in his heart, but she refused to give him the satisfaction of acknowledging him again.

*****

Before Achsah stopped at Sheerah's house, she took a raisin cake up the hill to the altar of Chemosh. It was a silly ritual, she knew, but she'd spent her young years, under the sacred trees of the high places, burning incense and bringing sacrifices to the gods. She'd been trained to do such things. Whether she married into an Israelite family, or not, she wouldn't neglect her duties.

She set the cake on top of the carved stone image and knelt before it. A small fire had been started earlier. She watched it burn as tendrils of smoke spiraled into the air.

She spoke the rote words of her prayer. "Chemosh, oh fish god, I present this offering to appease your anger. May peace and good things be given to me because of this sacrifice."

She stepped away and shivered. A chilly morning breeze stirred around her as she thought of the things she'd brought to the stone before. How many times had she prayed for peace and good things? Would the sacrifice be sufficient?

Lately, she felt anything but peace. There had been so many changes in her life. Much had happened.

A frown creased her brow. She'd left the unrest, in her own home, only to be forced to deal with Benaiah's confrontations. That horrid brother of Toi's was causing trouble for her. He was no better than Dinah.

It wasn't as if she hadn't dealt with others who were full of venom and hatred for her people before, but she was surprised to be encountering one of them in her own husband's home. Surely she'd done nothing to deserve this.

Denalah went about with pious airs, and denounced her people and beliefs, but he'd acted with less kindness than most of her Moabite friends. If this was what the Israelite God offered, then their God was no better than Chemosh.

What had Benaiah told his sisters? Before you know it, she'll be teaching you her ways. She sighed. Why did he think she cared to do such things? Who were these people to her anyway?

Achsah sat at the foot of the altar and pulled her outer scarf tighter around her. The breeze was chilly. A gloomy fog had come from the valley and drifted in patches on the shadowed hillside.

Chanting from others at the altars, higher up the hill, and around her, suddenly grew louder.

Something churned inside her as she listened to the rote voices encircling her. Her people called out in strange tongues while she cupped her hands over her ears to quiet the sound. The words rose in wisps and drifted away into nothingness.

She turned to watch her sacrificial offering burning, and she wrinkled her nose. She waved the smoke in a different direction with her hand. The smell was bitter and acrid.

She intertwined her hands together, in front of her, as she studied the cold, desolate block of stone that jutted up out of the ground. She sighed as she eyed the fish god's altar.

Though nothing ever seemed to be gained from her times on the hill, she was hesitant to ever cease the practices. She stood and backed away as a dark feeling swept over her. The thought of Chemosh's anger made her uneasy. She'd made light of the gods many times. What if they were not as she thought, but truly existent?

The god would most likely strike her dead for her thoughts. It seemed a good time to make her escape. A faint chill had stolen over her heart, and she shivered.

She looked beyond the hill to the quiet, soft meadows in the distance and took a breath. The skies were a dark blue. The risen sun sent spokes of light over the land.

She turned and started down the hill on her way to her friend's house. She walked in the direction of the town.

Maybe her visit with Sheerah would turn her attention to things less troublesome.

*****

Achsah went through the gate that led to Sheerah's house and entered the courtyard.

Sheerah was on the roof. She was hanging linen to dry. She stopped to wave at Achsah and smiled as she finished what she was doing. She took to the steps that led down to the area below. "Good morning, Achsah! It's so wonderful to see you. I was hoping you'd come!"

Once down, she crossed the courtyard and grabbed a scarlet-colored shawl which was lying on the edge of a stone cistern. It matched her dark red tunic. She tied it around her waist. "Let's walk to the market. We can talk along the way. We'll make some purchases."

"Yes, I've been looking forward to it."

Sheerah smoothed out the front of her skirt, and she slipped on her sandals. "My husband is with my father. They're overseeing the vineyard. I just finished my morning chores."

"Oh, Toi is with Shobach. He's cutting stone. He won't be home until later, but we might stop there. Since our house is farther from town, he works with Shobach. They must bring the stone to the city."

Sheerah nodded. They both turned and walked out of the courtyard.

They left through the gate and started down the town streets in the direction of the markets. The sun was high in the sky.

Sheerah gave her a mindful look. "You married very suddenly. There was no period of engagement?"

Achsah shrugged. "There was no need for waiting. Father wanted me out of the home, and Toi and I had our reasons."

"But I didn't know you had any intention to marry?" Sheerah looked puzzled.

Achsah smoothed out her tunic and then pulled her wrap tighter around her shoulders. "Don't repeat this to Tamar, or any of our friends, but there wasn't any intention. Toi and I had a business agreement. I accepted his offer after Tamar said that no one would have me." She smiled. "It was worth it to see the look on Tamar's face, after she was so cruel to me."

"Achsah! I thought you cared for him?" Sheerah looked shocked. "I saw the way you both looked at each other on your wedding day."

Achsah put her hand to her face to block the sunlight. She shrugged. "Toi's not without his redeeming qualities, and our agreement was to both our advantage. I've left my home and family, and I have money. He has business connections with my wealthy family."

She held up the bag which was next to her side. It jingled with coins. "He gives me shekels to spend and other good things. And his business will grow."

Sheerah stared at Achsah as if she were aghast. "You aren't afraid for what might come of such a thing? I thought you'd allow your family to choose a worthy man for you?"

Achsah smiled with a sly look. "You truly believe I would want who they'd have for me? They'd have taken any man, whether it was in my best interests, or not, for the purpose of ridding themselves of me. I had an offer, I believed would work to my advantage, and I could also prove to Tamar that she was wrong about me. Who knows what type of man my parents would have chosen? There's no going back."

"How did this happen? I didn't know you were acquainted with Toi."

Achsah swung her hands by her side as they walked. She gave a casual shrug. "We met briefly, in the marketplace, and at your place. He didn't appreciate the things Tamar and the women said to me. He felt the deal he proposed could work for the benefit of each of us."

Sheerah studied Achsah closely. "How do you know he's a good man, when you've only met?"

"I suppose I'll find that out in time. He seems happy enough with the marriage. His business won't suffer with my father's influence and money. He's making connections with the Moabite people."

Achsah moved off the path for a donkey and cart that rolled past them. It carried a man and his wife on their way to the market.

She pointed to a tent with handcrafted jewelry that was across the path. "Oh look, bracelets!"

She took her friend's hand and pulled her to the stand. She lifted up a bronze wrist piece with jewels molded into it. She examined it closely and smiled. "It's exactly what I want."

Sheerah put her hand on Achsah's arm. She had a solemn expression on her face.

Achsah shrugged off Sheerah's hand and pulled a couple coins out of her bag. She handed them to the jeweler. Then she slipped the bracelet onto her wrist, and she gazed at it with sparkles in her eyes. "Come now, Sheerah, don't despair. What's done is done. I'm well."

"But..."

"Please, there can be no regrets. The marriage is sealed, and there's no turning back." She shrugged. "I may as well enjoy the spoils of it. I'm free from Dinah, and the others at my home, and I have what I need."

Achsah pointed to the cloth tent farther down the path. "Come, we must see what Elpaal has. Maybe there'll be a pretty piece there."

As they neared the tent, Achsah spied Toi and Shobach, in Shobach's courtyard, where they worked. Together they lifted a large stone to put on another flat rock in the courtyard.

Toi looked up and caught her eye. He observed the handbag at her side, and his brow lifted as he went back to his work.

Achsah flipped her hair over her shoulder. She turned back to Elpaal and the cloth. What did she care what he thought? He'd agreed to the arrangement. He didn't seem the sort to go back on his word.

She lifted up a piece of red silk with sparkling jewels threaded through it. "What do you think, Sheerah? Do you like it?"

Sheerah nodded. Her voice was solemn. "It's very pretty, Achsah. I think you've made a good choice."

"How much for this, Elpaal?"

Elpaal smiled. "For you, I'll lower my original price. What do you say to five of your coins? It came from the orient."

Achsah reached into her handbag and pulled out three. "I'll give you this much."

"Four, and no less."

"It's your last offer?"

"Yes."

Achsah held the cloth up again. She laid it across the skin on her arm. "It is very pretty. I haven't seen this color before. I suppose I'll be able to use it for something." She smoothed her fingers across it.

She took out one more coin and laid it on the counter with the rest. "Here, take it. Now, I must make this into a pretty tunic."

"I think it's lovely, Achsah." Sheerah spoke softly.

Achsah smiled and leaned closer. "The color will be good."

She looked at Toi. He was busy talking to Shobach. He seemed unconcerned with her and her business. She might just take a stroll over there and find out when he'd be done.

Since moving to Toi's home, she'd noticed five large donkeys his father had brought with them from Bethlehem. They were quite unlike any others she'd ever seen. She wasn't fond of animals, but for some reason she was drawn to these majestic, sleek creatures. Their combed coat was shiny and well groomed, and they walked with a dignified gait.

The other day, Sapphira rode on one of them. Achsah was amazed at the donkey's speed and agility, and she had wanted it to have been her racing across the plains the way Sapphira did. She'd never ridden such an animal.

She thought about asking Toi, when he got home from the work he was doing, if he'd take her out, but she was afraid he'd refuse her after a hard day's work. If she stopped now, at the courtyard, where he and Shobach were, she might be able to convince him to take her on one of them later.

Elpaal handed her the cloth which she took into her hands. She smiled at him. "Thank you. I'll see you again."

He smiled and nodded. "I look forward to it."

Achsah nudged Sheerah. "Now, I must have words with my husband. Let's make our way over there, and then we might do some more shopping after that."

"It sounds like a good plan."

They locked arms and headed toward the gate of Shobach's family's home.

*****

Shobach turned the stone in his hands. He eyed it carefully and chipped away at the corner. "I thought you said you had no intentions to marry? And to Achsah? What were you thinking?"

Toi got up and lifted the rectangular stone he'd finished working on. He carried it to a cart and stacked it beside the others. He took another stone from a pile, near to where they worked, and lifted it onto the flat rock next to Shobach.

He brushed off his dusty hands and looked up at his friend and shrugged. "I didn't have plans, and you're right; I meant to stay far from her. I think I might have likened her to one of my uncle's concubines."

They both laughed as they watched Achsah leave the cloth maker's tent with her friend. Both women walked toward them.

Toi stopped what he was doing to watch her.

She lifted up the fabric and eyed it dreamily.

"She's bought some cloth." Shobach grinned.

Toi gave his friend an annoyed look. "I did promise her some things. I hope I don't live to regret it."

Shobach observed Toi watchfully. "You've been taken in by her?"

"Oh, I knew what I was doing. The deal was not made without my own interests being carefully considered. I've already made some connections with her people, which have benefitted my trade greatly, and her rich father is happy that I've taken her off his hands. She is pretty."

Toi raked his hand through his hair as Achsah unlatched the gate and came into the courtyard.

Her eyes danced while she made her way across the length of the area toward him. She seemed to be inwardly rejoicing over her purchases.

He spoke under his breath. "I just hope all my profits do not end up in the shelves of Achsah's room."

"I'll say prayers for you." Shobach could not help but laugh again. "I believe you'll need it."

*****

"Sheerah and I have been shopping. Did you see the pretty cloth I bought? Elpaal gave me a deal on it." Achsah held it out for Toi to see.

He looked over at the cloth maker's tent. Elpaal was counting his money and rearranging the remaining fabrics on the tables under the awning.

Achsah noticed that Toi's swollen cheek was more pronounced. She put her hand over her mouth and gave him a concerned look. "Oh…it's worse, the bruise?"

"You're stronger than I thought."

Shobach eyed the purple spot beneath Toi's eye. He looked from Achsah to Toi.

Toi gave Achsah a lazy smile and tugged on her skirt as he drew her nearer to him. "You're not tired from the celebration and the dancing?"

Achsah looked down at his hand which gripped her skirt, and she immediately pushed him away. She brushed her tunic off. "You've touched those rocks, and your hands are dusty. Now I'll need to wash this."

Both Toi and Shobach looked at each other and began to laugh.

Toi grinned good-naturedly. "It's what you can expect from marrying a stoneworker."

Achsah put her hands on her hips. "I came to ask you if you'd take me on one of your donkeys this evening."

"Donkeys?" Toi looked surprised. "You?"

Sheerah spoke quietly. "You want to ride tonight?"

Achsah nodded. "Sapphira was on one."

Toi put the tool, he used for chipping the stone with, on the brick he was forming. He looked surprised. "One of the animals we brought from Bethlehem?"

"Yes, I could do it. I know I could. The black one's pretty. I'd like to ride that one."

Toi lifted his hand to his chin and rubbed it. He eyed her clothing and the spangles on her wrist. He smiled. "You won't even allow your husband to touch your skirt. You'll get dusty on those donkeys, and they're not always predictable."

"This is one of my better tunics. I didn't come here to look like a stoneworker while I'm in the markets. I've other

100

faded ones which aren't so good. I want to ride the darker one."
Achsah wrinkled her nose.

"Take her on one of them. Let her try it." Shobach's eyes
shone with amusement. "But, I'd put her on the gray one."

"It's what she'd get, if I were to take her out. She can't
ride the dark one."

Achsah didn't say anything. Her cheeks heightened in
color.

Toi studied her face with sudden interest. "Before you go,
I want to know how my brother treated you this morning."

"Benaiah?"

"Yes, you didn't start anything with him, did you?"

She thought back to the morning and looked away. "I did
nothing, but he was much the same. He told Kezia and Sapphira
to stay away from me when I was looking at the little goat. He
wouldn't use my name. He called me the Moabitess again."

"And what did you do?" There was amusement in his
eyes.

"I told you, I didn't do anything. But your sister,
Sapphira did. She threatened to tell on him."

Her eyes narrowed. "But, I don't care what your brother
does. I wanted to go to town to shop, so I'd no time for him."

He looked over the wall of the courtyard in the direction
of the house. He seemed somewhat bothered by the information
she'd given him. "I'm glad Sapphira said something. I'll make it
known to him that Kezia and Sapphira are your sisters and that he
must leave you be."

She studied his face for an element of truth. Something
told her that it was in his plans to do as he said.

Achsah felt something turn in her heart, but she didn't
want to acknowledge how she felt. She looked down at her
sandals which she scuffled on the dry ground beneath her feet.
"Do as you please. It's no concern to me what your brother
does."

He pulled her closer. This time he ignored her protests.
When he kissed her, he watched her expression as he spoke softly

to her. "I'll be back later, and I'll take you riding after dinner. Although I must help father in the fields first."

Achsah felt heat rush to her cheeks as she quickly pushed him away. It wouldn't due to be taken in by his handsome looks and kind words. She didn't know what to say.

She brushed herself off again and took Sheerah's hand. "Come, before my skirt's totally ruined. I'll be back home for dinner."

She didn't look back at either Shobach or Toi. She didn't want to see the expressions on their faces or hear what they had to say.

*****

"I believe his heart's turned toward you, Achsah."

Achsah looked at the tents in the marketplace. She shook her head. "He can be kind, but he made it quite clear that it wasn't the case."

"Then why did he look at you and kiss you the way he did."

Achsah frowned. "I'm his wife, and he has the right. Why wouldn't he?"

Sheerah didn't answer her.

"Look," Achsah said. She wanted to push aside thoughts of her husband, whom she wasn't quite sure she understood herself. "Another tent. This one has perfume boxes. I'd like some."

A long, thin table held tiny containers of different shapes in neat rows. An aroma rose around the tent.

Achsah dreamily sniffed the air. "If I could buy them all, I would."

"They smell very nice, but I need certain oils. And after this, I should be getting back home."

Sheerah took a bottle of myrrh in her hands and one of lavender.

She gave coins to an old man who held out his hands. "Here, I hope this is sufficient."

102

The man nodded and put the coins in his leather pouch which hung from his shoulder.

Achsah turned and looked farther down the road. She made a face when she spotted Tamar.

Achsah groaned. "Oh no, not who I want to talk to."

"Achsah, you should be kind to her. It could help her to see you differently." Sheerah sighed.

Three other women stood next to Tamar giggling and talking. They made their purchases at one of the tents and then walked toward Achsah and Sheerah.

"She scowls at me and says mean things. I could never be kind to her. She doesn't deserve anything from me."

"Tamar would like to be as beautiful as you are. You have lovely clothes, and things, and her family's not so wealthy. The men flock to you, and they all vie for your attention. I'm certain that it's difficult for women who want this."

Achsah let out a snort. "Like Dinah, always angry and spiteful. I've no time for that."

"You see what's on the outside, but Adonai looks at the heart. He sees her hurting soul."

Achsah drew back with an odd look. She'd heard this before from Ruth. What did it mean? She sighed. Sheerah was a Moabitess. She and Ruth had learned from the Israelites. She'd no understanding of these people and their strange ways. She wondered at Sheerah's words.

She watched as the other women approached. Sheerah stepped forward and took Tamar by the hands. She smiled widely. "My dear Tamar, how good it is to see you. Achsah and I were shopping today."

Tamar smiled at Sheerah. "I'm happy to see you also. I wanted to ask you to join us later. We're sewing together." She turned and gave Achsah a dark look.

Sheerah smiled. "I must get home soon. Mother wanted me to help her with the meal, but you're very kind to ask. I won't be able to, but Achsah might want to."

Tamar drew in a breath. She didn't say anything.

Achsah shrugged. "Toi's taking me on one of his donkeys. We're riding tonight."

All the women looked shocked.

Tamar stuttered on her words. "You're riding one of those animals? Why?"

"My father never had the larger ones like the ones Toi's family brought from Bethlehem. They're beautiful."

"But why would he take you?"

"Because I told him I wanted him to."

Tamar suddenly got a sly look on her face, and her tone changed. She sounded as if she were about to burst with her next admission. "But, my brother said that Toi married you for business purpo…"

She cupped her hand over her mouth and smiled. Her eyes were full of glee when she said it. "Oh…sorry, maybe my brother didn't want you to know he knew this. He said it wasn't arranged by your parents and that you made a deal with Toi."

Achsah turned to Tamar in surprise. It took a moment for her to register what had been said.

Heat suddenly seared her cheeks. She cleared her throat but said nothing. It seemed that Toi cared little about what others thought of her. He'd very quickly told Tamar's brother, Judah, this bit of information which he knew she'd taken such efforts to hide. She wondered how many others had learned the truth of it.

Sheerah came quickly to Achsah's side. She took hold of her arm. "There must have been some mistake."

Achsah pushed Sheerah's arm off and sniffed. Who cared what Tamar thought, or what Toi had done, or what anyone else knew for that matter?

"Well, it's true, every bit of it. I've nothing to hide." She smiled as if Tamar had told a humorous piece of information. "Toi and I came to this agreement, on our own, no different had it been arranged by my parents."

Her eyes slanted at Tamar. "But, it seems your brother told only part of the story. Toi might have had his reasons, but I had mine too." She forced a knowing look on her face as she held

104

up her purchases and laughed. "You should know that I married h*im* for his money. And it was not difficult for me to get what I wanted. I always do."

Tamar looked as if she were totally disgusted. "How can you say such things? What kind of person are you?"

Sheerah looked uncomfortable. "Come Achsah, let's go. We can get the perfumes another day."

Achsah gave Tamar a sly smile. "It's true. Toi promised me many things, and it's what I want." She looked at Sheerah. "Maybe it's best we leave. Suddenly the perfumes don't smell so good. I'll come back another time."

Tamar's usual frown appeared. "You're a pitiful person. I feel sorry for your husband. You should treat him with respect." She made a small sound. "Yet, considering who he is, maybe you deserve each other."

"I'm happy with the arrangement, so it's all that matters to me." Achsah took Sheerah's arm. She turned to go, and she didn't look back.

She heard Tamar speaking to the other women, behind her, in exaggerated tones.

Let the woman say what they wanted. Nothing any of them did could hurt her in any way.

She spoke quietly to Sheerah. "I don't care what she thinks, or how much she's heard. She can tell the whole town, if it makes her feel better. None of it matters to me."

"Achsah, Tamar doesn't understand. I'm sorry she said those hurtful things. I don't want you to be injured by her."

"Please Sheerah, don't say more. I don't want to talk about her. I just want to go." She held the fabric in her arms closer to her chest.

"I'm sorry, Achsah. Truly I am." Sheerah looked chagrinned.

"Don't worry. She can't do anything to me. I don't care what she says." She released Sheerah and turned to go the other way. "I must go home now." She looked back once and waved. "I will see you again."

Sheerah sighed. "Are you sure you don't want to stay and talk, Achsah?"

"I'm sure. Nothing anyone said hurt me in the slightest." Achsah gave Sheerah an encouraging look.

Sheerah nodded. "Oh Achsah, we will meet again. Don't worry. Everything will be well."

Achsah gave her a half-smile and turned. She took quick steps toward her new home. She left Sheerah on the path behind her.

As she moved farther down the road, something churned inside when she thought of Toi giving Tamar ammunition against her. Surely, he would pay for what he did.

*****

That afternoon, Naomi came inside after working in the fields. She wiped a tear from her eyes as she crossed the room.

Ruth put her hand on her mother-in-law's arm. "I'm sorry you miss your husband. Elimelech was a good man."

Naomi nodded. "It's still difficult for me to believe he's gone. Each day I wait for the door to open, and he doesn't come through it. I miss the times we used to sit together in the evenings, in the courtyard, and talk."

"He cared very much for you."

"He did."

"Mahlon and Chilion are hard workers. Your sons will make sure your needs are met."

"Yes, but I worry that they'll be able to bear the load my husband did. Neither are as strong. They've had so much sickness in their lives."

"They love you, and so do Orpah and I. There's no need to worry."

Naomi's expression softened, and she smiled, even though another tear dropped onto her cheek. She wiped it away. "I have good sons and daughters. I'm grateful to the Lord for this. He's given me so much to be thankful for. He's the strength of my heart."

Ruth got up and went to the table. She picked up a bag of grain. "I'll start the bread. Orpah went to the fields to help. She'll be in later."

"Yes, I'll prepare the other dishes. My grief, it threatens to overwhelm me, but I must try to overcome the sadness. I do not wish to harbor bitterness inside me."

Ruth nodded as she took out a wooden bowl and poured the grains in. "I miss him, too. I'll do the same."

*****

Achsah went to the gate and opened it as Toi came home that afternoon from his work. She was quiet and didn't say anything.

Toi looked curious. "I see you changed into more appropriate clothing for a ride. I'll go to the spring and wash before dinner. We'll leave after the meal."

Achsah watched him take clothing from the servants and go out through the gate. She went back into the house where she smelled fresh baked bread and roasted lamb.

She sat at the far end of the table, next to Kezia as she waited for Toi to come back to join them. She listened to the others in the room as they discussed their day.

She looked across the table. Benaiah was staring at her darkly. She didn't give him the satisfaction of acknowledging him, but instead she looked down and kept her eyes fastened onto her plate.

She reached for a bunch of grapes and some lentil stew. She tried to choke down what she could. She was still upset over Tamar's words and the information her husband had given Judah.

Toi came into the room. He was washed and free of dust. He sat next to her.

Achsah looked away. She took another bite of lentil stew and swallowed drily.

Hannah's voice was quiet. "Did you see your friend today, Achsah? How was your day?"

Achsah put her silver spoon down. "I did see Sheerah, and it was profitable."

As she spoke, she wondered if Toi had told the family why he'd married her. In time, she might need to set them all straight.

"I like Sheerah." Sapphira's eyes glowed. "I'm glad you and her are friends. She's very kind."

Achsah smiled at the young woman. "Sheerah and I have been friends for some time. Her family and mine have known each other since I was young. I always enjoy spending time with her. We went to the markets today."

Benaiah sneered as he lifted bread to his mouth and chewed on it unceremoniously. "Judging from all the things you came back with; it seems it was profitable for you. Yet, I wouldn't say the same for Toi."

Achsah's eyes narrowed. Maybe it was time his family knew what Toi and her relationship consisted of, before he told them. "I suppose we both got what we bargained for in this marriage."

Toi turned to stare at her.

Benaiah looked interested.

Achsah frowned. "You shouldn't wonder, Benaiah, when the whole town seems to know that my marriage to Toi was a business arrangement between the two of us and nothing more. Tamar didn't waste any time letting me know she knew."

The whole table became silent as Toi turned to Achsah with a surprised look on his face.

She spat out her words. "You needn't stare at me like that. I'm sure you enjoyed telling Judah why we married, but I don't care. It matters little to me what you say or do."

Achsah got up from the table. Her cheeks were a crimson color. "My father's connections and money would've been enough to tempt most men."

"Achsah." He put his hand on her arm.

She shoved it off and pushed back the angry tears on her cheeks. "Please, I don't care what you told them. I set it straight with Tamar that I married you for the things you could buy for me."

The family all looked at Toi in shock. The table was silent. Even Benaiah regarded his brother as if he were surprised.

"Don't bother getting up." Achsah put her hand on Toi's arm. "I've changed my mind. I don't want to go riding."

Achsah could hear Josheb, Toi's father. He was chastising Toi as she crossed the room and left out the doorway.

She unlatched the gate of the courtyard and went out as she closed it behind her. She made her way to a rise that overlooked a deep valley. She sat down on a grassy area and watched some sheep farther out in the pasture.

*****

Hannah put her hand on Toi's arm. "You hurt her, Toi. I'm sure of it. I don't know how all this came about, but it's plain to see that she was humiliated and embarrassed by what was said about her."

"Achsah?" Toi blinked. "You heard her. She's no innocent in this."

Hannah sighed. "How could a son of mine do such a thing? Did you see the way she looked at you? She has to endure the ridicule that will come of this. Those women won't be kind to her."

Toi took a bite out of the bread in his hand. "Mother, if anyone can deal with it, Achsah can. She's not afraid of them."

"What are you saying?" His mother's eyes widened. "You would never have treated your sisters this way. What are you thinking, son? She's not happy with you."

Benaiah looked toward the door. He let out a snort. "He should have thought of these things when he married her. She'll always be a thorn in his side as far as I'm concerned."

Toi put down the food in his hand and got up. "Achsah isn't your concern, Benaiah." His fist tightened as he held it to his side. "You stay out of it."

Hannah wagged a finger at them both. "Not at the dinner table." She let out a breath. "Toi, you need to go talk to your wife. I don't care how your marriage came about. You've hurt her, and you need to make amends."

"Mother's right." Kezia piped in. "I saw it in her eyes. You can't treat Achsah like that. She might not show it, but she's hurt. You should be caring for her and not sitting here picking fights and eating." Her cheeks turned pink. "Achsah needs to see kindness in her life."

Sapphira's lips drew into a pout. "I feel bad that she ended up married to you."

Toi put down the bread in his hand. He let out a frustrated sound.

His father, Josheb, nodded. "Your sisters are right. You need to treat Achsah as a husband should."

Toi turned to his father. Then he looked up at the ceiling and laughed. "All right. Enough. You've said what you want to say." He put up his hand. "I see where all of your hearts lie, excluding Benaiah. I'll talk to her, if anything, to get all of you from turning against me."

Hannah let out a breath. Her brows drew into a frown. "I am not happy with you, but I'm glad you'll talk to her. Now, waste no more time and go and do this."

He went to the door. "Just let me alone, and I will." He chuckled to himself again. Then he turned and went outside to find Achsah. He left the others behind.

*****

A raw deep hurt swelled inside Achsah as she sat looking out over the meadow. She crossed her arms, and then she kicked at a pebble beneath her foot.

No one in her own family had ever cared for her, and now she was sure that none of Toi's would either. Maybe it would've been better for her father to have arranged a marriage, on his terms, as an acceptable transaction, rather than what had happened. She seemed to be no better off in Toi's home than she'd been in her own.

She sighed as she watched the shepherds farther out in the fields walking beside their flocks. The animals made soft bleating sounds as they occasionally stopped to watch their masters. They bent down to graze. She tried to take her mind from the family in the home behind her as she watched the men prod the sheep farther down the field.

A short time later, she heard footsteps behind her. She turned. Toi led two donkeys by leather reins which he tied to a nearby tree.

She looked back at the meadow.

"Achsah."

"I told you I didn't want to ride."

He came behind her. "I don't know how Judah knew. I didn't say anything to him. It's the truth."

"It doesn't matter. But, you should have told me, so that I'd have been ready for Tamar." She drew her shawl tighter around her. "She laughed at me again. You gave her a reason for it."

"But I told you that I never said anything to him. Shobach's the only person I spoke to, and he wouldn't have repeated it to anyone. The only other one I discussed it with was..." His words died in his throat suddenly.

Achsah turned around. Her eyes darkened. "Who?"

"It was the only way my father could convince your father to settle the agreement. He wanted something from it."

"My father?"

"It was said in confidence. He was told to not say anything to anyone."

Achsah let out a bitter laugh. She got up with a resigned look. "I suppose my family would've wanted to know why you'd marry me. I'm sure Dinah didn't waste any time getting the word out."

She shivered as she stared at the valley. "I shouldn't have expected more than I got. I'm sure none of them were surprised at my part in it."

"Achsah, I didn't intend for them to find out. If it makes you feel any better, my mother and sisters, and father, weren't happy with me. They told me I needed to learn how to treat my wife."

She let out a light laugh. "Which you should." She crossed her arms again.

"I suppose I wasn't expecting to be married so quickly." He regarded her with curiosity, and then he shrugged.

Achsah stared at him. "Then why did you?"

He didn't say anything, but he smiled and took her hand in his. He tugged on it. "Come, I know where Tamar lives. I'll take you riding there."

She eyed him warily. "Why?"

He lifted his hand to her cheek and wiped a tear from it. "I'll see to it that both her and Judah think again before they speak. Let's take the donkeys to the fields near her home. You can ride the black one, if you'd like."

"But, you said I couldn't have that one?"

"As long as Benaiah isn't aware of it, I see no reason why you can't. It's his."

"Oh." Achsah eyed the donkey from a distance. Her expression suddenly lightened.

"Then you'll go with me?"

"If I can ride that one. Can you help me onto it?"

He nodded and smiled. "Yes, but let's bring the donkeys to the meadow and start from there."

She watched as he untied the two large animals and took her hand. They walked down into the valley together while they led the donkeys behind them.

*****

Tamar's family was in the courtyard when Achsah and Toi rode into the fields near their home. Toi reached out and reigned in both donkeys. He got down and let his animal graze while he lifted Achsah from the other donkey's back.

He brushed her hair back from her face. "Look at me."

Achsah tipped her head upward. She turned to him quizzically. "But why?"

"I'll show you." He leaned down and whispered in her ear. "It's for Tamar's benefit, my dear wife, so that she might learn there's more to our marriage than a business deal."

As the evening sun dipped low in the sky, and spread colors of purples against the horizon, Toi leaned down and kissed her. Achsah blushed at the passionate nature of the kiss, and her heart felt lighter inside because of it.

She kissed him back, and she was struck with the thought that it was difficult to deny the great attraction she felt for him.

She sighed wearily with the knowledge that this display of affection was for Tamar's sake. Toi had made that clear to her. She knew she was treading on uncertain ground with him. It wouldn't due to allow for such feelings. He couldn't know how much he affected her.

She suddenly drew back, and she looked up. She attempted to appear unaffected. Her breath caught in her throat as she spoke with as much confidence as she could. "I'm sure Tamar was convinced. She'll certainly believe we have an attraction for each other."

Toi's first reaction was to show surprise at her remark, but then he took her hand in his. He lifted it to his mouth and kissed it while watching her.

Achsah felt the heat return to her cheeks. Her mouth drew open as she looked at him.

Toi's eyes sparked to life. He laughed, and he pulled her close again. "You might think those games will work with me, but they won't. You feel more for me than you are admitting."

"I don't deny an attraction of sorts." She turned away and started back to the donkey. "In all honesty, it's true." She petted the side of the great, black animal as a solemn expression crossed her face.

She looked back at him. "But you must know that my heart is not so easily swayed, and I wonder myself if you'll ever be fully privy to it. I can't say whether this will ever change."

"I'm sorry I hurt you. I didn't mean to. I didn't know these things would be said that were told in confidence."

She eyed him warily. She sighed and didn't say anything.

"Maybe someday you'll learn to trust me, my little Achsah." He came to her side and lifted her onto the donkey. "If you'd do this, I believe we might find things could be rather good between us."

She considered what he'd said warily. Something inside struck her deeply at his quiet words. A lump formed in her throat as she turned away and looked out over the expanse of the valley.

He got up on the gray animal and rode beside her.

Achsah hid the tears that fell onto her cheeks. She hoped the wind would dry them away.

*****

Chapter 6

Benaiah stormed out to the field when Toi and Achsah returned on the donkeys.

He grabbed the leather straps of Achsah's donkey. "Get down!"

Then he turned to Toi. "Why would you allow her to ride my animal? Dirty Moabitess!"

"Benaiah, watch what you say." Toi reached out to steady the black donkey. "You need to respect my wife, and it shouldn't matter which animal she's on."

Benaiah glared at Achsah. "I told you to get off!"

Achsah tried to find a way to get down. The immense height of the animal made it difficult. She looked at Benaiah with a puzzled expression. "If you let me alone, I'll figure it out."

Benaiah reached out and yanked Achsah's tunic. He pulled her so hard that she fell onto the dusty ground and hit with a thud.

Pain shot through her hip and ankle, and tears immediately sprung to her eyes. She made a wounded sound as she attempted to crawl from beneath the great animal's dancing hoofs.

Kezia came running out of the house. She went straight to Achsah. "Sister, I'm so sorry!" She looked up at Benaiah in shock. She pushed the donkey aside and tied it to the gate.

Toi jumped down from his animal and went to his brother. "I told you to leave her alone." His eyes were fixed on Benaiah, and he grabbed the front of his brother's robe and gave him a shove that sent him reeling backward.

Benaiah stumbled, but he caught himself from falling. "It's my animal she was on. She'd no right to it."

Toi's face darkened. His voice was a low growl. "You had no right to touch my wife."

"You purposely did this!"

Toi shoved his brother again. "I told you the other day to put an end to this."

Kezia got between them. "Stop this, both of you! Achsah's hurt, and no one's helping." Her cheeks were bright pink. "Toi, go to your wife. Help her up." She wagged a finger at them. "Don't either of you know how to treat a woman?"

Toi backed away with a frustrated look.

Then, he turned to Achsah and squatted down beside her. He put his arm around her. "Where do you want to go?"

Achsah pushed him away. "I don't need help. I can stand on my own." She winced in pain and got up. She began to walk away.

Kezia looked shocked. She put her hand to her mouth, and it seemed as if she were going to cry. "Take her somewhere to care for her, to her room."

Achsah put her hand out. "I can do it myself." She gave Benaiah a look of angst. Her eyes were dark and challenging. "I didn't believe Toi when he said it would be different here. You speak of your religion, and your ways, but it appears a home with the Israelite God is no better than a home with Chemosh."

Kezia blushed. "No, Achsah, it isn't the way it should be. Adonai wouldn't condone such things."

Benaiah didn't say anything, but he observed Achsah with a dark look.

Achsah took Kezia's arm and limped in the direction of the house. She could hear Toi and Benaiah arguing behind her.

Kezia spoke softly. "Lean on me. I'm sorry, Achsah. My brothers are horrible. I'll talk to both of them."

After taking a couple steps, Achsah's ankle gave out on her. She fell to the ground, and she grabbed her foot as tears dropped freely down her face. She made another sound, though she tried to hold it back.

Kezia backed away. She looked at her brothers. "Toi, you need to take care of your wife."

Toi went to Achsah and lifted her, despite her protests. "Achsah, let me help you." He began taking her toward the house. "It might be broken."

Something in his expression softened as he looked at her. He sighed. "You need to learn when to accept help. Must you always contend with everyone?"

This time she didn't say anymore. She put her arms around his neck as he carried her to the gate.

He took her through the courtyard and into her room off the second courtyard. He set her down on the bedding, and he got down beside her. "Let me see. I need to look at it."

She pulled her foot out from underneath her tunic.

He eyed the swollen ankle which was already forming a bruise, and he gently moved it in different directions. "You've turned it, but it appears it isn't broken. Is there anywhere else you're hurting?"

"My hip, but it's only sore." She sighed.

Toi nodded, and then he lifted his hand to the side of her face and outlined the curve of it. "I forget that I must care for you. I truly wasn't prepared to take a wife."

She propped herself up on her side. "But I don't need you to. I don't need anyone to care for me. I can do it myself."

"Achsah." He took her hand in his. "You'll need to allow it this time."

She frowned. "Why would you risk marrying me, when you knew what Benaiah was like? Kezia's sweet and kind. She's upset. Your family will suffer for it."

Toi reached out and took her hand in his. He looked at her with interest. He hesitated before he spoke again. "I'm not sure, as my profits don't seem to be growing, and you've caused me more trouble than your worth." He smiled. "Maybe the moon had an effect on me the night I made the proposal to you."

Achsah's lips drew up into a pout. She pushed his hand away. "Your brother hates me, when I've done nothing to him."

Toi reached out and put his hand on her arm. He looked concerned. "I didn't expect this."

Achsah sighed. "He's no better than Dinah. I left her for this."

There was a serious look in his eyes. "This was truly wrong of him, and it's the last time it will happen."

Achsah didn't answer but turned onto her side.

"Achsah, I mean what I say. He'll not touch you again."

"I don't care what he does." She pulled her foot closer to her and groaned. "I just want to be left alone. I'm tired."

"You can sleep, but I'll stay."

She pulled a blanket on the bed around her and closed her eyes as she lay there. She allowed herself to nod off to sleep while Toi sat at her side.

It wasn't long before she felt herself drifting away.

*****

Toi reached out and fingered a strand of Achsah's hair. He studied his wife's profile as she slept. He couldn't deny that she was very beautiful.

He watched while she drew in quiet breaths as her dark eyelashes fanned out over her cheeks. A faint blush colored her sun-browned complexion. It complimented the natural rosiness of her lips. Only in deep slumber, could this young Moabitess appear as peaceful as she did.

He smiled. He'd chosen a wife with spirit and willfulness. Life would certainly not be dull with her by his side.

He eyed her bruised and swollen foot.

Benaiah was wrong to have treated her so cruelly. Their father would never have treated their mother, or any of their sisters, the way his brother did.

Achsah may have deserved the consequences, she'd gotten for some of her actions, but there was no excuse for this. Such a thing wouldn't happen again.

He got up quietly and made his way to the door. He turned once to eye her thoughtfully. She was still fast asleep. He didn't want to wake her.

He left as he quietly closed the door behind him.

*****

"Mother, you must do something about Toi and Benaiah. They've been horrible to Achsah." Kezia put her hand on her mother's arm.

Hannah nodded. "I'll talk to them. I'm not sure where they get the idea that they can do the things they do."

Toi walked into the courtyard. He stared at his sister. "What do you mean? I took Achsah to her room and watched over her."

A blush stole over Kezia's cheeks. Her voice was soft. "It isn't what I meant. I think you know that your wife deserves better."

Hannah moved closer to Toi.

Toi shrugged. "What else do you expect? I checked her foot, and she's sleeping now."

Kezia's face was pale. She choked on her words. "Achsah wants more than this. Do you understand that she needs her husband's love? You must know how important it is."

Toi's brow rose slightly. "We had an agreement. Achsah's interesting enough, but hardly the woman a man can trust fully."

"But you chose marriage with her." Hannah sighed. "Once you make those bonds, Adonai's clear that you should love your wife, regardless of the circumstances. Your father's spared none of it. You should do the same."

Toi considered his mother and sister's words. "I cannot say I don't care for her, and I'll do my best, but it's all I can offer her at this time. As I said, it was an arrangement of our making. I'm sorry, mother. Achsah knows I'll provide for her. This much I'll do."

Kezia gave him a solemn look. "You might try prayer. Adonai can do more than you know."

"I'll do what I can and no more. Achsah strong. She's agreed to what I've proposed, so you needn't worry. She'll be fine." He grasped the door of the gate and opened it. "I need to go now."

He turned away from them. He didn't look back as he opened the door and went out. He had unfinished business at Shobach's to take care of.

*****

"It seems this whole marriage has caused quite a stir."

Shobach lifted a stone block and began to shape it. "What do you mean?"

"My family's divided over Achsah. I don't understand what it is they want of me. Benaiah's treated her unfairly. I tried to talk to my mother and Kezia, but they're not happy with me. They treat me as if I should be thrown to the lions, or much worse. And Sapphira hasn't spoken to me since this morning."

"So what has caused this?"

"I brought her home. And since the day she arrived, the whole place has been in an uproar."

Shobach smiled. "I recall a conversation we had earlier. I believe you were warned of the dangers of a union with her, but you didn't listen."

"And now it seems I'm paying for it." He stopped carving and dusted off his hands. He let out a breath. "Truly, I'm not sure what to do. No one in my family's happy with me."

Shobach grinned. "Maybe this will be good for you, the chosen one of the family. It's not profitable for anyone to hold that title for long. How might you learn your faults otherwise?"

"Faults?" Toi raised a brow. "I didn't think I had any." He smiled.

"Precisely." Shobach put his hand on Toi's shoulder. "And now you do." Then his expression grew solemn. "I'm hoping your mother, and the rest of them, are very tough on you.

You might see a bit of a need for Adonai in time and turn your heart to him."

Toi began working again to shape the precious stone into an idol. "Going to the synagogue is what you can expect of me."

Shobach looked concerned. "I don't mean to condemn, but you say this as you work on a stone for the Moabites' altars. You must know that the Torah speaks against this, Toi."

Toi shrugged casually. "I don't believe in the idols. It's my trade. I'm not worshipping them." He put the stone down and got up.

Shobach didn't answer.

Toi looked past the gate to the fields beyond the town. "I'm glad for our friendship, Shobach, but it might not be in our best interests that we argue this point. We've not agreed on this matter. In fact, we see it quite differently." He brushed off his robe again.

"You should read the Torah rather than listen to me."

Toi shrugged. "What you say holds weight with me. I'll think on it."

Shobach nodded. "We've known each other a long time. I hope you understand that I want the best for you."

"I'm sure you do. But, now our time here is running short. I must be going back home. Pray for our family."

"I'll do this."

Toi picked up his tools and put them inside a room off the courtyard. He came back out and waved to Shobach who was finishing his work. "Peace, friend."

"Peace." Shobach watched as Toi went through the gate.

*****

Jorah got on his donkey. Toi was meeting him later to work in the fields.

He clucked to the animal as he leaned down and spoke softly in its ear. "I suppose it's time we make our way back. The

caravan of merchants from the east has filled our empty sacks."
He patted the saddlebags loaded with various items for the family.

"But, first we'll get you a drink." He veered off the path
and followed a trail that led through a shaded, wooded valley with
a stream so that he could water his animal.

As he cleared a rise, he got down to walk the rest of the
way. He stopped short when he eyed Achsah's sister, Dinah,
walking along the bank of the river.

He watched as she picked clusters of flowers and slipped
them into her apron. She got up and walked over to one of the
river's trees and stood next to it. She took a rose from her lap and
held it to her nose as she breathed in its scent while she looked
toward the mountain in the distance.

Jorah led his animal the rest of the way to the river to give
it a drink. The donkey leaned down and began lapping up the
water.

Dinah turned and looked his way, but she didn't move
from where she was.

*****

Dinah gave Jorah a wary look. She hadn't considered
talking to him since he'd treated her so horribly at the wedding.
He didn't deserve as much as a glance his way after his what he'd
said to her, yet she didn't leave. She was curious as to why he
came.

"Dinah?" His voice was low and quiet. "I won't be long.
My animal needs a drink."

She didn't answer.

His brown eyes gentled as he stared appraisingly at her.
He reached out and patted the side of his donkey. "She's thirsty.
It's warm today." His look was encouraging.

She nodded. She was puzzled by his kind expression.
She couldn't help wondering if she had been too harsh in her
earlier assessment of him. He seemed quite different from the

previous night. She remembered him telling her he was more comfortable outside the social settings.

She smoothed out her skirt. The golden jewels on her upper arm slipped down, and she pushed them back into place while she held the edge of her apron so as not to tip the flowers in it out.

She still was unsure of his motives, but wanted to see what he had to say.

*****

Jorah let go of the reins as his donkey continued to drink. He stared at her with intent. "The flowers are very beautiful here. Do you come often?"

Dinah put the rose, that she'd been holding, in her lap.

He smiled. "You're not speaking to me. Did I offend you so terribly at the wedding?"

She played with the flowers in her apron. She touched the petals gently.

He laughed. "You didn't want me to protect Achsah and Toi's new marriage? What else might a good brother have done?"

"I didn't say it was wrong to do what you did. Though, our people wouldn't have cared so much."

"Then, what makes you so reticent to talk to me?"

Dinah looked at the fields in the distance. "You seem to ask a lot of questions, and I'm not one to speak openly about my thoughts with those I don't know well."

"But, how would anyone know you, if you didn't." Jorah studied her with an interested expression.

"I'm a difficult person to understand." Dinah sighed. "Maybe you should leave it at that."

Jorah left his animal at the river bank and stood next to her. "I've never claimed to understand any woman, especially a Moabitess."

Dinah picked up another flower from her lap and turned it in her fingers. "So, why would you wish to try?"

"I'm not sure." He laughed again as he patted the side of his donkey. A warmth lit in his eyes. "But, it seems I'm at the mercy of the Moabite women, in this place, and must try and understand them, and even more so, when I take an interest in one of them."

"Hmm, have I drawn your interest then, Jorah?" She suddenly gave him a practiced look. She slanted her eyes at him as her dark lashes swept onto her face coyly.

Jorah turned away. "Dinah, I'm saying that you're a part of my family now." He looked across the plains to the mountain.

"Ah, family. This is why you are taking interest in me." Dinah moved closer.

Jorah ignored her subtle looks. "Friendship."

Dinah giggled and brushed an errant strand of hair from her eyes. "Come now, an Israelite man wants friendship with me?" She gave him a curious look.

"Why not? You're like your sister. She's not so bad."

Dinah's eyes lit with a fiery glow, and she laughed aloud. "I'm sure Achsah would beg to differ with you, and she might not want you and I to be friends. I don't believe an alliance between us would be a good thing. You live in the same house as she."

"Then you believe I'd be your enemy because of it?"

"Oh, I don't know." She gave him an inquisitive look. "But, you might be someday."

"Our family is loyal to each other and to our friends. I'd treat you honorably as I do her." Jorah stared at the bubbling brook while watching the water as it moved swiftly in spots and slow in others. He picked up a small stone and skipped it across the surface.

"What do you want?" Dinah studied him closely. "You say friendship, but I don't believe it."

"My faith and beliefs are very important to me. I'd consider any Moabite woman as a friend, but nothing more. Our religions are very different. There would be difficulties for you and I, if we were more than friends. There are many things we wouldn't agree on, in the ways we live and think." Jorah gave her a solemn look.

"We should be able to rise above our differences."

"We could in friendship. But if I were to marry a Moabitess, I could not pray with my wife or take her with me to the synagogue. We'd worship separately, and I'd want to share this part of my life with her."

Dinah tipped her head thoughtfully. "I can see why you would want this."

"Toi takes his faith less seriously than I do."

Dinah lifted a rose from her apron and held it out to him. "Here take this. I might consider friendship with you."

He smiled and reached out to take the flower from her hand.

As she drew her hand away, a thorn scratched her finger. She stared at it as a drop of blood formed.

Jorah set the rose aside on a rock and took his headpiece off. "Here, let me see it." He tore off a piece of cloth from it and took her hand in his. He wrapped the fabric around her finger and then tied it so that it was secure.

She looked down at the roses in her apron and didn't say anything at first, but when she did, she spoke quietly. "I must take these home before they wilt. Mother expects me back."

"Is it possible I might see you again?" Jorah reached out to her.

Dinah frowned. The color in her eyes deepened. "It might be." She lifted the apron of her skirt with both hands and looked away. "But, I should go now." She turned and began to walk down the small footpath. She looked back at him once as she made her way up the hill and onto the road.

Jorah watched as she reached the top and disappeared over the rise.

He took the rose she'd given him. He was careful not to catch his fingers on a thorn.

He broke the longer part of the stem off and threw the piece with the thorns into the river. He wrapped the rose in the cloth and gently placed it in his saddlebag.

He looked at the top of the hill.

At the wedding, he'd willed himself to stay away from Dinah, knowing what he did about her and her family. It was true that such an alliance might lead to conflict and grief. It surely wasn't something he wished for, for her, or himself.

Now, he was not so sure. He'd seen a softer side to the young woman which he'd not seen the night of the wedding. He could understand how Toi was drawn to Achsah.

He took hold of the reins of his donkey and began leading it up the rise. Toi would be waiting for him at home. He supposed he shouldn't stay longer.

*****

The sun was over the horizon, and its bright rays sent their warmth through the town. Long, deep shadows stole past rocks, trees, walls, and houses as the day came to life.

The courtyard was full of life. Animals in the adjoining courtyard bayed and clucked and let out soft sounds. Some of their hooves padded across the hard ground while they feasted on their morning meal.

Achsah took the crutch Toi had carved for her. She put it under her arm and got up. She lifted into her arms two silken tunics, she'd sewn, for both Kezia and Sapphira. She handed each sister one of them. "I made these for you."

Kezia held the indigo tunic. Her eyes went wide. "Achsah, it's beautiful. I thought you were making it for yourself."

Sapphira stood. She circled once with a red shimmering tunic in her hands. "I love it. It's pretty. Thank you! I can't wait to wear it." Sapphira hugged her new clothing to her.

Kezia nodded. "I've never had anything so beautiful."

126

Achsah eyed them thoughtfully. She wasn't used to such responses. "They're only tunics. You can go with me to town next time and wear them. It's a small thing."

Achsah turned and noticed that Toi was watching her. He was on a stone bench, across from the women in the courtyard, carving the tip of a wooden spear.

She looked away and hobbled back toward the second courtyard where her room was.

She passed Benaiah who was sitting with Jorah. They were fixing the broken spoke of a wheel for one of the carts.

She sensed Benaiah's eyes on her. Lately, he hadn't been outwardly aggressive, yet she couldn't help feeling he hadn't changed the way he felt toward her.

"This one's almost ready," Jorah said to Benaiah. "When yours is done, we can fix it."

Benaiah nodded.

Toi put down his spear and went to where Achsah was. He walked next to her and whispered in her ear. "I thought you bought those pieces of material for yourself. Why did you give the tunics to my sisters?"

"Why do *you* think I did it?"

"I'm not sure. I'm interested to know it." Toi smiled.

Achsah shrugged. "I don't mind sewing and wanted to give them something, because they've been good to me." She steadied her crutch beneath her and turned to look at both Kezia and Sapphira who were still holding their new tunics with rapt expressions.

She thought how the fabric was a sharp contrast to the dull brown clothing, with leather ties, they were wearing. Neither flattered them in any way. At least now they'd be presentable in town.

"And besides, they can't go to market with me wearing those ridiculously drab tunics. The fabrics and colors are wearisome and worn. I can't have family appearing this way when I'm with them."

"Ah, the truth comes out." He laughed. "You wished to make them presentable."

"Your sisters liked them. It does make me glad to see them happy. And I can buy more, as it matters little to me. There's always a pretty piece at the market." Her eyes sparkled as she looked up at him. "They might want to go with me."

"And you'll not be alone in your ventures. I see." He shook his head. "More money out of my leather pouch." He shook his head.

"For a pretty wife."

He touched her cheek, and his eyes lit as he turned to her. "Yes, for a pretty wife."

Then his expression changed when he saw the way she was moving. He took hold of the walking stick.

"What is it?" She stopped and repositioned the crutch under her arm again. It was causing her some pain.

"Sit here a moment." He pointed to the stone stairs, on the side of the house, which led upward.

Achsah gave him a wary look, but she did as he said. She sat down on the hard, cool steps and brushed the dust off her hands. "There's no need for you to check it. It's better."

"Let me see." He reached out and took her foot in his hands. He untied her sandals.

"Truly, there's no need to look at it."

"Achsah, stop. You don't care for yourself, and you won't let anyone else. Someone has to."

Achsah straightened. She turned to see Benaiah watching from a distance. His expression was difficult to read. She wasn't sure what he was thinking. She looked quickly back at Toi.

Toi lifted her foot to inspect it. "It's still slightly swollen, but the color of the bruise is better. You mustn't keep trying to walk on it. You need to give it a chance to heal."

"But I can't lie in that room forever. I want to go back to the markets, or do something. I already made two tunics and wove a scarf for your mother. I must stay busy. I can walk on it now, without the crutch, but will favor it a few more days."

"I'll take you on the cart when the wheel's fixed. It should be ready about the time your foot is almost healed. Shobach's family's having a dinner and guests on the Sabbath. We'll go then. You won't need to do much walking for that."

Achsah looked relieved. "Can your sisters go, too?"

"You want both of them to ride there with us?"

Achsah nodded. "I would." Her eyes lit at the prospect.

"I don't see why they shouldn't. Shobach didn't say they couldn't."

"Good!" Achsah clapped her hands and squealed. She embraced his neck and kissed him as she laughed with delight.

Toi looked surprised. A sparkle lit his eye. "Maybe I should take you out more often."

Achsah couldn't help but smile. "I'm glad I'm feeling better."

Toi took her walking stick and sandals in his hand and lifted her up. "Rest, so you're ready for tomorrow. I'll take you to your room."

Achsah nodded. "I must decide what to wear. I've a few pretty tunics. I wonder who'll be there?"

Toi laughed. "I told you that you must rest. Figure those things out tomorrow, but do nothing more until then."

"I'll stay off my foot, if this is what you want, but I've plans to make. Your Sabbath will come soon enough."

He groaned, but said no more. He took her to her room and set her down. "Now, I must leave. I'll be back later."

Achsah smiled as he went out the door. She used the crutch to hobble over to her shelf and laid out the clothing and jewelry she planned to wear in the coming days. She couldn't wait for the excitement of the festivities to begin.

*****

Jorah's donkey quickened its pace as it neared Dinah's family's gate.

He wasn't sure why he'd come, but against his better judgment, he'd turned at the fork in the road before going home and made his way to her place.

He eyed the stone entrance, and the courtyard beyond it, as he watched two of Dinah's younger sisters as they chased each other, and giggled within the gated wall, while Laban's wives worked in the courtyard. One of the wives took bread from the stone oven with a long, metal tool. Another beat the dust, from a blanket that hung on an outer wall, while the third sat quietly and combed Dinah's brother's short, wavy hair. The boy sat on a stone bench while his mother gently tugged at his curls.

Jorah scanned the courtyard, for the young woman of his interest, but he didn't see her.

He was sure it had been a mistake to come this way, but he couldn't help wondering at the exchange between her and him days before. He stood behind a couple of trees, at a distance, where no one in the courtyard could see him.

The door of the house opened, and Dinah came out with a clay vessel in her hands which she lifted onto her shoulder and held by the handle.

"Dinah? I thought I told you to get water when you first got up this morning? And you've not braided or combed your hair. You look unkempt."

Dinah made a face. Her thick hair was loose down her back. "I combed it this morning, mother. And father wanted me to make Samla a special meal. I'm going to the well now."

"Well, you mustn't be long. Rachel needs your help finishing that blanket, and I've other chores for you."

Jorah fastened the ropes of his donkey to the tree and waited for Dinah to come out of the courtyard.

She closed the gate and adjusted the vessel onto her shoulder. She began walking down the road until she came to a bend in the path. She looked up.

Jorah stood next to his donkey.

She eyed him warily. "What are you doing?"

"I was on my way home. I wondered if I might see you."
He reached out and took the vessel from her hand. "Here, we'll
walk together. I'll carry it."

She gave him a chagrinned look. "You understand that I
didn't go to the river to meet you the other day."

He began to walk in the direction of the closest well. "I
didn't go there to meet you either."

Dinah didn't say anything.

He studied her hand. "I see your wound's healed. I'm
glad of it." He reached out and held up her fingers as if to inspect
them.

Her faced colored. She pulled her hand away and looked
down the path to one of the town wells. "I can carry the vessel.
I'll take it back."

"I believe the cistern's ahead. I'll get it for you." He
smiled. "You should accept a kind gesture when it's offered. I'm
willing to carry it." He kept the jar firmly within his grasp as he
walked beside her.

They were both silent as they made their way down the
path to the well. No other women were drawing water out of it
when they got there. The others had likely been there earlier to
avoid the hottest time of the day.

At a distance, other courtyards were lively and active with
women's chatter and children playing. Jorah let the ropes down
into the well and brought up the cool water to pour into Dinah's
vessel as she watched.

He set the container on the ledge of the well, and he
turned to her. "Your mother shouldn't have said what she did
about your hair."

She pushed back lengths of the thick, auburn pieces that
had fallen forward onto the front of her shoulder. "What do you
mean?"

"You don't need to braid it." He reached out and brushed
a silken strand with his fingers. "You shouldn't keep it bound."

Dinah moved back. She took hold of a piece of her hair,
once again, and twisted it in her hands.

He smiled. "You don't trust me, do you? Are we not kinsmen since your sister married my brother?"

She reached out to take the vessel from his hands, but he lifted it from the edge of the well and held it from her.

Dinah's brow furrowed. "We are, but I don't trust you."

"You said we might be friends, and I haven't done anything to compromise that. There's no reason for you to doubt my intentions." He winked at her. His voice held a hint of mirth in it.

She started down the path.

They walked for a time, until he finally broke the silence. "Why are there difficulties between you and Achsah?"

"Difficulties? Whatever made you think this?" She gave him an odd look, and then she giggled.

Jorah's eyes crinkled at the corners. "Some things my brother said might have led me to believe it."

"Well, whatever they are, you can put the blame on Achsah for them." Dinah turned to look out over the fields as they walked.

"I'm sure she'd disagree. I don't understand. What's caused this rift between the two of you? Sisters? You should enjoy each other's company."

"Maybe you should ask her?" Dinah drew in a short breath. She looked as if she had no desire to discuss the issue.

Jorah looked puzzled. "But, Achsah says so very little." He raked his hand through his hair. "I might never know."

She shrugged. "Then maybe you don't need to."

"Come, Dinah, I want to understand."

Dinah kicked at a pebble on the road and looked out over the valley. Her voice was matter-of-fact. "Things were different in our home when father began taking other wives. Neither Achsah nor I liked it much. I don't know what what happened." Her expression grew solemn.

He nodded. "Are things better since Achsah married and left home?"

"We don't see each other, if this is what you mean."
Dinah sighed. "Though she used to do half my chores so, in some
ways, it's more difficult with her gone. I complete her tasks, and
my own, in efforts to please my parents."

"And do you?"

"Do I what?" She sniffed.

"Please your parents."

She looked up at him warily and sighed. "Why are you
asking these things? Why must you know?"

Jorah reached out and put his hand on her arm. The tone
of his voice deepened. "I'm sorry, Dinah, but your family's an
enigma to me. And for Toi's sake, I'd like to know more. I live
in the same house as your sister and don't understand her. No one
does. Without this knowledge, it makes it quite difficult to have a
relationship with her."

She turned away. Her voice was resigned. "I never
have."

"Never have what?"

"Pleased my parents, and neither has Achsah."

He took her by the arm and smiled. "Come now? I've
seen how they care for you. I was at the wedding and have been
in town."

Dinah bristled and turned away from him. She resumed
walking.

"You're not speaking." He let out a breath. "Dinah, I'm
sorry. I don't understand."

She shrugged and walked on.

"I should have accepted your answer. Please, I do want to
hear what you have to say."

She pushed a length of her hair behind her ear and looked
up at him. "Maybe I'd like *you* to tell me how they care for
Achsah and I. You were at the wedding and know what you saw
of me in town. Tell me. I want to know what *you* think." Her
eyes darkened.

"Dinah."

She wagged a finger at him and stopped walking. "No, you don't want honest words. You want something else." She let out a breath.

"I didn't." Jorah gave her a concerned look. "I truly want to hear what you had to say."

"And you will, after you tell me your thoughts. I'll talk to you then. I promise."

Jorah studied her closely.

"I will." She brushed at the edge of her tunic.

"You're certainly both well-clothed and have many things. You're in town, quite often, visiting your friends, so you have freedom to what you want. And your parents are well thought of in the community. Others regard them quite highly."

She stared blankly ahead and tapped her foot against the hard path.

"You seem to have your needs met. And as I see it, you grew up in a solid home. You've had food and a roof over your head. Other than the arguments with your sister, all else seems quiet enough in your courtyard."

She didn't say anything, at first, and then spoke quietly. "I suppose it's why you might believe the way you do. What I say most likely will not carry weight, with you, or anyone else, so it might be best to say nothing."

Jorah shook his head back and forth. "Oh no. You promised to tell me about your family. It's your turn."

She shrugged. "Why should I, when you wouldn't believe me?"

"Because you promised."

Her eyes narrowed slightly, but she nodded. "Then I must choose my words wisely, I think, because even I don't understand it as I should." She looked away. "You're correct in saying that others have a great love for my father, and his wives. That includes Samla, and my younger sisters, and the people in town. And it is true that I've been given many things, and riches, as Achsah has. We have privileges others are not privy to. This is all as you have said."

She shivered as she looked out over the fields. She swallowed and spoke again. "But what if these things, that you speak of, were not as they seem? What if the truth were hidden, and all was not as it appeared outside of the house?"

"What do you mean?"

She looked across the plains to the town. "Have you noticed your Pharisees and Sadducees, quite beautiful in their long robes, as they parade past others and mercifully toss their coins to the poor, for the people to see. They can be quite noble, in their words and deeds. Yet, some appear one way, when they speak and act, but it is different with their hearts. I've seen them attempt to destroy their kinsman with a mere glance." She looked back at him.

"You're likening those in your family to this?"

"I believe they are much like it."

He nodded with a look of understanding.

Her voice quieted to a whisper. "What others notice, and applaud as honorable, is not always so. You see, the walls of a house can hide many things. I'm certain that evil can rein in a household, though others might not think it."

Jorah shifted the jar to his other arm. He set the vessel of water on a flat rock nearby. "It could be so."

Dinah nodded. "There's no love for Achsah and I there."

He watched her astonished. "But how can this be when your younger brother and sisters fare well enough? They are happy."

"If lies were told, within the family, to discredit one or more child, it would be easy to deceive the younger children, or others? Who would not believe their own mother? The little ones are afraid of Achsah."

"Have you told them how you feel about this?"

When honesty is frowned upon? She looked at him oddly. "Who would want to pay a price for such a thing?"

Jorah stroked her cheek. He had a gentle look in his eyes. "Children deserve their mother's love." He put his hand back to his side and picked up the vessel again. He took a place next to her as they continued to walk down the path.

She nodded. "I'll do differently with my own."

"It is possible to change your course."

She looked curious and nodded. "Yes, it is." She stared down the path. She suddenly stopped talking when the courtyard came back into view.

Jorah handed her the vessel filled with water. "Here, I must retrieve my donkey. I tied it at the bend in the road."

"Yes." She hoisted the water jar to her shoulder. She looked up at him. "I shouldn't be seen alone with you, I wouldn't want it to be said that my reputation is damaged, or that I encouraged it."

"Your sister doesn't care what others say."

"I believe she does, but she's found a way to escape it." Dinah sighed. "I suppose I envy her as she's lucky to be free. Maybe someday, I'll be free also. Though she has paid dearly for her forthright ways."

"You defend her? I thought she was your arch enemy?" Jorah smiled as he untied the ropes to his donkey. He turned back and looked at her.

"She is." Dinah put her free hand on her hips in mock defiance, but her eyes brightened, and she smiled. "But, despite what you might think, we are not so uncaring. She is my sister. She does make me angry, but I can't help wishing I had the same situation. Your brother seems to be a very good husband."

"Toi?" Jorah suddenly laughed aloud. "I don't know if you know what you're saying. He's a good brother, but as a husband, I'm sure Achsah is aware of his imperfections."

She put the jar down on the ground and went to him. Her eyes were wide. "Has he ever hinted that he might take another wife?"

Jorah gave her a reproachful look. "I believe Achsah's enough trouble for him. I wouldn't think too much on it. I'm sure Toi hasn't."

She backed away when he got onto his donkey. "He might not say it, so you don't know for sure."

"But, I know what's good for you, and it surely isn't coming between Achsah and Toi. It appears your rivalry with your sister might be clouding your judgment. You should give this some thought."

"What do you mean?" She lifted the water jar again as her eyes raked over him.

"That you should carefully consider your actions." Jorah shrugged. "Life with Achsah and your brother would not be as you would imagine it." He held the reins tighter when the donkey began to stir beneath him.

She put her hands on her hips, but backed away. "I don't know why you care so much."

Jorah's donkey circled and stomped. He turned back to her with an irksome stare. "Do as you wish, but there are things I need to tend to, so I must go. I've no more time for this, and I'm sure you're needed in your home."

Dinah didn't answer.

He dug his heels into his donkey's sides and turned his back to her as he trotted away.

Dinah's eyes darkened as she watched him disappear down the path. What did he know? Nothing. His family cared for him. She balanced the water on her shoulder and reached for the gate. She rolled her eyes when she heard the sound of her mother calling out to her.

"Dinah! Come! There's work to do!"

"I heard, mother. I'm coming!" She sighed as she closed the gate behind her.

*****

Jorah rode in the direction of his home. Clouds of dust stirred beneath him as the animal's pace quickened.

He let out an agitated breath. Dinah believed Toi might take her as a wife? Silly young woman. She was frustrating.

Clearly it was her competitive nature with her sister that had spurred these thoughts. The last thing Toi would consider would be to take in another of these women of such a rival nature.

He looked back at Dinah's house, and his jawline tightened as the sky darkened. A cloud had moved into the path of the sun. There was a hot desert breeze.

He supposed he couldn't blame Dinah for believing Toi might show interest in another wife, when her own father had three. Despite the difficulties these women had caused her, it seemed she'd grown accustomed to the idea.

He slowed the animal under him as he took another path that led to his home. The mournful cry of a bird from the shadowed limb of a tree caused him to turn for a brief moment, but then he looked back at the road. The sound mirrored his own quiet thoughts.

He recalled his earlier conversation with Dinah as he eyed the distant plains of Moab and the mountain rising behind them. Some of the things the young woman had said had struck Jorah inside. He'd seen the hurt in both her, and her sister, on more than one occasion, and couldn't deny their lack of trust and faith in others.

It seemed odd to say that it was possible that evil might reign in a home, yet Dinah had alluded to it, and who could say it did not?

His ears echoed with the sounds of Dinah's mother scolding her as he'd driven out of sight. At least this much was as Dinah had said. Things might not have been as they seemed.

He supposed much could be hidden behind the walls of a house. Though the family was well-dressed and mannerly, abounding in much wealth and position, it seemed they also possessed underlying flaws and hidden motives. He'd once heard that charm and wit might be the greatest form of deception and the best concealer of abuse. In this case, it most certainly might be true.

When he'd met the family, on the evening of the wedding, he'd taken great pains to introduce himself to Dinah's mother and father as Toi made it known that he wanted the family to make close alliances, and he did not want to disappoint his brother.

Being quite pensive at times, and attentive to detail, he'd studied them closely. People had always drawn his interest, and this family, more so, as they had suddenly become part of his own. In most cases, his observations had remained at a distance, yet this day he'd approached the family and had introduced himself to them.

Dinah's father, Laban, had been pleasant enough to talk to, yet Jorah had noticed, when they'd spoken, that the man's expressions had seemed less amenable when the topic of conversation turned to his eldest daughters, and this is what Dinah had implied.

Achsah's mother, had smiled wide as she'd tipped her head to him in a gracious, expected way. Her mannerisms had been properly executed, without error, the moment he'd met her. Yet, despite her notable efforts, he'd perceived something untrustworthy in her, a hollowness in her shining, grace-filled eyes. He believed her words to him to be flattery, rather than sincere, as if she were attempting to gain status with him.

Rachel, Laban's concubine, vied for her husband's favor, against the other wives, and had seemed less interested in Achsah's wedding ceremony than in promoting her own children.

And Matrid, the youngest concubine, who had sat next to Laban, had demonstrated pride in her eyes. There was an air about her which led Jorah to believe that she was aware of her youthful beauty and the effect it had on Laban.

On the surface, the whole family had seemed amiable enough, well-versed and conversant with others, yet underneath the surface, it seemed there were inconsistencies as Dinah had said.

Maybe this was what Dinah had meant, that the family weren't as they appeared? It was possible that she'd spoken the truth.

He supposed the Torah had an explanation for this as well in the beginning of time. Even the Devil himself had come to

Eve, as a beautiful serpent, with smooth speech and pretty lies. He didn't come as he was, but seduced the world, and sang a web of death as an angel of light. Why wouldn't the same happen today as it had then? It was possible.

In any case, some of the things Dinah had reluctantly shared with him held a ring of truth, and she'd trusted him with things she wouldn't ordinarily have shared with anyone.

He breathed a sigh and looked down the path. The sun was setting, and there was little time in the day left for such thoughts. His family waited for him.

*****

Achsah looked out from beneath the shaded canopy from where she sat at a low table. She eyed the people around her who happily conversed at low tables as the sounds of gentle harp music carried softly over the cool evening air.

She peered across the expanse of the area and past the gated entrance where Toi and Shobach sat as they conversed in an adjoining courtyard.

Achsah's foot was almost healed, and she no longer needed her crutch, although she kept it with her. The carved walking stick lay on a large, woven rug at her side.

She reached for a piece of barley bread and tore off a small chunk of it, then she dipped it into a wooden bowl which contained wine vinegar and oil. She savored the taste as she took a small bite. Food wasn't plentiful, at this time, but what was put out on platters was satisfying. There were summer fruits, roasted grain, and cheese.

She leaned over and put her hand on Kezia's arm. "I'm glad to be out of the house and taking part in the festivities."

Kezia smiled and nodded, though her interest seemed to be elsewhere. Her cheeks had a pale pink cast to them.

Achsah turned to see Toi's friend, Jair, a short distance away with Hezro. They were talking.

Achsah nudged Kezia. Her voice held a ring in it. "Jair would be a good match for you!" She had a light in her eyes when she said it. "He's handsome."

Kezia put her hand to her mouth and looked down. "Achsah!"

Achsah smiled. "You should let him know you're interested and smile at him."

Sapphira giggled from across the table. "I'll go tell him!"

"Sapphira, no!" Kezia looked mortified. She hadn't taken her hand from her mouth.

"I'm teasing." Sapphira laughed again. "But Achsah's right. He should know."

Achsah squeezed Kezia's hand. "Don't worry, we wouldn't do anything to hurt you." She took her walking stick and got up. "His sister's a friend of mine, and of Sheerah's. I'll ask him questions about her and include you in our conversation. If there's interest, he'll pursue a friendship."

"Achsah." Kezia shook her head.

"I promise. He won't know anything. But I'd like to make it known to him that you exist. You look pretty in your new tunic."

Kezia's cheeks were pink as Achsah got up from her seat. She looked in the direction of the two men.

Hezro's eyes were on two women at another table. There was a gleam in his eyes as he listened to Jair.

Achsah groaned. At least Kezia wasn't interested in him. Hezro's intentions, regarding those of the female persuasion, were not good. Any woman would do well to stay away from him if they considered deep ties of any kind with a man.

Achsah hobbled across the courtyard and made her way to both Hezro and Jair. She stopped short of them.

Jair turned and smiled. "Achsah? You hurt yourself? What happened to your foot?"

"I turned it, but Toi made a walking stick for me." She didn't want to be reminded of her horrible brother-in-law, so she didn't elaborate on what had happened.

"Oh." Jair nodded. "Well, I hope it's better soon."

"Thanks."

Then Jair looked over his shoulder in Toi's direction. He nodded to Toi.

None of the men seemed overly eager to speak to her since she'd married.

"So, what do you want, Achsah?"

"I've been looking for your sister. Where is she?"

He shrugged. "I believe she is coming with father later."

"Hmm, I suppose I must wait. I wanted to introduce her to Toi's sister, Kezia, at the table over there." She pointed to the feasting mat.

Kezia turned and looked at them. Her brown eyes widened, and the blush in her cheeks deepened. She quickly looked away and began talking to Sapphira.

Sapphira laughed.

Jair gave Achsah an amused look. "I haven't seen Toi's sister in some time. From what I remember, she's a very kind and gracious woman. She's very beautiful. You must tell her I said so."

Achsah smiled and gave him a knowing look. "I'll do that. And you might come to our home and see more of her in time."

Jair laughed. "I believe I might."

"Well, I must be going. My husband will be wondering what I'm doing."

"I'll bet he will." He grinned. "You must not stay here long."

Achsah nodded and waved him off. She put the stick back under her arm and made her way to the second courtyard to let herself in.

Toi studied Achsah, from where he sat on a huge slab of stone, as she came through the gate. He seemed to weigh his thoughts as he watched her.

Shobach smiled. He got up. "I suppose I should greet my other guests and leave you for now."

Toi nodded to him.

Achsah hobbled across the courtyard to where Toi was.

He moved over and brushed off a spot for her to sit on. "Here."

Achsah sat beside him. She took his arm to steady herself. Her sandals scuffed the ground beneath her.

He looked curious. "Jair and Hezro seemed glad to talk to you?"

"You saw us?" She smiled. Something inside her lightened at the thought of his having noticed. "You didn't approve?"

Toi didn't answer. Instead, he shrugged as his eyes met hers.

"I'm *your* wife." She reached up and stroked the side of his face. "You needn't worry. Kezia's interested in Jair, and I only made him aware of it. She's still blushing because of it."

Toi looked surprised. "Kezia?"

"Yes." She pointed at them.

Toi looked over the wall to where his sister was, across the courtyard where Jair stood.

Though Jair and Hezro conversed quietly, Jair hadn't taken his eyes off Toi's sister. It was obvious where his interest lay.

Kezia turned shyly away, yet there was a smile on her face as she spoke to Sapphira quietly.

Toi looked back at Achsah. "You were matchmaking?"

"And exchanging other pleasantries." She played with the folds of her emerald green tunic and the gold threads that ran through it. "Jair and Hezro are aware that I'm a married woman. They know who my husband is. They leave me be. I like it better this way."

"You want them to?"

Achsah let out an amused sound. "I never cared what they did, and I still don't." Her eyes danced as she spoke. "They served their purpose for a time."

Toi stared at her as if he wasn't sure what to think. "I hope you've found a more fulfilling purpose at our home."

"With sewing and helping with the meals, yes. I've found I can stand being there during the day. Your sisters are kind. Other than your brother, your family treats me well."

Toi turned. "My brother's still a problem? He's hurt you again?"

"No, but I don't know what to expect of him. He has little to say."

"He's not to touch you again. I've warned him of it. It seems since the last incident he's listened. Maybe he didn't expect the extent of your injuries to be as bad as they were."

Achsah's eyes narrowed, and she lifted her chin. "It doesn't matter to me what his feelings are, or what he does. He deserves every bit of what he gets."

"Maybe, but it might be good, if he attempts to make amends, that you treat him accordingly."

"I could never do that, not for him."

"For the family's sake?"

Achsah didn't say anything.

Toi leaned down to kiss her. "Ah, Achsah, you try so hard not to feel. Someday, maybe this will change also."

"But you don't care whether I do or not."

He shrugged and gave her an interested look. "I'm not sure. It might have an effect on me."

She drew back.

Then she took her crutch in her hand and got up as she turned to the opposite courtyard. "Can you help me open the gate? I've decided to take the small cart back early. You can bring your sisters later. It's doubtful Kezia or Sapphira will want to leave so soon."

He stood up, and he took her arm. "Are you ill? I'll take you back, if you'd like me to."

"Not ill, only tired. Shobach will want you to stay. It's a short ride and not dark yet. I'll be fine."

Toi unlatched the gate for her and took her to the smaller cart. He made sure the donkey pulling it was hooked securely, then he patted the side of the animal's neck.

He lifted Achsah onto the wooden seat on the cart and handed her the leather straps. "Are you sure you don't want me to take you? I'll do it, if you want?"

Achsah took the reins in her hands and looked down at him. She shook her head. "No, one of the servants will help me when I get back. They'll put the cart away. It's still early."

"Truly?"

She waved at him. "Yes, you stay. Take all the time you want. I'll see you when you get back."

She lifted the donkey's reins and held them in her hands. She sat up straighter as he moved away from the cart.

He watched as she rode off in the direction of their family's home.

*****

The evening rays streamed down into the courtyard of Achsah's home. She stood just inside the gate and watched the sunset as it spread colors of scarlet and orange across the expanse of the sky.

The animals were quiet. Only an occasional bellow of a camel, or the soft bleating of sheep, was heard while the rustling wind stilled their anxious cries.

The night air cooled the heat of the day. A slight chill had settled over the land. Achsah braided her hair into one long plait and tied a leather cord around the end of it as she waited at the gate for Toi to come back.

Ever since he'd spoken, to his mother and Kezia, outside her room in the courtyard, he'd been more attentive and watchful toward her. He'd tended to her injured foot and diligently saw to her needs.

There had been changes. She was certain of that much, though it was most likely due to his mother and sister's concern that he'd assumed the role of a dutiful husband. The tasks he carried out gave the appearance of husbandly affection, yet she was sure his heart wasn't swayed one way or the other. His attempts were awkward at best as he strove to fulfill his marital obligation.

She watched the colors in the sky darken, and she shivered as she drew her outer wrap tighter around her. She'd left early from the dinner, to rest, but what she truly needed was time alone. When Toi was near, it was difficult to think. The care he afforded, and physical attraction she felt for him, did not set well deep in the recesses of her heart. She feared she thought of him too often lately.

She looked down the path that led to the town. There was a man driving a cart with two women in the back. Two other men were on donkeys ahead of the cart. They were headed her way. In the shadows, it was difficult to see their faces.

The taller man had a cloth, over his head, which was tied with a cord. When he neared the courtyard where Achsah was standing, he got off the donkey and strode to the gate.

Achsah backed away. Who had come this late to visit? Why had the caravan stopped in front of Toi's house when the family was away? Other than a handful of servants, working in the fields, they'd come to an empty place.

The man opened the gate. "Achsah, you're home. I overheard Toi saying you'd left the meal early."

Achsah grabbed her crutch from the wall and took a step back. Ittai? What was he doing? He knew she was alone.

She drew in a breath. "What do you want? You mustn't stay. Toi will be coming. He doesn't want you here."

Ittai quickly closed the gap between them and took her by the arm. He clenched his hand around her wrist.

She let out a sound and dropped her walking stick. "What are you doing?" Her eyes narrowed as she attempted to escape his hold. "I told you that my husband will be back."

Ittai yanked her arm. He quickly lifted her, and put his hand over her mouth as he carried her toward the gate.

146

Achsah pushed and kicked at him, despite her hurting ankle. She attempted to bite his hand, but he tore off his headpiece and stuffed a portion of it in her mouth. He threw her in the back of the wagon and tied her hands.

"You thought you could treat me the way you did and get away with it, but there will be consequences for your actions. Toi won't come looking for you. He'll think you left him. You'll be as dead to him." He turned away.

She stared at him as he spoke to the other men.

"She's yours. She owes me for her past treatment, and the owners aren't home. They'll be glad to rid themselves of her. They'll believe she ran off."

"She's not family?" The older man driving the wagon tipped his head as he eyed her quizzically.

"She's a servant in the house and has been trouble for the family. You're welcome to sell her as a slave in Bethlehem."

The men nodded. They chuckled as the wagon lurched forward.

Achsah's eyes narrowed as she watched Ittai ride off in an opposite direction.

He'd given her to slave traders. She was unable to free herself or to call for help. She pulled on the leather cords that held her hands and struggled to loosen the ties as the cart rolled farther from her home.

*****

Chapter 7

Ruth looked around the family home. She wanted to make sure that everything was in place. Shadows danced against the wall next to the flickering oil lamp on a low, wooden table in the room.

Everyone, but her, was asleep. The room was swept and clean.

She moved quietly across the floor and went out into the courtyard.

One of the camels let out a loud bellow, and a couple of the sheep made soft sounds in their pens. The warm night air swept over Ruth as she looked toward the mountain peaks in the distance. A shadowed cart rumbled down the road, and into the darkness, while an orange desert moon rose above them. She wondered who might be on the path at this time at night. She watched the wagon disappear into the distance.

The crickets began to sing as she stood there and breathed in the balmy air.

She heard a cough behind her, and she turned. "Mahlon? I thought you were asleep?"

"I was, but I wanted to know where you were."

"It's peaceful out here and cool, so beautiful."

Mahlon nodded. He didn't say anything as he looked up at the stars.

Ruth turned to him. "You've given me a good home."

"I'm glad for it. You're a good woman." He moved closer.

Ruth smiled. Then a solemn look that stole over her face. Her voice was a whisper. "I'm sorry I'm still not with child. I wanted this for you."

Mahlon put his hand on her arm. "You mustn't blame yourself. It's the Lord's will, Ruth. He'll do what's best for us."

"I've appealed to Adonai, but he's the Israelite God. Why would he listen to the prayer of a Moabitess?" Ruth pulled her shawl tighter around her and shivered.

"He's your Creator, too. He's given Gentiles the privilege of choosing him since before Abraham. It pleases him when you go to him." Mahlon drew in a breath. "Continue to hope in him. Keep steadfast in your prayers."

Ruth lifted her eyes to his. There were questions in them.

Mahlon took her hand and squeezed it gently. "Remember when I spoke of Rahab, how our Lord honored her and included her in our heritage, because she demonstrated her love for him? Set your heart and soul on seeking him, as she did, and he'll listen."

"But, he hasn't given us a child?"

"It's true. I thought we'd have children too. I thought he'd allow us a son, or daughter, but we must keep in mind that our Lord knows what's best. You must believe that his will is being done, whether it's what we want or not."

Ruth sighed. "It's not easy to have such faith." She peered into the darkness.

Mahlon squeezed her hand again. "Sometimes, it isn't." He spoke quietly. "Yet, if you allow yourself to believe, anything's possible with the Lord. He'll do what he sees is best for us. If he chooses to bless you with a child, the generations after will surely benefit from it."

Ruth smiled when she looked at him. "I'll try to believe the way you do. I've seen your faith. I want to know Adonai also."

*****

Toi went straight to Achsah's room when he returned from her friend's home. He came back out, when he didn't find her there, and searched the rest of the house. He was surprised to find the place empty. She'd told him she was tired, so she couldn't have gone far, but he'd been in the house and around the courtyard. She hadn't been there either. The donkey and cart were tied in the outer area that housed the animals.

"Did you see Achsah?" He turned to his brother.

Benaiah was outside the gates brushing the fur of one of the donkeys as he gave Toi and indifferent look. "She isn't with Jair or Hezro? She seemed rather interested in them at the meal." He snorted. "You might try looking for one of them."

Toi's eyes darkened. "She isn't with either of them." He raked his hand through his hair. "She was tired and came back to rest."

"Ha! I don't understand what blinds you to that woman, or what you see in a daughter of Moab?"

Toi paced back and forth. "It doesn't concern me what you think, Benaiah. None of that matters right now."

Benaiah took the mule by the leather strap. He led it to the courtyard for animals and released it into the corralled area. Then he went back through the gate to where Toi was.

Toi looked at the ground. He squatted down as a frown drew over his brow.

Benaiah came closer. He stared at the items lying in the dust. "It seems she left in a hurry, and it's possible she went with someone." He gave Toi a knowing look.

Toi ignored his brother's silent insinuation. He took Achsah's crutch and a piece of her jewelry in his hand. "She used this to steady herself and would have kept it with her. She wouldn't have left her bracelet in the dust." He brushed his hand against the ground. "Here, there's larger footprints, and then hers are gone. It appears there was a struggle."

Benaiah studied the path that led out of the gate. He went to the stone entrance and pulled a piece of fabric off the latch. He handed it to Toi.

Toi took it and opened the gate and went out. "The wagon wheels, head north." He looked at the horizon.

He began pacing again as he breathed the crisp night air. He cleared his throat.

150

What had happened? Because of her size, and her ankle, Achsah would've had difficulty defending herself.

Toi looked around the courtyard. It seemed at least one of the servants would have been witness to a struggle, if there had been one. They'd have come to her aide. Why didn't anyone see anything and come forward? Had she been alone in the courtyard?

He looked back at his brother, and he reached up to loosen the neckline of his robe.

As much as he was loath to admit it, there was the possibility that Benaiah was right. Achsah might have gone willingly with another man. It was conceivable. He'd married her with the knowledge of her background.

His voice grew quiet. "Tell father and mother I'll be back after I find her."

Benaiah let out a breath. "I'll let a servant know, but I'm not sending you out alone. Get the donkeys ready. I'll be back."

Toi nodded. "Good, be ready quickly. Bring some water pouches and food."

"Father may want to come with us, so saddle two other donkeys, and one for Achsah." Benaiah strode in the direction the house.

Toi quickly headed to the stables while his brother went inside. He opened the door to the area which housed the animals, and he went where the donkeys were tied.

It was best they leave soon, if they wanted to find out where Achsah was. He wasn't going to wait a moment longer.

The donkeys had been trained for running distances. If they left immediately, they'd surely beat whoever it was, with Achsah, to the river.

*****

Achsah lips were parched after an evening of travel in the back of the wagon. She twisted the leather bands on her bruised hands and worked to free herself. It was night, and the wagon hadn't stopped yet. She was sure the men who had taken her, and the other women, would be setting up camp soon.

The cords had loosened, and she'd worked to slip her hands through them. If she escaped the wagon now, it would be difficult for them to find her in the darkness. The other women were asleep, but she still had energy left in her, and she was determined not to give in to slumber, while she was still close enough to her home to attempt escape.

As she wiggled her hands back and forth, and tugged at the leather one more time, she felt the ties slip and loosen. She struggled to pull her hand through it, and she breathed a sigh of relief when it came out. She used her free hand to untie her bound one.

She didn't say anything to the sleeping women for fear the noise would alert the men. Toi could help them later.

Achsah took a water pouch that dangled from the side of the wagon, and she crept to the end of the cart. She gingerly lifted herself over the edge and let go. She rolled into the ditch on the side of the road to ease the fall, but she groaned in pain as she tumbled to a stop. Luckily, the noise of the wagon was loud.

She quickly got up, staying in the shadows, as she strapped the water bottle over her shoulder. Although her ankle was still sore, she was able to walk on it. She'd need to look for something to support herself along the way.

She kept close to the road, yet she remained hidden in the underbrush as she hobbled back in the direction of the town.

She didn't believe these men would take the time to come looking for her in the dark. They wouldn't know when she'd escaped or what direction she'd taken.

The wagon wheels turned, and the cart made clanking sounds as it moved slowly away from her down the road.

Her heart beat wildly in her chest as she left in an opposite direction.

A dim light came from the full moon, and stars littered the sky. Other than that, the landscape was dark. There was little to hide behind but an occasional rock and dip in the terrain. She was

152

terrified of the thought of wild animals prowling the area looking for night prey, of which she was an easy mark.

The air turned chilly which caused her to shiver. She shook off thoughts of what might have become of her if she hadn't escaped. She was safe from the traders for now but might face other dangers just as formidable.

It seemed Chemosh was choosing to punish her again for her many sins, and on this night, he might even make her pay with her life.

*****

Benaiah, Toi, and their father moved quickly through the dark, shadowed countryside heading out of town. The donkeys clipped forward, without pause, over the hard, clay path that wound through the meadows and valleys of the plains.

The men said little as their animal's hooves pounded against the surface of the trail.

Toi made sure they'd brought swords and knives, along with their slings, and other provisions. He hoped they'd have what they'd needed to find Achsah and bring her back safely. Every now and then, he stopped to get down and study the path.

He slowed his donkey and called softly so that it came to a halt. "The wheel tracks head toward the river. These people will surely stop before they get there and camp for the night."

His voice was low and quiet. "She'd better be with them." He stared into the darkness with a creased brow.

"You'll find her." His father spoke softly.

Benaiah led his donkey next to his brother's side. "I don't understand why you care for her the way you do when she clearly doesn't love you?" He looked puzzled. "If she's in trouble, she most likely deserves what is happening to her."

Their father didn't say anything, but watched Toi with interest.

Toi took the reins in his hand and got back up on the donkey. "She has a troubled past, but she isn't as hardhearted as she'd have you believe. She's my wife. I want to know who she left with and what's happened to her."

His father nodded. "You've a right to know it. You can deal with her as you see fit."

Benaiah eyed his brother with a raised brow. "If you had chosen better, we wouldn't be in the desert in the middle of the night. Instead, you managed to get yourself a daughter of Moab who has difficulty staying out of trouble."

Toi looked into the darkness and slackened the donkey's reins. He gave a slight shrug of his shoulders and turned. "I suppose it wouldn't have been something I'd have done to consider a quiet, obedient woman. Achsah is who I've chosen. It is true, it *was* a business arrangement, and Achsah's not without her faults, yet there are advantages to such a marriage." A half-smile curved over his lips.

Benaiah scowled. "Such as?"

"Yes, I'd like to know." Toi's father frowned.

Toi looked over the plains as he spoke. "We're not beholden to each other the way others are. It suits both her and me. We do as we please, and there are no questions. We enjoy the benefits of our alliance without the burdens of it."

"But, son..." His father's voice held an urgent tone. "You've taken Achsah in marriage."

Toi shrugged. "I've no desire to discuss it anymore, father, with you, or Benaiah, or anyone else. What's done is done. It isn't going to change. It is true that she's my wife, but it's different with us." He dug his heels into the side of the donkey and urged the animal forward. He didn't speak again.

His brother and father did the same.

The men rode swiftly down the path again as darkness swallowed them while the night moved on.

*****

As the donkeys stormed the desert plains and raced down the road, Toi scanned the countryside for any sign of Achsah. She

154

was nowhere in sight, and he didn't seem to be anywhere nearer to finding her.

He adjusted the cloth bound to his head as he fixed his eyes on the road. Where could she have gone? What were the reasons she'd left their home? She hadn't been far from Shobach's. Who might have seen her, and what might have happened in the courtyard?

He searched the shadows of every hill, tree, and recess in the path as they rode swiftly along. He swallowed drily as possible thoughts of what might have happened ran through his mind.

He recalled some of the things Benaiah had said. Though he knew what Achsah's flirtatious behavior toward men had been, before he married her, for some reason, he didn't want to believe she would leave him willingly for another man when he'd taken the time to provide for her every need and see to it she was cared for in every possible way.

Maybe it was also the pride inside him that made him think it, but Achsah herself had made it clear to him, more than once, that she'd tired of the attention men gave her and was glad to have found herself free from it. She didn't seem to relish in such things, at least when she was near him.

He hoped his thoughts rang true. He didn't know what he'd do, if they weren't. He tightened his grip on the reins as a foreboding feeling ran through him.

Though he'd spoken, with confidence, to his father and Benaiah, regarding Achsah and his arrangement with her, beneath the surface, he was not so sure of how he felt about the possibility of discovering her with another man.

An inner turmoil brewed within him as he scanned the countryside. He was hard-pressed to find her, and his heart stirred at the thought of her possible infidelity. He couldn't imagine that she would do such a thing, in spite of her earlier actions.

His hands tightened on the donkey's reins as thoughts of her continued to race through his troubled mind. He let out a slow, uneven breath. The longer they looked, the more he realized that he might not be so unfeeling toward her as he had convinced himself that he was. He hoped they would find her soon.

*****

Achsah's foot bothered her. She stopped walking and sat on a large rock that jutted out from the ground. She reached for a stick that was lying next to her. It was solid and possibly could be used to help her walk. She took it in her hands, and she tore off the small branches that jutted off the side of it. She left a crooked handle at the top.

She worked quickly. She was still uncertain as to whether the traders would be back for her or not. She could use the stick, as a weapon to defend herself, in the event she would need it.

When the branches were gone, from the stick, and her foot was rested, she got up and made her way along the paths between the brambles and rocks, on the side of the road, as quickly as she could.

She shuddered as more than one animal's howl arose over the vast, shadowed terrain, and the sound of a hoot owl pierced the blackened air. She heard crackles in the underbrush and quiet hisses that arose from the fields. Everything was more pronounced at night without the protection of others around.

Town lights appeared in the distance. She breathed a sigh. She was sure she could walk to where they were. At least she might find her way back to Toi's house, outside the walled gates, by way of the lamps and torches of the town guiding her, if she were forced to leave the road.

A noise in the distance caused her to crouch down. It sounded like hooves, maybe gazelles, spooked by a night predator, or other travelers? She couldn't be sure. She sank behind a large boulder and steadied her beating heart with her hand. She gripped her stick tightly as she held it flat on the ground.

Four donkeys moved down the path in the distance.

Achsah's breath was unsteady as she peered around the rock from the shadows. Toi might have come for her, yet he would have been alone. His father would've been little help. And Benaiah and Jorah? Well, it was unlikely either of them would have taken the road with Toi to find her. Benaiah wouldn't have wanted her back.

If it were not Toi, she had no desire to meet anyone who might be roaming outside the town at night. She didn't want to fall victim to others who'd do her harm for the second time that day. She'd take her chances and find her way back home on her own.

She moved closer to the rock, in the darkness, and remained there as the pounding of animal's feet hit the hard surface of the road.

There were no voices, nor could she gather any clues, as to whether or not these were men she could trust. She listened as they moved past her in the black of the night.

She didn't call out to them, or give them any indication that she was within a donkey's length of them. Instead, she waited for their hoof beats to be swallowed up in the night.

She breathed a sigh of relief when they were gone and she was alone again. The deathly still, solemn sounds of the darkness pervaded the air once again. The only reprieve from the occasional, unnerving crackle of underbrush, and lone howl ringing out, were the crickets' song, trill and long. At least there was nothing to fear from them.

She took a drink of water from the trader's pouch. A dryness pervaded the inside of her mouth. She was thirsty. She let the water trickle down her throat as she savored the taste of it.

She got back up and began to walk. She decided to go by way of the road. She was far enough from the sounds of the travelers, and she would be able to hear wagon wheels, and hooves of donkeys, before they could see her. She'd make better time if she stayed on the road. She would surely find her way back faster there.

The lights of the town were slightly larger. She was determined not to stop walking until she reached her home. She was tired, but she kept moving.

*****

Toi peered into the night. He slowed his donkey.

His brother and father did the same.

Benaiah looked down the trail. His voice was low. "Whoever it is, they've stopped and set up camp. Let's use caution. We don't know how many there are."

Toi nodded. "They're most likely sleeping, but we can't be sure of it."

They all stopped. They quickly tied their donkeys to one lone tree that rose up in the shadows. The moon's glow was barely visible under the low-lying fog. All was still at the camp, and the forms of the men at the camp were lying quiet and not moving around the light of the fire.

Toi took a sword from his donkey's leather holder. He put a finger to his lips and motioned for his brother to do the same.

Josheb stayed with the donkeys.

Benaiah slipped his sword out of its sheath and edged forward beside Toi.

Both men crept to the site. They moved without noise as they surveyed the camp.

A couple of men lay on the ground next to the flames.

There was a cart which held two women who were asleep in the back.

Toi assumed Achsah would be with them, but he saw no sign of her, as he crept along the side of the wagon.

He motioned for Benaiah to come and stand by the men. Then he leaned over one of them and spoke in a low, gravely tone while he held his sword to the man's throat. "Get up, and tell me what you've done with my wife."

The man immediately jumped to a sitting position while the other man followed suit.

Benaiah pointed his sword in their direction.

The first man's voice shook. "We don't have her. We bought these women. They're slaves."

"I want the one you took from my home."

The man's face paled. "Ittai told me she was trouble and that the family wouldn't come for her. He said she was a servant."

Toi pushed the blade against the man's throat. "Ittai? He'd no right to give her to you. She's my wife. Where is she?"

"She's not with us. Look at the ties on the wagon which are dangling there. She broke free. There was no time to go back for her in the dark. She's most likely somewhere along the road attempting to find her way back."

Benaiah went to the wagon and held up the loose ties. The women in the back woke and sat up. He took off the binding that held them.

"You can't take them. We paid for them."

Benaiah ignored the man, but he motioned for the woman to leave the cart.

They got out quickly.

He lifted a purple scarf out of the back and brought it to Toi.

"It's Achsah's." Toi spoke quietly. He looked down the path. "But, we didn't see her on the road?"

Benaiah shrugged. "She most likely hid. It was dark, and she didn't know who we were."

Toi regarded the men. "You better hope she's back there." His voice was a low growl. "If I don't find her, this will not be the last time you'll see me."

"She'll take the path. I'm sure of it. She can't have gone far." The man breathed more easily when Toi took the sword from his neck. He rubbed his throat.

"Leave, and do not come back again. These women are Moabites. You've no right to take them from this territory. They belong with their families."

The men cautiously eyed both Toi and his brother. Neither of them had an advantage, both being slight in build. The shorter one let out a slow breath. "We'll not be back."

"See to it you aren't." Toi turned to Benaiah. "We have to go. I'm hoping we're not too late. For her to be alone, on that road at night, isn't safe."

Benaiah and Toi held their swords up and backed away from the camp. They motioned for the other women to come with them.

Both of them looked relieved as they moved quickly with them. "Oh thank you, sirs." They tipped their heads to both Toi and Benaiah.

Toi motioned to them. "My father brought an extra donkey you can ride. Come, let's leave this place."

Benaiah put his hand on Toi's arm. "It seems, at least this time, I was wrong about your wife." Then he shrugged. "Though, I wouldn't worry much. Achsah most likely has the wolves running in the other direction. We'll find her on the path."

"I hope."

They both turned when they reached their donkeys. Toi and Benaiah mounted their own animals.

Josheb allowed the two women to get on the extra donkey he'd brought for Achsah.

Toi looked out over the dark countryside. "The trouble is that she's not as strong as she thinks she is, and she's fearful of more than she lets on." He turned to his father. "We'll move together. Once we're farther from the traders, Benaiah and I will go on ahead. I don't believe those men will follow."

His father nodded.

They went back in the direction from which they'd come from.

This time they scoured the countryside in the light of the moon as they watched the path ahead. They moved slower and quieter while they made their way in the direction of the town.

Toi called Achsah's name occasionally. He hoped she'd hear and make herself known to them.

⫶ ⫶ ⫶ ⫶ ⫶

Achsah could go no further. She was exhausted after the day's events and after the grueling walk. Tension ran through her as she looked down the path. She was still a long distance from home. The darkened plains had taken its toll, and a great weariness had come over her.

The hard-packed earth looked like a soft place to lie. Even the howls of wolves, and occasional rustle in the underbrush, did not cause her concern. She searched for a place to close her eyes and a deep slumber to overtake her.

She came to a large, jagged rock and lowered herself onto the ground beside it, then she curled into the shadows. She held her walking stick in front of her and put her other hand under her head. Her eyes fluttered shut as she drifted off to sleep. The last thing she remembered were the soft sounds of the grassy field near her as they rustled in the light breeze.

*****

Sometime later, Achsah took a breath and was awakened by a wild, gamy smell. She opened her eyes and let out a sound as she gripped her walking stick tightly, then she sat up abruptly in the darkness.

In the light of the moon, only paces from her, a wild dog was circling. His mangy coat was stripped of fur in places, and his teeth were bared. His eyes glowed yellow. He watched her with interest.

She held her stick out and yelled, "Go away!" She pushed the weapon at him, and tried to sound strong and unafraid, even though she shook inside.

His low growls were loud in the quiet of the night. The fur on his neck stood up straight as he paced back and forth next to her.

She jabbed the stick at him again. "Leave! Please, go!"

Tears sprouted to her eyes when she realized he wasn't convinced. His growl got louder, and his eyes narrowed. He lowered his head and drew back his ears.

She held her place, even though she wanted to run. There was no where to go, and she couldn't turn her back on him.

His ears twitched suddenly, and he lifted his head to sniff the air. There was a wary look in his eye, even though he didn't turn from her.

Achsah heard the hooves of donkeys advancing from the direction where the slave traders had left. She wondered which was worse, this animal, or those on the path?

She yelled again, at the wild dog, and looked him directly in the eye as the donkeys came into view. "Go! Get away!" Her voice lowered.

The animal turned and spotted the riders.

A rock from a sling sailed past the dog which had bared its teeth. The stone had most likely come from one of the men who was in Achsah's view.

She jumped when the wild animal suddenly tore away from her, in the direction of the grassy field, across the road. The riders appeared to be more than the wild animal was willing to take on.

Achsah choked back a sob. Her hand tightened on her stick as the donkeys drew nearer. The dog was gone.

But another danger was at hand, the night travelers.

She lifted her skirt and turned to run in the opposite direction. She used her walking stick to move quicker.

The donkeys slowed and came to a halt behind her. "Achsah!"

She heard her name and stopped in her tracks. She recognized the voice. Toi had come from the opposite direction, and he wasn't alone. She turned and waited for him as tears flowed down her cheeks. After what she'd been through, it was difficult to believe he was there.

When he got down from the donkey, she ran to him and threw her arms around his neck and held tightly to him. She choked back a sob as she looked up at him. "You came for me?"

He brushed the hair back from her face. "You're surprised? You didn't think I would?" He looked amused.

"Ittai told me you wouldn't. He said you'd think I'd left you." She stared at him perplexed.

"I've been across the plains and back trying to find you." He smiled as he lifted her into his arms. "You're difficult to track down."

She wiped tears from her cheeks. "He gave me to those people, but I escaped. I tried to get home, and then there was the wild dog." Her eyes widened. "I didn't have a weapon."

He touched her cheek and shook his head. "Don't say anymore. I'll take you home, Achsah. You'll sleep well tonight. Kezia and mother will make sure you're cared for."

"I'm tired." She shivered.

He put her on the donkey and got up behind her. "Rest on the way back. There's no need to stay awake any longer."

She turned to a sound behind them when she saw Benaiah. He was with Toi? Surely not for her, but for his brother.

Benaiah eyed her guardedly. He didn't say anything, but he tugged at the reins of his mount and turned away.

Achsah shivered again. She looked back at the sound of more hooves beating against the desert sand. She tightened her hold on Toi.

"It's my father, Achsah." Toi pointed to Josheb and the extra donkey. "He has the women who were with you."

Achsah breathed deep and slow as relief swept through her. "I wasn't able to free them. I'm so glad. Thank you."

"We're taking them back to their homes."

Achsah loosened her hold, and the tension left her. The other women were free also, and she was safe from animals, the traders, and from the dark night alone in the plains of Moab.

She'd go back now and put what happened behind her. Toi would see to it that she'd be safe this night.

She laid her head on his shoulder and listened to the rhythm of the donkey's hooves as they moved along the road to the town.

After all that had happened, her eyes finally closed. It wasn't long before she could no longer stay awake.

*****

Toi held Achsah tighter. He leaned down and breathed in the soft scent of perfume in her hair and the sweet smells of cloves from oils on her skin.

The evening was quiet. The bright, full moon cast beams of light over the flat plains of Moab and beyond to the blackened mountains and cliffs in the distance. The four large donkeys trotted down the path, and the sound of their hooves overshadowed any other desert sounds of the night.

The tension eased from his shoulders as he rode down the trail.

Achsah rested comfortably in front of him. Her breaths were slow and even. She was holding him as she slept.

He fingered a silken strand of her dark brown hair. Her eyes were closed, and her thick lashes rested against her face peacefully. Her cheeks were rosy.

He'd been both surprised and touched by her lack of restraint when she'd first seen him. She'd gone to him willingly and without hesitation. It wasn't like his wife to allow herself such openness with him. He was sure it wasn't a trait he was likely to see again for a time.

The wild dog was within a donkey's length of her when Toi had come upon them. He'd seen the terrified look on her face, and he was relieved he hadn't been too late. The stone he'd shot had scared the animal away.

His hand clasped onto her more firmly as he looked out over the plains and then back again. He swallowed dryly.

What might have happened had he come later than he did? Would she have been able to fend off attacks of the animal for long? What would he have felt, if she had not?

As much trouble as she could be, the thought of losing Achsah to the traders, or to the wild dog in the plains at night, was something he didn't want to consider.

He breathed a welcome sigh of cool night air.

He looked down the trail to the lights that led to their house. It wouldn't be long, and they'd be back in the town. He was glad she was safe, and that they were on their way home.

*****

Chapter 8

Achsah tossed and turned in her sleep as nightmares of the previous evening stole over her.

"Achsah, wake up. You're dreaming."

Achsah's eyes opened, and she looked at Hannah. She let out a relieved sigh when she realized she'd been sleeping. She sat up.

The sun was streaming through a small window in the top of the wall. Toi's mother sat beside her on a short bench next to the bed. She'd brought a tray with food on it and set it on a stand.

Achsah turned to Hannah. "Where's Toi? Shouldn't he be home?" She drew a fur skin over herself in the dimming shadows in the room. "Judging from the sun, the day's nearly over."

Hannah had a worried look on her face. Her voice was quiet. "He left early this morning to find Ittai. We're waiting for news of him."

Achsah drew in a quick breath. "Ittai? Has anyone gone to check on him? Why hasn't he come back?" Achsah tugged on the sleeve of her mother-in-law's tunic. "It's late."

"Benaiah went. We must wait for him to tell us the news."

Achsah's face paled. "Toi was awake most of the night. He'll need rest. I must go see where he is." She started to get out of bed.

"You need to eat first, then dress. I'll tell you if we hear anything."

Achsah eyed the food next to her. She was terribly hungry. She took the tray in her hands. She pulled off grapes from a bunch and put them into her mouth. She ate them quickly.

Hannah got up. "I'll leave. You get ready, and if he comes, I'll send him to you."

Achsah nodded. Something sank inside her. She'd caused all the turmoil in the house and couldn't imagine what would happen to her, if Toi didn't return. How could the family even look at her again, if he were hurt badly or killed? How could she live with herself after such a thing?

She ate as much as she could and shoved the tray aside. She'd have to dress quickly so that she could find him.

*****

Achsah finished readying herself for a trip to Ittai's home. She was about to leave through the courtyard when she heard shouts coming from outside the wall.

Something ill stirred in her as she looked toward the gate. She drew a hand to her throat as the door swung open, and a group of men came in. They carried a stretcher made of tied branches with a woven, wool blanket thrown over it. Toi was on it. A cloth was wrapped around him. There was evidence of blood that had seeped through.

Achsah ran to him and grabbed his hand. Her words came out in a choked sound. "Oh...no." She moved with the stretcher as they carried it to one of the inner rooms of the house.

They placed it on the floor, near the edge of a straw mattress, and lifted him onto it. He groaned as they moved him.

Achsah's eyes were huge as she stared at the bandage and then at him. She moved his side and watched to see if he'd wake up.

When his eyes opened, a smile twitched at the corner of his mouth. There was a look of interest on his face. "Ah, little Achsah." He covered her hand with his own. "It seems you might harbor some feelings for me after all."

Achsah choked on her words. "You'd think me so cold and heartless that I wouldn't care that you were injured?" She drew her hand back. A flame grew inside her as she spoke. "I wouldn't want anyone hurt."

She stood back when his mother rushed in assessing the damage.

Hannah called for a fresh cloth, to wrap the wound with, and she worked to wrap the new bandage. Achsah watched as trepidation filled her heart. She avoided looking directly into Toi's eyes. She was sure he was still watching her. She didn't want him to see how afraid she was.

Sapphira and Kezia both came running into the room at the same time and went to their brother. They both stopped short when they saw him. They stood next to Achsah.

Sapphira turned to her mother. "Will he be all right?" There was hardly any color in her naturally rosy cheeks.

Hannah nodded. "The wound isn't too deep. As long as we keep it clean, and care for it properly, it should heal."

Both sisters let out a lengthy sigh.

Sapphira took Achsah's hand and looked up at her. "Don't be anxious. Did you hear mother? It isn't bad."

Achsah nodded. She didn't say anything, but she drew in a breath.

She suddenly felt overwhelmed by all that had happened, and a heaviness ran through her. She needed air. It was difficult for her to breath. "I don't feel so good."

Sapphira turned to her. "Achsah?"

"I need to go out." She turned, and made her way quickly to the open door as she rushed past Benaiah and the others.

She went into the courtyard, and opened the gate to the smaller courtyard, which housed her room. She sat on a low stone bench against the wall, in the corner, and she drew her knees to her chest. She sucked in the outside air.

She wanted to go to the high places to pray to Chemosh but didn't trust he'd listen. It seemed the god had marked her since birth and had not looked kindly upon her. Chemosh was, most likely, the reason Toi had been injured, and the reason she'd suffered as much as she had. So much had happened so quickly.

168

She balled herself up in the shadows of the wall and scuffed the courtyard ground with her sandals. An emptiness inside her grew as she sat there.

She choked on the thoughts that raced through her mind.

She remembered back to the weeks before this incident had occurred. Things had seemed better.

Despite Benalah's obvious dislike for her, Toi's family had treated her kindly. They'd included her in conversations, praised her for the things she'd done to help in their home, and saw to her needs because of the recent injury to her foot.

She'd spent considerable time with all three of the women in the house, including Hannah, Sapphira, and Kezia. After making new tunics for each of them, they truly seemed impressed by her work, and by the fact that she'd wanted to give them something she'd put great efforts into constructing for them.

She'd been reluctant to allow them entrance to her heart, yet she knew her distrust of them was beginning to erode. It had been difficult for her to keep up the pretense that she didn't care for them.

Achsah looked at the sky.

Two large birds circled overhead. She watched as the immense creature's wings opened. They dipped and soared against the cerulean, blue sky. They skimmed the edges of wispy clouds that appeared and disappeared for a time.

Might her life have been as uncomplicated as these creatures' lives were? If she had the chance, she would surely find her escape, the way they had, and lift herself above the fray of this life and beyond.

She looked back at the gate that led to the main part of the house. She drew her shawl tighter around her.

Would Toi's wound heal? What would happen to her if it didn't? She hoped it wasn't too deep. His mother had alluded to its being something that would improve with time, but what if it didn't?

She wanted to go back, to find out, yet it might not be wise. If she did, it could possibly do him more harm. If Ittai came looking for her, and she were with her husband, there'd be no telling what might happen. She didn't want to put him in more danger than he was already in.

Ittai could deal with her as he saw fit. Let him do what he wanted and be done with it. She was tired of worrying about him.

*****

The gate opened not far from her. Hearing the latch lift broke her thoughts.

"He wants you back there."

Achsah jumped at the sound of Benaiah's voice.

She backed away out of instinct and crouched further into the corner. She put her hand in front of her as a measure of protection.

Benaiah stared at her as if surprised. "You need to go to him." He let out a snort as he watched her. "Quit thinking about yourself for once."

"But..."

He took her by the arm and pulled her from the bench. He began dragging her across the courtyard.

She dug her feet into the ground and pushed him away. Then she sunk down onto her knees in the dust. "I can't."

"Get up. I told you he wants you there, though I don't understand why."

Her eyes darkened as she looked at him. "Ittai will be back, and nothing good will come of it. If I meet him at the gate, Toi will be kept from it. Ittai will want revenge."

Benaiah studied her, watchful. "Ittai's dead. He drew his weapon first."

"Dead?"

"Yes."

Achsah put her hand to her chest. She was most likely an underlying cause of this man's death. Her heart sunk inside her, but she showed little emotion. She didn't want Benaiah to know how much the news affected her.

"Come, you should be there for your husband. You owe it to him." Benaiah's voice was less gruff, but he was insistent.

Achsah spoke quietly. "I'll go, but for him. Not for you."

She got up and smoothed out the edges of her tunic. There was nothing more to say to this man who treated her as if she were dirt under his sandals. She straightened and lifted her chin as she walked past him.

She went in the direction of the main part of the house as Benaiah watched from a distance.

*****

Toi was asleep when Achsah entered the room. Curtains were drawn, and oil lamps had been dimmed.

She sat down on a stone bench next to the mattress he was lying on.

She eyed the calm expression on his face while he breathed deeply in and out. Even injured, as bad as he'd been, he seemed relaxed. He was resting peacefully as if he'd never gone out that day.

She observed the evenly sculptured lines of his face from where she sat, studying closely his well-proportioned features. His skin was tanned from long days in the sun, but there were few lines in it. Waves of hair, the color of desert sands, fell just below his ears.

She rarely had the chance to study her husband closely without his watching. If there were a man with more excellent features, at least in her eyes, she'd not been aware of it. She couldn't deny the attraction she felt for him from the first day she'd seen him.

His eyes opened. He seemed surprised to see her. He lifted his hand to her face and stroked the side of it.

She moved back as a faint color rose in her cheeks.

He smiled. "Benaiah didn't believe me that you'd come."

"I wouldn't for his sake, and I let him know it." Her eyes darkened.

Toi chuckled low, and then he took her hand in his. He gave her a tender look. "But you would for me?"

Achsah's chin lifted. She smiled. "Someone needed to be here. They've all gone out to the fields."

"So you're doing your duty to your husband?"

She sniffed. He was teasing her. "I wanted to make sure you weren't alone. I'm not so unfeeling as you believe me to be."

"I've never thought of you as unfeeling, my wife, despite the games I've seen you play with others."

He regarded her curiously. "Instead, I believe you might be distrusting and afraid to admit it. I saw you on the trail. You were not unhappy to see me. You keep these things from others, yet it's plain to see that you have a heart you don't share easily. Someday, maybe you'll trust me, little Achsah."

She stared at him. Trust? She wasn't so sure if she could trust anyone.

Her cheeks heated at some of the things he'd said. It was true. All of it. How he understood these things, when she tried so hard to hide them, she didn't know.

She exhaled slowly as she watched him.

She thought back to all he'd done for her in the past few days and what he'd risked. She'd deserved none of it.

She drew his hand to her and kissed the top of his fingers, in an uncharacteristic gesture, and looked down. She held his fingers in hers, but didn't say anything.

"Achsah?" Toi regarded her with surprise.

She lifted her eyes to his.

Her heart beat unsteadily, and she answered him quietly. "They want me to be here with you, and I want to stay, to make sure you have what you need, but I don't want to talk about what I feel." She wiggled uncomfortably in her seat. "I..."

He patted the side of the bedding he was resting on and gave her an easy smile. "Come, stay and have your wish. I'll ask no more of you."

Then his eyes glinted a light gray. "But, you still don't trust me. Am I so bad?" He jabbed her lightly in the side.

172

She gave him a look of chagrin. "I think you're mocking me, and you are very bad." She reached out and pulled a wool covering that had slipped down from his shoulders over him. "Trust is something that doesn't come easily for me. Maybe in time, but I'm not ready for it."

Toi smiled. "It's good to hear you say, 'maybe in time'." Then he turned and groaned. He looked down at his side.

Achsah got up from where she sat. She bent over him. "Do you hurt?" She should have let him sleep and shouldn't have talked to him so much. "Can I look at it?"

He reached for her shoulders and drew her to him. He laughed lightly. "You didn't know that I only wanted you closer to me." He pulled her near and enjoyed a tender moment as he kissed her.

She moved away from him and shook her head as she chided him. "You think yourself so clever?" She sat back in her seat. "You're to get well."

"Come, lie here, and we'll both rest. He pointed to the empty place next to him. "You need this as much as I do."

She nodded. "It's true. I am tired. Too much has happened, and I could use the sleep." She lowered herself onto the pallet and lay down. She relaxed as she closed her eyes and allowed herself the rest she so desperately needed.

*****

Chapter 9

Weeks had gone by since Toi had been injured. He was in the courtyard chipping away at a stone. He studied a carving he was working on.

Achsah came out the door and stood beside him. "What are you making?" Her eyes were intent on what he was doing.

"Things to sell. I'll soon be able to go back to town and lift and shape the bricks with Shobach, but for now I'll be content with small carvings."

"A goat god?"

Toi shrugged. "For a Moabite buyer. Money will be made from it, though I've no use for them."

"The image is a good likeness, and there are Israelites who would purchase them also. It's uncommon to see the detailed fur lines and the eyes with jewels. Your work is quite unique." She reached out and tugged on the sleeve of his outer robe. "I could use one for my morning devotions. I'd pray to it."

Toi gave her a disconcerted look. "I made it for the money." Then, he chuckled. "You believe I have the power to create a supreme being?"

Achsah looked at him with a puzzled expression. Then, she lifted her eyes to him. "I think it can become a god, and you can pray to it for protection and long life. Your wound might heal quicker with its powers."

"Achsah, there's no power in this stone. I made it with my hands."

She spoke quietly. "But maybe the carved image comes out? It has eyes, and a mouth, and ears."

"But what can it do. Can it move? Does it speak? Does it hear you? It was made with human hands."

"I tell it what I want." It was as if she were trying to convince herself. "Things might happen then. It's no different than your God, except mine has a form. I like these better. I can touch them. What has the Israelite God done for you?"

"He's done enough, but I know yours has done nothing."

She played with the dark braid which had fallen over her shoulder, and she drew her lips into a pout. "Your mother said he brought you forth from a dying birth. She said she prayed, and that your Israelite God set you apart when you were born, that you were special, and that Adonai made it clear to her that he stirred inside you when you were young."

"She tells this to everyone." Toi laughed. He chipped more pieces off the goat carving. "It's true I believe Adonai is the only Lord, the Creator of all." He smiled. "But I've little time for all the learning and prayers. I've seen no evidence that I was set apart."

"Your mother believes it."

He grinned. "Because I'm her firstborn. It makes me special."

Achsah rolled her eyes. "*She* might believe it, but I'm not so sure."

"Here." He smiled and handed her the goat image. "You can add this one to your collection."

Achsah looked surprised. She took it in her hands and looked at it in disbelief. "Truly? You're giving it to me?"

He nodded. "I've more to sell."

She hugged it to her and leaned close. She kissed him on the cheek. Her eyes sparkled. "I'll put it with my others and keep it there. It's well made and looks real. Thank you."

"Your welcome. I suppose I am good for something." Toi chuckled to himself.

"You said it. I didn't." Then, she straightened and spoke with excitement. "Now, there are some things I must do. I'll put this with my gods, and then I must go, but I'll check on you later."

He reached out and fingered the edge of her soft, red linen garment as she slipped out of his grasp. He watched her walk across the courtyard to the stone stairs that led to the roof. Her jewels, adorning her wrists and ankles, sounded like quiet bells as she walked. She was the picture of beauty and grace with each step she took.

When Achsah reached the stone staircase, that ran up the side of the house, she turned back to look at him. She gave him a smile, and adjusted the golden headdress that held her soft cascading hair behind her shoulders. She clutched tightly to her goat idol and took to the stairs.

Toi lifted another rock from the pile and looked at the work at hand. He shook his head slowly back and forth as he chipped away at it. His brow furrowed as he made the first markings, and he drew in a long, slow breath.

The pretty Moabitess he'd married was surely playing on his sensibilities as of late. Though he made it a point to maintain an indifferent stance toward her, since they'd wed; during the time he'd been forced to remain at home, and heal from his injuries, he was finding it more and more difficult to quell his more responsive side to her. Her vitality and good-natured teasing appealed to him greatly.

The more time he spent around her, the more he understood why so many other men had been willing to pursue her so diligently without regard, to themselves, or with regard to what might happen if they did.

Toi looked down at the block of stone in his hands. He stopped working. A thread of caution ran through him as he stared at the top of the roof.

Whether he allowed feelings for her, or not, Achsah wasn't willing to entrust anyone with her own heart. Her faith in others was as sparse the the rain in a drought.

Toi put down the idol and the tool in his hand. He got up and paced the length of the courtyard. He stopped and looked up at the cloudless sky as the dust beneath his feet stirred and then disappeared in the air.

Maybe someday, things would be different, but for now, he'd need to weigh his thoughts about her carefully. She'd not given her heart to him, or to their poorly orchestrated marriage. It

176

wouldn't due for him to grant her too much knowledge of his turning thoughts.

*****

Achsah crossed the roof to the corner where she'd hidden her other idols. There was a place where she'd stored them under a reed mat at the top.

She wasn't sure what the other family members would think if they knew she had them. For this reason, she'd kept them hidden. She'd only brought them out a couple of times for her morning prayers. Otherwise, she'd gone to the high places to burn incense to Chemosh where she wouldn't be disturbed.

She lifted the reed mat, under which lay a sun idol and the carving of a viper. She pulled out each of them and set them next to the goat idol in front of her.

She lifted her hands.

"Desert gods," she chanted. "Bring your good luck to me, and send harvest rains in this dry season for the crops."

She touched each of the idols, and she rubbed the tops. She bowed three times, in front of each of them, as she dutifully paid homage to them.

She looked around when she heard a noise behind her.

"Achsah? What are you doing?"

Sapphira stood behind her. "Those are Moabite idols in our home." Sapphira seemed surprised and puzzled at the same time. "You've kept them here?"

Achsah motioned for Sapphira to be quiet. "Shush, don't speak so loudly." She put her finger over her lips. "Benaiah will hear you."

Sapphira moved quietly across the roof to the place where Achsah knelt. She stopped and eyed the stone carvings with interest. "You brought these with you. But this one. Toi made it, didn't he?" She lifted the carving of the goat into her hands.

Achsah nodded. "He did. He gave it to me."

Sapphira set it back down and put her hand over her mouth. "Mother told him not to make them. It's why he goes to town to work. She said they'd turn his heart away. How can you pray to them? They're not real. They were made with human hands."

Achsah lifted the idol up. She pointed to the goat's eyes and face. "He was here all along. Toi only needed to bring him to life." Though she said the words, her heart questioned the truth of it.

Sapphira eyed the goat idol more closely. She looked skeptical. "But, he doesn't move. He does nothing without you."

"He might bring luck and fortune. Do you not realize that I have things, and a house, and food?"

Sapphira looked confused. "But the one true Lord does these things."

"I've never prayed to him, but I have these things and have more than most."

Sapphira sat down. She lifted each of the carvings and fingered the edges of them. "You believe this?"

"I think the gods might have supplied my riches. I've prospered. My family has also."

Sapphira eyed the carvings with interest. "I've seen other Moabite people in prayer to them."

"Yes." Achsah's head slanted upward as she looked at Toi's sister. She wondered what the other family members would think if they knew she was telling Sapphira about her gods. "I could teach you the chants. More gods might bring you more luck."

Sapphira looked curious.

Achsah leaned closer and whispered in her ear. "But don't tell your family. They might not be happy I shared this with you."

Sapphira took a deep breath and nodded.

"So, this is what I do. Come, kneel next to me. I'll show you what to say. We can meet here in the evenings before the others make their way to the roof."

Sapphira nodded again. She got down next to Achsah and fingered the idols.

Achsah took Sapphira's arm. She smiled. Maybe she wouldn't feel so alone now.

*****

The next day as evening drew closer, Achsah breathed in the cool desert air as she sat on the steps leading to the doorway of her house.

She smiled as Jair approached Toi's father. It hadn't taken the young man long to have found his way to their household. It appeared he'd taken Achsah up on her suggestion to see Toi's sister.

Kezia sat beside her.

Achsah reached out and took her arm. "It's a good thing you're wearing your red tunic, but I should've tended to your hair. It should have been braided."

Kezia looked down. She didn't say anything. Her cheeks turned pink, and she drew her shawl tighter.

"I can burn incense to Chemosh. He might look favorably upon you and grant you Jair as a husband."

Kezia looked shocked. "Achsah! Please don't pray to that god. It's abominable."

Achsah took Kezia's hand. "Come now, don't we have the same ancestors? Wasn't Moab one of the sons of Lot? Our gods cannot be so different from yours."

"From the Creator of all?"

Achsah frowned. "Someone surely created him also?"

Kezia shook her head back and forth slowly. "No. No one can create Adonai. It's not possible. He created us and the Earth. How could this world have come to be otherwise?"

Achsah looked up at the expanse of the sky and the landscape in the distance. Sheep bleated in the valley below. Grasses bent in the breeze. It was odd to her that there was so much of nature unexplained.

She shrugged wary thoughts inside her away. "Might it be that it's a tale contrived by a storyteller? Who can know the truth of it?"

"He was here before time began. He spoke us into existence and gave us our hearts and minds. Abraham, Moses, and others made record of it through Adonai himself."

Achsah swallowed drily. "But there are many gods."

"He's the only one. His teachings aren't deceptive philosophies, or religions, but truth."

"I've my own gods and my beliefs." Achsah wriggled in her seat uncomfortably. "Please say no more."

Kezia hesitated. "If it's what you wish." She gave Achsah a solemn look. "But, you might continue to seek the truth yourself. Speak to my Lord."

"I'll think about it." Achsah pointed to the door. "But remember, Jair's here. I'm certain he's come to ask your father for permission to see you. Look, he's brought a gift, a foal."

"Achsah, we don't know why he's here." Kezia looked away.

Achsah laughed. "Come, sister, don't be silly." She got up and took Kezia's hand and gently tugged on it.

Kezia smiled. At Achsah's urging, she stood.

"Come, dance with me." Achsah's eyes sparkled. She took hold of Kezia's arm. "Let's sing and celebrate that he's here."

Kezia drew back shyly. Her eyes widened as she watched Achsah take turns around the courtyard.

Achsah giggled with delight as she shook the spangles on her wrists and spun in slow, even circles.

Kezia looked at the door.

"Come, you should be dancing too!" Achsah motioned to Kezia. She sang a Moabite song. There was the bray of a donkey from outside the courtyard. She turned to the sound and she noticed Toi standing at the wall.

She smiled, but ignored him as she continued to dance and sing. Her sandals tapped to her own rhythm over the hardened earth.

There was a curious look in Toi's eyes as he watched her. He took hold of the rope on the donkey's neck that was beside him, and he brushed its coat.

Achsah stopped and let out quiet laughter. "What other reason could he have? He's with your mother and father."

Kezia smiled. "But, we must wait."

Achsah laughed again as she watched the door.

It hadn't been long when Josheb came out of the house and motioned to his daughter. He had a gentle look on his face. "Kezia, I must speak with you."

Achsah's smile widened. "See?" She pushed her braid over her shoulder and gave Kezia a gentle shove. "What did I tell you? Your father's asking for you."

Kezia got up as she straightened out the folds of her skirt. The rosy hue in her cheeks deepened as she made her way across the courtyard to go into the house with him.

*****

Achsah tapped her fingers against the folds of her tunic and stared at the door of the house. Kezia had been inside the house for a long time.

She looked up when the latch on the door moved upward. Her eyes danced when Kezia came out.

Kezia went to Achsah.

"Well?" Achsah's eyes were enrapt.

"It's true."

Achsah's eyes lit. She took Kezia's hands in her own and swung her around. "He's a good man. It's a good match."

Kezia tugged her hands free. "Achsah."

Achsah kissed Kezia's cheeks. "Come, now. You must tell Sapphira! She'll want to know. She's in town with a friend. You must find her. I'll tell Toi!" She got up quickly and made her way to the gate where Toi was still brushing the side of the donkey. She unlatched the wooden door and went to stand beside him.

He turned. "You have something to tell me. He's courting Kezia. Right?" He smiled and winked at her.

Achsah made a face. "I already told you this quite some time ago."

He laughed, and then he leaned down and kissed her. "Yes, at the dinner party. It seems you've made a match."

She wagged a finger at him. "You mustn't look the way you do. I did a great thing."

She took his hand. "Now wash up, and come into the house. You should be there to see what your father has to say."

Toi watched her as if entertained. "I'll finish with the animals first."

"Your sister will be very happy, but I need to go now. After this is said and done, there'll be new tunics to make, and jewelry to buy for a future marriage!"

Toi smiled and shook his head again. "And more money out of my pockets for fabric and pretty clothes."

Achsah gave him a reproachful look. "You're ridiculous. I must get back to the house."

He laughed and took the donkey's rope and led it to the stable inside the second gate.

Achsah made her way to the house as she left him to tend to the animals.

*****

Sapphira giggled. She held up a bracelet. "Your idols! They did this! I've all these beautiful things, and I'm having so much fun, Achsah!"

"Yes, more gods. See, I told you. It's better to pray to a lot of gods."

Achsah suddenly shivered and looked upward. After talking to Kezia, she wasn't sure Adonai would appreciate her

182

talking to Sapphira about other gods. She quickly turned her thoughts to the vendors on the streets instead. There were purchases to make.

Sapphira skipped alongside her in the marketplace. "What more can they do? What might we do?"

"Come, and I'll show you. I'll take you to another tent. There's more to buy and friends to visit. Tol won't be in from work until later."

"But, my parents?"

Achsah shrugged. "We'll be with my friends, and as long as Benaiah doesn't know, there's certainly no problem with you spending time with me."

Sapphira smiled. "This is true, but I don't think I'll tell them where I've been."

"I suppose." Achsah took Sapphira's hand and pulled on it. "Come, follow me. We'll have some fun."

Sapphira nodded. "I believe we will."

*****

Achsah giggled as she held up her chalice. "See what I told you. It's harmless here. My friends will treat you kindly. This is Merab, Basemath, and Maacah. We've spent our childhoods together."

Sapphira nodded to each of the women. She looked around the large, ornate room. Wealthy families congregated to talk and eat together here. The house was one of the finest in the town. A few rich Moabites were there as they watched the young women dancing in a group in the middle of the house.

She eyed the young women there. Achsah's friends were covered in jewels and brightly colored tunics with ornate stitching. They were very beautiful and full of life as Achsah was. They laughed as they tasted the food and drink.

Achsah's friend, Basemath, had a veil covering her face.

Basemath took the silk cloth down, and she laughed. The ring of her voice was lilting. "Achsah! You've brought a friend.

Come and sit with us! Maacah's making painted designs on Merab's hands. The artwork's beautiful."

Basemath's dark eyes had a mischievous glow to them. Thick, black lines around them made them appear very large. Her braided and piled hair was arranged carefully. She turned back to the other women.

Achsah took Sapphira's hand. "Sit by me. We'll have ours done next."

Sapphira moved closer. She took another drink.

Maacah looked up from what she was doing. "She's an Israelite."

"She's Toi's sister, and her name's Sapphira. It doesn't matter that she's an Israelite. She worships Chemosh, and my household gods, as we do, and she's descended from Abraham, like us...other than our being somewhat tarnished because of Lot."

The others laughed.

Sapphira smiled. "You're not to blame for your ancestor's past."

The women seemed intrigued. Basemath took rings from her finger and placed them on Sapphira. The others followed suit with spangles from their wrists.

Maacah giggled as she lifted her chalice to her lips and took a drink. "As sisters of the plains, you're one of us now."

Sapphira eyed her newly acquired jewels. Her cheeks glowed with warmth. "I love them."

Merab held up her hand to show Achsah and Sapphira the intricate paintings on it. "Look, Maacah's an artist. Her work is beautiful. Stay and have yours done."

"The flowers are pretty." Achsah smiled. "I want those same colors for mine, but we must be back before it's too late. Toi will be leaving his work before sundown."

Basemath nodded. "Maacah works fast. Mine was done earlier. Sit and enjoy the music while you wait. We'll watch the dancing."

Sapphira leaned forward. "I was told not to do this."

184

"Paint designs? But, it's pretty."

"Yes, but it's in the Torah. Kezia said our focus should not be on ourselves, but rather on the Lord. She said that, in time, we might value our bodies over our Lord." Sapphira spoke softly. "And that it's better to work on our inner beauty."

Merab smiled widely. "My work isn't permanent. It will fade in time."

Achsah caught Basemath's eye.

Basemath smiled at her with a knowing look. She lifted her tunic from her shoulder to reveal a small printed flower. "I see no harm in it. It is a small thing?"

Achsah turned to Sapphira. "It is pretty." Yet, she couldn't help wondering whether Kezia's words might contain some truth in them. Kezia's inner beauty shone without adornment on the outside. She had no need for embellishments of any kind.

"I might watch instead." Sapphira smiled.

Achsah's friends went back to their work. They left Sapphira and Achsah to look around.

Sapphira turned and watched the women dancing in the room while she waited.

Her eyes rested on a beautiful woman who was sitting further away in the corner. The woman's dark eyes were large, yet she wore little kohl around them. Her other make-up was almost non-existent. She had a natural beauty quite different from the other Moabite women in the home. Though her tunic was simply made, nothing about her was plain.

"Who is she?" Sapphira looked at Achsah and pointed to the woman.

Achsah turned and made a face. "Oh, Anah. She's the other sister. She's very pretty, but rarely spends time with Maacah, Basemath, and Merab. She prefers solitude with her animals."

"Hmm." Sapphira smiled. "Yes, she is very pretty, but not as fun as you and your friends."

All women smiled and lifted their glasses.

They watched as Maacah went back to her work.

*****

Visits to Achsah's friends' homes had become more frequent. Sapphira had come to know the other women quite well, and Achsah was enjoying her time with this youngest sister of Toi's.

They giggled and laughed as they came back from their last visit to town.

Sapphira reached for the gate. She let go and put her finger to her lips. "Shh, mother might hear."

Achsah lowered her voice. "They're most likely in the fields. There's no need to worry."

*****

Kezia eyed the sun which lowered in the sky as she opened the gate. She hoped Achsah and Sapphira were on the other side.

When she saw them, she breathed a sigh, though her stomach churned inside her. She took Sapphira's hand. "Where have you been?"

It was late afternoon again. Achsah and her sister had slipped out in the mornings and had not come home for most of the day while their mother and father worked in the fields. Kezia had taken extra chores for their sake.

"What are the purposes of these visits you're making? What have you done?"

Achsah groaned. "Why must you keep watch over us?" She stared at Kezia. "We bought things for you and spent time with friends."

Kezia stepped back to let Achsah pass. She tugged on Sapphira's arm. "I don't need cloth or jewelry. Sapphira, you're only fifteen and unmarried. Why are you going out everyday?

You're spending too much time with these women in the daylight hours. What's the meaning of it?"

Sapphira let go of her sister's hand. She waved her off. "If you'd come with us, you might find out what we do is not so bad. There's nothing to keep me here. The servants tend to our needs, and mother is at Ruth's."

"Mother's in the field, and Jair wouldn't approve of my going with you. I wouldn't want to take part in these things. You could sew with me. I miss your company, Sapphira. And Achsah's too. We used to spend time together."

Neither of them answered. They both turned away from her.

Kezia spoke quietly. "You're changing, Sapphira. You've darkened the lines around your eyes like an unchaste woman. You should wash it off so Benaiah doesn't see you."

Sapphira's eyes narrowed. "Ha! I'll be asleep before he gets back, and I don't care what he thinks. He's an old burr in the dust anyway."

Achsah laughed. "That's true. We don't need to listen to what he says."

Kezia sighed. "Adonai's forgiving and kind, but he's also just. You might push the bounds too far someday. You're running after idols of a different kind. In the Torah, it says that those who are wicked will chase after their heart's desire. You must be careful."

Sapphira turned away. As she went inside, she called out over her shoulder. "Ha! Wicked? You need not worry. Things are not as bad as you think. I'm tired."

Achsah nodded. "I'm wanting rest also. You mustn't be afraid for us. Nothing will happen to your sister while I'm with her."

*****

Achsah couldn't help but notice the pained look on Kezia's face as she turned to leave. Sapphira's sister was clearly distressed over the matter, yet it wasn't something Achsah wanted to think about. What harm could come from a little fun with friends?

Though a stab of guilt crept into Achsah's heart, she pushed the feeling away. It was true that Sapphira was drifting from the family who loved her. But, Achsah was enjoying her company and didn't want her time with Sapphira to end.

She went through the gate and closed it behind her.

Hopefully, with Jair, coming around more frequently, he might keep Kezia occupied so that she and Sapphira would be able to go about their business unhindered.

Toi had been busy with his work, since his injury had healed. He'd attempted to make up for lost time, and Achsah had seen little of him, other than spending a few quiet moments talking to him, before he dozed off at night to sleep. He was unconcerned with her undertakings. His thoughts had been tied to his business and work. Maybe in time he'd be home more.

*****

Benaiah studied Sapphira from across the room. His younger sister had certainly changed in the last couple of months.

Her naturally bright, inquisitive nature had dimmed, and she'd become sullen and moody.

Her mode of dress was different. She was less modest. Her jewelry was excessive, along with her makeup. Benaiah noticed that she was gone during the day and that she spent less time with the family. She wasn't doing her chores.

He snorted with disgust as he watched Achsah from across the table. Toi didn't seem to notice the way his wife behaved. The woman caused more difficulties than his brother knew. Even Kezia, as accepting as she was of others, seemed troubled over the matter.

As far as he was concerned, after this day, Sapphira would no longer dabble in the Moabite culture. He'd seen enough, and he was determined that it wouldn't continue. He'd go to where they'd been spending their time and have a talk with Achsah's so-called friends. Then he'd fix it so that Sapphira would never go back.

Both hers and Achsah's time was running short. His youngest sister would learn some valuable lessons about these Moabite women and how much they truly cared for her.

*****

Kezia looked over the grassy plains. Her stomach rumbled. She'd fasted day and night and prayed for her sister, and for Achsah.

She thought of Sapphira, her sweet, full-of-life sister, with a heart for others. Sapphira was turning from Adonai. Her actions appeared to be stealing the beauty and life from her.

When she thought of Achsah, Kezia lowered to her knees and bowed to the ground as she wiped a tear from her cheek.

Kezia was sure Achsah's harsh words and offhand remarks were a fortress around her as a result of little love. Her escape, from their home, was most likely a refuge from her troubled past.

"Adonai, loving Father, and Holy One, care for Achsah and Sapphira. Keep both of my sisters safe, and help them to know your love for them."

Kezia didn't move. She allowed Adonai's peace to radiate through her as she trusted that he'd answer her prayer in due time. Her heart was humbled by his greatness. Adonai's abilities were larger than her own. She'd have faith in him.

She'd believe that he'd do good things for her and her family.

Adonai was true to his word. He was to be trusted.

*****

Kezia looked down the road.
Ruth was coming from town.

189

Kezia got up and waved to her. "Ruth! So good to see you. Mother wanted to talk to you. Would you like to come inside for a visit?"

Ruth quickened her steps and made her way to the gate. She smiled. "Peace, Kezia. I'd love to come in, but I can't stay long. Mahlon's been sick. I must leave shortly."

"Mahlon?"

"Yes, and Chilion, Orpah's husband too. They're both coughing."

"Oh, I'll pray for them. Come in the house. There's something I could give you that might help them." She motioned to Ruth.

Ruth adjusted the basket on her arm. She followed Kezia through the gate and into the courtyard.

Hannah sat near a stone oven as she watched the flat bread baking. She looked up when Ruth and Kezia took a place next to her. "Peace, Ruth. Tell me how Naomi is. I've been meaning to visit your home."

Ruth leaned down and kissed Hannah's cheek.

She stood back up. Her expression was solemn. "She struggles with the death of her husband. She has had such sorrow in her heart. Yet, each day there are less tears, and she's more accepting of what's happened."

"Tell her that my prayers are with her."

"I'll do this."

Hannah lowered the shawl that was around her shoulders. "Where are Achsah and Sapphira? I haven't seen either of them today."

A veiled look came over Kezia. "They might be on the roof. At least Sapphira was. I'm not sure if Achsah was with her though." She didn't say anymore.

Ruth studied Kezia's face. She seemed to contemplate something.

Hannah looked curious. "Lately, they've been gone a lot. Have they been shopping?"

"I'm not sure, mother." Kezia spoke softly. "I believe they've been with friends of Achsah's. They told me they were going out later."

Hannah nodded. "I suppose Achsah will be making some new tunics." She smiled. Then she got up as if she suddenly remembered something. "Are those herbs inside? I should add them to the lentils we're having today."

"Oh mother, could you bring some oils for Ruth? Mahlon and Chilion are sick. They need something that might help their cough."

"Sick?"

Ruth sighed. "Yes, for some time. I'm hoping they're better soon."

Hannah looked sympathetic. "I've things that might help them. Wait here."

She went inside the house and left Kezia and Ruth to talk.

When Hannah was out of range of hearing, Ruth put her hand on Kezia's arm. "Are Achsah and Sapphira in trouble? I thought I saw them on the road the other day. Where have they been?"

"They've been at Basemath's father's home. Sapphira's placing her trust in things with little value. She wants little to do with Adonai. I don't quite know how to tell mother. I am distressed at the thought of it. I've prayed."

Ruth put her hand on Kezia's arm. "If you're speaking to the Lord, you can be assured that Adonai's plans will prevail. You must not fret, as this is for unbelievers. But leave this in his hands and go about your business. We mustn't fear anything when our Lord is watching out for us. Everything he does and allows is for our good." She looked hopeful.

Kezia nodded. "Thank you, Ruth. Sometimes I wish I had your faith. Mahlon's taught you well."

"He's a strong, godly man as is Jair. You'll do well with Jair."

Kezia looked up. "You've chosen to be a servant of our Lord, and of your husband. A strong couple gives themselves to the service of the other. I hope it can be the same for Jair and me someday. He wishes to marry me. Mother says marriage can be, difficult, but rewarding."

Ruth stared at the plains of Moab, and a warm look came into her eyes. "This is good, and it's true. Mahlon and I have chosen to be willing servants of Adonai and of each other. I trust Adonai to lead Mahlon in right paths. As it is easy for me to serve Mahlon. His love is one of a godly man. He cares for me very much."

Kezia smiled. "I hope to have the same loving marriage."

"You will, Kezia. Adonai will provide it for you."

"Thank you, Ruth."

The door opened, and Hannah stepped out with a clay vessel in her hand. "You might add this oil to your cooking pot and allow the steam to rise for Mahlon and Chilion to breathe. It'll help their coughs."

Ruth got up and dusted off her tunic. She took the container in her hand. "I'm grateful to you, Hannah. I'll do this."

"A couple times a day should make them feel better."

"Thank you. I suppose I must get back now. Orpah's there. She's watching over both our husbands and providing Naomi with the comfort she needs."

Hannah nodded. "I'm glad you were able to come."

"Yes, I'll stop by again when I can." She was careful with the clay vessel in her hands. She held it gingerly as she crossed the courtyard and turned to wave.

Kezia and Hannah watched as Ruth went out the gate and started down the path toward her home.

Kezia's heart lifted with Ruth's words. A peaceful feeling enveloped her with the thought that Adonai was watching over Ruth and her family.

*****

"What are you doing, Benaiah? Put those down!"
Sapphira moved closer to him. She was on the roof as he took
Achsah's idols in his hands and made his way toward the stairs.

Benaiah scowled. "Sorry, but you can't have them.
You're done following that Moabitess around and dabbling in her
worthless rituals. You were happier before she came, but you've
changed. You've lost your sweetness and that smile you used to
come running to me with. What's happened?"

Sapphira stared at him sullenly. She reached out and tried
to take the carved images from him. "Give them back! They're
not yours, Benaiah. I'm telling Achsah. Toi made one of those
for her."

"I don't care who they belong to, or who made them.
Mother and father wouldn't appreciate the fact that they're in our
home. And you've paid homage to them! No wonder you're
acting the way you are. And it's all because of that Moabite
woman. I told Toi not to bring her here. She's done exactly as I
said she would."

"I asked to see the gods. I wanted to go with her. She had
nothing to do with it. It was my choice."

Benaiah turned. He stared at her in disgust. "Sapphira,
I'm ashamed of you. You're covered in bracelets and rings. Your
sweet face is painted in all those hard looking colors and lines,
and your clothes are without modesty. You look no different than
one of the harlots at the town gates. No decent man would have
anything to do with you. You've fallen to the depths. You should
return to Adonai with your whole heart."

Though Sapphira was taken back by his blunt words, she
met his eyes brazenly. "What makes you think you can speak to
me the way you do, when you're no better than I am? You've not
been a good example to follow."

For the briefest of moments, there was an uncomfortable
silence. He crossed his arms in front of him and spoke in a gruff
tone. "At least I'm not praying to a worthless piece of stone
which I'm determined to put an end to. The idols are going.
There's no life in them. There's no power in them, and I say this

with confidence. Don't even try to come after me. If you do, mother and father will know what you've been doing. I'll tell them."

Sapphira stood back as she watched Benaiah carry the idols down the stone steps that ran along the side of the house. Her mother and father could never know that she worshipped the Moabite images. How could he threaten exposing such a thing?

And harlot? This is what he'd likened her to? Why would he say this? She looked down at her clothes and jewels.

Her anger over his words simmered within her as she sat in silence. She took off the spangles on her wrists and ankles and laid them on the roof.

What did he know anyway?

She rubbed at her cheeks as she eyed the rolling plains in the distance.

Then she sighed.

Though she wanted to deny it, some of the things her brother told her bothered her more than she cared to admit. She wondered why he thought so much about what she did.

Lately, he seemed to be on every street corner watching her with a scowl on his face. Didn't he have better things to do?

She hadn't sat at the town gates. Was she so bad? Truly what he told her was not what others were thinking. Surely, Benaiah had exaggerated the whole matter in his mind.

Things had certainly changed since they'd moved from Bethlehem. Their family had changed. Not all of it for the better. If Benaiah had accepted Achsah, and her ways from the beginning, things might not have been so stirred up.

Sapphira went to the stairs and started down them. Maybe getting out of the house would do her good. Toi was at Shobach's working. Achsah was most likely in her room.

After dealing with Benaiah, and listening to his rant, she was ready for a diversion. She didn't want to think of any of the things he said, or accused her of. She only wanted to spend time with Achsah and her friends.

Her sandals hit the last step on the ground below. She moved quickly in the direction of her Moabite sister's room. She'd find Achsah, and they'd leave to take their mind from their troubles. Anything was better than sitting and stewing about a brother who clearly meant to cause trouble.

⁂⁂⁂⁂⁂

Jorah untied his donkey from a post in front of his friend's home. He was curious when he looked across the street and saw Dinah in the midst of a group of Moabite women. They'd stopped to show each other their market purchases.

One of the women looked up and noticed he was there. She nudged Dinah in the arm and pointed. "Who's that? He's looking at you."

Dinah turned. She studied Jorah a moment. "It's Achsah's husband's brother. His name is Jorah."

Jorah started across the path with the donkey ignoring the stares of the other women. He stopped in front of them and took Dinah aside. "If you're on your way home soon, then I can walk with you?"

Giggles erupted from her friends. One of them whispered in Dinah's ear. She gently pushed her away.

"I was finished and had plans to go back soon, but I don't believe my father would approve of your going with me." She flicked a length of hair behind her shoulders.

Jorah smiled. "It's daylight, and we'll be on the road in plain sight. Come, I'll tell you what's happened recently to your sister and Toi. I'm sure there are things you haven't heard."

"What things?" Dinah leaned forward as her eyes widened.

"If you come with me, I'll tell you on the way." He took her hand and gave it a gentle tug.

Dinah turned to her friends. "I want to hear what he has to say. I'll see you tomorrow."

Her friends looked curious. They giggled as they watched Dinah take a place at Jorah's side.

She ignored them and began walking next to him. "What's she done? Is she still in your home?"

"Who?" He tugged on his donkey's reins and clucked to it.

"Achsah, of course! Who else? You told me that you knew things."

He smiled. "Oh, yes. Ittai gave her to slave traders, and Toi brought her back."

Dinah's eyes widened. "Slave traders? When did this happen?" She gave him a puzzled look.

"A few days past."

"But your brother went after her? I would've thought he'd be ready to sell her by now."

Jorah laughed. "She's his wife. He went in the night and tracked them down. He brought her back safely, and there was a confrontation with Ittai."

"Was Toi hurt? What happened?"

"He was wounded, but he's well now, though Ittai's dead."

"Ittai?"

Jorah nodded. "Yes."

Dinah looked shocked. She moved quickly to get out of the way of a cart that was rattling toward her down the road.

Jorah took her arm. "The road's busy."

"It's been like this all day."

Jorah reached out to take her from the path, before another wagon rolled past. "Here, ride on the donkey. I'll lead it."

She started to move away. "There's no need. I can walk."

"From what I see, if you ride, you'll be one less traveler on the road, and there's too many already."

"I suppose it is true, and it is hot today." Dinah brushed a strand of hair from her eyes.

Jorah stared at her with interest. Dinah's cheeks were flushed, and her wind-tossed hair was in disarray. A brightly colored tie hung loosely around her waist, and the sandals on her feet were slightly large for her tiny, dust covered feet.

She was quite different from her sister who hardly allowed a hair, or piece of clothing, out of place. Achsah would have frowned at Dinah's appearance. Dinah seemed less skilled in this area.

He took a breath, and he smiled. He reached out and brushed at a smudge of dirt on her cheek.

Dinah drew back as she studied him. At first, there was mistrust in her eyes, and she seemed to regard him with a certain amount of skepticism.

Jorah looked uncertain. "I suppose I shouldn't have done that. We'll have friendship, remember?"

Dinah smiled and suddenly moved closer, and her expression changed. There was a knowing look in her eyes as she tipped her head to him.

Her innocence was suddenly lost in the art of her culture and in her practiced words, though she was unaware of the repercussions that might come as a result of such behavior.

Her speech became smooth, and her voice was soft. "You think I'm pretty, don't you, Jorah?"

The sun came from behind a cloud and streamed down on the path. A heated breeze stirred the dust around them as Jorah's donkey let out a quiet bray.

"Dinah...I."

Dinah reached up and fingered the golden necklace that swung freely from her neck.

The donkey let out another whinny, and Jorah reached out to steady it. He turned back. He suddenly regarded her warily.

He couldn't be taken in by the Moabite influence and its women. Dinah didn't understand the differences in the ways they lived or in their beliefs. There was much to consider in allowing his thoughts of her to wander.

He swallowed drily and lifted her onto his animal reluctantly putting her on. "I'll take you back. It is time for you to be home again."

He turned away as he took the reins and began walking.

*****

Dinah put her hands on the mane of the donkey while she watched Jorah from behind. She studied him as he led the animal down the path.

It seemed he took an interest in her for more than friendship after all. Yet, it was obvious that he was conflicted at the thought of forming an attachment to her, most likely because of his religion and culture. Dinah wasn't surprised at this, though Jorah didn't strike her as the type of man who'd consider such things lightly.

The donkey clomped steadily along on the hardened earth. She put her hands on its mane again and held the thick, coarse hairs in her fingers.

She watched as Jorah guided the donkey down the path. He held the reins firmly in his hands. The animal swayed neither to the right, nor the left. The sounds of the hooves striking against the ground beneath it brought forth an even rhythm. The ease at which Jorah led the great animal seemed to mirror the steadfast way he lived his own life.

Dinah sighed. Given the right circumstances, she'd be interested in this man. The care he'd afforded her, and protection he'd given, on more than one occasion, did not go unnoticed. He was honest, respectable, and considerate, and his quiet, thoughtful manner attracted her more than she cared to admit.

She turned away and looked into the distance toward the horizon. An Israelite, such as Jorah, would surely wound her heart in the end, and she'd be worse off for it.

Though he'd treated her kindly when they'd been together, she knew it was foolish to set her sights on him. Even though his brother had married Achsah, it generally wasn't the

198

custom with these men to attach themselves to a Moabitess for long. Encouraging his attentions would surely be a mistake she'd regret.

*****

Neither spoke much on the way to her family's place.

Jorah took Dinah from the donkey when they reached the bend in the road near her home.

She looked up at him as he helped her down. "The road's less busy here."

He nodded. "Yes, I'm glad I could see you safely back."

Her eyes turned a deeper shade of brown as she watched him turn the animal around.

He looked back at her.

She lifted the edge of her tunic and backed away. "I thank you for bringing me here. I'll go before my father sees me."

Jorah bowed. "Yes, I have no desire to bring trouble upon you."

He supposed it was the wrong thing to have done, to bring her back. Yet, when he'd seen her in the marketplace, he'd been glad to see her and had wanted to make sure she got to her home safely.

She nodded and looked away.

He watched as she went into the courtyard of her home while the gate swung shut behind her, and then he turned in the direction of his own place. He didn't look back again.

It would do no good to allow his thoughts to stray her way after this. He and Dinah came from different cultures. The incompatibility of their beliefs would ultimately cause heartbreak for them both. It was best to leave well enough alone.

*****

Achsah closed the gate behind them as she and Sapphira set out on the path on the way to town. She turned when she spotted Sheerah walking toward them.

"Achsah! Sapphira! It's wonderful to see you both." Sheerah was coming back from the markets. She swung a basket of figs on her arm.

Sapphira stopped and waited with Achsah.

Sheerah smiled. "You're on your way to town?"

"We're going to see Basemath and her sisters." Achsah nodded.

"Oh! I was with Anah."

Achsah's brow rose a notch. "We'll be spending time there, but not with that desert shrub. I intend to enjoy myself."

"Achsah." Sheerah's cheeks colored. You mustn't say such things. Anah's a good woman. She's been a friend to me as much as you've been."

Sapphira moved closer. "The other sister?"

"Yes." Achsah frowned. "The one Basemath and the others have little to do with."

Sheerah's eyes widened. She gave Achsah a chiding look. "I'd be careful which of those sisters you spend your time with. They've been unkind to her. Reuben would say it's wrong. You should consider this, Sapphira, and look to the Lord for wisdom."

Sapphira turned away and looked at the ground.

Achsah shrugged. "Why do you care, Sheerah? You and I are not Israelites."

"It's true, we're not." Sheerah's cheeks colored. "But Adonai cares for the Moabite people too, even though he's chosen the Israelites to represent him. They're to keep his statutes as a witness to others."

Achsah gave her an odd look. Then she laughed aloud. "Toi and Benaiah? Ha! These are who he's chosen for his purpose?" Her eyes sparkled as she spoke. "I'd be no better off following them as I would Basemath."

Sheerah sighed. "You'd do well to follow Ruth, or Kezia, or Toi's parents, who attempt to faithfully carry out what Adonai's purposed them to do."

"And you believe this?"

Sheerah nodded. "Reuben's revealed many things to me. You should consider Adonai in your heart."

Achsah studied Sheerah more closely. It seemed her friend *had* accepted the Israelite God. Achsah wondered how any Moabitess could speak with such conviction. Ruth had done the same.

She smoothed her fingers along the folds of her tunic and turned to look toward the town. "Our Moabite gods are sufficient for my needs." She motioned to Sapphira. "Come, sister. Basemath told me that they'll have dancing. I wouldn't wish to be late for it."

Sapphira turned to Sheerah. "I apologize, but we must be on our way. Maybe another day Achsah and I will have more time to talk."

Sheerah smiled warmly. "Yes, we will. You're both invited to come to our house. Mother and father would be happy to see you again." She put her hand on Achsah's arm. "I miss you. You haven't visited for some time."

Achsah nodded. She fidgeted with her hands. "I miss you too, Sheerah. I'll come again when I can." She took hold of Sapphira's arm. "It's unfortunate we can't talk longer, but our time is limited, and we must be on our way."

Sapphira watched as Sheerah turned to go.

Sheerah looked back once and smiled. "Peace to you both."

"Peace, Sheerah." Sapphira smiled back.

Achsah tipped her head. "Yes Peace, Sheerah."

Achsah and Sapphira left down the path to find their way to the market and then to see Basemath.

Achsah looked up. At least the sun was above them. There were many things they still needed to do.

*****

Ruth entered her home as she closed the door behind her. Her husband and his brother were still coughing. Their sickness had gotten worse. Mahlon's face was a pale color, and he appeared as if he'd lost weight. Ruth hadn't noticed this before, but the sunken look around his eyes was deeper.

"I brought special oils from Hannah's. She told me to boil them in a pot over the fire. They're supposed to help with breathing ailments."

Naomi's face looked strained.

She took the container from Ruth's hands and set it on the table. "I'll start the water to boil. Maybe this will help them."

"Don't worry, mother. Adonai will care for us in his way."

Ruth went to Mahlon and put her hand on his forehead. "Lie back down." She pulled a warm coverlet over him. "We must do something for this."

He smiled at her. "Ruth?" Between coughs he spoke softly.

"What is it, Mahlon?" Ruth leaned closer.

Mahlon's eyes softened. "Before I sleep again, I would like you to continue to think on the things I taught you."

"About the Lord?"

Mahlon coughed again. He nodded. "Yes."

"Adonai is my foremost thought. I can no longer breathe without his presence in my life." She smoothed back the hair on his forehead. "Have no fear. Your family's my own."

He looked at her tenderly. "I can rest easily knowing this. Adonai's good."

"He is."

Orpah was sitting on a bench by the fire. Her eyes were dull and lifeless as she stared into the flames.

Ruth sat beside her. She took Orpah's hand in hers. "All will be well. You'll see. Mother's fixing an oil for them both. They'll get better soon."

Orpah squeezed Ruth's hand. "You're a kind sister. I take heart in your words. I'm glad to have you in my family."

"And I you." Ruth sat quietly and breathed in the pungent scent which permeated the air as Naomi added drops of oil to the boiling water.

A soothing smell calmed her as she inhaled deeply. Maybe things would be better soon in their household.

*****

Time slipped away from Achsah and Sapphira. Dusk was closing in on them as they made their way back home from Basemath's. Time in town had been well spent with music, dancing, and laughter. It would soon be time to retire for the evening.

Sapphira raised her chalice in the air as she looked off into the sunset from the road where she and Achsah walked.

She giggled when she spilled some of the contents of her cup onto the road. She'd certainly had enough to drink. She supposed she should have eaten more. She observed the sun which had lowered in the sky. "Let's take a different path. There's a rocky ridge that leads to our home. It's faster. It's a climb, but once we're over the rise, the house is just on the other side. It takes longer to go by the road."

Achsah smiled. "We should, if it's shorter? It would be an adventure."

"Come with me." Sapphira took Achsah's hand and led her off the pathway to climb the rocky hillside. "I know the way."

Achsah's face lit at the prospect of the climb and at the fact that she was learning a faster way home. She followed behind.

*****

Benaiah stormed into Achsah's friends' home. He planned to have words with these women who wreaked havoc in his sister's life. He'd asked questions around town and found out where his sister and Achsah had spent most of their time.

It was getting late. The others were still feasting and dancing in their absence. Music and laughter came from inside. Sapphira and Achsah had most likely gone home.

He looked around the courtyard as he moved through it. He stopped occasionally to ask questions. Where was Merab, Basemath, and Maacah? These were the names he'd heard most often.

He went to the front door of the house. It was open.

Jeuz, one of the Moabite men, he'd met earlier, came to greet him. "Benaiah, someone said you wanted to talk to Achsah's friends?"

"You know them?"

"They're at that corner table, in there."

Jeuz pointed to three women just inside the doorway. They were seated on mats as they lifted their cups in a toast. They all laughed.

Benaiah nodded. "Thank you. There are things I must say to them. I'll talk to you another time."

He made his way to the back of the room where the women sat. He stood next to the table.

The women stopped talking and looked up. They stared at him curious.

Basemath's heavily kohl-lined eyes were dark and large. They sparkled with delight as they moved over the length of him. "Ah, what have we here, a handsome Israelite who's come to see us?"

She put her cup of wine on the table. "You must be Sapphira's brother. I wondered when one of you would pay us a visit."

The other women giggled as they watched him.

"And you're Basemath?"

She lifted her chalice to him and nodded. "Would you like some wine?" Her voice was soft and inviting.

His eyes darkened. "I want only one thing from you."

She looked interested. "And what is that?"

"That you'll have no more to do with my sister. And I mean what I say. Do you understand?" His mouth was set in a grim line as his presence filled the room.

Merab gave him a sharp look. "She was here earlier. Sapphira said your mother was waiting for her. She and Achsah left to go home." She smiled at her friends.

The other two women giggled again.

Basemath shrugged. "Your sister does as she pleases. If she shows up at our gate, we won't turn her away."

Benaiah's voice took on a dangerous tone. "You won't see her again." His eyes darkened. "And you'll listen to what I have to say. With what I tell you, you might change your mind."

"Ha!" Basemath laughed. "You have no say here. You're in my home." She played with the bracelets on her wrist as if his words were meaningless to her.

"You might think differently when you know what's at stake." He scowled.

Basemath shrugged. "I might, but you must tell me what you came here to say first."

Benaiah reached up and straightened the collar of his robe. "Your father does business with my family, I believe."

"I've seen your father at my home before. It's true that he and my family have a connection in this way."

"And I believe you've prospered since we've come." Isn't this correct?" He gave her a confident smile. "The past year has been better for you. Your food is plentiful, and you have many things."

Basemath shifted in her seat. "Your father's been generous, with the livestock he brought from Bethlehem, and he's harvested large amounts of grain in the short time he's been here. He seems to understand how to work the land to get the most out of it."

Benaiah smiled. "It's true. And I don't believe your father would appreciate it if we severed our business connections with him." He crossed his arms.

The smile on Basemath's face turned downward. "What are you saying?"

"I want you to tell my sister to leave when she comes to visit next time. She's not welcome here, and neither is Achsah. Is this clear to you?"

The women looked at each other.

"I don't need to listen to your ridiculous threats." Merab lifted her cup to her mouth and took a drink. She turned to her sisters. "Tell him it doesn't matter whether they visit us or not."

The other sisters didn't say anything.

Basemath's eyes narrowed. She frowned at Benaiah. "They don't need to come here as far as I'm concerned. Achsah thinks a little highly of herself anyway. I'm tired of her flaunting her jewels and clothing in front of me. They won't be missed."

"We had more fun before they came." Maacah agreed. "And Sapphira's like a shadow. She follows Achsah around like a little goat with its mother. She wants to be a woman of this land, but we all know it isn't possible."

"Then I need not say more. I wouldn't wish it on anyone to be a Moabite."

Benaiah gave them a satisfied look. "I'll leave you to your fun, and my father will continue to do business with yours, as long as you keep to the agreement."

Basemath shrugged. "I can live with this."

The women didn't say anymore but turned away. They laughed between them.

Benaiah scowled. He was astonished that Sapphira had spent time in a place like this with these women.

Achsah had introduced their carved images to his sister, and also to her Moabite friends. No wonder Sapphira had been led so far away from what she believed. They spent their time and energy on their pleasures, rather than on things that mattered.

He stalked out of the house and into the courtyard.

Those who had been outside had moved into the house. Storm clouds approached.

Benaiah quickly strode past a well in the shadows. He was staring at the ground as he walked and thinking about his sister and Achsah, the ungodly Moabite woman Toi had brought into their home. He wasn't happy with either of them at this moment.

When he looked up, he didn't have time to react when another young woman stepped into his path. He knocked her to the ground unwittingly as water from her pitcher spilled out onto the path in front of him.

He immediately got down beside her. He reached out apologetically. "I'm sorry, I didn't see you."

The woman turned suddenly. Her large, dark eyes met his with a surprised expression. Then she quickly looked down as her rose-colored cheeks brightened. She lifted her pitcher so that it was upright.

Benaiah drew in a breath.

The woman was captivating. In the brief moment she'd turned to him, he was struck with her beauty. Her thick eyelashes rested against her sun-browned cheeks, and when she looked up at him with her huge eyes, she was the picture of innocence. She wore no dark lines of makeup, or any rouge on her cheeks, but she possessed a natural beauty instead. Her dark, unbraided hair fell in thick waves over her shoulders.

He couldn't deny his attraction to her. "I'm sorry. Here, I'll refill your pitcher." He took the container from her and brought it to the well.

He set it down when he realized he'd left her there. He should have checked to see whether he'd hurt her or not. He went back. He was embarrassed by his jumbled thoughts.

"I should have helped you first. Are you injured?"

He reached down to take her arm, and he lifted her to her feet. She smelled of myrrh and cloves. He leaned closer and drank in her sweet scent.

She moved back as if suddenly alarmed. Her voice was soft. "I can fill it myself. There's no need for you to do it." She gave him a wary look.

Benaiah couldn't take his eyes from her. She was nothing like the others here. He wondered what she was doing at the gathering.

When she reached to retrieve the vessel, he quickly took it back into his hands and held it from her. "I caused you to spill it. I'll draw more water for it."

She blushed at the way he was looking at her. She didn't answer him, but she waited as he went to the well and pulled the rope from inside it.

He didn't take his eyes from her as he worked.

He was intrigued by the simple style of her clothing which clung to her natural curves and enhanced her beauty. Her ankles and neck were unadorned. Only one pretty bracelet encircled her wrist.

Despite her modest restraint in her clothing and jewelry, she was none the less beautiful. Her skin was a flawless, dark tone, and her features seemed near perfect. Her cheeks had a natural rosiness to them. In his eyes, he'd never seen a woman so lovely.

"Are you a servant?"

She put her hand to her mouth and giggled. Her eyes shone as she looked at him.

Though she was shy, he noticed that there was also a playful side to her. He was intrigued by this and wondered who she was.

He continued to pull on the ropes at the well and draw the water out. "What are you doing here? Are you a friend of someone in the home?"

She shook her head. "No." She began to fidget with her hands which were clasped in front of her.

His curiosity was even more aroused as he watched her. "Please, I'd like to know."

She cleared her throat and watched as he drew the container out of the well and over the side. "I'm a daughter."

"Of the house?"

She nodded. "Yes."

"But this is where Basemath lives. It's her father's home." Her answer puzzled him. The music and laughter, coming from inside the place, suddenly seemed louder.

She brushed her hands on her tunic and played with the ties on it. "Basemath's my sister. I'm Anah."

Benaiah stared at the young woman. He set the container of water on the edge of the well. "But she's a Moabitess." His brow drew inward as he turned to look at her more closely. "Your father's Moabite?"

A knowing look came into her eyes as she studied him. She lifted her chin higher and moved closer to take the container from him. She nodded.

Benaiah ran his fingers through his hair with a puzzled frown. "But, you can't be? Your people are detesta..." He looked upward and groaned. "But, how can this be?"

She sighed as she watched him. "I can take the water jar now." She reached for the container and rested it on her hip. She turned to leave. "My father will be waiting for me. I must go."

As she made her way across the courtyard, Benaiah stood there in shocked silence as he watched her.

A Moabitess? Surely it wasn't possible. In his eyes, the Moabite women were far beneath any women he'd known. They were despicable worshippers of Chemosh. They were uncultured, strange foreigners. Her people were unchaste, immodest, and rude. No good thing ever came from them.

She stopped and turned back to see if he'd left. She didn't say anything but waited at the door as she watched him.

Benaiah immediately regretted his words when he noticed the hurt expression on the young woman's face. As much as he despised the women in the land, and their customs, it bothered him that he'd had injured this one with his unkind words.

Moabitess, or not, he couldn't deny that he was drawn to her beauty. Her cheeks were still pink, and she appeared modest and very sweet.

The woman held the water jug next to her side. She looked at him expectantly, though she made no move to come closer.

Benaiah backed away. The longer he stood there, the less comfortable he felt. He let out a breath in frustration, and then he turned and unlatched the gate to go out.

She was a foreign woman. He could have nothing to do with her. It was better to walk away and not see her again. Anything else would lead to his downfall.

He shook his head at the twist he felt in his heart as he got on his donkey and rode away in the direction of his home. He only wished he would not have set eyes on her.

As he took the path, farther down the road, he couldn't seem to erase the woman's gentle, dark eyes from his mind. He kicked the side of his animal and urged it to pick up speed. He needed to leave the vision of the beautiful woman behind.

*****

Achsah laughed loudly while she put one foot directly in front of the other. She was dangerously close to the edge of a cliff. She lifted her arms to balance herself. "What a lovely place, Sapphira! See this!"

Sapphira followed closely with a smile. "I used to come here when I was young. It's a challenge, but walking along the ridge is much quicker."

"And beautiful!" Achsah twirled around as she stood precariously close to the edge. She laughed as she swung her arms out to her sides.

"Watch what you're doing. The rocks are soft there." Sapphira leaned closer to Achsah. She moved over to take Achsah's arm. "Here, let me help."

But, before either of them could respond, Achsah's foot slipped, and she screamed as it went out from under her. "Sapphira!" She began to topple over the edge.

Sapphira tried to take Achsah's hand, but they fell together. Both of them tumbled onto a lower ledge just below them.

Achsah managed to slow their momentum and keep Sapphira from going farther.

They crouched near the edge.

Sapphira put her hand on Achsah's arm. "We might have gone all the way over. Are you hurt?"

"No? Are you injured?" Achsah eyed Sapphira closely.

"Maybe a bruise, but other than that I'm not."

They both looked up.

Achsah's brows drew together. "We can't climb. It's too far. And it's farther to go down." She drummed her fingers on the folds of her tunic and looked out over the horizon. There were storm clouds approaching.

Sapphira took Achsah's hand. "I'm sorry I wanted to come this way. Now, I'm not sure how we'll get back. Toi would remember this path, but I don't know if he'll think of it."

"We better hope he does. We can only be stranded here for so long." Achsah brushed the dust off her skirt and sat up against the side of the rock wall.

"When the storm gets here, we should use that chalice to collect rain water." Sapphira pointed to the bronze cup which she'd dropped onto the ledge. "At least there'll be that."

Achsah pulled at the leather tie on her braid. She readjusted it in the back. "I'm not sure I want to be here, when it comes, or in the wind that will be with it." She stared at the place in which they'd fallen from. "If it were a tiny bit closer, we could climb up there, but there is nothing in the rock to put our feet in."

Sapphira took a loose stone in her hand. "We might chip away at the face to make some footholds."

"We might." Achsah eyed the jagged rock in Sapphira's hand, and then she looked at the side of the cliff. "I suppose there's nothing else we can do, at least for now."

"It's true, and if Toi comes, we'll have places to step into so he might help us out of this." She chipped away at a place with a natural groove in the wall. She blew on the dust as she made progress.

Both women took turns working on the rock face while the storm rumbled in the distance.

*****

"Where's Achsah and Sapphira?" Hannah spoke quietly as she looked beyond the gate of the house. Dark clouds rolled in while a hot wind stirred up dust in the courtyard. "I thought they'd be back by now."

Toi shrugged. "I haven't seen them. They might have decided to stay at their friend's home until the storm passed."

"Sapphira told me she'd help with dinner." Hannah gave him an odd look.

"They aren't here?" Benaiah frowned. "Her friends told me they'd left the gathering some time ago to walk back to the house. I didn't pass them on the road. I assumed they were on the roof, or out back."

"You went to her friends?" Kezia stared at him. "What were you doing there?"

Benaiah scowled. "Looking for them, and making sure they'd never go there again."

"Never?"

"It's what I said."

Kezia put her hand on her chest. "You spoke with the women there?"

"I did, and they'll stay away from Sapphira and Achsah, if they know what's good for them."

Kezia breathed a sigh of relief. "Adonai's answered my prayers. Oh Benaiah, you're a good brother."

212

"Good brother?" When he thought of Anah, the Moabitess he'd met, and the thoughts that had run through his mind concerning her, he gave a sardonic laugh. "At least for ending their business there, I am."

Jorah eyed him curiously as if something were amiss.

Toi moved closer. He looked up as rain fell, and lightning crackled. He considered the darkening plains. Dust was stirring in wisps. "It seems we can do nothing until this passes. We should move into the house until then."

Benaiah and Hannah nodded, and the four of them made their way inside.

Toi stood at the window and looked out as the sky turned dark. "I can't imagine where they might be. They'll have some explaining to do." He raked his hand through his hair as he watched the rain coming down. "We'll look for them after the storm breaks."

*****

Dark clouds had thickened over the expanse of the valley, and the wind lashed against the rocks where Achsah and Sapphira were. A cold rain came heavily down upon them.

The water droplets turned into small pellets as the wind grew even stronger, and the sky around them disappeared into a torrent of blackness.

Both young women huddled together against the side of the cliff. They wrapped their scarves around them as lightning crashed loudly. Thunder echoed with earsplitting drumfire on all sides of them.

Sapphira drew in a breath. Achsah's gods were not with them. There were no household idols, to speak to, or pray to, and she'd turned from Adonai. She wondered if he'd even listen to her after having strayed so far from him.

The roaring of the wind hadn't slowed, and the sky turned darker still. The valley below had become a black mass of rain. Lightning struck, and thunder rattled the ledge on which they sat.

They both jumped when vibrations ran through the ground beneath the rocks.

Sapphira huddled closer to Achsah as she gulped back a sob. "Adonai, great Maker of the universe, bring us through this storm. Shield us from the winds, and ease our troubled hearts."

Achsah took Sapphira's hand. "It will stop soon. It will blow over."

Something told Sapphira that Achsah seemed less sure than she pretended. Achsah trembled, and there was a catch in her voice as she spoke.

They both crouched closer to the side of the cliff.

Sapphira squeezed Achsah's hand as they waited and watched the storm move slowly across the plains. Darkness surrounded them as flashes of light continued in rapid succession above them.

It seemed as if time stood still before the wind finally died, and the sounds of rumbling grew farther from the lightning strikes. The bent grasses, in the valley, settled to a still whisper as sunlight suddenly spilled out of an opening in the clouds, and the rain slowed to a drizzle.

When the last drops of rain ended, and the clouds formed a line, in the distance, both young women sat up and looked around. They eyed the retreating storm and shivered from the blackness of it.

Sapphira breathed a sigh of relief. Adonai had listened to her, despite her sins against him.

She bowed again and began to pray when she realized it might be a while before they were found. Would Adonai answer one more prayer and lead Toi to them? Did the Lord see that she was contrite of heart and ready to return to him?

*****

Achsah sat up. She wrung out her wet hair. The storm had disappeared into the distance. She looked down at her dripping clothing as she eyed the large desert sun which was

214

slipping farther across the sky. It wouldn't be long before night set in.

"Come, we'll start chipping away at the rock again. You've made one foothold. We need at least one farther up." She took the rock in her hand and pounded against the partially dented surface. "We're making progress."

"Will you climb it, if we finish? We're very high."

Achsah glanced at the top. She eyed it warily. "I'll try, and then I'll get Toi to come back here. Otherwise, we'll never get out of this place."

Sapphira looked relieved. She took the stone from Achsah. "Here, I'll do it." She struck the rock against the side of the cliff as she knocked out a large piece of the crevice. "It's bigger. It might be large enough now."

Achsah suddenly stood when she heard a noise in the distance. "Wait." She put out her hand.

Sapphira quit working and sat quietly listening as she turned her head upward. "I hear it too."

*****

Toi and Benaiah turned to each other. They reined in the donkeys they rode along the top of the ridge.

Toi spoke softly. "Hear that? Those sounds?"

Benaiah nodded. "Sapphira used to come this way. Maybe it's them."

*****

Achsah and Sapphira both called out. "Over here! This way!"

The voices and the clomp of donkeys grew louder. It wasn't long before Toi and Benaiah came into view.

When the two brothers reached the ridge where Achsah and Sapphira had fallen over, Toi looked down. "How in Moab?"

"You found us! Achsah! It's them!" Sapphira called out excitedly.

Benaiah stared at them reproachfully. "They're lucky we knew where to find them." He pulled on the reins of the donkey and got down.

Toi did the same. He looked concerned. "You're not hurt?"

"No, it wasn't far, but we couldn't climb it. I was hoping you'd remember this path." Sapphira shook her head.

Achsah wiped at the dirt on her face and smoothed out her wet tunic. She played with the spangles on her wrists as she looked at them. Her dark brown hair was in tangles down her back.

Toi studied her. A smile formed on his face, and he suddenly laughed. He turned to his brother. "They look like a couple of drowned wolf pups."

Benaiah couldn't help but smile.

Achsah's brow arched. "You'd look this way too, if you went through what we did. It couldn't be helped." She crossed her arms over her chest. "And we have little time for talk if we want to be home before dark."

Toi's eyes sparkled as he spoke. "You believe you deserve our help after the trouble you caused? Maybe we should leave you here." He laughed again.

Sapphira wrinkled her nose. "You shouldn't make light of this, Toi. It's not funny."

"Maybe a night here would do them good." Benaiah grunted.

Achsah lifted her foot into the first groove and reached for the next one. "I'm not staying here. I can climb, with, or without either of your help. The footholds are all I need."

Toi let out a breath. "Hold on. Wait, or you'll hurt yourself."

Achsah wiped more dirt from her face. She didn't answer.

216

Toi looked down and eyed the grooves in the cliff wall. "It appears you've been busy." He got down at the edge of the cliff face and lowered his hand over the wall. "Here, step into the first notch and take hold of my hand."

Achsah gave him a wary look as she turned to the face of the wall. She put her foot into the crevice while Sapphira steadied her from behind. Achsah grabbed hold of Toi's hand with both of his and took steps upward.

"Here." Toi gave a tug, and he pulled her over the top beside him.

She crawled away from the edge and moved aside. She brushed herself off. "I thought you'd never come."

"You're lucky we did. You could have been here for some time. We might never had found you."

He leaned down to offer a hand to his sister. "Here, Sapphira, grab hold."

He helped his sister over the ledge.

She looked somewhat shaken as she crawled beside Achsah. She studied both her brothers. "I was so afraid. I'm glad you came."

Toi smiled. "I'm glad we did, too."

Achsah got up. She raked her fingers through the strands of her disheveled hair. When she found it too difficult to separate the pieces, she put her hands to her side. She let out an agitated breath. "I want to bathe and get out of these clothes."

She began walking down the road, but she was surprised when Toi came beside her and took her hand.

"Here." He lifted her onto the donkey. He started leading it down the path. "Rest now. I'm glad neither of you were hurt."

Achsah looked at him, but she didn't say anything.

"Hold on so you don't fall." Toi steadied the donkey with the leather reins.

She held to the donkey's mane as he led the animal along the top of the ridge. Sapphira followed on her brother's donkey.

*****

As they neared the courtyard, Toi looked back at Achsah. Her hair was still damp, and darkened tendrils lay in wild disarray over her shoulders. She was shivering, and her lips were less rosy than usual. There were smudges of dirt on her cheeks, and her tunic was clinging against her skin.

How had she managed to do so much damage in one afternoon, he'd not a clue. He smiled.

Yet, despite her ragged, rain-lashed appearance, disheveled hair, and rumpled shawl, held tightly in her hand, he couldn't help but feel a great sense of admiration for her.

Aside from all the difficulties she'd faced, her head was still held high, and her shoulders were straight. Her emerald eyes were watchful and determined. She didn't seem to allow any situation around her to cause her to falter.

He smiled. It seemed he'd chosen a wife he could appreciate for more than her physical beauty. Her strength of mind, and character, her strong fortitude, and willfulness were also admirable qualities.

He reached out and fingered the spangle which dangled from her ankle. It appeared that she'd added a new piece of jewelry to her collection.

When his hand brushed against her skin, Achsah moved her foot as a wary look entered her dark eyes.

He looked up at the uncertain expression on her face. He assumed by now she might have begun to trust him, yet the apprehension in her had not seemed to have lessened much since they'd married.

Though he'd certainly softened toward Achsah, since he'd brought her to his home, she seemed less inclined to do the same for him. He'd seen glimpses of a tender heart, yet for the most part, it was rare and protected.

He let go, and then he tugged on the reins of the donkey. The animal's stride widened as they neared the entrance to their home.

As he looked back at her again, he wondered what their marriage would be like if she ever willingly opened her heart to him and brought down the walls she put up to protect herself. He supposed, if she did, it would be more difficult for him to remain distant with his own feelings, and wasn't sure if he truly wanted to allow her this much.

*****

Chapter 10

"Tell Benaiah to go back and undo what he's done. None of my friends will talk to us. I've been to their homes, and they won't see me." Achsah's cheeks reddened. Her fist was clenched to her side as she looked up at Toi. "Tell him he can't do this to us."

Toi brushed off the side of his donkey. He turned to her. "Sapphira doesn't need to be exposed to the poor influences you've introduced her to. She's young, and mother doesn't approve of such things. Maybe it would be good for the two of you to turn your thoughts to things at home for a while."

"You can't be serious?" She gave his arm a tug.

Toi frowned. "You do as you please, but Sapphira isn't free to do as she wishes. Father has put an end to her trips to town. I won't come between him and her. This decision stands, so I won't be speaking to your friends."

Then he looked at her and laughed. "What will you do without your social outings? How will you survive?" He watched for her reaction. "You won't be able to stand a day at the house without going somewhere."

Achsah's eyes narrowed. She let go of his arm. "I can go, or stay. There's no reason for that look on your face. I've been doing chores here also."

Toi shrugged and eyed her lazily. "We'll see. I only hope you don't cause more trouble for mother than is necessary."

"I'm certain your mother won't have any difficulty with me." Achsah laughed to herself. "Having raised you, I'd consider any dealings I have with her would be easy for her."

She turned and walked away. She left him standing at the gate. Let him think what he might. She could have fun without her friends. There were other things she could set her mind to here. It mattered little where she spent her time. This place would be as good as any.

*****

Benaiah stood outside the gateway of Basemath's father's home. He waited for Jabin to come into the courtyard. One of the servants went inside to get him.

He tapped his fingers against the stone wall he was leaning against. He had business to attend and planned to do what was needed and be on his way.

From a distance, he eyed the door as it opened. Jabin wouldn't have seen him from the courtyard, where he stood, so he opened the gate to go in. But, he suddenly stopped when he realized it was Anah who came out instead.

Anah didn't look at the gate, but she made her way to the goats, who bayed in a pen, near the courtyard. She was barefoot and dressed simply. Her hair was unbound. It fell in thick, dark waves down her back.

Benaiah let out a low gasp. The woman was beautiful. She wore a simple tunic, and her face was freshly washed. Her dark skin and large brown eyes complemented her dusty, lavender tunic. He couldn't take his eyes from her.

She approached the door that led into the pen and smiled as she called each goat by their name while she fed them. She giggled as they pushed against her.

She was so at ease with the animals.

Benaiah was intrigued by the way they responded to her. He couldn't help but marvel at her gentle voice. It was hardly above a whisper. Her manner was, as before, kind and thoughtful.

He turned when he heard the door open.

"Anah! What are you doing in that filthy pen again? You must leave those goats alone!"

Anah pushed her hair over her shoulder and went to the gate. She let herself into the courtyard from the adjoining pen. Closing the door of the small enclosure, she ran to her father with a smile. "I'm sorry, papa, but they were hungry. I heard them crying."

He shook his head, and he wagged a finger at her. His eyes crinkled at the corners. "For this we have servants. You should be inside with Basemath and the others." He looked down at her bare feet. "What am I to do with you, my youngest daughter?"

She kissed his cheek and took his hands in hers. "I'll try harder, papa. I'll put on my sandals. But you cannot ask me to allow my goats to go without full bellies." She smiled at him again.

Jabin turned to see Benaiah standing at the gate. "Ah, I almost forgot. Benaiah! How good it is you've come!"

Anah's eyes widened when she saw Benaiah, and she quickly looked at the ground. Her cheeks reddened. She spoke softly to her father. "I'll go find Basemath, but I want to walk the goats later." She let go of his hand.

"I've business to tend to, so I'll speak with you another time. I'm glad you'll be with your sister."

She stepped back inside the house and didn't look back.

Benaiah stared at the closed door.

Something turned inside him at her hasty exit. He wished he'd treated her better the last time he'd seen her. For a reason he couldn't understand, the young woman had made an impression on him he hadn't been able to forget.

Since the day he'd spoken with Basemath, and her friends, he'd thought of Anah more often than not. He'd tried to forget her, but it had been to no avail. Everything about the young woman was as fresh, in his mind, as the first day he'd laid eyes on her.

He'd imagined the scent of spices that had surrounded her, and he thought of her sweet voice, which was gentle and soft. Her rosy cheeks were natural, and there was a quiet grace about the way in which she carried herself. He'd revisited his musings of her more times than he'd care to admit.

Yet, Anah was Basemath's sister. How could he allow his feelings for a Moabite woman to have been swayed in such a way? How was it possible?

222

"Benaiah?"

Jabin patted him on the shoulder. "My daughter's pretty, isn't she?" He eyed Benaiah keenly.

Benaiah directed his attention back to Jabin.

"Anah." Jabin smiled.

"I'm sure she's captured more than one man's attention." Benaiah's brow rose above his eyes. "But, it's not why I've come. I'm here to talk business."

Jabin nodded while he put out his arm to sweep it ahead of him. "Then, you must come into my home to talk. My wife has food and drink. We've much to discuss."

Benaiah walked with Jabin into the house.

Jabin took him to a low table in the largest room where they sat down. Servants immediately brought them platters of choice food. Their goblets were filled.

Benaiah looked across the room to where Jabin's daughters and wife sat. The women worked on pieces of cloth.

Anah refused to look at him. She was intent on her work with her head bowed. She had a look of reservation on her face, and her eyes were solemn and dark.

She turned to her mother. "May I go take the goats out to the field? They've been penned for two days."

Benaiah listened to both Jabin and to what the women said at the same time. He couldn't help being intrigued by Anah. She was so different from the rest of her family.

Basemath let out an annoyed sound. "She shouldn't take those dirty things anywhere. Tell her no, mother. She should stay and help us."

"Anah can do as she pleases, Basemath. We've never dissuaded you from doing the things that interest you. Anah doesn't enjoy the same things. Let her be."

Basemath's mother patted Anah's arm. "You may, but stay in the field out back. Go no further."

Anah smiled wide. "Oh, thank you! They've been waiting."

Basemath wrinkled her nose. She went back to her work as she shook her head with a look of disgust. Then turning, she gave Benaiah a haughty look.

Benaiah frowned.

Anah got up and smoothed out her tunic. She didn't look to where Benaiah and her father were, but she took quick steps to the door and went out.

Benaiah turned back to Jabin, yet the man's words settled in the back of his mind as he listened and nodded. He couldn't get the image of Anah out of his thoughts.

When Jabin finished talking, Benaiah nodded. He finished the discussion, then got up, and made his way to the door. He looked out and eyed the trail that Anah had taken.

Jabin put his hand on Benaiah's arm. "I'm glad we made plans. I can see we'll do a great business with each other."

Benaiah nodded. "Yes, I look forward to return visits."

*****

Kezia spoke quietly as she stitched the cloth evenly and in a straight path. "This is for Benaiah. I believe he'll be pleased."

Achsah rolled her eyes. "I'm sure he has enough robes. I could think of better things to do."

Sapphira lowered her head and quietly worked.

Kezia looked up. "He hasn't been kind to you. I'm sorry my brother's treated you the way he has." There was a gentle expression in her eyes.

"He can do what he wants." Achsah shrugged. "I won't ever please him, and have no desire to."

Kezia hadn't taken her eyes from Achsah. She spoke softly. "You're not so hardhearted, Achsah, as you would have us believe. You're distrustful, but not unfeeling."

Achsah didn't say anything. Toi had said the same thing once. She reached out and took two lengths of fabric from the basket and began to stitch the sides together.

"It's not what we do, but who we are in our hearts that matters." Kezia rested her work in her lap and looked up. "It's our inner thoughts and motivations that Adonai sees. He knows when we're truthful and whether we put others before ourselves. He knows why we do what we do."

Achsah kept making neat, even stitches without speaking.

"You are kind, Achsah. I've seen it. I'm certain Toi knows this too. And you have a lively spirit, which is why I believe my brother wanted to marry you. When you're in a room, you bring color to it, and the music follows you."

Achsah looked up. A frown drew over her eyes. "But, you don't like those things. You wanted Sapphira and me to stay home. We danced and laughed with our friends. Now we make tunics at home."

"Who you are goes with you." Kezia smiled. "There's color in this room as we speak. Adonai's blessed you, Achsah. He's created you for a purpose. I'm certain he's chosen you when he brought you to our family."

Achsah tipped her head to the side. "Chosen? Ha! The Israelite God? He couldn't possibly choose me." She laughed. "I've been trouble since my birth. My family has as much as cast me out. I've been a burden to them. How could this Lord choose someone such as myself?"

"Achsah, you must not doubt what I say. Adonai searches the hearts of man and has seen how you've been downtrodden and rejected. You are what he wants so much for his own. He loves the brokenhearted above all else. Because of your difficulties, you'll love him all the more when you see what he's done for you."

Achsah's brow lifted. "I've done wrong things."

"Maybe not so wrong. But, that you are willing to admit to your faults and are repentant of them is what matters to Adonai. Those who blame and condemn, and are unwilling to see their own faults, or do not wish to, should be more fearful. He loves us all, though he will exact his judgment upon unrepentant sinners. He is just."

Achsah put the cloth she was working on in her lap. "You speak of your Lord as if he were here." She looked around as the shadows in the room deepened. She shivered.

Kezia's dark eyes shone with warmth. "Adonai's all, and he's with us wherever we are. He's not an idol made with human hands."

"This God, you speak of, is in this room? Even though he's unseen?"

"We walk, not by what we see, but by faith. With him, there is no need for a carved image or the conjuring up of visions of him. Our vain imaginings could never begin to discern the hidden things of Adonai. We can take comfort and faith in the fact that his presence is with us."

Achsah picked the woven cloth back up in her hands. Her breath was soft, but slightly uneven, as she worked the stitches into the fabric. "He's very strange and difficult to understand. He's unsettling."

Kezia nodded. "He shakes the Earth and brings down mountains. He's powerful, but just. It's right to fear him and good to humble yourself before him."

Achsah put up her hand.

"Achsah?"

Achsah shook her head back and forth. Something inside her made her feel very afraid. "I'm not certain I wish to hear more. Please, let's speak of lighter things and keep our thoughts on our work."

Kezia and Sapphira both looked up. There were questions in their eyes as they watched her, but they remained silent.

Then, Kezia smiled. "Look." She pointed at the stitches she'd formed in the shape of pomegranates. "It's the hem of Benaiah's robe. I'm giving him color." She giggled.

Achsah let out a light laugh. "I might weave some stitches into this one also. You can give it to Benaiah, too. He'll need it."

Laughter spilled out among the young women as they went back to their tasks that lay ahead of them.

226

*****

Benaiah waded through the tall grass and moved onto a small trail that led to where Anah walked. Her flock of goats pressed up against her. They vied for a place near her side.

She cooed softly to them. She stopped often to pet each of them on their heads. Her voice was quiet as she spoke. Her loosened hair danced behind her in the light breeze as she walked next to them. She seemed carefree and relaxed.

Benaiah stepped onto the path and studied her with interest. He gathered that she spent much time outdoors by her sun-browned skin and dark, streaked hair. Her gentle, sweet manner with the animals tugged at his heart.

Farther down the path, she turned and stopped when she noticed that he was following her. She waited for him to make his way over the rocky path toward her.

The animals crowded around as they pushed for a space to stand next to her.

Benaiah took long strides to reach her and then stood outside the circle of animals. He smiled as one of the goats wedged its way between her and him.

"Why did you come?" Anah's dark lashes fanned over her rosy cheeks. She lifted her chin.

"That I might see you, and that we might talk."

"You wish to speak to a daughter of a Moabite?"

Benaiah shrugged. "If you'd call off your goats, I might get closer. I've thought of you often. You are very beautiful."

Anah gave him a disconcerted look. "What do you mean by closer?" She put her hands on her hips.

He laughed. "I only wish to know you better, Anah."

She took a step back. Her voice lowered to a whisper. "You think because I'm Moabite, and my culture is different from yours, that I am willing to give myself readily to you?"

"Anah, I have heard...." Benaiah looked down when a goat shoved against his side and pushed him further away from her. He gave it a cross look and brushed off his robe.

"You're wrong about me as others have been. The Israelite men are much the same."

Benaiah gave her a questioning look. "Others?" His voice was suddenly gruff.

"You know nothing of me, yet you say 'you have heard...' I want nothing to do with you, if your intent is what I believe it is."

Her cheeks reddened. Her dark eyes met his. "I'm sorry, but I must go. I see no reason to call off my goats. I expect to be treated properly, and for men to approach my father for permission to speak to me. Unless I've taken vows, there will be nothing between us. I intend to remain chaste until I'm married."

Benaiah's mouth opened, as he watched her take quick steps from him while the goats moved down the path.

He studied her as he drew in a breath.

She expected him to approach her father? A Moabitess?

He shook his head as his brows drew inward. He'd made it clear, more than once to his family, that he'd never bring home a daughter of Moab.

His eyes trailed after her as she reached the pen where the goats were kept. She locked them in the gate. She looked back in his direction and then turned to the house and went inside.

Benaiah shook his head warily and let out a sound. He gave her an incredulous look. Ha! How could she expect as much as she did? Go to her father to win her affections? What was he to do now? There seemed to be no easy answer.

She could not be as proper as she said she was. There had to be a way. A Moabitess? What was she thinking?

*****

Achsah looked up when Benaiah angrily shoved the gate open in the courtyard.

228

"What's aggravating him?" She sat on a stone step that led to the roof. She was next to Toi.

Toi was sharpening a stone tool.

Achsah moved closer to him.

He leaned down and brushed his lips against her hair.

She wrinkled her nose as she looked up at him. "Your brother has been better, but I'm not so sure now." She turned to stare as Benaiah stalked past.

He gave a grunt when he saw them, and he went into the house.

"Whatever it is, it doesn't seem things went his way today." Toi put down his stone tool and sharpener and got up. "Come." He put out his hand to take hers. "Let's go in. Mother said the meal was ready. There are things I must discuss with Benaiah."

Achsah shrugged. "I'll help your mother while you talk to him. Since I've been all but shunned in the town, I am finding other things to do."

Toi gave her an odd look, and then he laughed. "At least I've seen more of my wife, and you're keeping out of trouble. I haven't had to rescue you in a while."

She took his hand in hers and looked up at him. "Don't think too much on it. Trouble seems to have a way of finding me no matter where I am."

Toi pulled her closer as they went in through the doorway. He leaned down and whispered in her ear. "I don't mind trouble, or you." The tone of his voice was tempered with affection.

Achsah pulled back. She eyed him quizzically. Was he beginning to care for her, or was she only imagining it?

Lately, he had given her that impression. She wasn't sure why. What could he want from her?

As they went through the doorway, he tugged on her skirt and then fingered a piece of her hair. "If you wanted to do something, I could take you to see your parents. It would be a diversion from this home."

Achsah's brow arched above her eyes. She pushed his
hand away. "Visit them? But, I don't ever want to go back."

"They're family, Achsah. I've talked to your father, and
he told me he'd like to see you."

She laughed. "Ha! He's too busy trying to appease his
wives among other things. I have no time to listen to their
arguing and complaints, or to listen to them mock me."

"I'd protect you." He smiled. "You know how much I
love you."

"Oh, stop it." She pushed him away and crossed the room
to where Toi's mother was and took a platter of bread from a table
against the wall.

Toi sat down next to his brother.

Achsah felt her husband's eyes on her as she moved
across the room. She put the bread on the table and took a place
on a stone bench, carved into the wall, close to where Hannah
worked at a low stand. She returned Toi's gaze squarely, and
taking a bowl of grapes in her hands, she pulled off the stems.

Toi gave her a sidelong glance. Then he pointed to where
his heart was and then to her, and he smiled.

Her brow shot up, but then she couldn't keep from smiling
back at his endearing gesture.

He grinned at her, and then he turned to his brother.

Benaiah took a bite out of a piece of bread. He chewed
unceremoniously as he watched them.

Achsah couldn't help noticing that Benaiah had been less
critical of her and Toi lately. It was as if something had triggered
a change in him, and he was attempting to make sense of it.

Surprisingly, as of late, he'd made attempts to speak to
her. She wasn't sure what had happened to him, but he seemed to
regard her differently.

Though still reserved in his nature toward her, quite often
he'd give her a slight nod of assent when he agreed with her. She
still couldn't trust that he had her best interests in mind and was
suspicious of his motives.

230

She sighed and looked down at the grapes she was working on.

What did it matter what he thought and felt? Benaiah meant nothing to her.

She got up after she finished working on the last of the grapes. She took them to the table and placed them next to Toi.

"Thank you, Achsah." Toi smiled at her.

She nodded.

Benaiah didn't say anything but took a couple of the grapes while he observed her closely.

Her eyes narrowed as she looked at him. She backed away from the table and left them to their meal. She had other things to think about and do to occupy her time in a busy household. She'd eat later when the men were finished.

*****

Achsah crept out of her sleeping quarters, early in the morning, determined to catch the first rays of the sun coming over the horizon. She pulled her wrap around her as she stole across the quiet, dark expanse of the courtyard.

She turned and watched when she noticed Kezia sitting on a bench with her head turned upward. Her lips moved. Kezia's eyes were open as she quietly prayed to Adonai. Achsah listened to Kezia's words.

"Bless you, Adonai, for giving me Jair. Allow your will, and not my own, to direct my thoughts. Speak to me, throughout the day, and help me to hear you. Let me feel your presence."

Achsah stopped. "There's no incense or sacrifice. You speak plainly to your God as if you would to a friend."

Kezia turned. "Achsah?"

"Why don't you chant?" Achsah swallowed drily as she looked at Kezia. "Why are your words not directed toward the sun? Or to an idol? Do you see Adonai in your mind?"

Kezia eyed Achsah with a puzzled frown. "I told you before, that he's unseen." She smiled. "How might I do this? Such a thing would be more than I could know."

"By stirring up an image, of your own making, or by picturing him in your mind. Could you not find a way? Then you might have a form to worship."

Kezia shook her head. Her eyes widened. "Oh, no, there's no need for such a thing. He makes his presence known when he wishes it."

Achsah scrunched up her brow. "And if he does not?"

"Then we walk by faith, not by sight, as I said before. I'm assured that he hears when I speak plainly to him."

Achsah frowned. "The Israelite God is very different."

"I told you that he's the one true God and is good." Kezia put her hand on Achsah's arm.

Achsah looked around the courtyard.

The sun was moving over the horizon and shone around them. The day lightened, and the warmth of the morning enveloped them.

She didn't say anything at first. Then she spoke quietly. "I'll leave you to your prayers, and we can speak later."

"Are you sure? I can tell you more about him."

Achsah smoothed out her skirt and let out a long, quiet sigh. "No, I must find Toi and see when he'll be leaving for Shobach's."

Kezia nodded. "I think he went to the goat pen. You might find him there." She smiled and went back to her prayers. Her voice was a whisper as she closed her eyes and bowed her head.

Achsah watched Kezia, for a time, and then she left to find Toi so that he could take her out.

*****

Benaiah stood at the threshold of Jabin's home. He tapped on the door impatiently.

The door opened, and Jabin came out. "Welcome, Benaiah. Come, please take a meal with us."

"No, thank you, but I must speak to you. Could I have a moment?" Benaiah put his hand on Jabin's arm.

Jabin stepped outside. "Yes, tell me why you've come."

Benaiah drew in a breath. He hesitated as he looked toward the door of the house.

"What is it? It cannot be so bad."

Benaiah tugged at the neckline of his shirt. "It's concerning one of your daughters. I want to speak with her, but she isn't willing. I've tried lately, many times, but she won't allow it."

"Basemath? Which one? I've four."

"Basemath?" Benaiah gave Jabin a surprised look. "No, Anah."

Jabin's eyes crinkled at the corners. He chuckled to himself. "Ah, Anah. I see."

"She leaves when she first notices me. I only want to talk to her."

"What has made her dislike you, my friend?"

Benaiah raked his hand through his hair. Frustration edged his voice. "Your daughter is very beautiful, and when I found out she was Moabite, I was disappointed, as I took a great interest in her. As you most certainly know, Israelites are not encouraged to pursue the daughters of this land. I said things I regretted and was immediately sorry for it. Now, I wish to engage myself to her and take her as my wife, but she won't have me."

Jabin gave Benaiah a surprised look. "Engage yourself to her?"

"Yes, she is a modest young woman and an innocent, yet she knows her own mind. I admire her greatly for her strength of spirit."

Jabin leaned forward and studied Benaiah closely. "Then you care for my Anah?"

"Very much, and I want her to know this."

Jabin seemed to be contemplating something as he nodded slowly. "You would be a good match for my daughter. Your family prospers greatly in Moab." He looked down at the money bag attached to his waist and then at Benaiah again. "I'll speak to her, in order that she might talk to you."

"I'd like this." Benaiah let out a sigh.

Jabin chuckled. "My daughters were raised to be self-reliant. Anah makes her own decisions. I cannot say she'll listen to me, but I'll make attempts to convince her. Come back tomorrow. It'll give her time to think things through. She'll be out with the goats at early light."

Benaiah nodded. "Thank you. I'll come back then. I appreciate that you'll talk to her, Jabin."

"I'll do what I can. After that, it's up to her."

"Thank you again. I must go now. I've work to do."

Benaiah went out through the gate and got on his donkey as he turned in the direction of his home. Maybe Anah would see him the following day? He hoped this would prove to be true.

He glanced back at her house, one more time, as the music and laughter of her people, coming from inside, began to stir in the air around him. Jabin had said he would talk to her. He'd seemed pleased with the thought of an engagement. Maybe Anah would change her mind.

He didn't care anymore that their lives were so very different. What could it matter that their customs and beliefs were not the same? Surely Adonai would bend his rules for this one exception. Anah was not like Basemath or her other sisters. She lived to higher standards, and she didn't take part in the things the others did.

He swallowed drily as words from the Torah struck him deep in the recesses of his heart. He knew Adonai's statutes didn't change and that there were no exceptions. What he planned to do was not what he'd been taught. A separation from the people of the land, and their rituals and beliefs, was what their Lord commanded. These commands were put in place to benefit both Anah and himself. Neither would have to contend with each other's differences within their marriage.

Benaiah looked toward the mountains, in the distance. He groaned inwardly. But, Anah? Surely, this woman had struck his heart. The first time he'd seen her, he'd been captured by her beauty, and he had not been able to stop thinking about her.

The heat of the day beat down on him, and he wiped the back of his neck with the sleeve of his robe. He drew in a breath.

How could he not feel and think the way he did? How could Adonai expect him to be obedient when thoughts of Anah had tormented him day and night? What was a man supposed to do?

He dug his heels into the side of the donkey and pushed it to move ahead and race across the plains. He wanted to escape what he knew to be right and true. He didn't want to believe it.

He leaned forward as the donkey kicked up trails of dust behind it. He put his sights on the path ahead and didn't look back again.

He only wanted one thing, that Anah would be his own someday, and that they would live as husband and wife, in spite of the statutes and laws and rules of his people.

*****

Achsah stared into the night sky from the window in her room. Her eyes shifted to the side of the house. Kezia was outside and was climbing the stone steps that led to the roof of their home. Achsah was sure Toi's sister was going there to pray.

The young woman quietly ascended, in the late evening hours, with little or no sound. Achsah wouldn't have known Kezia had done this, had she herself not spent time looking at the stars each evening.

She happened to notice that it was a habit of her Israelite sister to pray at night. It impressed her that prayer was not something Kezia did for show, so others would know, but rather, Kezia made it a private affair between her and Adonai.

Achsah watched as Kezia stepped onto the roof and disappeared from her sight. After having followed her up, the other evening, she'd seen the extent of Kezia's love for Adonai and her faith in him. Kezia hadn't been ritualistic, or repetitive in her prayers, but she'd spoken to Adonai as if he were real, and as if he stood on the roof beside her. What would it be like to know a God, so intimate, yet so powerful? Was such a thing possible?

She shivered as she wrapped her scarf tighter around her. She wondered how this God, Adonai, had created the universe. The expanse of it suddenly seemed too wide and too deep for her to comprehend. She shuddered at the thought.

And why would Adonai have anything to do with her, a Moabitess, who had done so much wrong in her life? Her brow furrowed, and she took a deep breath. Kezia had told her that Adonai was willing to accept her as his own, if she opened her heart to him and his great love. She wondered if it were possible.

When she'd told Kezia about her sorrow over her troubled past, and the things she'd done, Kezia had regarded her with an astonished look.

"Achsah," she'd said. "No one, not even my sweet mother and father, can say they are without a troubled past. No one can say they are free from wrongdoing."

But, Achsah had fretted how Josheb and Hannah had lived a life going to Sabbath and teaching good things to others. They'd been an encouragement to their children and had lived worthy lives.

Kezia had shook her head back and forth. She'd spoken quietly to Achsah, "None of that matters. All have sinned, even those who have spent a lifetime in good works. Even in the heart, or in subtle, sly actions, there's sin. The Lord expects us to be honest and sorrowful for these things. Without this, it's impossible to know him, no matter how well you've lived your life. You're precious to him because you recognize your weakness and are willing to admit that you're sorry for it."

Achsah had looked out over the countryside in bewilderment. She'd questioned Kezia further. "You say that the only thing you need to do is to believe in him? This should not be so difficult."

Kezia's expression had been solemn. "Yes, but remember, to believe is more than to acknowledge that he exists. Father Abraham believed, and it was credited to him as righteousness. His belief was a deep faith. Father Abraham was willing to put his old ways and life behind him and trust the Lord to lead him to unknown territories. He committed himself to Adonai wholeheartedly and it resulted in action. This is the belief that is spoken of."

The things Kezia told Achsah about the Israelite God was puzzling to her. She wondered if such things could be true. Was the Israelite God truly the Maker of the Universe and the One True God? How was Kezia so sure of it? Could he possibly accept a Moabitess, such as her, as his own?

She was not so certain, but the idea was intriguing.

*****

The next morning, Benaiah pushed his way past a long-haired goat on the trail. He attempted to get closer to Anah who was encircled by a flock of nervous animals. "Anah? I know your father spoke with you. I'm sorry if I offended you in any way."

A color rose in Anah's cheeks. She looked away.

Benaiah sighed. "I've no ill designs toward you, truly."

"None?" She turned back. "But, you don't even like the Moabite people. What would you want with me?"

"I do business often with your father. How can you say I don't like your people?"

Her eyes grew larger, and her expression was wary. "Some time ago, I overheard Achsah tell my sister that you said she was a dirty Moabitess and that you pulled her from your donkey. She was hurt badly."

Benaiah let out a breath. There was silence. "You must listen to me, Anah. I wasn't pleased when my brother married

Achsah, and am not sure I'll ever fully understand why he chose her. But I also must tell you something I haven't told Toi, or anyone else. And you must know it." His brow furrowed.

Anah drew in a breath. "I don't want to hear how terrible Achsah is. I can imagine what you're going to say."

"No, I want to be truthful about it. I'm not trying to discredit Achsah." He cleared his throat.

She didn't say anything.

"Truly, I pulled Achsah's tunic so that she'd get down from the donkey, but it didn't happen the way I intended. Achsah is petite, and my strength was more than I expected it to be. I was surprised when she fell and was hurt, but I was too angry to admit it. I shouldn't have done what I did, and I knew it. I've never intentionally hurt any woman before this. I've suffered with the guilt of it, but I've been too proud to admit to the truth. I haven't wronged her since, and I'm sorry for what I did. I know you might not believe this, but I've changed, and I'm willing to make amends."

Her look was one of distrust. "But how can I know your intentions? My papa wants me to see you, but I'm not so sure."

"You trust your father, Anah. I wish I would've done things differently. Your father works with me. He knows my character."

She leaned down to touch one of the goats, and then she pulled her hand back when another one vied for her attention.

"Please, Anah. I'd like to make you my wife. I've asked your father."

She stood up abruptly and put her hands on her hips. Her eyes widened. "Wife? What do you mean? You know nothing of me. How can you say this when we've never spoken? My father allows me to have my own thoughts and make my own decisions."

Benaiah gave her an exasperated look. "I want to know you, but you won't let me. Then, you speak of wrongdoings, yet you've judged me, before you've given me a chance. You don't know me. How is this better?"

"I've judged you for what you've done and how you've treated me."

"But, I'm not as you think. Truly, your father knows it, otherwise he wouldn't have allowed me to speak to you. He trusts that I would treat you well."

Anah lifted her head. A blush set into her cheeks, and her hair slipped into her eyes. She pushed it behind her shoulders.

Benaiah sighed. "Could we meet with your father present? Would you be willing to do this?"

She looked at the goats. She seemed unsure. "I don't understand why my father wants me to talk to you. I don't know why he'd do this."

"He knows me and knows my family. You'd be treated well."

"But, I don't understand. Why would you be interested in me, a Moabitess?"

Benaiah's eyes gentled when he looked at her. "I've been humbled by you. I wish to make amends because of it. If you would meet with me, one time, I might begin to prove this to you."

Anah was quiet. She reached out and pet a goat on the head. She sighed as she looked at him.

"Please, allow me this one chance, Anah. I'm sorry how I treated Achsah. Surely, I'll make efforts to right this wrong. Meet with me, this once, and I'll prove to you that I'm not who you think I am."

She was hesitant to say anything but spoke softly. "For my father, I might meet once, because he believes you to be as you say. I trust him, but am not so sure myself. After that, you must promise me that you won't ask again, if I don't want you to."

He smiled. "I can't promise I won't ask again."

Anah looked up at him. "You say that papa will be present?"

"He said he would. You can ask him."

"Then, I'll meet with you tomorrow, in the morning. But now, you must leave me to finish my task alone. Let me see to my goats. I must get them back to their pen unhindered. Father must be present when I talk to you."

"So, you *will* see me?" Benaiah gave her a surprised look as he backed away from the path.

She nodded and wrapped her scarf over her head. She made a sound to the goats to move them along.

A surge of hope ran through Benaiah as she walked past. He let out a relieved sigh. Tomorrow couldn't come soon enough.

*****

Achsah tipped her head. She eyed Benaiah suspiciously as he walked by her. He was in an unusually jovial mood. He even glanced her way with a smile. She wondered what he was up to.

She took the wooden platter of raisin cakes, to the doorway of the house, after having pulled them from the rounded stone oven in the courtyard.

She turned to Kezia who was also watching her brother. "Where is he going this early? Did you ask him?"

Kezia eyed her brother curiously. "He wouldn't say. He has on his new robe."

Benaiah unlatched the gate to go out. His step was unusually lighter, and his expression seemed to convey a measure of hope.

Achsah tapped her fingers against the side of her tunic. Hmm. He hadn't even told Toi what he'd been doing as of late.

She turned and followed Kezia into the house with her platter of cakes. "Whatever he's up to, he's behaving very strangely. I've never seen him this way. I'm afraid to say it, but he seems almost pleasant to be around."

Kezia took her arm. "Achsah, he hasn't always been the person you've known. Before Toi married, he and his brother were very close. They were both happy when they were together. He was very different and not so unkind."

Her face was pained. "It was difficult for Benaiah to see Toi marry outside our cultural beliefs. I know he misses the comradery he's had with Toi in the past. Unfortunately, he seems to have blamed you for it."

"Well, whatever he's done, and felt, maybe he'll be happier in future days." Achsah shrugged. "I doubt he'll ever care much for me. But I've no great love for him, either."

"I hope in time things will be better for you and him."

"I'm not holding my breath. Things are never that easy."

Kezia sighed. "Maybe, but it's always good to hold out hope."

Achsah took the raisin cakes to the table and laid the platter down. She turned to Kezia. "I suppose we should get the rest of the food. The others will be here soon and will be hungry."

Kezia nodded. "I'm glad for your help. I'm happy to see you home."

"It hasn't been as bad as I thought it would be. I suppose I might get used to it in time."

Kezia smiled. "Maybe you will. It would be a good thing." She brightened. "Jair's taking tomorrow's evening meal with my brothers. He brought me bracelets. He's a good man."

"He is, and I'm glad of it. You deserve someone who treats you well."

"As you do. Toi may not show it, but I believe he's beginning to care for you."

Achsah tipped her head to the side. She looked unsure. "Toi and I have both benefitted from our marriage. It hasn't been without its advantages."

Kezia nodded solemnly. "I pray for you both. I think Toi needs love as much as you do."

Both women went back to the courtyard to finish their work.

*****

Benaiah sat on a bench outside Jabin's house while a servant went inside.

He looked up when Jabin opened the door.

"Ah, Benaiah! You've come." Then Jabin chuckled to himself. "I'm surprised my Anah's agreed to this. She weighs affairs such as this one very carefully, and rarely anyone will be afforded a second chance."

Benaiah turned and looked at the house. "She won't change her mind?"

"She'll be here, if she said she would. She's trustworthy." Jabin smiled. "Look, it's her." He pointed when the door swung open.

Anah came out and ran to her father. She kissed him on the cheek. "Good morning, papa." She didn't look at Benaiah.

"Good morning, Anah. Benaiah's here. I'll be in the adjoining courtyard with the animals."

He turned to Benaiah. "You may speak with my daughter now."

Benaiah nodded. He watched as Anah took a place on the bench. One long braid swung over her shoulder as she leaned forward.

Jabin went through the courtyard and moved to the other side of the gate. He went about his work without looking back.

Benaiah took a place beside Anah. He breathed in her soft scent of myrrh and cloves as he leaned closer. He smiled at her reddened cheeks.

She pointed farther down the bench. "You sit there."

"Anah."

She pointed again. "You told me we'd talk."

"I did." He smiled and moved away. He studied her with interest. "You didn't take the goats walking today?"

"I went early. They've been fed and cared for."

"Before I came?"

242

She nodded. "Those and the other animals. My papa allows me to tend to the camels also."

"You take good care of them. They're healthy."

"I make certain they're clean and combed everyday. My papa says it's unnecessary, but they seem content this way."

"It appears you're right. Look how they bray quietly."

"It's true, and they come to me when I enter the pen.

Benaiah looked over at Jabin. "Your father's a good man. He's been kind to me." He turned back to her.

"Yes." Anah swung her feet under her. She played with her long braid. She looked curious. "Do you and your father work the fields together?"

"Along with the servants. Our family's done well with Toi's business and our crops."

Anah glanced at Benaiah. "You seem to be a very close family. We don't have brothers, but I have uncles. They help father with his land."

The door opened, and Basemath came out. When she saw Benaiah on the bench, sitting next to Anah, she burst into laughter. "This is who you've chosen, when you could have stayed the other night with me?" She sidled over to them and eyed Benaiah flirtatiously. "Too bad."

Benaiah scowled, but he held his tongue.

Anah spoke quietly. "You're on your way to market?"

"To meet my friends." Basemath laughed again. She fingered a length of hair that fell over her shoulder. "And to see what fabric we might purchase. I want something pretty."

Her eyes raked over Benaiah with interest. "If you tire of your conversation with Anah, come to the east gate. I'll be there." She gave another little laugh.

Benaiah's brow rose. He spoke quiet and low. "I've chores to do, and any time I have this morning will be spent with your sister."

Basemath's dark eyes narrowed as she looked at him. "Do as you wish." She turned and went to the gate. "There are plenty of other men who will oblige me."

Benaiah muttered under his breath. "I'm sure there will be. I pity them."

She opened the gate and left through it.

Anah shook her head. "Don't say that, and don't look that way. Basemath's not so bad. She doesn't know what's good for her."

Benaiah wanted to move closer, but he stayed where he was. He gave her a curious look. "You're so very different from your sisters. I would never have guessed that any of them would be your siblings."

Anah seemed uncomfortable. She didn't speak at first as if she were not sure how to answer him. "They're my half sisters. Basemath, Merab, and Maacah have a different mother."

"But Jabin has only one wife?"

"My papa married his first wife and had my three sisters." She drew in a breath, and color came to her cheeks as she looked back at him. "Then he took a concubine who died in childbirth. She was my mother. I never knew her."

"A concubine?" Benaiah gave her a look of disbelief.

She nodded. "Yes, she's the reason we're different. My papa says I favor my mother."

"I see that you're special to him."

"I believe he loved her very much."

"I'm sure he did."

There was a brief silence before either said anything again.

Then, Benaiah suddenly chuckled to himself as he spoke aloud. "A Moabitess, and the daughter of a concubine. Ha!" He couldn't believe she was both. What would his family say to this?

Anah slowly rose from the bench as if his laughter had suddenly injured her. "I'm sorry, I should have said." Her eyes grew large.

She turned to leave and reached for the door.

"No, Anah." Benaiah got up and went to her. "Please, there's no need for you to go." He suddenly felt sick inside. He'd been thoughtless.

She looked back at him. "But, you don't think much of me because of what I told you."

"No, you've captured my every thought as of late. I can think of little else. I think very highly of you."

She tipped her head upward. Her eyes held questions in them.

He took her hand and led her back to the bench. "It's my family that has caused my laughter. It's only that I said many things I regret. I made so many wrong assumptions. If you allow me someday, to bring you to my home, they'll never let me forget how foolish I've been." He smiled as he said it. "I can only imagine what Achsah will have to say. I'll never be able to live too easily around her after this."

Anah sat back down. She watched as he took a seat farther away. She covered her mouth with her hand as if she were trying to hold back a smile. "I'm sorry for this. I've not meant to cause you trouble."

"You've done nothing. Any trouble caused was my own fault." Benaiah laughed again. "But, I'm not sure how sorry you are."

She turned without saying anything. Her hand was still held to her mouth. She looked back at the goats by the fence, and she smiled again.

Benaiah pointed to the gate. "You like animals? Would you like to see the donkey I brought from my homeland? It's a different breed."

She immediately got up and looked at him. Her eyes lit. "I would, please."

"They're from Bethlehem. They're larger than the ones here, and they run faster when they decide to cooperate. They're loyal and affectionate."

"Will he bite?"

"This one's gentle."

Benaiah took her hand and led her outside the gate to where his animal was. He unleashed the leather ties from the post and led the donkey to her. "His name's Snowrah."

"Snowrah?" She gave him an odd look as she reached up to pet the side of the donkey's cheek.

He grinned. "Sapphira named him. He got into a sack of barley grain that wasn't meant for him, and after that he became Snowrah."

"I see." She petted his mane and down his neck. "We've only had the shorter breeds."

"I'll take you for a ride if you'd like."

She continued to pet him. "Near papa?"

Benaiah smiled. "If you'd like."

"Yes, but how do I get on?"

"Here." He reached out and lifted her onto the donkey's back. Then he took the leather reins in his hands and began to lead the animal with her on it.

She looked at the ground. "He's very tall."

"They're a different breed."

"He doesn't seem bothered that I'm riding him?"

"No, he's not as stubborn as some."

She nodded. "I believe I'll enjoy this ride."

"I hope so."

*****

The morning went quickly. Benaiah was surprised at how much he and Anah had in common and how quickly the time passed. Though she was a shy, quiet young woman, he found she was less so, once she was comfortable. The more time they spent together, the more convinced he was that she would eventually be the one he would bring home with him.

He sighed. Marrying a Moabitess would go against the wishes of his parents, and culturally, there would be differences in his and Anah's beliefs. Was he willing to forgo what he knew might lead to complications in his and Anah's life later on? Would it be so wrong? Anah was sweet and kind and was not as the other Moabite women he'd met. Surely, there would be no harm in it?

246

His conscience pricked slightly. Yet, despite, he pushed thoughts of Adonai from his mind, justifying the reasons for his choice. He wouldn't allow anything to get in the way of what he felt in his heart to be right. Anah was the wife he wanted. She'd left an impression upon him he couldn't ignore. She had to be right for him, even in the Lord's sight. He had to believe it. There was no other woman who would ever compare to her.

Later in the day, Benaiah left to go back to the fields.

His father was waiting. Josheb eyed Benaiah as if he was interested in what his son had been doing.

For now, Benaiah didn't know what Anah's thoughts were, so he said nothing. He would need to wait until Anah agreed to come home with him. Then the family would learn the truth.

*****

Chapter 11

Toi stopped the donkey and cart in front of Achsah's families' home. "You have not been to see them since we married. I visit your father frequently. Your mother and father would like to see you, Achsah."

"You told me we were going to Sheerah's. I said I didn't want to see Dinah, or any of them."

"Achsah, we can visit Sheerah's later. You must miss Vashti?"

"Yes well, Vashti's a sweet girl, but it's no good seeing her, if I have to spend time with the others, or listen to father's wives argue."

"But your mother, Mara? Achsah, you should see her."

Achsah let out a breath. "I told you. I don't want to see any of them."

She held tightly to the donkey's mane. "My father shouldn't have married as he did and brought the trouble he did upon us. It never ends. All of his wives are secretly at each other's throats. I left home for a reason and have no desire to go back."

Toi smiled. "Come now, Achsah. It can't be as bad as you say."

"Truly?" Achsah bristled, her eyes darkening. "I thought you were more perceptive than this. You've seen none of it?"

"Difficulty between your father's wives? They seemed amiable enough when I visited."

"Amiable?" She reluctantly allowed Toi to take her from the donkey after he got down. Achsah laughed. "Ha! You know nothing. You don't understand."

She sighed. There was a solemn look in her eyes. "I suppose you've not been subject to their constant tirades and plots as I have and haven't had the occasion to see it for yourself. Most of them aren't honest in their dealings with others. But, you might not see it."

Toi didn't say anything. His expression was one of interest.

"Rachel was not in the household when my sisters and I were born. We are nothing to her, and there is no pretense in this. She and her children consider us beneath them, even though we were the eldest children in the household."

Achsah looked at the house. "And you've seen Matred, the pretty, barren one. You must have noticed how she parades around the household while listening intently to father's every word as if he were Moabite royalty. She's the favored one in his eyes but not well liked by the others. I can say this much is true."

"But, your mother? Surely, you'll wish to see her? She seems kind enough."

Achsah scuffed her sandaled foot on the ground and stared at the dust stirring around it. She turned to Toi. Her eyes were large and dark green. She was hesitant to speak at first. "Why should I when you wouldn't believe me?"

Toi's eyes lightened as he took her hand in his. "I'd like to know. Please, tell me."

Achsah tried to pull her hand away, but he held it fast. She gave him a weary look. "You mustn't allow her to fool you. She's not what you think, or what you believe."

"What do you mean?"

Achsah sighed. "You mustn't allow what she says to sway your sensibilities. I tell you, that you must weigh what she says very carefully. She's very adept at flattery. Her sweet words, are edged with the sharpness like a knife, and her words are insincere. She'll cut your heart out one day with it. You can count on it."

"I suppose it will be best to be careful then." Toi chuckled. "I'd like my heart kept intact."

Achsah's look was one of warning. "The other wives are like her, and the children, except for Vashti, and Dinah, I might add. I trust the two of them to tell me the truth, though Dinah's honesty is rather like a bad wine."

"Dinah asked to see you. She wanted you to come."

"Ha! You believe this?" Achsah shook her head. "If I know my sister, she's more interested in doing what she can to secure your affections to get back at me. She's likely dreaming of becoming your next wife."

Toi looked at her in surprise. He leaned down and brushed his lips against her hair. "I've no intentions of taking other wives, Achsah. I have my hands full with you." He laughed and pulled her close as he winked at her.

She pushed him away and gave him an exasperated look. "Leave me be. You're ridiculous."

He took her arm. "Come, they're waiting for us. Please make attempts to keep to polite conversation. I told your father you've changed."

"Changed? We'll see about that. Maybe if they keep their thoughts and oily words to themselves, I'll behave differently."

She turned when her brother came out of the house. She drew in a breath. "Oh, great grains, it's Samla, the concubine, Rachel's son. I suppose Helah won't be far behind him."

Almost immediately, Samla's sister, and Vashti stepped out of the house. Helah was laughing. She grabbed Vashti's hand and pulled her along behind her. Vashti had a look of delight on her face. They trailed behind Samla.

When Vashti saw Achsah, she stopped short and put her hand to her lips. Her mouth opened wide. She seemed hesitant to come forward.

Achsah shook her head. "Hmm, it seems even my little sister isn't speaking to me. I can only imagine what they've said to her. More of the same I'm sure. Lies and more of them. It isn't difficult to sway the minds of young children."

Toi threaded his arm around her waist and guided her in the direction of the house. "Come, it's family. There must be something they've done to demonstrate their love for you."

250

Achsah laughed. "No. There isn't, but you can think it, if it makes you feel better." She called to her sister. "Vashti, come! Take us inside!"

Vashti nodded and put out her hand. "Achsah." Her voice was soft and quiet. "Father and his wives are waiting. I'll take you to them."

Achsah gave Toi a perturbed look. "You knew I wouldn't have come, if you had told me we'd be coming here. Now you'll see why. It should prove an interesting afternoon."

"Surely, things aren't as bad as you say?"

Achsah made a face as she followed Vashti inside the house.

*****

Achsah's father, Laban, was at the end of the table. Rachel, Matred, and Mara stood at a distance watching him. No one said a word when Achsah entered.

Dinah had a half smile on her face. She smoothed out her hair and straightened her tunic as she looked at Toi.

Samla took a seat next to his father.

Achsah let go of Toi, so he could join the men.

He looked back at her as he made his way to the table and sat down.

A feeling of trepidation came over Achsah as she stood at the doorway next to Vashti. She lifted her chin and set her shoulders back as she eyed the others there warily.

The room was unnaturally quiet. No one moved at first. It seemed as if they had momentarily lost their ability to speak.

Then Achsah's father motioned to his first wife. "Mara, go greet your daughter. She and Toi plan to stay for dinner."

Achsah's mother looked somewhat annoyed, but she nodded dutifully. She went to Achsah with a half-smile. "Daughter, you've come. How good of you."

Achsah took a step back. There was an edge to her words. "I didn't ask to and had no plans to stop."

"We're happy you did." Mara spoke in a dry tone. She critically assessed Achsah with darkened eyes, even though a smile was still wide on her face. "It was right of you to come, to make up for past grievances. Forgiveness hasn't been one of your strongpoints."

Achsah didn't respond. She turned to Vashti. "Could you put my cloak somewhere safe?" She took it off and handed it to her sister. The bracelets on her wrist jingled as she lowered her hand to her side.

Her mother sniffed as she stared at Achsah.

Achsah couldn't help wondering at her own mother's ability to forgive. Though many times, Achsah had offered an olive branch and buried past mistakes, Mara had never shown remorse for her own sly remarks and inuendos, and her apologies always cast the blame on others.

Vashti bowed and did as Achsah asked. Then, she poured wine while the others conversed quietly with each other. She brought a cup to her sister. "Here, Achsah."

"Thank you." Achsah lifted the cup to her lips and took a small drink. She watched as Vashti filled the rest of the cups in the room. Then Achsah turned back to Toi and stared at him, from across the room. He shouldn't have brought her here.

There was something dark and vile in this house, a presence Achsah couldn't escape. Though it was buried in politeness and smiles, and light-hearted banter, beneath the surface it simmered. It tore at pieces of her heart.

Achsah's mother's eyes narrowed slightly as she turned to the other women standing next to Laban.

Laban extended his hand to his youngest concubine. "Matred, come here, my beauty. Take a place beside me while I speak to Achsah's husband. I'd very much like to look upon your pretty face."

Achsah watched as a myriad of dark emotions played out over her mother's face. There was a smile on her lips, but the look in her eyes could not hide her true feelings. There was simmering dislike for the other women.

252

Matred bowed slightly and gave her husband a coy smile.

Achsah sighed. What she'd expected would happen hadn't taken long to come to pass. Surely it would not be long before the subtle games would be played between the women.

Matred, the youngest of her father's wives, and the favored one, quickly went to Achsah's father's side. A playful smile lit her face, and she giggled. "I'm glad to take a seat beside you, master."

She got down next to him, and she tucked her knees up under her. She rearranged her jeweled tunic with a prideful expression as she turned to Mara. Her eyes danced.

Laban grinned as he adjusted the sleeves of his robe. Then he reached out and took Matred's hand in his and squeezed it. He back at Toi. "I'm glad I took this second concubine. She's somewhat younger than the others."

Toi seemed at a loss for what to say. He smiled, though his eyes had questions in them.

Achsah sighed. Her own mother, Mara, and her father's other concubine, Rachel, stood at a distance. Neither said anything at first.

Laban's voice lowered. "Mara, get me a dish of food, not too much on the plate."

Mara begrudgingly moved away from Achsah and left through the main door. Moments later, she came back with a dish in her hand to take to her husband. She squatted down next to him. "It's roasted lamb, your favorite." The spangles on her wrist jingled as she placed it on the table. "I made it earlier in the day for you."

Laban grinned as he took the meat into his hands. "This is the wife who cooks for me. She never fails to appease my appetite." He chewed the succulent morsel slowly as if savoring each bite.

Rachel spoke. The tone of her voice was dry. "There's more in the courtyard if you're hungry later. I can get it for you."

Laban turned to Toi. "My women are good to me. It pays to have more than one woman." He rubbed his waistline and smiled.

Achsah rolled her eyes. Her father loved being the center of attention. If Toi ever took another wife, she'd not vie for his approval the way these women did. She'd want nothing to do with such ridiculous behavior. She couldn't imagine taking part in the schemes her mother and the other women played. She looked away and smoothed out the edges of her tunic.

Dinah picked up a basket of bread from a long bench. She smiled and took it to the low table. She leaned close to Toi as she allowed her hair to drape over her shoulder next to him. "Would you like some of mother's baked goods?"

Her eyes sparkled as she looked at Achsah and then back at Toi.

Achsah gave her sister a bored look, even though Dinah's antics incensed her. Dinah was no different from her mother and her father's other wives. She'd learned from them.

"Maybe later, thank you." He put up his hand to her and shook his head. There was amusement in his eyes when he looked at Achsah.

Dinah broke a piece of the bread off and put it on his plate, even though he'd made it clear he didn't want any. She backed away, but her eyes didn't stray from him as she continued to hold the basket in her hands.

Achsah wondered why Dinah thought her silly antics would have any effect on her. What did she think she might gain from them?

She went to where Dinah stood and put out her hand. "I'll have a piece. We've not eaten since early morning. I'm famished, and since you're willing to bring the bread around, like a common household servant, you can wait on me."

A cold, dead stare erupted from Dinah's eyes. She suddenly appeared as if she wanted to dump the bread over Achsah's head, or beat her with the basket, but she refrained. Instead, she held out the container.

254

Toi was still watching them both as if they were entertainment.

Achsah broke off a piece from the loaf and put it in her mouth. She took a bite and chewed it with a smile. "It's good. Did you make it too?" She reached for another piece, but Dinah pulled the basket back.

The others in the room suddenly grew quiet. There was only the sound of Vashti's feet swinging under the bench as they nervously scraped against the floor. Interesting what happened when she called them on their games. A little bit of honesty was not handled well in this place.

The edge of Laban's jaw tightened. "Achsah."

Achsah laughed inwardly at the way they stared at her. They'd been witness, too many times, to hers and Dinah's quarrels, which had often gotten out of hand. She was sure they feared a scene, but they felt they could no longer intervene as they had in the past.

"Women are supposed to wait, Achsah." Dinah put out her hand.

Achsah laughed. "Ha! A guest. Since you offered it to my husband first, I see no reason why I should put off my empty stomach any longer. You can't allow your own sister to go without. Here, give me another one."

"Achsah." Her father's voice growled low. A ridge formed above his brow, but he didn't get up.

"Father, tell her to go away." Dinah's eyes darkened.

Toi suddenly got up and went to Achsah's side. He leaned down and kissed her gently on the cheek. "Achsah, come, I've more than I need." He broke a piece of his bread off and held it out to her. "What's a husband for but to provide for his wife?" There was subtle humor in his eyes.

Achsah gave him an annoyed look as she took it from him. She chewed on a piece of it.

When Toi pulled her close, Achsah sent Dinah a guarded stare and then turned away.

Toi grinned. "You didn't tell me your daughter had such a lively spirit when you allowed me to marry her." He reached up and brushed a crumb off Achsah's cheek. "My family enjoys the color she adds to our household. It seems the gifts my father brought you, in exchange for my bride, were well worth it."

Laban looked from Achsah to Toi. He gave Toi an odd look, and then he laughed. "Anyone who could say the things you do, and bring gifts, in exchange for my daughter's hand, must see something in her we did not. Maybe you are the right one for my Achsah."

Toi pulled Achsah closer to him as she rolled her eyes.

The others all laughed and turned back to each other in conversation. Even Dinah backed away without a fight. The mood of the room was somewhat lighter as the rest of the meal was served.

Toi left Achsah's side and sat back down next to Laban again. He winked at her from across the room.

Achsah leaned close to Dinah and whispered in her ear. "My husband's not unaware of your schemes." Her voice lowered. "Yet, if he ever took you as a second wife, just remember, that I'd make your life miserable."

Dinah backed away with narrowed eyes.

Achsah smiled. She strode across the room to where Vashti and Helah sat on a stone bench that jutted out from the rock wall of the house.

Both young girls quickly made room for her. They seemed more relaxed, when she sat next to them, away from Dinah.

Toi watched her as he spoke to her father.

Achsah turned away.

She wished he hadn't brought her here. Not much in the home had changed since she'd left. She was reminded why she'd been so eager to marry a man she barely knew and live elsewhere. There'd been little she'd lost since she'd left and little to be desired. She looked forward to the afternoon meal coming to an end.

256

*****

"Achsah." Toi extended his hand to her as he pulled the donkey down the path.

She took a place beside him but refused to take his hand. "Why did you take me there? You saw how they were. They would rather I wasn't there."

"But they're family."

She shook her head. "It wears on me to be near them. It's pretense. I didn't want to go. I told you this, and I am sure they speak unkindly of me at this very moment."

"But if you spent time there, things might be different. They asked that I bring you."

"No, I have spent time there, but it has only brought division and strife. I believe Abraham separated from Lot and his family for that very reason. I don't think your Lord wants this in families as Kezia says Adonai is the God of peace."

Toi stared down the path and nodded. "It is true that Abraham lived separately from his divided family. I hadn't considered this." He turned and reached out and took her hand in his. "He went his own way for the sake of peace, so I suppose in some situations, such as your own, it might be best for them, and you, that you did the same."

Achsah didn't answer.

Toi smiled. "At least I didn't have to separate you and Dinah as I had to in the past."

Achsah gave him a dark look. She stopped walking. "If you took her as a wife, you could expect it. I wouldn't be as civil as I was today."

Toi let out an exasperated sound. He stared at her in surprise. "Achsah, I told you, I'm not taking other wives." He stopped and took her hand. "I said this before. In any case, Dinah would give me more trouble than you do. Do you truly believe I'd want this?"

"She's pretty."

He laughed. "For this, I would invite such ruin? No, Achsah, your sister would be the death of me. And you're pretty."

Achsah's eyes questioned his. "But, if there was a woman you loved?" She stopped walking.

He smiled. "Ah, little Achsah, I told you once, I didn't believe myself capable of love. Are you thinking it might be possible for me now?"

She looked up at him with questions in her eyes. What had he meant by what he'd said? 'Did she think it possible?' Did he feel more for her than he was willing to say?

"I don't know what you think, or plan to do." She sighed as she spoke quietly. "But, I don't want to go back there again."

He tugged on her arm and smiled. "Come, I told you I'd take you to Sheerah's. The evening's still young. Reuben wanted to see me, and Shobach will be there. It's Sabbath."

Achsah walked beside him. She stared at the path that led to town. She shivered and pulled her wrap closer as she quickened her steps to keep up with him.

She breathed in the fresh evening air as she pushed thoughts of her family and Toi aside. She didn't want to think about what she didn't understand.

*****

Time spent with Sheerah that evening more than made up for the meal at Achsah's parent's home. Toi was right to have brought her to her friend's. It had been a night of laughter and dancing and time with Sheerah. Sheerah was full of gladness in her marriage with her new husband's family. There were no disparaging remarks or discord in their home. It was enough to lift Achsah's spirits, and send her off, having forgotten the meal with her own family.

When they returned home, later that evening, Achsah left Toi in the courtyard to care for the animals while she went inside to work on a tunic she'd mended earlier. She sat next to Kezia.

258

Josheb, her father-in-law, was at the table. He was talking to Hannah.

They all turned when a noise sounded in front of the house.

Benaiah came through the arched stone entrance. He pushed the door shut behind him. He sat at the table next to his father.

Josheb eyed him curiously. "You've been gone longer than usual today." He handed Benaiah a basket of fruit and bread.

Achsah put the fabric in her hands down. She'd stitched the edge of an outer robe for Toi while sitting on a stone bench against the wall. She leaned forward to listen.

"I've been at Jabin's house. There's something I need to say to you." Benaiah's sentence was hurried as he took a piece of bread and held it in his hand.

"They need more feed?"

"No, this doesn't concern our business with them."

Achsah's ears perked. He wouldn't tell Josheb about Basemath, and and her friends, and the meetings they'd had with Sapphira?"

Sapphira sat down next to Achsah. Her eyes grew large as they looked at each other. Then, she turned back to Benaiah.

Benaiah cleared his throat. "It concerns one of Jabin's daughters."

Achsah blinked. A daughter? Basemath? Or Maacah or Merab? What was the reason for this? Would he betray her and Sapphira?

Josheb put his hand on Benaiah's arm. "What have you done?"

"It's only that I've taken an interest in one of them."

Achsah's eyes grew large. Benaiah?

Jorah was at the table. He'd eaten, but he turned to listen. "A Moabite daughter?" He put down a piece of bread he was about to bite into.

Achsah turned quickly to Sapphira who stared at Benaiah in disbelief.

Josheb made a sharp movement. He pulled his hand from the table. He didn't say anything as a look of astonishment came over him.

"It's true, father. I like this young woman very much. I want her for my wife, and she has agreed to it. She's told her father she's willing."

A hushed silence suddenly fell over the room. Everyone stopped what they were doing.

Achsah's mouth flew open wide, and she almost dropped the fabric on the floor that lay in her lap.

"A Moabitess?" Josheb's face registered shock. "You?"

Jorah looked stunned, but he didn't say anything.

Benaiah nodded. "Yes, father."

Achsah could no longer contain herself. She cupped her hand over her mouth and started to laugh. Was it Basemath? Which one?

She laughed again. "Who? Basemath?" Her eyes sparkled as she said it.

Benaiah turned and silenced her with a dark look.

Sapphira was quiet, but her mouth drew open as she watched her brother.

He turned back to Josheb. "Her name's Anah, father. She's very different from the other Moabite women." He gave Achsah an annoyed look.

Ah, Anah. Achsah took her hand off her mouth. It made sense. He was interested in the beautiful, quiet young woman who stayed in the shadows at Basemath's home.

Achsah wasn't surprised at his choice. What had he said? Not like other Moabite women. Ha!

Benaiah's voice quieted. "If you meet her, you'll understand."

Hannah came into the room. She didn't say anything, but the expression on her face was evident that she'd overheard from the doorway. She put a wooden bowl, filled with lentils, and a dish, laden with bunches of grapes, on the table next to them. She stood watching them.

Josheb couldn't seem to get over his initial reaction. He kept staring at his son in a state of shock. "But, you said…"

"I know, father, but I met Anah. You must go to Jabin and arrange it. He knows my intentions. Take many gifts, and assure him I'll treat her well. I want her as my wife."

Achsah made a choking noise. Him? Treat this woman well? A Moabitess? She didn't believe it.

Benaiah scowled. "Please, father. Anah knows my intent. She is willing."

"My son, you're allowing a pretty face to sway you from your beliefs. People shouldn't come together in marriage who hold such different faiths. Though I hold nothing against Achsah, as she's not to blame in any way for what Toi has taken it upon himself to do, a marriage, such as this, is bound to have many difficulties associated with it. You don't hold to the same traditions, and she will worship different gods. Your heart will be divided in the things that are most important to you. Anah's upbringing was not the same."

Achsah couldn't disagree that the cultural differences had driven a wedge between her and the family, despite her willingness to accept the family, and them her. She sometimes wondered if she'd ever understand Toi's people. Benaiah and Anah might not be so tolerant, as Achsah and Toi had been, regarding their different faiths. Anah believed in Chemosh and the idol gods.

Achsah's eyes lit as she thought of the misery such a marriage might cause Benaiah. A Moabitess? She smiled to herself.

"But the Moabite people shouldn't be held accountable for their ancestor's actions. Anah's people have done nothing to deserve our scorn." Benaiah got up and began to pace.

"I don't look down upon her, or her people. I consider them part of our Lord's creation, and as you do, our ancestors. I only want you to be aware of the difficulties you will face by such a union. I believe you that Anah is a good woman."

Toi came through the door. "Anah? Who's Anah?" There was a look of interest on his face.

Achsah ignored Toi. She looked at Benaiah in disbelief. Did he say what she thought he did, that her people didn't deserve his scorn? Ha! The young goat herder must have influenced his thinking. She giggled again.

Benaiah turned to Toi and answered. "She's one of Jabin's daughters."

"The pretty one with the dark eyes, I'm assuming?" Toi went to Achsah and brushed his lips against her cheek. He took her hand in his, and he chuckled to himself.

"You mustn't say anything to hurt Anah, Toi." Benaiah's voice held a stern warning.

Toi looked curious. He didn't respond.

"You'll speak to Anah's father?" Benaiah turned back to Josheb. "You'll secure her hand for me?"

"You're marrying a Moabite?" Toi's look was one of shock.

"I am, and why shouldn't I?" Benaiah let out a long, slow breath. "It didn't seem to be a problem when *you* did it. Father?"

Toi laughed.

Josheb eyed Achsah who was still holding her hand to her mouth and smiling. He shook his head. "It seems your mind's made up. I suppose I've no choice but to give my blessing. Though our cultures are very different. I hope you can see this. She has different beliefs."

"I understand. I'm willing for her sake. I love her very much."

Toi sat down next to Achsah and Sapphira. He stared at Benaiah incredulously as if he were still trying to make sense of the whole matter.

Josheb spoke quietly. "Tomorrow morning, I'll see Jabin. I've an extra camel and some goats. He should be pleased with these animals."

Benaiah nodded as if satisfied. He looked down at the platter of food in front of him. He took bread from a basket and began to chew on it. "Good, we'll eat now. Anah will be a favorable daughter to you and mother. You'll see this in time."

Josheb turned back to the food. "We'll accept her as our own as we have Achsah. Now, let's eat before the food gets cold."

Toi sat down with them, and they turned their conversation to business as they ate and drank and spoke of their future plans.

*****

Chapter 12

After awaking early, Achsah climbed the stairs before the sun had risen. She sat on the top of the roof and stared at the stars. The dark expanse of the universe spread its canopy above her like a blue-black, glittering blanket. The moon still hovered on the horizon moving slowly across the desert sky.

"Adonai, are you there?" Achsah's voice was soft and quiet. "Would a God as great as you listen to me?" She breathed out the words as her heart thumped in her chest. Though Kezia told her it was possible, she wondered why she felt she had the right to call out to this God, the Maker of the world.

She waited and listened as the quiet sounds of the early morning hours faded away, and the desert plains came alive with a shivering wind and a dove's song. Other birds lit on the edge of the roof. They chirped full morning sounds as the horizon lightened, and the moon disappeared.

Kezia impressed Achsah as having had a true faith. The young woman spoke of the Torah and the Israelite God as if he were real.

The old ways were leaving Achsah. She'd prayed and opened her heart to the possibility of Adonai's existence and sovereignty.

She looked across the Moabite plains as the light around her slipped out of the darkened shadows. Trees appeared on the horizon in the deep valleys. The great river, that ran along the edge of the town, appeared out of the mist as the last star made its exit from the dark morning sky. Cliffs rose in the distance, and the majestic mountains suddenly took shape against the sunlit horizon. Everything was visible. Everything was plain to see. The creation was real, and it was noticeably before her.

As the sunlight spread light over the fields and throughout the land, Achsah wondered if Adonai, the Israelite God, would ever seem to her like the plains of Moab did when the light awakened the morning Earth? Would she know Him? Would she understand Him as Kezia did?

She wondered if someday it might be possible.

*****

Anah and Benaiah married quickly. It wasn't long before Anah came to live at their home.

As Achsah guessed, Kezia and Benaiah's wife became fast friends. Both modest, hard-working young women, they spent time quietly pulling threads at weaving looms or spinning wool for yarn. They tended to the animals, baked bread, and cooked the meals together.

Sapphira was quick to accept Anah. She adored Anah for her kind spirit and natural beauty. She spent her time tagging along behind Anah. Sapphira seemed happy to learn all she could about Benaiah's new wife.

Achsah stood back and watched from a distance. She smoothed the wrinkles in her tunic and adjusted the leather cord that held her braid together.

Anah got up and came to her. "The animals need to be fed. They're more active in the morning hours. Come with me." She put her hand on Achsah's arm.

"You should have the servants do it."

"But I enjoy taking care of them." Anah smiled. "Come, there are new sheep."

Achsah gave her a reproachful look. "You and Sapphira are always trying to get me to touch those dirty things. You'll have me smelling like them."

Anah took her hand and tugged on it. "They're young and clean. You'll like them. Benaiah just brought them yesterday from town. Besides, there are things I want to ask you."

"I'll look at them, but don't give me any feed. I don't want them butting up against me."

Anah laughed. "You can watch."

They went through the gate as Achsah stood looking around. A small, white lamb came toddling over to her. It began to chew on her skirt.

"You're going to the wrong person, little one. I've no food to give you."

The lamb stared at her and tipped its head upward.

Achsah frowned. She reached down and pet the top of it's head. "Oh, all right. But don't think I'll be coming to see you tomorrow. I've better things to do."

She sat on a bench while Anah held sweet smelling hay out for the sheep to munch on.

Anah's voice was soft. "Would you like to go to the high places this evening with me?"

Achsah shook her head from side to side. She looked up from where she sat. "I've prayed to the Israelite God. I rarely pay homage to Chemosh anymore. And of course, Benaiah got rid of my idols, so I've quit that too."

"You don't worry that you'll anger the gods?"

Achsah shrugged. "Chemosh, or the idols? I never really believed in them."

"Achsah! You shouldn't say that." Anah's eyes widened. She put her hand to her chest. "You should come with me tonight and make amends. It isn't good to think the way you do."

The little lamb nibbled at Achsah's fingers, and she pulled them away. She laughed. "Chemosh has no hold over me."

Anah lowered her arm. She let hay drop onto the ground. She brushed off her hands. "I've visited the high places since I was young. I'd feel wrong if I didn't. I suppose I'll have to go alone."

"I understand. I know what it's like for you."

"I wish Benaiah understood, but he isn't Moabite."

"He isn't quick to accept things."

"But he *is* good to me." Anah took more hay and fed the sheep that encircled her. "I suppose neither of us can expect the other to embrace these differences so easily."

"It seems he loves you, whatever you believe."

"Yes."

Achsah moved away from two sheep that pushed against her. "I think I've had enough of these animals for now." She smiled.

She backed toward the gated entrance and squeezed through it "I'll leave you here. Talk to Kezia. You may find what she has to say is encouraging."

Anah looked up from what she was doing. "I'll do that. I'll find her later."

Achsah nodded. "I'm going to town to take Toi food his mother prepared for him, and, of course I'll look at the fabric and perfumes. I'll be home later."

"I hope your morning's profitable." Anah petted the sheep around her and then turned to feed more of them. She waved to Achsah.

Achsah smiled. "I hope yours is, too."

Achsah turned toward the gate. A trip to town would do her good.

*****

Jorah sat in the courtyard of their home as he watched Achsah leave for the town. Anah was still in the pen with the animals. There were two Moabite women in their household now. He couldn't blame Benaiah for taking Anah as his wife. She was lovely and sweet of spirit. With few Israelite women in the land of Moab, it was difficult not to be swayed in this direction.

Yet, since Benaiah's wedding, Jorah was as determined as ever not to set his heart on a daughter of Moab.

He'd seen the disappointment in his father and mother's faces when both Toi and Benaiah had announced their engagements to foreign women. He knew what it meant to the family, that they were to remain separate from the people of the land, and their cultures, so as not to lose their own way of life while they sojourned here.

And as much as he'd thought of Dinah, he realized it was best not to see her again.

*****

Chapter 13

Toi and Shobach chipped away at their stone carvings. Achsah watched them both. She had come early and was waiting for the marketplace to awaken.

Shobach got up from where he sat. "I've a few tools I need. I'll be back."

Toi nodded as Shobach made his way to the door of his home and disappeared inside.

Achsah sat down next to Toi. She looked up when Benaiah came into the courtyard and approached them.

A flicker of Benaiah's old nature brewed as he gave Achsah a guarded look and then turned to his brother. "What is she doing here?"

Achsah looked down at her feet and readjusted the straps on her sandals. She wanted to tell him to leave, but squelched the words that threatened to escape her lips.

"My wife?" Toi lifted the basket onto his lap and took bread out of it. "She stays. What you tell me will be kept between us."

Benaiah let out a breath. His voice was gruff. "I've nothing to hide. She's heard it before."

Achsah turned from him. She didn't give him the satisfaction of answering.

Toi looked puzzled. "What's happened? Why aren't you in the fields with father?"

"He says we need to wait a day. I've come to trade in the marketplace."

"And this has darkened your mood?"

Benaiah frowned. "No, it's Anah. She was at the high places and is storing those idols in our room." His voice was low and deep. "She refuses to give them up. She won't listen to me, even when I tell her they're worthless."

Achsah couldn't help but smile inwardly, even though she knew it was wrong. Benaiah's perfect wife, Anah, was contradicting his wishes.

Achsah was glad she'd put away her practice of praying to the Moabite gods. It did her little good, and Adonai seemed much more real to her since she did. In time, she hoped Anah would see the benefit of leaving them behind also.

She looked up at Benaiah. She could hold her tongue no longer. "If you don't like it, why don't you smash her idols like you did mine?"

Toi shook his head. "Achsah."

Benaiah didn't say anything. He looked at the courtyard gate.

Toi reached out and took Achsah's hand in his. "You might speak to Anah about what you've learned."

Achsah looked at him in surprise. "I tried this morning. But, if she won't listen to either of you, why would she listen to me? You're the Israelites." She let go of his hand.

Benaiah scowled.

Toi ignored them both. "Then why do *you* listen to Kezia?"

Achsah looked in the direction of the home. She shrugged nonchalantly. "Your sister genuinely practices her faith. Neither of you listen to Adonai like she does. You talk of it, yet have nothing to show for it, other than going to the temple on your Sabbath, or to your ritualistic festivals, or doing good deeds."

"We have our beliefs."

"But, I'm not sure what you mean by that?" Achsah gave them both a puzzled look. "I haven't seen you in prayer, at the altars, or studying the Torah. You talk of faith, yet it seems you have little time for your God."

Both Toi and Benaiah stared at her. Neither said anything.

"Kezia truly loves Adonai and is willing to put aside her own interests to take up his. She says that her life isn't to do with as she wants."

270

She looked away from them. "You carve images of stone for the Moabite people, yet you tell them not to worship them. You treat others with little regard for their feelings, and you don't see your own sin. How will Anah ever know anything from either of you? You admonish others when you have no connection to him yourself? You've become like them."

"Like who?" Toi stared at her interested.

"Like the idols. Kezia says they don't speak, or see, or hear, but neither do you."

"Achsah, the people in my family are good. Shobach's my friend. He studies the Torah and speaks of prayer. He's spent much time caring for others." Toi got up from where he sat and dusted his robe off. "My mother and father have done many good things also. I'm part of a godly family. They pray diligently, and they spend much of their time at the temple."

Achsah pushed her dark braid behind her. She turned sharply, and then she sighed. "They might do many things, but what about you? What have you done? You live through your family and friends. But, what do *you* have to do with the one true God? Truly? Do you know him? Do you seek him like your sister does? Do you study the Torah? If you were doing these things, wouldn't there be evidence of it. You go to the temple, but when do you go to *Him*?"

Achsah took hold of the empty basket on the ground at Toi's feet. "Where do you stand?" She straightened. "Adonai wants your heart. He wants more than rituals. Kezia tells me that your heart and the intentions of it are what is important to him. This is what he wants from you." She choked on her last word.

She put her hand to her mouth. "I'm sorry, but I must go. I've said too much, and I've things I must do. I truly know so very little and can't help you with Anah. I'll see you at our home later." She turned and left quietly through the gate.

*****

Toi stared at the entrance to the courtyard where he worked. He looked down at the carved image in his hand and set it down.

A thread of discomfort stirred inside him. He dusted off his hands and turned back to his brother. "None of us know enough about it. I suppose Achsah's right. You might get Kezia to speak to Anah."

Benaiah frowned. "You allow your wife too much freedom to do and say as she wishes."

"We're in Moab." Toi shrugged. "Achsah has always spoken her mind. I knew this when she became my wife."

"Yes, but I couldn't condone such a thing."

"So, Anah must keep her true feelings from you. She must do things in secret. Neither of you trust the other."

Benaiah didn't answer at first. He gave Toi a wary look. "She doesn't keep her feelings from me. In fact, most of the time, it's the opposite. But, if she trusted me in this, she'd have no reason to do the things she does."

"We've chosen women who believe differently and don't know our ways. We can't expect the same from them as we would from an Israelite woman."

Benaiah began to pace. He raked his hand through his hair. "Nothing is as it should be. It's not what I thought it would be. I thought Anah would very quickly accept our ways and adopt them."

"Benaiah, even women of our faith harbor their own thoughts. You can't force what you believe on her. She's been raised very differently."

"Than how will she ever understand?"

Toi laughed. "Understand what? Your deep faith? Come now, brother. Did you hear anything Achsah said?"

"What?"

Toi picked up the Moabite idol and began shaping the side of it. He shook his head. "It seems Kezia is our only hope for both of our wives. There's a better chance they'll learn something from her."

"I only wish Anah would listen to what I tell her. It seems my influence isn't as great as I thought it would be." He looked toward the gate. "I should go. I've things to do, and she'll be waiting."

Toi nodded. "I'm almost finished. You go, and let mother know I'll be back soon."

"Ha!" Benaiah laughed. "And she will believe that." He turned to leave.

Toi smiled. "I'll try for her sake." He watched his brother go out of the courtyard, get on his donkey and ride in the direction of their home.

*****

Later in the day, Toi looked at the stone carving in his hand and set it on the bench next to him. Achsah's words had taken a turn inside him.

What *had* he done to for the sake of Adonai other than to take part in rituals and Sabbath ceremonies? Was it enough? And what did she mean that he needed to *know* the one true Lord? Could she have any understanding of it herself? She wasn't even an Israelite. What was Kezia teaching her?

He got up and and brushed his hands off. The day was beginning to darken, and the sun was sinking over the horizon.

It was time to make his own way home and time to put his mind on other things. He'd talk to Shobach before he left and then be off.

Even though it hadn't been long since he'd eaten, his stomach had rumbled at the thought of the women's meal. Achsah would be at home. There would be good food and drink to give him his fill.

*****

Chapter 14

Achsah inwardly laughed as she watched Benaiah from across the room.

He was standing beside Toi, who'd come in shortly after him. A frown wavered over his brow as he looked at Anah. He was obviously still affected by what had been said earlier.

Anah went to him and handed him a bowl filled with lentils. He took the bowl to the low table where both he and his brother sat side by side.

"Autumn's been mild this year." Toi lifted a spoon to his mouth and took a bite of the stew-like meat. "The storms have been few."

Benaiah turned from his wife. He nodded. "Enough for the crops to do well. It's been a good growing season."

"Yes."

Josheb and Jorah sat down beside them.

Conversation was, as usual, talk of the harvest and town happenings. There was very little in the way of anything any of them had not heard. Sabbath was drawing near. Trading had been good that day. Toi's business was thriving. Nothing had given them reason for much concern.

So, when the door flung open, and a Moabite servant they'd not seen before entered, everyone turned.

The whole group looked up from their plates and waited for the the man to speak.

The Moabite held a spear, and he was out of breath. He put his free hand on his chest. "I'm sorry to interrupt your meal, but I have news." He straightened when his breathing slowed.

"Tell us." Josheb looked interested. "What's happened?"

"The King of Moab asked that the people here are informed of what's happening at the border. Amorite spies are there, and the king's requesting the help of all able-bodied men."

"How many are there?" Toi listened intently.

"They're not sure, but for our protection, the king is sending a large company."

Toi got up from the table.

The room suddenly grew silent. "What needs to be done?" Toi took hold of the man's arm.

"Supplies have been sent." The servant waved his hand. "Ready your mounts, and I'll take you to the others. We're not sure what will take place."

All three brothers immediately got up from the table.

Benaiah went to the man and put his hand on his arm. "Wait, and we'll get what we need."

"Yes, this situation could affect our homes and families. We should be there." Toi nodded.

Josheb put his hand on Jorah's arm. "We'll need you to stay here for mother's sake. In the event that there's trouble, there needs to be one of us at home."

Josheb didn't say anything, but nodded. He didn't look particularly pleased that he wouldn't be going with them.

Achsah's mouth opened as she watched Toi and Benaiah both take up weapons and extra robes and leave through to the door to go out into the courtyard. She looked across the room. "Hannah, they're not Moabites! You're not going to let them go? Will you please tell them to stop?"

Hannah and Anah stood there stunned. They didn't say anything, but instead they followed Achsah outside.

Achsah ran to Toi as he was readying one of the donkeys to leave. "But, you're Israelite. Why would you go?" She tugged on the sleeve of his robe. "You don't need to do this. It isn't your battle. Please, Toi, stay here with us."

Toi gave her a gentle shove aside. "Come now, Achsah." He smiled. "We live with the Moabites. It's our duty to go and fight if they need our help."

"Duty? But it's not. You're not Moabite." A worried frown formed over her eyes. "Please, we need you to stay here with us. There will be plenty of men at the border without you. You don't need to go."

"Achsah, why are you carrying on so? Can't you see that I can't stay? It would be wrong."

She reached out and took hold of his arm. "But I don't want you to. What will happen to us, if you and Benaiah leave? If one of those men came here, Jorah can't defend us alone. Stay and protect us?"

"Ah, little one, I see now. You're afraid. But, Jorah's a man. He can protect the household from harm." He brushed her hand back. "I'm needed at the border."

He reached out and took one of his larger knives from a leather container he'd strapped to the saddle of his donkey. He gave it to her. "Here, take this. Protect yourself with it, and if necessary, the others. It's one of my better knives. I put my confidence in you. Use it if one of those Amorites find their way here."

Achsah looked at the knife in her hand and frowned.

Anah went to stand next to Benaiah. She looked up at her husband. Her voice was soft and quiet. "Be careful, Benaiah, and come back to us."

The expression on Benaiah's face softened. He bent down to kiss her goodbye. He got on his donkey. "Don't worry, we'll be back."

Achsah watched their exchange, then she rolled her eyes. She turned back to Toi. "I can't protect anyone, and I don't want to." She held the weapon to her side and watched as Toi got onto the donkey. She reached out and took hold of the reins. "Please Toi, stay here. Don't do this."

Benaiah turned to his brother. "We've no more time. Tell her to keep quiet."

Achsah's brows drew inward as she looked at Benaiah. "You go help them, but leave my husband be."

Toi took her hand from the donkey's reins and lifted it to his mouth to kiss it. He smiled widely. "It seems my little

Achsah will miss me." His eyes sparkled as he said it. "It's good to know you'll be waiting for my return."

She snatched her hand away. Her green eyes narrowed. "You'd better not believe for a moment I'll shed tears for you, or be covered in sackcloth, if you don't come back. You have chosen to leave with little consideration for me."

She backed away from the donkey and watched him as he looked down at her.

Dust from the donkey stirred beneath the animal's feet. Toi lifted his hand. "Don't worry. You have the knife." He dug his heels into the donkey's side and the animal moved in place beside Benaiah's mount. Toi straightened in his seat, and he didn't look back again.

Achsah watched as the two brothers took the path that led out of town. She put the knife into its leather holder and took it with her back into the house. Her hands shook as she held it.

Didn't they understand what they might be getting into? The Amorites were a fierce people. She drew in a breath. The last time this happened, things had not turned out so good. Two of her uncles had never made it back.

She wanted nothing more to do with war and the effects of it. Toi and Benaiah should have left this to the Moabites.

*****

Darkness had set in. An eerie mist enveloped the plains which separated the rolling hills in the distance from the desert beyond. A strange cry of a bird echoed over hundreds of men who waited in the shadows near deep ravines. They watched the flat lands where enemy tribes might find their way through.

Toi lifted his fingers to his mouth and put a hand in the open air behind him.

Whispers ended when shadowy figures emerged from the shrouded hills.

When the signal was given, the Moabites, and their Israelite comrades, stole out of their hiding places and attacked the enemy tribes who charged them. Toi helped lead them.

*****

Achsah sat up bolt right in her bed. She pulled her woolen coverings around her and shivered. How many days had it been since Toi had left for the front? She'd lost track.

Her ears were trained on the noises outside. Her heart pounded inside her chest.

The sheep, in the gated courtyard for the animals, stirred. Nervous bleats pierced the still night air. Achsah heard the sound of a donkey's gait and a quiet snort outside the courtyard. Was someone there?

It was dusk, and the others had gone inside to retire for the evening.

She reached down and pulled on her sandals as she tied the leather laces around her ankles. She took the knife, Toi had given her, off a stone ledge, and held it tightly in her hand. She crept outside and stood beside the gate.

At first it seemed she'd been mistaken, that there might be an intruder, as the night grew suddenly quiet. The wind whistled low, and the cricket's song rang out in unison across the wheat fields beyond the gate. She turned to go back into her room, and then she distinctly heard hooves again pawing and dancing. It brought her to a halt.

She leaned against the stone gate behind the entrance. Her fingers curled around the knife. She waited as her heart pounded louder. The darkness of the night hid her from whoever was behind the wall.

Someone got down from the donkey and slowly turned the latch on the gate.

Achsah's breath slowed, and she shivered as the opening grew wider. She held the weapon closer and gripped it with both hands.

278

When a tall, shadowy figure entered the courtyard, and turned in the direction of her home, Achsah stepped behind the man. "Don't go any farther. I'm holding a knife."

Her heart skipped, and her breath came in gulps as she held the knife in the air behind him. She shook so bad she could barely hold it steady.

The man didn't move. "It's Jair, Achsah?"

"Jair?"

He turned, and the moonlight caught his profile.

Achsah could see his face. "What are you doing? It's night, and we've all turned in to sleep. Why have you come so late?" She put her hand on her chest and took a breath. "You scared me."

Jair gave her a look of consternation. "There are things I must ask of your family, and I came to see that Kezia was safe and that the family was well."

"But, I could have harmed you."

"I was with Benaiah and Toi at the border. I stopped on the way to my house to give you news of them and to ask for things."

Achsah put her hand on her hip. "But they didn't come back with you? Where are they?"

"Not everyone could leave. I was sent, but I'll be going back."

They turned when the main door of the house opened.

Achsah took a step back when Josheb and Hannah came outside, followed by Kezia, Anah, and Jorah.

Kezia's face paled when she saw Achsah standing in the courtyard alone with Jair. She moved from behind her parents. "Achsah? What are you doing?"

Jair looked from Kezia to Achsah. His words were jumbled. "I came from the front. To see…"

Josheb and Hannah were both looking at the two of them with questions in their eyes.

Hannah stepped forward. "What are you doing out here with Jair, Achsah?"

Jair was clearly rattled, and the family was waiting as he struggled with words.

Achsah gave them an annoyed look. She lifted the knife. "He's here for Kezia, and he's lucky he's alive. When I heard a noise, I went to the gate. I'd plans to use this. Toi and Benaiah didn't come with him."

Kezia eyed the knife with relief. The color came back into her cheeks. She breathed a sigh and spoke softly. "I'm glad you're unharmed, Jair."

Hannah turned. "Achsah, put that away."

"He shouldn't sneak around at night with what is happening." Achsah shrugged. "He should know there could be problems."

Everyone seemed to breath more easily when Achsah put the knife down.

Josheb took Jair by the arm. "Come, you must tell us what's been happening."

They all went into the house and gathered around Jair. "Toi and Benaiah were unharmed when I left. There were more of us than there were of the Amorites, and we were in a better position to fight. I was sent back to town to ask the households for more food and provisions. I can't stay, but if you have supplies to spare, I'll take them back there with me."

Achsah brushed off her tunic. "I thought they'd be home by now."

Jair turned to her with a look of impatience. "It'll be a few more days. The Amorites want the land and are willing to fight for it, yet they're outnumbered. It shouldn't be difficult to push back."

"But, Toi and Benaiah shouldn't be there. What business is it of theirs to have gone?" Heat reddened her cheeks as she tugged on his sleeve.

Jair drew in a breath, then he suddenly smiled and looked amused. He pulled his arm away. "They told you why, but I'll let them know you miss them."

She let out an exasperated sound as she looked outside one of the windows of their home. "They should be protecting us and not warring in a matter that doesn't concern them."

"Achsah, we live in Moab. We're willing to help your people."

"But..."

Jair put his hand on her arm. "They'll do what they feel they need to."

"It's true." Josheb nodded. "I see no reason to continue to argue about it."

Jair looked at the door. "I need to take the cart back with supplies. I'll need to leave as soon as I can."

"Here, take these to them." Hannah lifted sacks of grain and dried foods off the shelves. "We'll also send fresh water from the cistern if they need it."

Jair nodded. "That will be good. We'll take it to the cart."

Others took oils and various items from the shelves. They carried them outside.

Kezia moved behind Jair. She tugged on the sleeve of his tunic.

He turned. A warm look entered his eyes. "Kezia?"

"Tell my brothers I'm praying for them."

"I'll do this."

Achsah moved beside Kezia. Her eyes narrowed slightly. "Tell them I'm doing the same."

He nodded and smiled. "I will."

Kezia's voice softened. She looked at Achsah. "Achsah and I will go to town. Are there more supplies you need?"

"Buy what you feel we could use for food."

Kezia tipped her head. "We'll have someone take it to them."

"Thank you. The skirmish shouldn't last much longer, and we'll be back soon."

Kezia stepped back and nodded again.

After the family loaded the supplies, they left a lamp with her at the gate, so that she might say goodbye to Jair.

Achsah reluctantly went back to her room in the adjoining courtyard.

Tomorrow, she and Kezia would leave for town to get more supplies. At least she'd feel she was doing something to help rather than sitting and waiting. She was tiring of pacing and her nervous thoughts.

*****

The next day, the marketplace was quiet and empty, except for a few vendors who traded and offered goods alongside the town paths.

Achsah looked across the road as she and Kezia carried their traded goods in the direction of their home.

Naaman, one of the Israelite priests, turned and stared down the length of his nose when he saw Achsah.

Kezia put her hand on Achsah's arm. "Come, Achsah. You need not start anything."

Achsah crossed her arms. She gave the man a look of disgust. "I've never done anything to him, but I shouldn't have to suffer, every time I see him, because I chose to marry Toi."

"The priest holds power. Naaman is one of the elders. You should watch what you say to him."

"Hmm, I think he's an old goat. He should watch what he says. He frowns at me, even when there's no reason for it. I don't understand what I've done to deserve his harsh criticism of me?"

Kezia bent her head and looked at the ground as they walked past. "He doesn't see you the way our family does, and looks for reasons to condemn you. What he sees on the outside is what matters to him. He watches for mistakes to be made, sins to be committed. The other priests are kind, but Naaman is prideful. Please, Achsah, watch yourself around him."

Achsah stopped walking. She tightened her grip on the sack of grain she carried. "He has no hold over me. I'm a Moabitess, and I don't have to follow his silly rules. He won't let me into the synagogue, so what does it matter?"

"You're married to my brother, an Israelite. For some reason, the man's more vigilant than ever to find fault with you. I tell you that you must be careful, Achsah. He's not kind."

Achsah gave Naaman a disgruntled look. "Well, I don't like him."

The crease in Naaman's brow furrowed. He called from across the road. "Your pagan ways will get you in trouble, Achsah, and if I were you, Kezia, I'd be careful around that woman. Your sister-in-law will cause you to falter. This Moabitess is not a good influence."

Achsah waved a hand at him. She lifted her chin with a haughty air. "Oh, go back to your chants and good works for show. You do these things for others to see, but it doesn't mean you're a kind and caring person as Kezia is. She gives to others, because she trusts Adonai and wants to please him, not for her own benefit, or any other reason."

Kezia put her hand to her mouth, and her eyes widened. "Achsah, you mustn't answer Naaman this way."

Achsah let out a breath. "I don't care if he's the pillar that supports the King's palace. If your Lord is who you say he is, I can't imagine him honoring such a man. That priest pretends to be pious, but he gives no thought to the truly needy or poor. He a gossip and a fake. He admonishes others, when he's no better."

Naaman's fists tightened, and the veins in his neck formed ridges. "You'll pay for your detestable words, woman. Our Lord will find you out in the end, and no good will come of it. You speak, so openly, in our Lord's name. It's sinful, even more so, when you're a Moabite with little understanding of our faith."

"Oh, go give an offering! Do something to help others rather than hindering them. Take care of your own dark and aging heart, rather than trying to find fault with others!"

Achsah shook the dust off her robe and gave Kezia a gentle nudge in the direction of home. "Come, Kezia, we've better things to do."

Kezia looked as if she would shrink dead away. Her dark eyes were large, and her cheeks were pale. She began walking down the dusty path.

Achsah lifted her chin as she moved closer to her sister-in-law's side. She didn't look back. Ha! That priest could stew over her words. There'd be no more talking to that scoundrel.

*****

"Achsah, you shouldn't have spoken to Naaman that way. It's wrong. He's in a position above us, and our Lord has appointed him to be there."

Achsah shifted the grain sack she held in her arms. She blinked. "Even when he says things that aren't true? Should I keep silent when he accuses me wrongly? I've been faithful to Toi and haven't strayed. I've quit praying to the Moabite gods and am listening to what you say. Why does he treat me this way when I'm making efforts to learn your ways?"

"Naaman's been given a position of authority by the Lord. He'll give account for his deeds, if he chooses wrongly. The Lord knows the truth of it. There is no need for us to speak to him in unkind ways."

"But..."

"Achsah, we're to be obedient to Adonai. We need to allow him to guide our thoughts and actions. He'll see justice done with his appointed."

"I don't understand your beliefs. They're odd." Achsah wrinkled her brow. "How is it possible to treat a man, such as Naaman, with such care when you know what you do about him?"

"The Lord is the one who's good. I can do nothing without him."

Achsah didn't respond. Instead, she looked in the direction of their home. She swung the bag of grain at her side by the leather straps that were tied to it.

She scuffed her sandals against the road as she walked. It might be best to follow in Kezia's steps instead of Toi's.

Kezia was kind. She loved others. There was peace and patience in her heart, and there was no pride. She wasn't self-seeking, and she spoke of changes inside, rather than worrying about her outward appearance. Spangles and precious jewels meant nothing to her.

Achsah sighed. Toi and she both needed whatever it was Kezia had. What would it take for them to live differently and listen to the voice of the Lord? How might they see that this was something they might benefit from too?

She looked at the sun which was above them. We must be getting back. We've chores to do. If we quicken our steps, we'll get there in time to help mother."

Kezia nodded and smiled. "I'm glad we're almost there. Now, we have supplies for my brothers."

"They'll have what they need."

They hurried as they made their way down the path to their home. They stepped inside the doorway.

*****

Jorah scanned the countryside. He eyed the mountains of Moab in the distance which were a natural border of their country. Toi and Benaiah were there somewhere. He hoped they'd be back soon and that the matters at the edge of the land would finally be settled.

He looked to where the valley had formed a depression near the river. The brook bubbled as it moved along swiftly.

Upon closer inspection, he saw movement. There was a lone figure at the bank of the creek. A young woman playfully called to a small donkey. Her back was to him so he couldn't see her face, yet he recognized her bright scarf, of shimmering gold, which was fastened to her waist.

Jorah blinked. Dinah?

He eyed the hills beyond and the vast plains that stretched out in the distance. Sounds of birds echoed overhead in the silent back country. He wondered was she doing so far outside of town alone.

He let go of his donkey and watched Dinah as she chased the animal when it began to trot away. Her feet were bare, and her bright, auburn hair flew behind her as she ran.

When she caught hold of the donkey's rein, she pulled the small animal close and petted the top of its head between the ears. She nuzzled it as she reached down and picked a flower to weave into its mane.

She talked to the animal, but Jorah couldn't make out what she was saying from where he was.

He'd seen her before, by the riverside, picking flowers at the edge of the water. She was light-hearted and carefree, not the closed young woman he'd spoken to on the road.

Here, Dinah played with the animals. Her affectionate hugs around the donkey's neck and laughter revealed a young woman who seemed much more free-spirited than she'd allowed others to see.

He sighed as he studied the way she moved and danced along the river's stream occasionally dipping her sandaled foot into the water. She pulled the donkey alongside the bank as she made her way farther from him in the direction of her home.

He untied his own animal and walked along the edge of the path as he trailed her from the top of the ridge. He wanted to make sure she made it home safely. She'd obviously little understanding of the dangers a young woman posed walking in the countryside alone. She should have known the necessity of keeping to the safe paths.

*****

286

Dinah glanced quickly at the top of the rise and then back at the river. She heard donkey's hooves and hoped the rider would do her no harm. She breathed a sigh of relief when she realized it was Jorah who had been following her.

What was he doing?

Lately, their paths had crossed quite often. She wasn't sure she knew what to think of it.

She didn't look back at him as she didn't want him to know that she'd seen him. She supposed it was better for him not to know. Pursuing an Israelite could lead her on a path to heartbreak, one she was best to avoid. Though the Israelite men were friendly to her people, it was not often a man, like Jorah, would consider bringing a foreign woman to his home. He was quite different from his older brothers.

It was best her thoughts went no further than the friendship they'd forged and that she would remain content with the fact that he was near and that he would see her safely home.

*****

Chapter 15

Toi lifted his hand to his shoulder and held it there. He winced. He attempted to turn over, but couldn't move.

Blood seeped from a wound on his upper left arm. He'd lost and regained consciousness, more than once, as he lay on the ground and listened to the sounds around him.

Where was Benaiah? Was his brother injured as well?

He though of Achsah, and he let out a groan.

He hadn't treated her well when he'd left his parent's home. Though she'd not admitted it, he knew she'd been afraid when she'd asked him not to leave.

He closed his eyes and then opened them again. She'd not deserved the offhand remarks she'd gotten from him at the gate as he rode away.

Now he wasn't sure whether he'd make it back alive. He might never see her, or his family, again. If the Amorites overtook Benaiah, and the others, he'd surely die.

He thought about praying, yet after all the things he'd done, and how he'd treated the Lord, could he even hope that Adonai would listen? He breathed in deeply and closed his eyes.

He'd not been careful in the way he'd lived his life. Achsah had told him that he'd had no faith, or belief, and that his was a religion no better than her Moabite rituals. She'd been right. He'd never put forth an effort to understand the Israelite teachings, and he hadn't inquired of the Lord for guidance.

Though he'd gone to synagogue with his family, and worked everyday providing for his own, there were things he hadn't considered.

He'd been taught the Torah was of utmost importance in knowing truth, yet he'd read little of it, and hadn't attempted to study the verses, other than in rote memorization. Nothing he'd done had been in servitude toward the Lord. He'd rarely inquired of the Lord. It hadn't been his desire.

The direction his life had taken, and how he'd spent his days, had been without thought to the Lord. By his actions and words, he'd surely made jests of what was sacred. He'd turned it into a game. If he'd been set apart at birth, he'd misused the gifts he'd been given by making idols for his own profit. What Achsah had told him and Benaiah, the one day in the courtyard, had been right.

He put his hand to his aching shoulder and clasped it there as he listened to the eerie howl of hyenas in the distance. He drew in a breath of cool desert air.

An uncomfortable feeling swept over him as he murmured a prayer. He'd nowhere else to turn.

He prayed for his warrior friends, and for his family and asked Adonai for victory over the Amorites. He prayed for a chance to speak to Achsah and assure her that she'd be safe with him. He would show her greater care, if he were given the opportunity.

He made another attempt to turn over, but he was unable once again.

His prayer stuck in his throat while he thought of the few times he'd listened and obeyed the calling of the Lord. Until now, he'd trusted in his abilities, but he suddenly realized it wasn't possible. If he died this day, there was little he'd done to deserve the blessing of the Lord.

As darkness closed in, he shut his eyes. He'd no strength. He spoke quietly. "Adonai, nothing I've done merits your help. I've not given my heart to you before this. I haven't acknowledged my sin, but now I do. I fearfully place my life of disobedience into your merciful hands. Allow me a second chance. Return to me, oh Lord."

*****

Days passed since Kezia and Achsah had come from the town.

Kezia took Achsah's arm after she walked through the doorway. "Ruth needs us. There's trouble in her home. Both she and Orpah's husband's, Mahlon and Chilion, are very sick. Their health is failing. Ruth's mother-in-law is beside herself as she can't afford to lose either of her sons, and Ruth and Orpah are doing what they can to care for both their husbands and her as well."

"The men are worsening?" Achsah drew in a breath. "Oh, no."

"Yes, and Ruth and the other women need rest from it."

Sapphira piped in. "I'll go! I can help."

"And I," Anah spoke softly.

"We'll go in shifts." Kezia echoed her thoughts. "It won't due to all be there at once. They'll need this. Sapphira and Anah will go when Achsah and I return. Mother will take a turn also."

Sapphira and Anah nodded.

Anah put her hand on Kezia's arm. "We'll take our turn when you return."

"Yes, there's no time to spare. Let mother know our plans. We'll come back to you in the morning."

*****

Ruth sat down next to Achsah on the front steps of the house. It was evening, and the night stars appeared on the horizon. The house was quiet inside.

Achsah reached out and took Ruth's hand. She squeezed it gently. "They'll be well soon. Don't worry. Your Lord's powerful."

Ruth nodded. "Yes, and I believe in Adonai, yet Mahlon's not doing well. What if the Lord's answer is that Mahlon is to do? I fear that my husband won't make it through the night. I'm afraid, Achsah. Chilion's no better."

"Don't despair. They'll surely come around."

"It's the custom that if anything should happen to my husband and he doesn't live, I'd marry Chilion. Yet, Chilion's sick also. There are no other brothers. There'd be no hope of heirs for Naomi. We'll be widows with no prospects. I'm not sure what we'd do."

"Marry the brother? This is what the Israelites do?" Achsah choked on Ruth's words. If something happened to Toi, she'd marry Benaiah? She put those thoughts away as it wasn't the time or place.

She turned back to Ruth. "They won't die, Ruth. Believe this. Things will work for your good. You'll see."

Ruth got up. The dark circles under her eyes betrayed her weariness. "I'll keep praying and watch over Mahlon. I'll sit by his side all night. Come, let's go back inside."

"Yes, let's. You've nothing to fear."

*****

Despite, Ruth's brave words, both Orpah and Ruth lost their husbands, that evening, and Naomi, her sons. Mournful sounds rang out in the household throughout the night and through until morning.

Achsah and Kezia stayed for a time, but then left the women to grieve with other friends. They sent for Hannah. Ruth and Orpah had sat at their mother-in-law's feet as they'd rocked back and forth and cried.

When they closed the gate behind them, Achsah looked back. "What will they do? We can only give them so much of our store. We've given so much to Jair and the men on the field. They're alone. They've little food left. How will they survive?"

"I don't know. They're destitute. There are no men to care for them. Unless Ruth remarries, there will be no hope for them."

*****

Anah, Sapphira, and Hannah returned the next day. They'd been at Ruth's home all day.

Anah sat down, on the stairway in the courtyard, next to Achsah. She spoke quietly. "Ruth and Orpah left with Naomi. They're going to go back to Naomi's homeland together."

Achsah sighed. "I heard that Ruth didn't want to leave Naomi. Orpah went back to her family so she will be able to remarry."

"Yes, Naomi wanted this for her. But, Ruth has embraced the Israelite God as her own. After living so long in Naomi's family, she couldn't deny what she saw in her husband's family. She wanted this also. She loves her mother-in-law very much and won't leave her destitute. She's taken a great step of faith."

"She has, and I pray that they're cared for in Naomi's homeland."

"I too."

Achsah got up when she noticed a couple riders in the distance. They approached the house. "Who is it? Who's coming?"

Both Kezia and Anah got up and walked to the gate.

"Benaiah!" Anah called out as they reached the latch and opened it.

Achsah stood and watched as the donkeys neared the house. Benaiah and Jair were back, but Toi wasn't with them.

Benaiah got down as Anah went to him and embraced him. She looked up. "Is it over? Are the Amorites gone?"

"Yes, they are." He nodded. "They won't be coming back, though it wasn't easy. We lost men."

Jair also got down and tied his donkey to a tree by the gate. He began to go in, when Achsah reached out to stop him.

"Where's Toi?" She eyed Benaiah warily as her breath went out of her.

Benaiah spoke drily. "You care whether he's with us or not?"

She choked on her next words. "Where is he?"

Benaiah tipped his head in the direction of the field from which they'd come. "His donkey's foot was sore. He had to get off the animal." He gave her a curious stare.

Achsah looked down the rock-strewn path. A lone figure led a donkey by its reins. She let out a sound as tears sprung to her eyes.

She didn't say anything else, but she lifted her skirts and ran down the road. She passed the home and quickened her pace as she got closer to Toi.

When she reached him, she said nothing, but threw herself at him and hugged him tightly.

Toi wrapped his arms around her and leaned down to brush his lips against her hair. "My little Achsah missed me. Could it be?"

She spoke quietly while she held on to him. "You didn't come back when Jair did."

"You wanted me to?"

Achsah let go and looked up at him. "You left me with a knife, and I almost killed him with it. You shouldn't have gone away."

His eyes lightened as he looked at her. "And you were truly worried that I might not come back?"

"If you had died, I would have been given to Benaiah as his wife. What kind of custom is that?" Achsah stared at him angrily.

He laughed. "I didn't consider the two of you together ever."

"You would have left me in an impossible situation. I'd have nothing, and my family…! Did you give any consideration of what might have become of me?"

He took her hand and held it tightly in his. "I'm sorry, Achsah, that you were afraid. I'm back now. I won't leave you again."

She straightened and gave him a wary look. "I wasn't…afraid, that is. Truly."

He gave her hand another gentle squeeze. "I don't believe you'd tell me if you were, but I thought of you when I was gone. I'm sorry for the way I left you. I might not have seen you again."

She sighed. Then, she noticed his shoulder, and her mouth drew open. "What did you do to yourself?"

"I'm quite sure it was a spear. Things happened so fast it was difficult to tell. It's smaller than I thought it was and it did bleed a lot. It's good that I'm back home."

"It doesn't look small." She took the donkey's leather strap from his hand and began to lead the large animal down the path. "You must get back so you can rest. Come, your mother and father will want to see you."

He walked with her until they reached the gate. After putting the donkey inside the courtyard for animals, he tugged on her hand and pulled her close. "I'll be with mother and father soon enough. It's been too long since I've seen you." He tugged on her hand.

"They'll want to see you."

Toi shook his head back and forth. "We'll have time for them later." He didn't let go of her and pulled her with him.

They both slipped inside the arched doorway leading to the courtyard and closed the door behind them.

He'd finally come home.

*****

That evening, Achsah stole out into the night air.

She looked into the dark, star-lightened sky and drew in a breath. The air was crisp and fresh as it entered her chest.

"Are you there, Adonai? Do you speak?"

She listened and waited for an answer as she'd done countless other times, but there was none.

She shivered and drew her scarf tighter around her.

The hushed solitude of the night affirmed the vastness of the dark universe that surrounded her. An errant cloud swept past the moon and darkened the courtyard. The trill sound of crickets rose out of the blackness.

"I suppose I shouldn't wonder why the Lord of the heavens doesn't answer. I'm a Moabitess, despised by my own family. What should I expect?"

She heard a sound and turned. Toi was standing behind her.

"He might, if you trusted him, Achsah. And maybe if you learned this, you could trust me."

Achsah looked out into the darkness. "How long have you been there?"

"I heard your prayers."

"And you didn't say anything?"

"I couldn't sleep. I didn't mean to intrude."

"You tell me to trust, but you haven't done it yourself."

He looked at the stars. He didn't say anything at first as if he weighed his thoughts. "It's true, I hadn't before I'd left you. I suppose lying in a pool of blood, on a battlefield at night, makes a man reconsider the path he's on."

"You might have died? You said it was a small wound." Achsah looked shocked. She went to him and put her hand on his arm. "I told you not to go. You should have listened."

Toi reached out and touched her cheek. "But I did, and I'm beginning to believe now that the Lord had reasons for it, that I needed to be there, even though I didn't see it at the time."

"What are you saying?" She looked up.

He didn't answer, but looked thoughtful.

"Tell me. What other reasons?"

"Ah…Achsah, you must know that things have changed. Thanks be to Adonai."

"What things? What do you mean?"

"Remember when you spoke to Benaiah and I once about our faith, or lack of it? I considered what you said. I looked at my life, very differently, when I had time to think things through."

"But you had no desire to change? You had no intentions of it?"

"Not at the time. But, as I've said, things have changed."
His eyes crinkled at the corners. "I plan to do the Lord's will
instead now. I want to start living for him rather than for myself."

She looked at the wound on his shoulder, and a frown
drew over her brow. She didn't know what to think. "But, *you?*"

He laughed at her astonishment.

She backed away, and her eyes suddenly narrowed.
"Kezia has this type of faith, but I don't believe you could.
You're different than her."

"I suppose I don't know much, not like Kezia. But, I plan
to learn. You'll see." His brow curved slightly. "I've made
commitments. I see my life differently now."

Achsah drew back. She gave him a wary look. "But,
there are things you do that your Lord would not approve of that I
don't believe you'd ever give up. I'm sure of it."

"Achsah, I saw things I didn't see before and want to
follow him." His expression was solemn, yet resolute. "You
might doubt it, but I know it's true. I'll do anything he asks of
me, from now on. His life is my own."

She looked at him puzzled. He was different, yet she
wasn't certain he was completely serious. Surely he'd be unable
to break the ties he'd had to his past which had done so much for
him.

Her thoughts turned to his work, and all the things he'd
accomplished that had given him success, his crafting of idols.
Toi wouldn't give these things up, for anything, even if the
Israelite God disapproved. It'd be too costly for him. It would
ruin his livelihood for him to quit fashioning the stone into
Moabite gods. But, surely, if he wanted to give wholehearted
devotion to Adonai?

He said he'd changed. But could he trust in the way he
said he wanted to? Could he put aside these things, for his
newfound faith? If not, he couldn't fault her for her lack of it.

She went to him and smiled. "Anything?"

He nodded.

"You allowed Benaiah to smash my idols, yet you continue to make them. Do you believe Adonai would want you to do this?"

Toi turned suddenly. He looked conflicted. "Achsah, this isn't what I meant."

Her eyes gleamed when she saw his hesitation. She was right. He would never give up making the idols. He couldn't do it. Wealth meant too much to him. It was his first test, and he'd already failed.

"Making the idols is my trade. It's how I earn money for the things you buy. I don't worship them."

She put her hand on his arm. "But you make them. Do you truly believe your Lord would condone such a thing? I thought trusting the Lord was important to you, since you've come back? Isn't it what you said?" Her eyes glinted green.

He hesitated.

"You said you wanted to do his will. I'm sure he wouldn't want you making idols."

He stared at her as if deep in thought. Then, he lifted his hand to her face and outlined the curve of it as he smiled at her. "You think I would listen to a Moabitess about such things?"

She slanted her eyes at him. "And why not, when that Moabitess is your wife?"

"My wife, yes." His eyes sparkled as he looked at her. He smiled again. "It would be a first step in following him. I suppose you're right. It is what Adonai would want, so I will do as you say. I won't make the idols. I want to do what would please him."

"But..."

"Achsah, I told you I'd give up what I thought would be out of line with Adonai's will, and you're correct in saying that making the idols is clearly not what Adonai would want. I keep my word, Achsah. It is one thing you can depend upon."

Achsah pulled back from him. "But you wouldn't. You can't!" He was willing to go this far? He couldn't be serious. How would he make a profit? Where would her silk fabrics, costly perfumes, and fine jewelry come from? How would he support her? "It's your trade."

"I must have faith that my business will not falter because of it, and if it does, I must trust him."

She stared at him as he leaned down to kiss her. He couldn't mean it? Could he?

She wondered at his words and at the ease at which he said them. What was he thinking? Had he lost his mind?

Was he willing to throw away everything for this newfound faith? She wasn't sure she wanted to find out.

*****

Chapter 16

Achsah sat on a long mat, in the courtyard, where the family was eating. She eyed a platter of fish in front of her but took a piece of dark bread from a basket instead and dipped it into oil. She took a bite and chewed slowly as she watched her husband.

He was talking to his father about the fields and the work that needed to be done. He stopped to pour goat's milk from a container into his cup, and then he filled hers when he was finished. He nodded as he listened to his father's answer.

He'd changed since he came back from the skirmish at the border. He'd been more watchful of her, and he seemed as if he wanted to make amends for any past behavior for which he might have wronged her.

He'd given up the trade of making idols as he said he would. He told her that other aspects of his work were being considered instead.

He turned. "You seem to be contemplating something. I hope it's good." He smiled.

"I was thinking of how you've changed, and I'm glad of it." She took a drink.

He looked as if he were amazed at her words. "I never thought you would feel this way. Aren't you afraid my business, and the money I bring in, will suffer from not making the idols? I did quite well in that trade."

"You've done well in many things. I've confidence you'll find other ways to bring shekels in for my benefit." She grinned at him.

His eyes shone as he looked at her. "Adonai will surely be with us in whatever comes."

Kezia smiled from across the mat.

Josheb and Hannah both chuckled as they listened.

They all turned when Benaiah and Anah came through the gate and made their way to where everyone was eating.

Anah gestured to Achsah. She spoke quietly. "Benaiah has something to tell you."

He nodded. Then he turned and looked at her.

Anah nudged him.

He swallowed. His voice was low and quiet. "I want to apologize, Achsah."

Achsah put down the cup of milk in her hand. She opened her mouth slightly in surprise. "For what?"

Hannah and Josheb lowered the food in their hands. Hannah's eyes widened as she looked at her son.

"I was quick to judge, and I shouldn't have treated you wrongly in the past." Benaiah raked his hand through his hair. He cleared his throat. "I must make amends by way of an apology. It won't happen again."

Achsah's look was one of surprise. She didn't know what to say. She just nodded.

Toi took her hand in his and squeezed it gently.

Anah turned to Hannah and Josheb. "There's another thing."

"Benaiah?" Josheb put down the raisin cake in his hand.

"We're with child. There will be a new member in the family shortly." Benaiah smiled. He turned to Anah and put his arm around her shoulders.

Hannah stood and went to Anah. "It's true?" She put her hand over her mouth and laughed when Anah nodded. "Oh, the Lord has blessed us!"

Kezia, who had been quiet for most of the meal, got up from the end of the mat and went to Anah. Her eyes sparkled as she spoke quietly. "It's wonderful news."

Achsah watched the family curiously. She wasn't quite sure what to think of a baby. She took a bite of her bread. Babies could be difficult, yet they also could be rather sweet.

Toi glanced at her with a knowing smile. "You could make brightly colored tunics for it and cover it in sweet-smelling oils. You have enough perfume for it." He winked at her.

"Oh, stop it." Achsah pushed on his arm. She smiled good-naturedly.

Everyone laughed.

Anah took Benaiah's arm. "I've more to tell the family."

"Anah?" There was concern in his voice. "Are you well?"

Everyone turned to look at her.

"I have decided to not worship Chemosh and my Moabite idols. I've chosen the way of my husband and family."

Benaiah's eyes widened. "Truly?" He looked at her as if he were amazed.

The others in the room smiled.

"I've listened to your mother and father, and Kezia, and Achsah. Adonai's done many things for you, and Toi, and for your family. I want your Lord to be my own also."

Benaiah looked relieved. "I've not been a good example, but it's what I hoped to hear."

Hannah put her hands to her cheeks. "So much has happened to be thankful for."

Achsah eyed the family cautiously as they celebrated the news. She wasn't sure about what to think. She'd offered prayers to Adonai, yet Anah had taken a step, she herself was still unwilling to take. Achsah hadn't placed her trust in Adonai. She hadn't fully accepted him as her own. She wasn't sure what held her back, but things weren't as easy as it seemed.

Toi leaned down. He whispered in her ear. "My family has accepted you, Achsah. You need not be anxious about anything."

Achsah didn't answer. Toi had changed so much since he'd come back from the front. She wasn't sure what to think of him either.

Benaiah looked around the courtyard. "Where's Sapphira and Jorah? They'll want to hear this."

"Mother sent them to town for more grain." Kezia let go of Anah's hands. "The stores were almost empty. So much went to the border and to Ruth for their journey. They'll be back later."

Hannah and Kezia both sat back down.

Hannah smiled. "I'm sure you can't wait to tell them. Sapphira will be dancing around the place, and Jorah will be pleased."

"I look forward to it." Benaiah nodded.

Josheb held out his arms and gestured to the food. "Come and sit. Let's finish eating. It's a time to celebrate."

Benaiah and Anah sat next to Toi and Achsah.

"The meal looks wonderful. We'll see the others in time."

*****

The market was busy. People moved shoulder to shoulder carrying their purchases past tents set up on the path.

Jorah put his hand on Sapphira's arm. "I believe we've bought enough. We'll need to get back, Sapphira. I'm sure we've missed mother's meal."

Sapphira looked up from the grain sack she'd just bought and pointed over his shoulder. "Isn't that Achsah's sister?" She tugged on her brother's sleeve.

Jorah turned and looked across the path. His brow furrowed. "Dinah." He sighed.

Dinah sidled up to Sapphira and smiled. "You're from my sister's family?"

"Yes, I'm Toi's sister. I saw you at Achsah's wedding."

She gave Jorah a quick glance and then turned back to Sapphira. "And this is your brother, Jorah?" She pretended not to know him. "I believe we spoke at the wedding."

Jorah's eyes trailed from her face to the lengths of hair that had fallen over her shoulder, and then finally to her hand which had been pricked by the thorn. His frown turned to a smile. "I haven't forgotten you."

A blush arose in Dinah's cheeks, but she didn't say anything.

Sapphira gave them both an odd look. "Yes, this is my youngest brother, although he's older than I am."

302

Dinah turned back to the road. "You're on your way home? I'll walk with you if you'd like. I'm on my way to my father's."

Jorah held his hand up. Maybe it was not a good an idea to allow Dinah access to her sister. The young woman was unpredictable. "We might have other things to purchase."

Sapphira gave a sack to Jorah to carry. "Mother said grain was all she wanted. That's what she gave us money for." She turned back to Dinah. "You can come with us, and yes, we're going back now."

He lifted the leather ties over his shoulder and began to follow behind them. He didn't say anything.

Sapphira looked out over the fields of Moab as they made their way down the path.

Dinah was the first to break the silence. "How has my sister been? I haven't seen her for some time."

Sapphira's face lightened. She looked at Dinah. "Achsah's become a good friend to me. She's very happy."

"Happy? I'm surprised."

"She and I have spent much time in each other's company."

Dinah frowned. "I wouldn't have thought it. What does Toi think of her?"

"I'm sure he loves Achsah. He's very attentive to her."

"But he didn't love her before?" Dinah's eyes narrowed slightly when she said it. She stole a glance at Jorah who was still behind them.

Jorah let out a long, slow breath.

Dinah ignored him. "Something must have changed."

"I don't know how he felt, when they first married, but she prays to Adonai now, and he likes that." Sapphira smiled.

Dinah's eyes narrowed. "But what about Chemosh and her idols?"

"Oh, she quit going to the high places, and Benaiah smashed her idols."

Jorah broke in again. "Sapphira, you mustn't gossip."

Sapphira put her finger to her lips. "Jorah, please." She sighed. "I don't know why mother wanted you to come with me." She gave him an exasperated frown.

He let out a snort. Then, he turned and stared at the fields.

Dinah ignored him. She looked back at Sapphira as if shocked. "What did Achsah do?"

"She got angry." Sapphira smiled. "She told him her thoughts on it."

"Yes, I can imagine. My sister will speak her mind and isn't afraid to."

"She wasn't happy when he got rid of the special goat idol Toi made for her."

Dinah reached up and wound a piece of dark hair around her finger. "What do you mean, special?"

"It had carved lines on its sides and eyes with jewels. It was very different from any other idols. The work was unique."

"Is that so?" Dinah stopped walking.

Jorah reached out and took his sister's arm. "Sapphira, I'm sure neither Achsah, nor Toi, would appreciate your repeating these things."

Sapphira shrugged him off. "I thought I told you to leave us be."

Jorah scowled. There was a perturbed sound in his voice. "I've things I need to do at home and have no time for this." He strode ahead of them and looked back once. "I'll see you back there." He gave Dinah a dark look.

Sapphira ignored him. "What were we saying? Oh, yes, Toi's very talented."

Dinah looked down the road as she listened to Sapphira rattle on.

Sapphira looked thoughtful. "But he doesn't make idols anymore because Achsah doesn't want him to."

Dinah took another piece of hair in her hand and twisted it. "He did this for her?"

"Yes, she told him to stop making them."

"Hmm. I'm surprised he listened to her. I'm sure she's been trouble for him."

Sapphira's eyes widened. "Oh no. Toi and she have been good for each other. My brother needed her."

Dinah made a face. "For now, I suppose. It's still early in their marriage." She eyed the fork in the path ahead, and she stopped walking. "Oh, it seems we must part. The path has split."

Sapphira nodded. "Yes, please tell your family we wish them well. I must go my way."

"I'll do this. Tell my sister I'll make efforts to see her again. Peace to you."

"Peace."

*****

Sapphira waved as Dinah left to go on the other trail. She breathed a sigh. She'd spoken freely about Achsah and Toi, and hadn't intended to say as much as she did.

She supposed she should have listened to Jorah. He'd warned her, yet at the time, it hadn't seemed wrong. Now, she feared her gossip might cause problems later on. Dinah seemed to be digging for more information than she herself had been willing to give, and she had been the one to supply it.

She was silent for the remainder of the walk. She wanted no more to do with idle chatter of any kind.

Luckily, the path was short, and she wouldn't have to ponder her conversation with Dinah, and the things she'd said, for long.

*****

Dinah hummed a tune while walking the path. She eyed the hilly rock formations in the distance. Their triangular mounds were etched with lines and revealed the layers of sediments in them. She studied the patterns as she passed.

A traveler might think that the terrain was a blend of desert rock without much variation, but having lived her whole life, in the country of Moab, attending to the most minute detail, on her walks to town and back, Dinah saw a vibrancy in them that others, less acquainted with the area, might fail to grasp.

Rose colored rocks, with shadowed lines of every shade of brown and gray, spread out beneath a light blue sky while dusty green bushes dotted the countryside. She stared at the scene before her. It never failed to appeal to her sensibilities.

When she looked up she jumped slightly.

Jorah was around the bend of the road and was waiting for her.

"What are you doing here?" Her voice rose a notch as she made her way to him. "I thought you were going home?"

Jorah ignored her questions, but asked his own instead. "Why didn't you want Sapphira to know that you knew me? You pretended you'd never met me."

Dinah gave him an odd look. "I didn't think you wanted her to know. It didn't seem you wanted to walk back together, or acknowledge that you knew me."

"I didn't want the two of you together, and there was good reason for it." He moved closer. "You and Sapphira should not have been discussing such private matters of Achsah and Toi's. I don't know why you wanted to know about my brother's affairs?"

"Why wouldn't I?" Dinah scuffed the path with her sandaled feet. She leaned down to pick up a feather that lay on the ground and twirled it between her fingers as she studied its colors. "My sister's married to him. It's important that she's treating him as she should, so that our family name isn't tarnished." She ran her fingers along the edge of the feather. She looked up at him and smiled.

Jorah's jawline tightened. "You need not look after Toi. He can take care of himself. And Achsah's done nothing to tarnish your family name."

"Why does it matter so much to you, if I have an interest in your brother and my sister's marriage?"

Jorah let out an agitated breath. "I don't want to hear about Toi anymore. And you shouldn't either. He wants nothing to do with you."

Dinah stared at him with fascination. She suddenly reached out and traced the outline of his face with the feather.

He took a step back. "Dinah, stop. You should listen and stay out of Achsah and my brother's life."

She waved the feather in the air at him and laughed. "I think I know why you're angry. There's another reason you don't want me to talk about Toi, isn't there?"

"What are you saying?"

She giggled. "You're jealous, aren't you Jorah?"

*****

He pushed her hand away. "Toi's a married man. I've no reason to be jealous. My brother would not consider you. He wouldn't take another wife. It isn't our family way."

Dinah gave him a teasing smile as her lashes lowered coyly. "But *you* would consider me? And you have, haven't you?" She moved with a natural grace toward him. Her voice was smooth.

He stared at her. Though she played games, she had a powerful effect on him, and he was certain that she knew it too.

"There would never be competition between my brother and me, in your case."

"No?"

"No, because as I've said, he has a wife."

Dinah tipped her head to him. She spoke quietly. "But you don't have one?"

He breathed in the sweet scent that surrounded her. As the sun streamed down on them both, the heat stirred in him. He couldn't deny his attraction to her. He'd never felt such strong feelings for a woman before.

He hesitated, at first, but despite the warning signals that were going off inside him, he leaned down and kissed her.

Though he knew it was something he'd regret, he ignored the misgivings he had concerning her.

Dinah responded warmly to his touch.

She looked up at him, and her eyes widened. "Jorah?"

Upon hearing his name, he just as quickly moved back from her. He wondered what he'd been thinking to have kissed her. She wasn't Israelite, and the Lord had warned against attachments to those of contrary beliefs. He'd kept his distance from her until now.

A smile curved over her lips as she studied his conflicted expression. "It's as I thought."

Jorah sighed. He quickly let go of her. He supposed he should have left things the way they had been. He had not wished to cause her harm, in any way. "Dinah, I…"

She regarded him with surprised expression.

Then, her brows knit together when she saw the way he was looking at her. "What is it you want from me? What are your intentions?" Her cheeks turned a darker shade, and she eyed him quizzically.

"I don't want to hurt you. I told you that friendship was what you could expect from me." He tugged at the collar of his tunic. In taking the liberties that he had, he may have given her the impression that might be more for them. "I'm sorry if I've led you to believe differently."

"You wouldn't hurt anyone. How would you hurt me?"

He cleared his throat. He couldn't bring a third foreign woman home to his parents. They'd expected differently from him. "It was wrong of me as we've different beliefs. You're Moabite, and I'm not."

Dinah gave him a curious look. Then, she laughed and took hold of his hand. "Surely you've noticed before this?" She moved closer to him. "Your brothers didn't seem to be bothered by it. It didn't stop them from marriage to what you might call, 'foreign' women."

The heat of the warm sun wrapped around Jorah as he stood looking at her. Rich, auburn hair framed a dark, lovely face that seemed almost as perfection to him. He wanted to reach out and draw her closer.

Instead, he let go and pushed her away. "I told you, it is not the way of my people to intermix with other cultures, despite what my brothers did. And you shouldn't encourage such things with your manner of speech and in your actions. You're not listening to what I've said."

Dinah stared at him in astonishment. "Ha! Me? I'm the cause of of your dilemma?" Then, she made a sound and laughed again. "*You* waited for me as I recall."

"You were alone and should be walking with someone."

"But I've always walked this way by myself." Dinah shook her finger at him. "You took this path knowing I'd be here. And you were also at the river the other day. You followed me there, too."

Jorah turned. "You knew about it but did not say?"

"How could I not know? You followed me back with that donkey lumbering along the ridge above me. It should not be a surprise to you that I heard."

"I wanted to know that you arrived home safely. You were in the wilderness without an escort. I don't know why your father allows it."

She smiled. Her dark lashes swept against her cheeks again as she tipped her head upward. "And you offered your protection?"

Jorah gave her a frustrated look. "I'd do this for any woman I saw walking in these places alone. You shouldn't be taking risks like this."

Her lips formed an upward curve. "Any women?" She gave him a flirtatious look.

Jorah's voice lowered. "I'm sorry for my behavior. I shouldn't have allowed what I did to happen." He looked back once. "Go home. Take someone with you the next time you're out."

The spangles on Dinah's wrists spun downward as she dropped her arm to her side. "I don't need you to watch over me, or anyone else." Her eyes narrowed. "Now, I must go. My father and mother will be waiting for me."

"Dinah, I am sorry if I've hurt you. I didn't mean to. It's only that our homes and customs are so very different..."

"Jorah, stop. You said what you wanted. Now, you must go and not come back. You mustn't keep following me."

"Dinah..."

"Please. We've nothing more to say."

Jorah frowned. "I'll go, but you must bring someone with you when you're out next time, your brother or your sister, Vashti. You're a young woman and aren't safe alone. Something could happen to you."

She just stared at him. She didn't respond.

He sighed. "I hope you'll listen to what I have to say. I must leave now. Please go home. See to your safety."

He turned and walked away. He didn't look back.

*****

Chapter 17

Toi held up a ring to examine the intricate cut of the gem fastened to it. He spoke quietly to Shobach. "The jewelry should give us the additional business we're looking for."

Shobach laid a large brick on a pile after smoothing out the edges. "And you can get us more of the gems?"

"I can get many precious stones which will be greatly admired."

"Achsah might be interested to know what you've done."

Toi nodded. "She'll have my first finished piece. I'll give it to her soon."

"But not yet?"

"Until know how our business fares with these changes, I'd rather wait to tell her."

"I suppose it would be best." Shobach handed Toi another gem. "We'll fashion these and cut the bricks and decorative pieces for homes."

"Let's not waste time. I believe I'll be staying late until I make up for the losses we've taken."

"Yes, I'll do this also, and in time, I believe we'll not suffer for it."

*****

Chapter 18

Achsah and Sheerah both eyed the plains of Moab from the top of the rise. The evening sun, on the day of Sabbath, had lowered over the valley and spread its colors of pink and orange hues in streaks across the expanse of the sky.

"I'm glad we could walk the path from my home."

Achsah nodded. "Yes, it's been some time since I've seen you."

"It has." Sheerah voice was hushed. "It's beautiful here, isn't it? I come often to watch the sun when it rises and sets. It's very pretty."

Achsah's expression was guarded. "It is." She sighed and gazed into the distance. "Although the colors will fade eventually. Nothing lasts forever."

Sheerah turned. "You understand that your life with Toi is secure. He's attentive to you."

Achsah flicked a long braid over her shoulder, and she straightened. "He's been this way, since he came back from the border, but lately I wouldn't know. I don't see him until evening, and he's tired when he gets back. I'm not sure what he's been doing."

Sheerah patted Achsah's arm. "He's your husband. He's busy with his business. You only need to see his face, when he looks at you, to know he takes a great interest in you."

A small piece of wheat drifted on the breeze and landed on Achsah's tunic. She brushed it away and shrugged. "Maybe, but he didn't marry me because he loved me."

"He's been at Shobach's. I saw him there yesterday. I believe their business is prospering. The Moabite women, in particular, seemed very interested in bartering for deals."

Achsah turned. "Women?"

"The buyers." Sheerah's voice suddenly died when she looked at Achsah. "They were doing business."

Achsah bristled. There was a dry tone to her voice. "Toi was most likely using his charm to persuade them."

"It wouldn't matter as he seems to only have eyes for you."

Achsah stared at the plains. "I'm not so sure. Our marriage was hasty. No promises were given."

"Achsah," Sheerah sighed. "I didn't mean to plant doubt in your mind. I believe Toi's changed."

"Maybe, but I suppose time will tell."

"All will be well. You need not worry."

Achsah rose to her feet and looked down the path. She needed to get back to help with the preparations for dinner. "I suppose I should leave now, but I'll surely visit again."

Sheerah got up and stood next to Achsah. "Come, I'll go as far as my own home. We can part there."

Achsah turned and walked with her friend.

The air was still and silent.

Sheerah spoke softly. "I'm sorry if I said things that might have caused you injury. All will be well. I'm sure of it."

Achsah smiled. "Nothing you've done has hurt me. Don't be anxious. There's been much to think about lately. Another day, and I'll come visit again."

Sheerah stopped at the end of the path that led to the gated door of her home. "I look forward to it. Be careful on the way back."

"All will be well. It's a short distance." Achsah smiled again. "Peace, Sheerah."

"Peace."

Both waved as Achsah left for her home.

*****

Achsah continued down the path from Sheerah's.

She heard the sound of a donkey and cart behind her, and she moved aside to let it pass. She turned and looked. Her sister was driving it.

Dinah slowed the animal, and then stopped when she spotted Achsah.

Achsah backed up a step. "Hmm, it's you." There was sarcasm in her voice.

Dinah looked annoyed. "Ha! First the market, and now this."

"Market was fine for me." Achsah played with spangles on her wrist. "I got what I wanted there. Toi makes sure of it." She studied Dinah. Though her sister appeared cool and composed, it was clear she wasn't. She was holding taut to the donkey's reins, and there was a dark look in her eyes.

Achsah supposed she should have taught her younger sister a better way and treated her with kindness as Toi had told her once. But, for some reason, whether she'd prayed to Adonai, or not, Dinah brought out the worst aspects in her.

A sudden tinge of guilt ran through her. She'd been better at controlling her temper, as of late, but with certain people it seemed impossible, Dinah being one of them.

*****

Dinah sighed. Achsah treated her as if she were not worth her time. What was it that caused such friction between them? Why did their encounters with each other always end in such misery for them both?

Yet, it didn't seem fair, that Achsah seemed to thrive, when she herself was left in a ruinous guise of a well-bred family. Achsah, Achsah. It seemed to be all Dinah had heard lately from everyone. She was tired of the sound of her sister's name.

Though she empathized with Achsah, with regard to what she'd experienced in the home, she had little sympathy for her now.

She'd take that self-assured smile from her sister's face.

Dinah let go of the reins and put her hands on her hips. She looked back at the marketplace, and tipped her chin upward.

"Toi does have a unique way of carving idols. You may get what you want, but my friends and I are enjoying his work also."

Achsah stared at her. "He gave up that trade. He's not making the idols anymore." She seemed less sure of herself.

"Is that what he told you?" Dinah turned to Achsah with a sly look. She suddenly laughed. "You might think so, but I know the truth of it."

*****

A sick feeling ran through Achsah as she watched Dinah's confidence rise with her words. "You don't know what my husband does."

Dinah's face lit. Her eyes danced. She brushed imaginary dust from the sleeve of her tunic. "Are you so sure? Only yesterday, he gave me a goat idol. It was beautiful."

"He did not." Achsah scowled at her sister. "He quit making them, I tell you."

Dinah laughed again. "His work was quite unique. The idol had interesting lines, and there were jewels added to the face. He wanted me to have it."

Achsah's heart skipped a beat as she heard what Dinah was telling her. She shook her head. "He wouldn't have done such a thing. I'm sure of it. He keeps his word."

"For me, he would make one." Dinah lifted her chin. Her eyes sparkled with delight. "I'm one of his special customers."

Achsah's cheeks turned a deep crimson. A wave of sickness ran through her. Toi might not have been as honest as she'd thought.

She reached out and took hold of the edge of her sister's cart, and her voice shook as she spat out the words. "If he did, it's of no consequence to me. He can do as he wants. I knew when I married him what he was like. It was a business arrangement and nothing else." Achsah held back tears that threatened to spill from her eyes. She let go of the cart and backed away. Her mouth was suddenly dry. She couldn't allow Dinah to know how she really felt. She smoothed her skirt out as the color in her cheeks deepened. "You don't believe me? Ask Toi. Nothing he does matters to me."

Dinah studied Achsah closely. "Are you certain of it? I'm not so sure."

"Well, it's true." Achsah turned and stared into the distant fields. "I don't want to fight you anymore, Dinah. I can't see any point in it. Do what you must. I told you what I think. I must be going."

Dinah took the reins back in her hands. "I have things to do at home, as I'm sure you do. I suppose it's one thing we can agree on."

"Yes, I suppose it is."

Dinah snapped the reins of the donkey. "Ha!" The cart moved forward as the wheels began to turn.

Achsah watched Dinah's cart roll down the path and disappear into the shadows.

*****

The courtyard of Dinah's home came into view. She shivered as she drew her wrap tighter around her shoulders. Her mother would be waiting for her with a list of chores while the other children played games outside the house. She sighed at the thought of her father watching her from the door. She was growing tired of his dark, brooding looks which he'd very specifically reserved for her, since Achsah had gone away.

And now, after she'd had the unfortunate encounter with her sister, she wasn't sure what to think. Things had not gone exactly as she'd first thought they would. Achsah hadn't reacted the way she would have in the past.

When Dinah had first seen Achsah, on the path, she'd immediately bristled at the thought of speaking to her. The last time they'd been together, Achsah had gloated over her marriage to Toi, and demanded that bread be brought to her at their families' table. Yet, this time, things seemed different.

316

Dinah, at first, had relished the thought that she might be able to convince Achsah that Toi had strayed from her, by the information Sapphira had provided her with. Yet, when she'd lied about the goat idol, and about her relationship to Toi, somehow it hadn't felt as satisfying as she thought it would.

She'd seen the puzzled look on her sister's face and heard the quaver in her voice when they'd spoken. Achsah wasn't as self-assured as she'd attempted to appear. It seemed her sister had more feelings for her husband than Dinah had originally thought.

Dinah sighed. Though Achsah had thoroughly incensed her at times, not everything between them had been entirely bad. There had been times that they'd found comfort in each other's company, and a comradery of sorts.

Though Achsah took the blame for much of their family's difficulties, Dinah was not without her own constant criticism. Neither found solace in their home.

A sick feeling roiled within Dinah. She'd wanted to wound her sister for escaping with Toi, but instead, she was left with feelings of doubt.

She was unsure of what caused her to say and do the things she did when she might have made attempts to reconcile with Achsah instead. How could she ever expect sisterly affection, when she treated Achsah the way she did? She'd wronged her sister cruelly. Sometimes her actions seemed no better than her parents.

She knew things hadn't been easy for Achsah. Marked as a troublemaker from the beginning, and blamed for the discord in the family from the time she was a young child, Achsah had truly fought a difficult battle. No wonder she wanted little to do with the family.

Achsah couldn't possibly have conformed to the high standards they'd set for her.

She supposed much of her own dislike for Achsah stemmed from her own inability to break her way free. Maybe Achsah wasn't so much the problem, but rather an easy mark for her own frustrations with the struggles she faced on her own.

She eyed the sun lowering in the distance. A sinking feeling settled within her as she looked back at her home. Maybe someday she would escape the confines of those thick stone walls, as her sister had. She'd little patience for the trials and vexation she'd faced there.

*****

Achsah looked down the road. The dust from her sister's cart shrouded the path behind her and kicked up a bitter scent.

A lone lizard scurried past. Achsah's brow wrinkled as she watched the small animal disappear underneath a desert shrub. She clasped her hands together and held them to her chest as she stood on the dry, barren road.

How had Dinah known about the handcrafted goat god and its unique craftsmanship when Benaiah had smashed it? Toi hadn't made anything like it since. Or at least he said he hadn't.

Achsah's doubts grew when she thought of Dinah's triumphant smile and the information her sister had provided. Toi hadn't come home until late in the evenings, and he'd seemed distant. What had he been doing?

A frown curved over her brow. Had he made Dinah a special carved idol similar to the one he'd made her? Had he been taken in by her sister's tricks?

Achsah straightened and drew her shawl tighter as she watched the settling dust in the distance. Her eyes turned a smoky green.

A hollow emptiness ran through her as she stood in the middle of the road and contemplated what Dinah had told her.

Toi had managed to penetrate beneath the surface of her heart and draw her in, as of late, with his kindness and concern. Yet, maybe it wasn't as it appeared. What if it were nothing as she imagined, and she were being terribly mislead?

A picture settled in her mind of Toi and her sister as a second wife. She imagined Dinah laughing and casting sly smiles her way, and she was sure Toi would find it amusing. A troubled feeling stirred in her at the thought of it.

She crinkled her nose to the smell of the bitter herbs along the path. Her eyes suddenly narrowed. She'd allowed too much trust in her husband. She'd need to be more careful.

She kicked a pebble on the side of the road and let out a breath. Ha! What did it matter?

Dinah could have him for all she cared. He'd surely be preparing his own path to ruin if he chose to bring her sister into the family. His caressing smiles would amount to nothing as she wouldn't share them with Dinah.

If what her sister had told her was true, about the goat idol, and his interest in her, Toi would suffer in the end for it. Achsah would not allow him to make a mockery of her.

*****

Chapter 19

The next morning, Toi got up and readied the donkey. He reached for Achsah's hand.

She straightened and unloosed her fingers from his. She'd silently brooded over what her sister had told her the day before. She reached up to adjust a crease in her robe and then quickly look away.

Toi turned to her. "What's wrong? I thought you wanted to go to Sheerah's? Come, we'll go together."

"I do want to, and nothing is wrong."

He lifted her onto the cart and got up beside her. "Are you sick?" He put his hand on her forehead and felt it.

"I'm not sick, and I told you that things are fine." Achsah pushed his hand aside and looked down the path.

Toi didn't answer her, but instead he clucked to the donkey and slackened the reins as the donkey ambled along.

They rode in silence the rest of the way. There was a gloomy fog that had arisen over the valley. Shades of gray obstructed the view on the path ahead.

Only when they finally reached Sheerah's house, did the fog begin to lift. It ushered in the warmth of the sun which had risen in the sky.

She sat up straighter when she spotted the house ahead.

Toi pointed down the path. "Sheerah's outside the gate. Look."

Achsah nodded without answering.

Toi stared at her. He seemed to be contemplating whether or not she'd told him the truth.

She didn't look at him but turned back to the road as they neared the place where her friend was standing.

*****

Once there, Achsah got down from the cart.

She put her hand on her friend's arm as they went inside. "Sheerah, are you well? You must tell me what you know."

Toi stood behind Achsah and watched as she walked away with her friend.

Achsah ignored him. He could find Shobach on his own.

"Yes, there are things I must relay to you, things you should be made aware of."

Achsah listened as Sheerah rattled on about her family, home, and friends. Much had happened since she'd last seen Sheerah. They'd been apart for quite some time.

Sheerah sighed as she spoke softly. "There's another piece of news, Achsah, you should know about."

Sheerah bent down and whispered it in Achsah's ear.

Achsah leaned closer while she looked around the room full of people. "You're certain of it?"

Sheerah nodded. "Yes, but don't say anything."

Achsah's mouth drew open. "But, how could Tamar have done this? She's aware of the repercussions of such things."

Sheerah put her finger to her lips. "Achsah, not so loud. I don't want Reuben, or any of the men to know. It could be bad for her. You and I are the only ones who are privy to this information. Hezro used his smooth words. Tamar was taken in by him, and she thought he cared for her."

"But, she hasn't told him?"

"No, she did, but he's denying the child's his."

Achsah drew in a breath. Her eyes widened as she leaned closer. "But, soon others will know. What will she do?"

"If Hezro marries her, within the month, he might save both her and the baby."

Sheerah put her hand on Achsah's arm. "Achsah, he's not listening. I'm not sure what to do."

"So, why are you telling me this?" Achsah frowned. "You're not saying…"

Sheerah sighed. "Hezro listens to you. All the men do. I'm not sure who else I can trust, or who might be able to sway his thoughts."

Achsah stared at her.

"Please, Achsah. I understand your feelings concerning Tamar, but there is no one else." Sheerah hesitated, then she spoke quietly. "Could you please speak to him, just once, for me?"

Achsah groaned. She rolled her eyes. "Tamar's treated me terribly. You know what she's been like. You truly believe that I would do this for her?"

"Achsah, he won't listen to anyone else. I don't know who else to ask."

"Does Tamar know what you're asking of me?"

Sheerah sighed. "No, but I trust you. You'd put aside your dislike for her, for the sake of her life, and the baby's. Your heart is kind, Achsah. I know you'll do what is right."

Achsah's brows drew inward. She never understood how Sheerah put such faith in her.

"Please, they'll take the baby's life too."

Achsah sighed. "There's no one else who can talk to him?"

"You should know that there isn't. I can't tell this to anyone, and Hezro isn't cooperating with Tamar. You're the only one he might listen to."

"But…"

"Please, Achsah…for the child."

Achsah shifted in her seat and looked across the room. "I don't know."

"Achsah, please. The baby will die, and so will Tamar. You're the only one who might be able to save their lives."

Achsah let out a deep sigh. "It *would* have to be me who is asked to go to him. I suppose it is only right that I talk to him, but only because I know he persuaded her to do this, and it's not fair. He needs to take responsibility for his part and protect them both. There are lives involved."

322

"I know he's responsible." Sheerah looked relieved. "Oh Achsah, you're a good friend. It's the right thing to do."

Achsah looked out one of the windows in the house. "Tell him to meet me at Chemosh's stone early tomorrow morning, before daylight. He knows where it is. I used to go there regularly, so no one should see us. There are never Israelites there."

"I'll tell him."

"Thank you."

"I'm not doing this for Tamar, but for the child's sake. Now, I must go find Toi. We should leave soon so I'm able to rise early enough for this."

Sheerah stood back. "Thank you again, Achsah."

"We'll meet another time." Achsah smiled. Then she turned to go.

She didn't look forward to the ride home. It bothered her to keep secrets from her husband, especially one of such magnitude.

She hoped Toi wouldn't ask her too many questions. She didn't want to talk to him, or to anyone else.

*****

Achsah shut the door behind her. She turned to cross the room. The sun was lowering in the sky and shadows fell over the room.

Toi reached out to her, but she pushed him away.

"Achsah, you haven't spoken to me since yesterday. I don't understand. Something's happened."

She put her hand on her head. "I've a headache. I want to lie down." She sat on the bed and gave him a cross look. "I haven't felt well."

Toi eyed her skeptically. "I don't believe it."

"I told you my head hurts. I want to be left alone." Achsah crossed her arms. She didn't move from where she sat.

"Achsah." Toi cleared his throat. "I don't believe you're sick. It's plain to see how you feel. You're not happy with me."

"How would you know? You aren't the one who feels the way I do."

Toi gave her an impatient look. "I only wish I knew what happened. I'll make amends if I've said or done anything to offend you. Please, you must tell me. What's happened?"

"I said I don't want to talk about it."

He let out a breath and made a move for the door. "For now you'll have your wish, but eventually, you'll tell me what's bothering you."

Achsah turned away from him. She could hear the door closing behind her. She breathed a sigh of relief when she realized she was finally alone.

*****

After Toi left the next morning for work, Achsah stole down the path to meet Hezro. It was early. The moon lit the trail. There would be time before others came.

Hezro's feet were planted apart on the path as he stood watching her. "What do you want, Achsah? It's certain that you didn't call me here without good reason. Toi wouldn't appreciate it."

Achsah lifted her chin. "He doesn't need to know about this. But you must hear what I've come to say."

Hezro leaned forward. "I've no time for women's talk. I've work to do."

"But, you'll listen, because it concerns Tamar."

The wind whistled over the tops of the stone altars. A slight rustle, of the field grass below the hill, stirred around them.

Hezro's eyes narrowed. He didn't say anything at first, then he leaned down and spoke dangerously in her ear. "Whatever you heard, you must forget it. It's her doing. She might have chosen differently, but she didn't."

"What?" Achsah's cheeks colored. "It's not all her fault. What about you? You can't place the blame solely on Tamar. You must take responsibility for what you've done. It's your child, too."

Hezro wiped at a bead of sweat that trickled down the side of his face. He looked away. "How do you know it's mine when she might have been with another man?"

Achsah stared at him incredulous. "Tamar? Another man? As much as I can't stand defending that woman, I know there was no one else involved, and you know it too. You persuaded her to do this." She reached out and took hold of him. She wanted to shake him. "This is your doing, and you should be owning up to it."

Achsah shivered and wrapped her shawl tighter around her. She gave Hezro a chagrinned look when he didn't answer. "Truly? You would allow your own child to suffer death along with Tamar?" She leaned closer. Her fingers dug into his arms.

Hezro didn't say anything.

Achsah scowled. "You encouraged her in this. You should marry her. It's wrong of you to desert her."

"She knew what could happen."

Achsah leaned closer. "But Hezro, they'll stone her and your child. Marry her, and you'll not have this on your conscience. It's still early enough. Please don't allow this to happen."

Hezro turned back to Achsah with a wary look. "Why do you care what happens to her? Tamar means nothing to you."

"She has been nothing but trouble, in my eyes, but this concerns her life and the life of a child. You must not allow harm to come to them. Tamar's an Israelite. You're not doing right by her when you're as much to blame."

She shook his shoulders gently. "Please, Hezro. Think of your child. You will regret it if you don't take measures to save the little one. You'll never forget. In the years to come, you'll think of this son or daughter of yours."

He turned from her. "People will know. I will be an outcast because of it. Tamar wasn't…"

Achsah put her hand on his arm and held it there. "A baby will die…your baby." She looked up at him.

"But, I've been with her outside of marriage. You don't understand. Adonai's just. I'll suffer punishment."

Achsah observed him with a furrowed brow. She put her hands on him and held onto the sleeves of his robe. "They say your Lord is all seeing. He would know what you did. If he is loving and just, as Kezia says, he would want you to save Tamar and your child from certain death and accept his consequences."

"But, you don't know what this would do to me."

"Hezro? But, Tamar. The child. What would become of them?"

Hezro took a step back. He suddenly growled low as he let go of her hand. "Please, Achsah, I don't want to hear about Tamar and the child again. You've said what you came to say. There's no need to go on about this. I won't speak of it anymore."

Achsah let out a breath. "Then I've done what I can for the child and for her. I hope you will see, in time, that what you are doing is wrong. I must go now. I must not be seen here with you."

Hezro turned. He gave a quick glance back at her. "I must leave also. I have things to do." He strode quickly away from her without speaking again.

Achsah watched as he made his way to the field below. She walked past the high places which were set aside for Chemosh.

She sighed as she eyed the burning incense on top. She pushed away thoughts of things she knew had taken place there. Not only incense was given this god. There had been much worse for the sake of this stone idol which had given her people nothing but grief. She'd seen the faces of the tear-streaked women who were forced to hand their babies over to Chemosh.

What Hezro was doing was no better than the child sacrifices she'd known to have happened at these very altars. He would surely regret everything one day, if he allowed this to happen. Taking the life of his own child, made no sense to her.

*****

Chapter 20

The sun beat onto the dusty path as the donkey trudged slowly along. Achsah and Toi neared the middle of the town as they wove through the small alleys that led from one courtyard to the next in the middle of the city.

Achsah sighed. She'd had a day to think about the conversation she'd had with Hezro. An ache settled deep inside her with the thought of what might happen to Tamar and the baby. Hezro hadn't seemed convinced that he would change his mind over the matter. How could anyone take such a coward's way out and not take responsibility for their own child? What was he thinking?

She clenched the fabric of her tunic in her hand and then let go as Toi urged the donkey forward and lightly snapped the reins. Her thoughts turned to her sister.

Though she still fumed over what Dinah had told her, there were other things on her mind more unsettling. She couldn't dwell on what was said or allow it to affect her.

She looked ahead and observed the busy streets as they drew near to the market.

A line of bawling camels with ornaments that hung from their necks pulled carts filled with silks and precious wares from the east. Merchants stood on the side of the path as they held out colorful fabrics for people to buy. Each of them vied for position in the crowd while their voices rose and fell in unison.

Achsah spoke matter-of-factly. "We'll get fruits last. Elpaal has new fabrics that came all the way from the Orient. There were silks, and I want to see the cloth weaver near Shobach's."

Toi stopped the cart as a flock of long-haired goats passed in front of it. The animals took quick, nervous steps as the goat herder prodded them with his staff in hand and waved to Toi.

Toi took Achsah's hand while they sat and waited. The goat-herder smiled.

Achsah glanced sideways at Toi and gave him a distrustful look. She looked away. A gray-haired man was walking next to the cart as they began to move forward again. The man was leading a donkey with a thick, brown saddle blanket. He stayed next to the cart until he disappeared down another path and into the crowd.

Ahead of the cart, there was a crowd gathering, and some men shouted.

Toi spoke quietly. "I wonder what's going on."

Achsah didn't say anything, but watched the commotion forming. She was puzzled when she realized the people were turning their way and staring at them.

Toi sat up straighter in the cart. He continued to drive toward the disturbance, despite the crowd that was blocking the path.

Achsah straightened the folds of her tunic. She shivered as she eyed more than one priest. It appeared they were waiting for the cart to draw closer. Others watched as if curious about what was about to happen. The lines in their faces deepened as Toi and she drew nearer.

"I told you she'd be here!" A man shouted and pointed. It was Naaman. His long, purple robe, embroidered with golden pomegranates and green palm trees snapped back and forth in the breeze as he marched toward them angrily. "She's with her husband!"

Toi let go of her hand and held firmly to the reins. "Do you know what's happened, Achsah?" He slowed the donkeys to a measured gait.

"I've no idea."

The priest's mouth formed a grim line as he stared at her.

Achsah put her hand on the edge of the cart when she realized that she was the object of his contention.

Her eyes narrowed. What did that horrible man want this time?

Toi pulled on the reins of the donkey and drew his animal to a halt.

A huge throng of people encircled them as they yelled and chanted on the street. Dust stirred under the cart's wheels as it was brought to a halt.

A couple of women near the cart stared at Achsah from the edge of the circle while a group of men blocked the path so that the animals could no longer move.

Naaman moved to the front of the cart and pointed to Achsah. "She's the one. Take her from the cart."

Toi put out his hand. "Wait. What are you doing?"

A tall, heavyset man next to the cart pointed at Achsah. "I'm sorry sir, but your wife's been seen with another man. There's been word on the street that she's been unfaithful to you."

Achsah eyes widened as stared at him in disbelief. She pushed her hair behind her shoulders and sat up straighter. "That's preposterous. What are you talking about? There's no truth in this." She turned to Toi. "I didn't do anything?"

"Achsah?" Toi gave her a questioning look.

"I told you, it's not true."

"Take her off the cart!" Naaman yelled. "Get her down!"

The man, next to her, reached up and grabbed hold of her arm. "You must come with me, Miss." He tried to yank her from the cart, but she held tight to the seat.

"Come now, woman."

Toi tugged on the reins of the donkey. "Whoa!" he shouted.

Achsah shoved at the man, attempting to shake herself free. "Let go! I've done nothing." She looked back at Toi. "Tell him to take his hands from me."

But the man suddenly dragged her from the cart and pulled her to the ground. Achsah fell hard. She let out a sound.

The man quickly took hold of her arm. He yanked her toward him.

Toi got down from the wagon. He pushed through the mob to get closer, but two other men took hold of his arms and held him back. His look was one of disbelief. "What's the basis for these accusations? Who said this? I want to know."

330

Achsah straightened her tunic and pushed her hair behind her. "Yes. This is ridiculous! I didn't do anything!"

Naaman scowled. "Be quiet! You were seen early this morning before the sun was up at the high places. There were two witnesses."

She began to speak, but her voice was drowned by a mob of angry voices, and she was yanked through the streets away from the cart. She attempted to look back, but wasn't able to. She tripped on masses of feet and the cobblestone beneath her.

Someone shoved her down on the dusty path.

She rubbed her knee where she hit. "Ow!" She quickly sat up and pushed her hair from her face so that she could see.

She drew back, as a frenzied mob of angry men encircled her.

Naaman stepped into the center of the crowd. His eyes were set upon her like a hawk. He reached out, and his gnarled hands gripped her by the shoulder.

Achsah winced in pain. She turned and she saw Toi from a distance. The same two men held Toi at a distance from her. He was clearly agitated by the look on his face.

Toi turned to the priest, and his eyes darkened. "I asked who accused my wife of this? I want to know."

Benaiah came out of the crowd and took a place beside him.

The people gathered around them.

Benaiah put his hand on Toi's arm. "Wait, until this is straightened out. You must hear them out."

Toi turned when Naaman began to speak.

"She's kept her indiscretions from her husband. It would've been better for her if he'd have been able to provide a reason for her behavior. But, in this case, it seems he cannot. He's not heard and cannot vouch for her." Naaman's dark eyes shone with secret pleasure as he stalked past Achsah. He paced with his hands clasped behind him.

The crowd quieted.

"Let everyone see you, young woman." Naaman suddenly grabbed a fistful of Achsah's hair and yanked her upward.

Achsah groaned but said nothing. She wasn't about to give him the satisfaction of hearing her cry out. She looked away.

Toi shoved at one of the men, but they held fast to him. "This is preposterous! She's done nothing. It's your word against hers."

Naaman's voice lowered. There was a feral sound to it. "I'm not surprised, and you shouldn't be either. I was certain it was only a matter of time before she'd find herself here." Naaman scowled. He took Achsah's chin in his hand and lifted it. "Tell your husband what you've done, and be truthful. The Lord is watching."

Achsah looked at him in disbelief. She shook his hand off her. "How can I tell him anything when I don't even know what you're accusing me of?" An angry tear spilled over her cheek which she quickly wiped away.

"Liar!" Naaman scowled. "You do know!" His hand struck her across the cheek.

Achsah fell back. Her elbow hit the hard ground. When she caught herself, she sat back up and glared at him. "You're the liar! You've no proof!"

"That's not true, and you know it." He swung around to the crowd. There was venom in his voice. "Don't listen to her, or be swayed by her tears, as I've heard differently."

The people listened intently as the dust on the street settled.

Achsah's eyes grew large. "Heard what? What are you talking about?" She looked over at Toi. She rubbed the side of her face.

He tried to move, but couldn't.

Benaiah put his hand on his brother's arm. He was neither accusing, nor in defense of Achsah. "Wait."

Achsah turned to Naaman. "Whoever told you this nonsense, they're wrong! It's not true! I've done nothing!"

Naaman scowled. "Dirty Moabitess!" He lifted his cloak off the path as he paraded past her. "You've played games with your husband, but they will end soon. You've betrayed those who've trusted in you."

Achsah's voice was laced with a bitter thread. "You're the one who's lying!"

Abigail and Rizpah came out of the crowd. Abigail shook her head. "No Achsah, you know he's telling the truth, and Rizpah and I can attest to it."

Achsah gave them both a bewildered look.

Tamar watched from the edge of the circle. She was standing next to Hezro. Her look was one of horror. She lifted her hand to her mouth.

Abigail turned to Naaman. "What I told you was true. Rizpah and I saw her yesterday morning at the high places with her hands on a man. They were close. There was no denying that they'd been together. It was before the sun had risen, still dark. She's a married woman."

Achsah's heart suddenly lurched at the realization of what they'd seen. It was as if the blood drained from her. Her meeting with Hezro had not gone unnoticed.

She turned to Toi. Her dark eyes met his warily.

"Achsah?"

"It's not what…they don't know what they saw." She put her hand to her chest. Her words stuck in her throat. "I tell you, I've done nothing. It's true, I was there, but not for the reasons I'm accused of."

She pushed aside tears that formed in her eyes, and she looked at Toi again. "I swear by the heavens I would have nothing to gain by such a thing, but I can't tell anyone why I was there."

Achsah caught Tamar's eye briefly. She glanced at the loosely-fitted tunic the young woman wore. Tamar's abdomen was slightly rounded. If what had transpired with her and Hezro at the high places was told to the crowd, the baby's life would surely be compromised.

A lump formed in her throat. She blinked back tears.

Toi stared at Achsah. Then he turned to Benaiah. "I believe her. Something's happened." He shook his head. "She's done nothing. There's no proof, other than the word of two women who dislike her immensely. This is ridiculous."

Rizpah wagged her finger in the air. "No, you're wrong. She admitted to having been there. You heard her."

The people in the marketplace began to chant. "The husband lies for her! She's admitted she was there!"

Naaman yanked Achsah's arm and turned. He waited until the crowd quieted before he spoke again. "There's no reason for these women to lie. She didn't deny she was there, and in his arms at dawn, before the sun had arisen." He gave her a shove. "She's attempting to save herself, and other wives will do the same, if she isn't made an example of."

He scowled again. "She admitted to being with a man who wasn't her husband in the early morning hours. She'll give us no answers as to what transpired between them." He pointed to the side of a stone building. "Put her there."

Achsah tried to break free as two men dragged her across the path. "He's wrong. He doesn't care about the truth! He hates me! You must believe me!"

The men ignored her pleas. None of them spoke. They left her where Naaman had directed them and then moved quickly away.

Achsah stared at them angrily and then glanced across the walk to where Tamar and Hezro were.

Tamar continued to hold her hand over her mouth. Her other hand was on her slightly rounded belly. Tears dropped onto her cheeks, and her eyes were huge.

Achsah turned back to Naaman. "I swear. I did nothing wrong. You must believe me."

Naaman ignored her. His voice carried over the crowd as the people chanted and waved their fists. "We're done listening! Stone her! We'll have no more of her lies."

One rock whizzed past the priest's ear and hit the wall next to Achsah.

Achsah ducked. Her body shook as she braced herself against the bricks behind her.

"Stop!" Toi called out. "These are accusations. It's wrong what you're doing. There's been no trial."

Naaman put up his hand, ready to give the signal.

A cold terror suddenly passed through Achsah. She put her hands over her face.

"I said to let her go." Toi shoved one man backward, but two others grabbed onto him and held him steady.

"One day you'll consider it a blessing that she's not with you." Naaman sneered as he looked at Toi.

Benaiah left Toi and pushed his way through the crowd to Naaman. "We shouldn't be so quick to judge and take a life. Give her a fair trial before you do this."

Toi strained to loose himself. "She wouldn't have done this. You're wrong."

Achsah sat up. "I'm telling the truth. I've no interest in anyone but my husband. I've told him this." Anger threaded its way through her as she turned to the men in the crowd. "I'm innocent, but cannot say the same for the rest of you who chant and raise your fists at me! You believe it right to take more than one wife or concubine. What you do is no better than what you accuse me of. And I'm innocent." Her cheeks heated as she looked at Toi. She twisted a length of her hair in her hand.

Toi gave her a puzzled look.

She wiped away more tears that fell onto her dust-smudged cheeks. "I tell you, I had no part in this." She pushed her hair behind her and looked at Toi. "You took me as your wife when no one else would. Why would I do something so foolish?"

"Achsah?" Toi stared at her.

She covered her face in her hands. "They should all know how I feel." Her words were barely a whisper.

Toi frowned. "Please, I don't care what you say that she's done. Let her go."

"What she says changes nothing!" Naaman voice rose above the others. "Ritzpah and Abigail have no reason to lie."

The mob stirred again. Shouts rang out.

Achsah crouched lower. She put her hands over her ears as she waited for the stones to be hurled. Her heart thumped wildly against her chest.

Toi spoke quietly to her. "Achsah, our Lord's just. Be still, and he'll fight for you! Talk to him."

Her eyes met his briefly, and a glimmer of hope rose in her. She closed her eyes and bowed her head, though she knew her sins against Adonai were great. She was sorry she'd done so much wrong.

She quietly asked Adonai for his strength and presence, and she trusted him for her good. She wasn't afraid of either life or death, because she believed in him.

She looked around as the people chanted louder.

Something stirred in her heart. 'Don't fear...you're mine. You're loved'. The words filled her and strengthened her. The words were clear. 'I'll fight for you'.

Achsah drew in a breath. Adonai had spoken to her. She put her hand to her chest. Surely the Israelite Lord would keep her safe.

Naaman suddenly cried out, "Strike her dead! We'll have no more of this ridiculous banter."

But before anything could be thrown, Tamar stepped in front of them. She put up her hand. Her face paled as she called out to the crowd. "Wait!" She choked on her words.

A hush suddenly fell over the people. Those around her lowered the stones in their hands and listened. They seemed shocked by the fact that Tamar, Achsah's greatest adversary, was stepping between her and the others there.

Naaman took Tamar by the arm and tried to yank her aside. "Woman, do you wish to be injured?"

"No, I don't." She put her hand to her chest. She gulped before she spoke again. "But this must end. I know what happened! I must tell it and clear Achsah's name."

336

Naaman scowled. He took hold of Tamar and tugged on her arm. "Stop it. You must move out of the way."

"No, the people must hear what I have to say. I told you that I know the truth." She pulled her arm away from him. "Please, you must not throw one stone until you've heard my testimony. Achsah's innocent!"

The people's mouths dropped open in surprise as Tamar stood in front of Achsah holding out her arms. Some of them grumbled as they watched her.

"But they hate each other." A woman spoke loudly enough for everyone to hear. "Surely Tamar will not speak for Achsah?"

Achsah shook her head. "Tamar, don't." She sat up as a worried look came into her eyes. "You mustn't. Please."

Naaman lowered his arm along with the other men in the crowd. "Tamar?"

Tamar took a deep breath. Her cheeks colored, and her voice was raspy and quiet. "Achsah has influence with the men in the town. My friend asked her to speak to him. There was a personal matter of my own I wished to resolve. She was asked to go to him for me. She's innocent. None of this was her doing."

Naaman's eyes narrowed. "But, you could have sent your father to this man instead."

Tamar's voice dropped to almost a whisper. "It was a private matter. I didn't want to endanger this man's life because of it."

"Private? Come now. What could be so..."

Before he could finish his sentence, someone in the crowd gasped and pointed. "She's with child! Look at her hand where it rests. Surely, she's in the way!"

"No!" Achsah shook her head adamantly. They couldn't know this. They'd kill the child and Tamar. "It isn't true!" Her words were jumbled. "Tamar didn't send me! Please don't believe her!"

Naaman reached out and put his hand on Tamar's rounded belly. "She was trying to convince the man to marry this woman. Tamar's with child. It's why Achsah was sent."

Achsah got up and ran to the priest. She tugged on his arm. "No! They were right. I did what they said!"

Naaman shoved Achsah to the ground and kicked her aside with his foot.

Achsah's voice quavered. "Please! Listen!"

Benaiah gave Toi a surprised look.

At that moment, Hezro took a place beside Tamar. "Leave them." His voice was low and quiet. "If you want to place blame, it should be on me. I should have stepped forward before it came to this."

"Hezro?" The priest faltered on his words. "What...?"

"Tamar's my responsibility, and the child's mine. Achsah's innocent. She came to me to convince me to marry Tamar."

Tamar moved closer to him. She took hold of his arm as if to steady herself.

"I'm asking Tamar to be my wife. I will engage myself to her this very moment, if she'll have me. She'll be protected in marriage, as the baby is mine. Achsah convinced me to see justice done. There'll be no stoning. Tamar?"

Tamar breathed a sigh of relief. "I will accept you as my husband from this day forward."

Naaman circled around. He looked displeased, but he didn't say more to Hezro. He looked at the ground for a moment as his fist tightened. There was a wary expression on his face.

Then he spoke reluctantly and quietly to the crowd. "It seems there's been a misunderstanding. Things were not told as they should have been. The situation was not as it appeared. Achsah should have been forthright from the beginning."

Achsah frowned at him.

He turned to her and gave her a grim look. "You must be careful. Your reputation does nothing for you."

He dropped the stone in his hand and dusted off his palms on his outer robe. He turned to the mob which had quieted. "It appears we should resume the tasks we set out to do this morning. The Moabitess is innocent, after all, at least for now."

He gazed darkly at Achsah. "It would be wise for you to go back to your husband and stay out of trouble. You mustn't be so foolish in the future. You almost got yourself killed over what was not your business."

Achsah got up and brushed off her hands. Her green eyes were dark as she turned to the priest. She said nothing but walked quickly past him.

She stopped to speak to Hezro and Tamar. "The baby's safe. I'm glad of it."

Hezro lowered his head. "I should have stepped forward sooner. I'm sorry, Achsah. I understand if you will not forgive me for it."

"You had the baby and Tamar to protect. You'll suffer enough for this and for your baby also. I understand why you waited. All is well now."

Tamar reached out to Achsah. "I'm sorry for all I've done and said in the past. You've deserved none of it."

Achsah let out a breath. "You and the baby are safe. It's what matters. It seems that your Israelite God wants your child and you to live."

Tamar let go. She lowered her eyes. "He's good, but he's your Lord also, Achsah. I know you prayed to him. Hezro and I will live in disgrace in the eyes of our people, yet no lives have been taken. It's all I can ask."

Hezro took Tamar by the arm. "Come, we must get back to your father's house."

Achsah turned when she heard Toi's voice behind her. "Are you hurt?"

She looked up at him and saw the relieved expression on his face. She shook her head wearily. "No, I just want to go home. I don't want to be here."

Benaiah came forward. His voice was low and quiet. "I've a blanket. Here, I'll put it on the cart." He took it to where Achsah would be riding and folded it into a cushion. Then he got on his donkey. "I'll go ahead to tell mother and Anah to wait for you."

Achsah didn't answer. She just nodded in surprise at the kindness he showed.

"Here." Toi lifted Achsah onto the cart. "Are you sure you're well?"

She nodded. "I only want to leave this place." There was an urgency in her voice as she watched him climb onto the cart and sit beside her. "But I don't want to talk about what happened."

Toi turned to her. "I'll take you back, but first, there are some things that were said that need to be addressed."

Achsah closed her eyes and took hold of the side of the cart with her hand. "I don't want to talk about any of it."

Toi took her hand in his and squeezed it. "You need to trust me."

"But..." She eyed him warily.

"Achsah, you said something in the marketplace. I want to know what you meant by it."

She pulled her shawl around her, and she sighed as her eyelashes rested on her cheeks. She turned away from him.

"When you said it was wrong for men to take more than one wife, you looked at me."

She didn't say anything, but her cheeks grew red.

Toi studied her. "I told you that I had no desire to have more than one wife. I thought I made this clear to you." He watched when she stiffened and sat straighter. "It's true."

Achsah fidgeted with her hands in her lap.

"Achsah? Do you truly believe I had intentions of it?"

She looked at him, and her eyes suddenly flashed a dark green. "When you made Dinah an idol, a special one like the one you made me? Why wouldn't you?"

Toi looked surprised. "Dinah? What? I didn't make an idol for her, or for anyone else."

"She told me you did. She said it was a goat god, with the carved lines and eyes with jewels. You told me you weren't making idols anymore."

"I didn't give her anything, and I'm not making them."

He reached for her hand, but she pulled it back.

"Achsah, I didn't make her one. You must believe me."

"Then how did she know what the idol looked like, the one that Benaiah smashed? She told me you made one like it for her. She described it in detail."

"Achsah, I don't know how she knew this. Sapphira was talking to her on the road the other day. You could ask her. This is where Dinah most likely got the information. Jorah was with them."

Achsah smoothed out her skirt. "I'll ask. I want to know."

"Ah, so now I understand why you've been short with me." Toi began to smile. "You've listened to your sister, who I'm sure plotted this little scheme to injure you."

Her brows turned inward. She didn't answer him.

He looked at her perplexed.

"But it's not only Dinah." She choked on her words. "I've heard other things."

"Achsah, what have you heard? You must speak plainly to me. I need to know why you're upset."

Her lips formed a pout as she turned to him. Her eyes had questions in them. "Sheerah told me that there were women at Shobach's. You've been late coming home. There have been distractions, and you've had no time for me. There are reasons to distrust you."

"You're jealous?" Toi gave her an astonished look. Then he laughed as he watched her. He leaned down and kissed her cheek. "Is it true that you do love me, little Achsah?"

Achsah looked at him. "You're impossible. Come now, take the reins and let's go back home. We're wasting time in this place."

He pulled her close to him and spoke softly. "There are no other women, not Dinah, or any other. There's a reason for my being late, and for the women at Shobach's, but it has nothing to do with what you might be thinking."

Achsah turned sharply. She didn't say anything.

"I have something to show you which I've saved for you. It's in my money pouch. Just a moment, and I'll get it out."

She watched as he reached into a small, leather bag that was attached to his side and took a ring out of it.

"Here." He held it out to her. "For you."

She looked down at the ring and then back at him. "But…"

"I wanted you to have this." His voice was steady and sure. "I believe I've grown to love you, little Achsah."

Her eyes widened. "But I thought you said that it was impossible."

"I never said impossible." His eyes crinkled at the corners. "I said I didn't believe I could ever love this way, but I never said it couldn't happen."

Achsah didn't say anything. She looked at his hand.

"Here." He held out the ring again which he'd made from a rose-colored gem. It was carved in the shape of a desert flower. "The heart of Moab. Now you have my heart."

Achsah took it in her hand and put it on her finger. She touched the delicate petals of the intricately carved flower.

She studied him with an astonished expression on her face.

"I made it from gems we've taken from the caves in the cliffs. It's the first jeweled piece. I fashioned it for you." He smiled. "The women were there to see our work and buy pieces from us."

Achsah scrunched up her brow. She put the ring on her finger and studied it. She looked at Toi with a puzzled frown.

Toi took her hand in his. "Achsah, despite what you might think, I know that you are kind, and that you care for others, and I wanted you to know my feelings for you."

Achsah held up the ring. "This is what you've been doing?"

"Yes, Shobach and I. You must know, that our work has been for business purposes only."

Achsah looked surprised. Then she spoke quietly. "I believe *I* might have been considered a business purpose once." Her lips drew into a pout.

He laughed. "You were, but you're also the pretty Moabitess I married." The expression on Toi's face gentled. "I don't regret it, Achsah. I want you to know this."

She took his hand in hers as she allowed him to tenderly kiss her, and she responded in kind.

He drew back and suddenly looked curious. "Was your prayer to Adonai, a prayer of faith? Could it be?"

"I wanted him to save me. I trusted he would keep me safe."

Her voice choked as tears came to her eyes. She wiped them away before they dropped down onto her cheeks. "Kezia said she thought he'd chosen me." She looked at him with a puzzled expression. "But, how is this so? I've been so wrong, such trouble. I'm the least of those he'd want as his own, and yet I felt his love in my heart. I knew it was him and that he would care for me. I wasn't afraid after this."

Toi smiled. "He knew you'd be repentant and love him all the more for what he's done for you. I know this, because it's so with myself. Who we are will always pale in comparison to him. His love is unfathomable. He chooses those who are despised, and those who feel unworthy, because they will love him more this way."

She nodded.

Toi took her hand in his. "It'll be dark soon, and I must get you back to our place. I'm glad I could share this with you. I hope you like your gift."

Achsah's breath caught in her throat at the way he was looking at her. She pushed tears away that came to her eyes. "I do, very much."

She took his hand in her own. "No one, except for Adonai, has ever done as much for me. You've been kind. I'm without words."

"You don't need to say anything."

Achsah stared at him with a look of incredulity.

He smiled and brushed the tears from her cheeks. "Will you trust me now, little Achsah?"

She nodded. "I will."

*****

Chapter 21

Achsah got down from the wooden cart and watched as Toi gave the donkey's reins to a servant.

He turned to her and took her hand in his. "Come, the family will want to see you back with us."

Achsah went in through the gate with Toi.

Sapphira ran to her first. "Oh! Achsah! You're safe and not hurt." She walked alongside them. "I was so afraid for you, and wondered if I'd ruined everything between you and Toi, after I talked to your sister. She kept asking me questions about Toi and the idols he made. I didn't want her to come between you and my brother."

Achsah looked up at Toi.

He laughed. "You see? It was her. I didn't know what you were talking about."

A blush rose in her cheeks. She turned to Sapphira. "Dinah told me that Toi was making idols and made one for her."

Sapphira shook her head adamantly back and forth. "Oh, no! She knew that wasn't true." She turned and grabbed Jorah by the arm. "You know it, too. Isn't that right, Jorah? Dinah was causing trouble."

Jorah gave her a perturbed look. "I can understand why you and she have little sisterly affection for each other. She needs someone to set her straight."

"Dinah? I wouldn't waste my time on her, and won't."

He shrugged and didn't respond, but went into the courtyard set aside for the animals and untied one of the donkeys.

He turned to his mother who went to the gate behind him. His voice was low and quiet. "I'm going out. I'll be back before dark. I've things I must do."

Hannah nodded. She backed away as she watched him leave.

The family gathered around Achsah and drew her in. They all talked at once.

"Come inside," Hannah said. "We must get you food and drink."

Sapphira and Kezia nodded. Kezia took Achsah's hand and tugged on it. "You need rest, and some clean clothes. I'm sorry for what Naaman did to you. We heard the news and were ready to leave for town, but the messengers said the matter has been resolved."

"Naaman was wrong." Achsah let out a relieved sigh. "I'm happy I'm home, and that Tamar came forward. I do need rest, but will take time for family first." She looked back at Toi and smiled.

He gestured to the doorway of the house. "Naaman won't bother you again. I'll see to that."

He followed Kezia and Achsah inside while the others stepped through the doorway behind them.

Achsah breathed a sigh. She was glad to be home with the family.

*****

It didn't take long for Jorah to make the path to Dinah's father's house. He went in through the gated entrance and walked past three of Laban's wives and their children playing in the courtyard. He knocked on the door and then lowered his hand as he waited.

When Dinah opened the door, she looked surprised. "What are you doing here?" She peered around the gated area while the other women watched from a distance. "My father might see you."

"I saw him in the fields on the way, so there's no reason we can't speak freely. We've a matter I wish to discuss." He took her aside as he stared at her impatiently. He raked his hand through his hair. "Why did you do what you did, Dinah? I don't understand."

"What do you mean? What are you talking about?" She shook her arm free from his grasp.

Jorah frowned. "You lied to Achsah and told her things that were clearly not true. There are no explanations for it."

Dinah looked over the courtyard wall. She didn't answer him.

He took her by the shoulders and turned her to face him. "I told you that Toi had no interest in other wives, and you knew it. Does your sister mean nothing to you?"

"Let go of me." Dinah unsuccessfully tried to work her way free from his grasp. She looked away.

"No, you'll listen to me. There were people in my family hurt because of your actions." He held onto her arm firmly. "I want to know why you did what you did? How could you treat your sister the way you did? Why would you tell her things that were clearly untrue?"

Dinah's brows took a downward turn. "I told you to let go."

"Oh, no. This time, you'll answer my questions. You won't run away from them."

She tried to break away, but couldn't loosen his grasp, so she stomped on his foot, and he let go. She quickly ran toward her mother and stood behind her.

Mara rose from her seat while Jorah stalked over to where they stood. She looked at him with a raised brow. "What do you want with my daughter? What's the meaning of this, Dinah?"

Jorah frowned. "I'm Toi's younger brother. Dinah needs to answer to some things that she's done that have caused our family harm. I must speak with her."

"Toi's brother?"

"Yes, I've come to settle some things. She spoke in haste, and I want to hear why she did it."

Dinah broke in. "He doesn't need to know my business with Achsah! That's between her and me."

Mara ignored Dinah. She turned to Jorah. "It seems a reasonable enough request. She should answer to what she does and says that causes harm to others."

Dinah stared at Jorah as her cheeks flamed with color. "But I don't want to talk to him, mother, and no one can make me, including you, or him."

"Don't ever talk back to me." Mara's eyes narrowed. "This man isn't violent or unstable. I believe you owe him some explanation and possibly an apology. Now, go and discuss what you need to, and don't come back here until Jorah says you're finished with your discussion. Your father will hear about this when he returns. You'll not defy him."

Dinah gave them both an angry look. She suddenly ran toward the gate, unlatched it and went out. She could hear her mother behind her.

"Go after her! Get this matter straightened, and bring her back. She'll need to answer for what she's done."

Jorah went through the gate. He took the rope of his donkey and followed after Dinah. When he reached her, he began walking beside her. "Dinah."

"I said I don't want to talk to you." She stopped walking, but wouldn't look at him.

"Come now. Stay until we set this matter to rights. Dinah, what's wrong? Why have you done this to my brother and to your own sister?"

Dinah didn't answer.

Jorah used a softer tone. "Achsah was hurt by it. My brother had to convince her that she was wrong. You caused trouble in their marriage, until they were able to come to an understanding."

Dinah looked away.

"You came between a husband and wife. Toi clearly doesn't have an interest in other women. He doesn't want other wives."

"But, you don't understand."

"I know you lied to your sister and put doubts in her mind that were untrue. My brother has been honorable towards her. How did he deserve what you did, maligning his name?"

Her cheeks reddened, and she looked away. "I didn't mean to hurt him by this. It was between Achsah and I."

"But, you did, and you might have done great damage to her marriage."

Her voice was a whisper. "I was angry with her. You wouldn't understand. No one would."

Jorah sighed. "Please, help me to understand. My family should know, so they can put this behind them."

Her eyes misted over with tears. "It's only that she's gone, and I'm still here. She's escaped them, but I haven't. Achsah always finds a way out. It's not fair."

"But, she's been hurt as you have been, even more so than you have. Can't you see that she's dealt with great trials? Today, on the street, she was accused of adultery by Naaman the priest. She was almost killed, and you could have lost her. Did you know this? What would you have thought if you had never seen her again?"

"How do you think I'd feel? I was there, and I saw it all. You don't know me, or what I think." Dinah reached up to wipe a tear that had suddenly fallen from her eyes.

Jorah didn't say anything at first. There was a thread of hope in his voice when he finally spoke. "You were hurt by this?"

She shook her head despite the tears that ran down her face. She tried to push them away.

Jorah leaned down and kissed the top of her head. He held her close. "It seems she means more to you than you've allowed others to see."

"I saw the whole thing from the crowd. All of it." Her voice cracked and then broke. "I knew it was wrong of them to do what they did. I wanted to defend her. You see, I do care for her, but I didn't know the truth of it."

"I'm sorry you were witness to something so terrible."

"I wanted to help, to say something, but I didn't know what happened. I thought she'd done what they said. There was

349

no proof she hadn't. But, even if I'd have known the truth, Naaman wouldn't have listened to me, a daughter of Moab."

He stood back and eyed her thoughtfully. "I'm glad you do care for your sister. It's good to see this."

Dinah nodded. Through more tears she answered him quietly. "I've been hateful and jealous. I know this. I see that Toi cares for her, but I have had no one. They care nothing for me, but only pretend to."

"Your family?"

She nodded again.

There was another muffled sob, and then she spoke quietly. "I've done what Achsah has, and I've prayed to your Lord for help."

Dinah drew in a breath. She looked up at Jorah. "I had no peace until I spoke to him. I saw nothing clearly and blamed Achsah my own bitterness and pain. When I saw her on the street, I realized that she found a measure of peace with your Lord which I wanted myself."

"So, you put your trust in him?"

"After I heard what she said, and after seeing all that happened, I couldn't help but be affected by it. She spoke from her heart, and I saw how kind she was to Tamar."

Jorah regarded her with a look of incredulity. At first, he seemed as if he didn't know what to say. "Would you tell Achsah this? Would you be willing to make peace with her?"

Donkeys neighed in the distance. A quiet breeze stirred the dust of the plains.

Dinah looked in the direction of her house. She sighed. "After what I witnessed, as difficult as it would be for me, I believe I would. My sister spoke with integrity, and Toi stood behind her. It was beautiful. I wanted to have what they did."

Jorah's eyes lightened, and a smile tugged at the corners of his mouth. "Our Israelite God swayed your thoughts?"

Dinah drew back from his teasing manner, but she nodded. "He has, and he's made me his own."

Jorah smiled. "I'm glad of it."

She wiped more tears from her face and smiled through them.

"Do you know what it means that you've told me this?"

She looked surprised. "What?"

"That I can ask you something I've wanted to from the day we met." Then his expression abruptly changed, and he looked concerned. "But, I'm not sure I should."

"Why?"

"First, I must know something. You asked, once, if Toi would take another wife? I need to know if it is something that you'd still consider?"

Dinah stared at him as if surprised. "Your brother?"

"Yes."

"You want to know if I'd have him as a husband?"

"If he asked you?"

Dinah's expression softened as she looked up at him. She took hold of his hand and squeezed it gently. "What do you think?" She smiled.

The grass in the meadows stirred quietly as he let go of her hand. His eyes darkened slightly. "You seemed rather determined he'd have you?"

"Would you be bothered by it if he did?" She laughed suddenly. Then, she gave him a teasing look. "If you want to know the truth, it's what I wanted my sister to believe, but I've never thought it possible, after the things you told me. I've seen how Toi looks at Achsah and listened to what you've said, and I haven't given a thought to your brother since. I never knew him, and didn't really want to."

She reached out and took his hand in hers again. "But, I think there *is* a man who truly cares for me and has waited that I might know the Lord he worships. I can say that I have thought of him quite often."

Jorah began to smile as he looked down at her hand. He gave her an interested look. "A man?"

Her cheeks heightened with color when she spoke, and her eyes began to shine with light. She spoke softly. "I believe it's you."

Jorah didn't say anything at first, but instead he reached into the money bag he'd slung around his neck and pulled out a folded piece of cloth. He carefully opened it and held up a beautifully, well-preserved, dried desert rose. "You once gave this to me. I assumed there was significance in the gesture."

Her eyes suddenly misted with tears. She pushed them away. "You kept it?"

Jorah nodded. "It's what's given me hope. I've prayed that you would know my Lord, and that I could someday bring you home with me."

"The thought makes me very happy. I only hope that your family and Achsah will be accepting of me and forgive me for my waywardness."

"They will love you as I do."

He leaned down and kissed her tenderly. He smiled when he finally let her go.

Dinah unwillingly moved out of his embrace and gave him a solemn look. "I must go back now. Mother will be asking for me, and my father will be back."

Jorah didn't say anything, but instead he nodded and lifted her onto his donkey. He took the reins as he began to walk in the direction of her home.

*****

The harvest had ended and winter was coming. The family surrounded both Dinah and Achsah. The women dashed forward to shower them with kisses and hugs.

"My dears!" Hannah's face was beaming as she turned and cried out. "It gladdens our heart that you're both together and happy."

Kezia spoke softly. "I'm relieved also."

The others nodded with warm smiles.

Achsah studied them closely. She didn't say anything.

Toi grinned and pulled her closer to him. He whispered in her ear. "Achsah, my family's honest. They've claimed you both as their own. There's nothing false in them. It's true. They love you and your sister."

Achsah choked on her words. "It's too much." She swallowed before she spoke again. "Adonai's family has given us more than we deserve." Tears welled up in her eyes, and she pushed them away.

Dinah nodded.

"It's what he wanted for you both from the beginning. You only had to see it. You're his daughters, and he's chosen you both."

Dinah and Achsah smiled as Toi's family gathered around them.

Achsah's look was one of astonishment. She and Dinah had been willingly accepted by Toi's family. This family's capacity to love touched her heart in the deepest of ways.

Toi smiled at her. "Adonai will never turn away from you. He won't condemn you, nor forsake you. He's given you a new home and a new beginning."

His mother added. "Yes, he provides." Her face lightened.

Achsah let go of her sister and turned to Toi. She gave him a puzzled look, and then she smiled as she outlined the edges of her ring. "Your heart has changed." She took his hand in hers.

He nodded. "Adonai's been good to me, even though I hardly deserve it. I am quite a different man."

"It led me to believe that your Lord can do great things." A teasing smile formed on her lips.

"Ah, my little Achsah." Toi lifted her hand and kissed it. "I believe you're right, though I might have embraced it sooner."

Laughter and talk filled the courtyard as the afternoon sun spread its warmth around them.

Achsah took Toi's hand in hers. So much had changed since she'd come to know this family. Her life had taken turns, and those around her had changed also. News came concerning Ruth and Naomi. Ruth had married into Naomi's family and was with child. There were so many blessings.

Achsah had learned to depend on her relationship with the one true God for his grace, his all-consuming love, and the peace he afforded.

He'd given her and Dinah a family, a loving one of which they'd not known before. Toi's family saw what others had not, that Dinah and she had a propensity for love. They'd been accepted and cared for by the Lord. Adonai had made all things new.

For this she was grateful. Neither Dinah, nor she, would ever turn from him. Adonai offered them charity in the land of Moab, a love they would have never known without him.

He'd given his heart to them in Moab, and he'd given them a new life and home.

*****

LOVE

Charity suffereth long, and is kind;
charity envieth not;
charity vaunteth not itself, is not puffed up,
Doth not behave itself unseemly,
seeketh not her own, is not easily provoked, thinketh no evil;
Rejoiceth not in iniquity, but rejoiceth in the truth;
Beareth all things, believeth all things, hopeth all things, endureth
all things.
Charity never faileth:
but whether there be prophecies, they shall fail;
whether there be tongues, they shall cease;
whether there be knowledge, it shall vanish away.
for we know in part, and we prophesy in part.
But when that which is perfect is come,
then that which is in part shall be done away.
When I was a child, I spake as a child,
I understood as a child, I thought as a child:
but when I became a man, I put away childish things.
For now we see through a glass, darkly;
but then face to face:
now I know in part;
but then shall I know even as also I am known.
And now abideth faith, hope, charity, these three;
but the greatest of these is charity.

1 Corinthians 13: 4-13
King James Version of the Holy Scriptures (KJV)

*All quotes taken from the King James's Version of the Holy Scripture

****

Dear Reader,

If THE HEART OF MOAB, was a book you enjoyed and learned from I'd love it if you could tell your friends, pastor, church and family about it or consider giving any of my books as gifts. I have other women's fiction books and children's books on-line on Amazon that you might also be interested in. I would also appreciate it if you would let me know your thoughts on my book on Amazon in the comment and star section or on your Facebook page, website or blog.

Thank you! In Christ's love,

Kara McKenzie